A Darker Domain

Set in Scotland, Val McDermid's brilliant exploration of loyalty and greed intertwines the past and present in a novel that was chosen as a *New York Times* Notable Crime Book of the Year and a finalist for the *Los Angeles Times* Book Prize.

HARPER PERENNIAL OLIVE EDITIONS

This book is part of a special series from Harper Perennial called Olive Editions—exclusive small-format editions of some of our bestselling and celebrated titles, featuring beautiful and unique hand-drawn cover illustrations. All Olive Editions are available for a limited time only.

A Darker Domain

Also by Val McDermid

The Vanishing Point
Trick of the Dark
The Grave Tattoo
Cleanskin
Killing the Shadows
A Place of Execution

Tony Hill and Carol Jordan Novels

How the Dead Speak
Insidious Intent
Splinter the Silence
Cross and Burn
The Retribution
Fever of the Bone
Beneath the Bleeding
The Torment of Others
The Last Temptation
The Wire in the Blood
The Mermaids Singing

Inspector Karen Pirie Novels

The Skeleton Road
The Distant Echo

Kate Brannigan Novels

Dead Beat
Kick Back
Crack Down
Clean Break
Blue Genes
Star Struck

Lindsay Gordon Novels

Hostage to Murder
Booked for Murder
Conferences Are Murder
Deadline for Murder
Common Murder
Report for Murder

Nonfiction

Forensics – The Anatomy of Crime (2014) [34]
Bodies of Evidence (2014)
A Suitable Job for a Woman (1995)

A Darker Domain

A Novel

Val McDermid

HarperCollins books may be purchased for educational, business, or sales promotional use. For information, please email the Special Markets Department at SPsales@harpercollins.com.

FIRST HARPER PERENNIAL PAPERBACK PUBLISHED 2009.

FIRST HARPER PERENNIAL OLIVE EDITION PUBLISHED 2019.

ISBN 978-0-06-295754-2 (Olive edition)

19 20 21 22 23 LSC 10 9 8 7 6 5 4 3 2 1

This book is dedicated to the memory of Meg and Tom McCall, my maternal grandparents. They showed me love, they taught me about community, and they never forgot the shame of standing in line at a soup kitchen to feed their bairns. Thanks to them, I grew up loving the sea, the woods, and the work of Agatha Christie. No small debt.

Wednesday, 23rd January 1985; Newton of Wemyss

The voice is soft, like the darkness that encloses them. "You ready?"

"As ready as I'll ever be."

"You've told her what to do?" Words tumbling now, tripping over each other, a single stumble of sounds.

"Don't worry. She knows what's what. She's under no illusions about who's going to carry the can if this goes wrong." Sharp words, sharp tone. "She's not the one I'm worrying about."

"What's that supposed to mean?"

"Nothing. It means nothing, all right? We've no choices. Not here. Not now. We just do what has to be done." The words have the hollow ring of bravado. It's anybody's guess what they're hiding. "Come on, let's get it done with."

This is how it begins.

Wednesday, 27th June 2007; Glenrothes

The young woman strode across the foyer, low heels striking a rhythmic tattoo on vinyl flooring dulled by the passage of thousands of feet. She looked like someone on a mission, the civilian clerk thought as she approached his desk. But then, most of them did. The crime prevention and public information posters that lined the walls were invariably wasted on them as they approached, lost in the slipstream of their determination.

She bore down on him, her mouth set in a firm line. Not bad looking, he thought. But like a lot of the women who showed up here, she wasn't exactly looking her best. She could have done with a bit more make-up, to make the most of those sparkly blue eyes. And something more flattering than jeans and a hoodie. Dave Cruickshank assumed his fixed professional smile. "How can I help you?" he said.

The woman tilted her head back slightly, as if readying herself for defence. "I want to report a missing person."

Dave tried not to show his weary irritation. If it wasn't neighbours from hell, it was so-called missing persons. This one was too calm for it to be a missing toddler, too young for it to be a runaway teenager. A row with the boyfriend, that's what it would be. Or a senile granddad on the lam. The usual bloody waste of time. He dragged a pad of forms across the counter, squaring it in front of him and reaching for a pen. He kept the cap on; there was one key question he needed answered before he'd be taking down any details. "And how long has this person been missing?"

"Twenty-two and a half years. Since Friday the fourteenth of December 1984, to be precise." Her chin came down and truculence clouded her features. "Is that long enough for you to take it seriously?"

Detective Sergeant Phil Parhatka watched the end of the video clip then closed the window. "I tell you," he said, "if ever there was a great time to be in cold cases, this is it."

Detective Inspector Karen Pirie barely raised her eyes from the file she was updating. "How?"

"Stands to reason. We're in the middle of the war on terror. And I've just watched my local MP taking possession of 10 Downing Street with his missus." He jumped up and crossed to the minifridge perched on top of a filing cabinet. "What would you rather be doing? Solving cold cases and getting good publicity for it, or trying to make sure the muzzers dinnae blow a hole in the middle of our patch?"

"You think Gordon Brown becoming prime minister makes Fife a target?" Karen marked her place in the document with her index finger and gave Phil her full attention. It dawned on her that for too long she'd had her head too far in the past to weigh up present possibilities. "They never bothered with Tony Blair's constituency when he was in charge."

"Very true." Phil peered into the fridge, deliberating between an Irn Bru and a Vimto. Thirty-four years old and still he couldn't wean himself off the soft drinks that had been treats in childhood. "But these guys call themselves Islamic jihadists and Gordon's a son of the manse. I wouldn't want to be in the chief constable's shoes if they decide to make a point by blowing up his dad's old kirk." He chose the Vimto. Karen shuddered.

"I don't know how you can drink that stuff," she said. "Have you never noticed it's an anagram of vomit?"

Phil took a long pull on his way back to his desk. "Puts hairs on your chest," he said.

"Better make it two cans, then." There was an edge of envy in Karen's voice. Phil seemed to live on sugary drinks and saturated fats but he was still as compact and wiry as he'd been when they were rookies together. She just had to look at a fully leaded Coke to feel herself gaining inches. It definitely wasn't fair.

Phil narrowed his dark eyes and curled his lip in a good-natured sneer. "Whatever. The silver lining is that maybe the boss can screw some more money out of the government if he can persuade them there's an increased threat."

Karen shook her head, on solid ground now. "You think that famous moral compass would let Gordon steer his way towards anything that looked that self-serving?" As she spoke, she reached for the phone that had just begun to ring. There were other, more junior officers in the big squad room that housed the Cold Case Review Team, but promotion hadn't altered Karen's ways. She'd never got out of the habit of answering any phone that rang in her vicinity. "CCRT, DI Pirie speaking," she said absently, still turning over what Phil had said, wondering if, deep down, he had a hankering to be where the live action was.

"Dave Cruickshank on the front counter, Inspector. I've got somebody here, I think she needs to talk to you." Cruickshank sounded unsure of himself. That was unusual enough to grab Karen's attention.

"What's it about?"

"It's a missing person," he said.

"Is it one of ours?"

"No, she wants to report a missing person."

Karen suppressed an irritated exhalation. Cruickshank really should know better by now. He'd been on the front desk long enough. "So she needs to talk to CID, Dave."

"Well, yeah. Normally, that would be my first port of call. But see, this is a bit out of the usual run of things. Which is why I thought it would be better to run it past you, see?"

Get to the point. "We're cold cases, Dave. We don't process fresh inquiries." Karen rolled her eyes at Phil, smirking at her obvious frustration.

"It's not exactly fresh, Inspector. This guy went missing twenty-two years ago."

Karen straightened up in her chair. "Twenty-two years ago? And they've only just got round to reporting it?"

"That's right. So does that make it cold, or what?"

Technically, Karen knew Cruickshank should refer the woman to CID. But she'd always been a sucker for anything that made people shake their heads in bemused disbelief. Long shots were what got her juices flowing. Following that instinct had brought her two promotions in three years, leap-frogging peers and making colleagues uneasy. "Send her up, Dave. I'll have a word with her."

She replaced the phone and pushed back from the desk. "Why the fuck would you wait twenty-two years to report a missing person?" she said, more to herself than to Phil as she raided her desk for a fresh notebook and a pen.

Phil pushed his lips out like an expensive carp. "Maybe she's been out of the country. Maybe she only just came back and found out this person isn't where she thought they were."

"And maybe she needs us so she can get a declaration of death. Money, Phil. What it usually comes down to." Karen's smile was wry. It seemed to hang in the air in her wake as if she were the Cheshire Cat. She bustled out of the squad room and headed for the lifts.

Her practised eye catalogued and classified the woman who emerged from the lift without a shred of diffidence visible. Jeans and fake-athletic hoodie from Gap. This season's cut and colours. The shoes were leather, clean and free from scuffs, the same colour as the bag that swung from her shoulder over one hip. Her mid-brown hair was well cut in a long bob just starting to get a bit ragged along the edges. Not on welfare, then. Probably not a schemie. A nice, middle-class woman with something on her mind. Mid to late twenties, blue eyes with the pale sparkle of topaz. The barest skim of make-up. Either she wasn't trying or she already had a husband. The skin round her eyes tightened as she caught Karen's appraisal.

"I'm Detective Inspector Pirie," she said, cutting through the potential stand-off of two women weighing each other up. "Karen Pirie." She wondered what the other woman made of her—a wee fat woman crammed into a Marks and Spencer suit, mid-brown hair needing a visit to the hairdresser, might be pretty if you could see the definition of her bones under the flesh. When Karen described herself thus to her mates, they would laugh, tell her she was gorgeous, make out she was suffering from low self-esteem. She didn't think so. She had a reasonably good opinion of herself. But when she looked in the mirror, she couldn't deny what she saw. Nice eyes, though. Blue with streaks of hazel. Unusual.

Whether it was what she saw or what she heard, the woman seemed reassured. "Thank goodness for that," she said. The Fife accent was clear, though the edges had been ground down either by education or absence.

"I'm sorry?"

The woman smiled, revealing small, regular teeth like a child's first set. "It means you're taking me seriously. Not fobbing me off with the junior officer who makes the tea."

"I don't let my junior officers waste their time making tea," Karen said drily. "I just happened to be the one who answered the phone." She half-turned, looked back, and said, "If you'll come with me?"

Karen led the way down a side corridor to a small room. A long window gave on to the parking lot and, in the distance, the artificially uniform green of the golf course. Four chairs upholstered in institutional grey tweed were drawn up to a round table, its cheerful cherry wood polished to a dull sheen. The only indicator of its function was the gallery of framed photographs on the wall, all shots of police officers in action. Every time she used this room, Karen wondered why the brass had chosen the sort of photos that generally appeared in the media after something very bad had happened.

The woman looked around her uncertainly as Karen pulled out a chair and gestured for her to sit down. "It's not like this on the telly," she said.

"Not much about Fife Constabulary is," Karen said, sitting down so that she was at ninety degrees to the woman rather than directly opposite her. The less confrontational position was usually the most productive for a witness interview.

"Where's the tape recorders?" The woman sat down, not pulling her chair any closer to the table and hugging her bag in her lap.

Karen smiled. "You're confusing a witness interview with a suspect interview. You're here to report something, not to be questioned about a crime. So you get to sit on a comfy chair and look out the window." She flipped open her pad. "I believe you're here to report a missing person?"

"That's right. His name's—"

"Just a minute. I need you to back up a wee bit. For starters, what's your name?"

"Michelle Gibson. That's my married name. Prentice, that's my own name. Everybody calls me Misha, though."

"Right you are, Misha. I also need your address and phone number."

Misha rattled out details. "That's my mum's address. I'm sort of acting on her behalf, if you see what I mean?"

Karen recognized the village, though not the street. Started out as one of the hamlets built by the local laird for his coal miners when the workers were as much his as the mines themselves. Ended up as commuterville for strangers with no links to the place or the past. "All the same," she said, "I need your details too."

Misha's brows lowered momentarily, then she gave an address in Edinburgh. It meant nothing to Karen, whose knowledge of the social geography of the capital, a mere thirty miles away, was parochially scant. "And you want to report a missing person," she said.

Misha gave a sharp sniff and nodded. "My dad. Mick Prentice. Well, Michael, really, if you want to be precise."

"And when did your dad go missing?" This, thought Karen, was where it would get interesting. If it was ever going to get interesting.

"Like I told the guy downstairs, twenty-two and a half years ago. Friday, 14th December 1984 was the last time we saw him." Misha Gibson's brows drew down in a defiant scowl.

"It's kind of a long time to wait to report someone missing," Karen said.

Misha sighed and turned her head so she could look out of the window. "We didn't think he was missing. Not as such."

"I'm not with you. What do you mean, 'not as such'?"

Misha turned back and met Karen's steady gaze. "You sound like you're from round here."

Wondering where this was going, Karen said, "I grew up in Methil."

"Right. So, no disrespect, but you're old enough to remember what was going on in 1984."

"The miners' strike?"

Misha nodded. Her chin stayed high, her stare defiant. "I grew up in Newton of Wemyss. My dad was a miner. Before the strike, he worked down the Lady Charlotte. You'll mind what folk used to say round here—that nobody was more militant than the Lady Charlotte pitmen. Even so, there was one night in December, nine months into the strike, when half a dozen of them disappeared. Well, I say 'disappeared,' but everybody knew the truth. That they'd gone to Nottingham to join the blacklegs." Her face bunched in a tight frown, as if she was struggling with some physical pain. "Five of them, nobody was too surprised that they went scabbing. But according to my mum, everybody was stunned that my dad had joined them. Including her." She gave Karen a look of pleading. "I was too wee to remember. But everybody says he was a union man through and through. The last guy you'd expect to turn blackleg." She shook her head. "Still, what else was she supposed to think?"

Karen understood only too well what such a defection must have meant to Misha and her mother. In the radical Fife coalfield, sympathy was reserved for those who toughed it out. Mick Prentice's action would have granted his family instant pariah status. "It can't have been easy for your mum," she said.

"In one sense, it was dead easy," Misha said bitterly. "As far as she was concerned, that was it. He was dead to her. She wanted nothing more to do with him. He sent money, but she donated it to the hardship fund. Later, when the strike was over, she handed it over to the Miners' Welfare. I grew up in a house where my father's name was never spoken."

Karen felt a lump in her chest, somewhere between sympathy and pity. "He never got in touch?"

"Just the money. Always in used notes. Always with a Nottingham postmark."

"Misha, I don't want to come across like a bitch here, but it doesn't sound to me like your dad's a missing person." Karen tried to make her voice as gentle as possible.

"I didn't think so either. Till I went looking for him. Take it from me, Inspector. He's not where he's supposed to be. He never was. And I need him found."

The naked desperation in Misha's voice caught Karen by surprise. To her, that was more interesting than Mick Prentice's whereabouts. "How come?" she said.

Tuesday, 19th June 2007; Edinburgh

It had never occurred to Misha Gibson to count the number of times she'd emerged from the Sick Kids' with a sense of outrage that the world continued on its way in spite of what was happening inside the hospital behind her. She'd never thought to count because she'd never allowed herself to believe it might be for the last time. Ever since the doctors had explained the reason for Luke's misshapen thumbs and the scatter of café-au-lait spots across his narrow back, she had nailed herself to the conviction that somehow she would help her son dodge the bullet his genes had aimed at his life expectancy. Now it looked as if that conviction had finally been tested to destruction.

Misha stood uncertain for a moment, resenting the sunshine, wanting weather as bleak as her mood. She wasn't ready to go home yet. She wanted to scream and throw things, and an empty flat would tempt her to lose control and do just that. John wouldn't be home to hold her or to hold her back; he'd known about her meeting with the consultant so of course work would have thrown up something insurmountable that only he could deal with.

Instead of heading up through Marchmont to their sandstone tenement, Misha cut across the busy road to the Meadows, the green lung of the southern city centre where she loved to walk with Luke. Once, when she'd looked at their street on Google Earth, she'd checked out the Meadows too. From space, it looked like a rugby ball fringed with trees, the criss-cross paths like laces holding the ball together. She'd smiled at the thought of her and Luke scrambling over the surface like ants. Today, there were no smiles to console Misha. Today, she had to face the fact that she might never walk here with Luke again.

She shook her head, trying to dislodge the maudlin thoughts. Coffee, that's what she needed to gather her thoughts and get things into proportion. A brisk walk across the Meadows, then down to George IV Bridge, where every shop front was a bar, a café, or a restaurant these days.

Ten minutes later, Misha was tucked into a corner booth, a comforting mug of latte in front of her. It wasn't the end of the line. It couldn't be the end of the line. She wouldn't let it be the end of the line. There had to be some way to give Luke another chance.

She'd known something was wrong from the first moment she'd held him. Even dazed by drugs and drained by labour, she'd known. John had been in denial, refusing to set any store by their son's low birth weight and those stumpy little thumbs. But fear had clamped its cold certainty on Misha's heart. Luke was different. The only question in her mind had been how different.

The sole aspect of the situation that felt remotely like luck was that they were living in Edinburgh, a ten-minute walk from the Royal Hospital for Sick Children, an institution that regularly appeared in the "miracle" stories beloved of the tabloids. It didn't take long for the specialists at the Sick Kids' to identify the problem. Nor to explain that there would be no miracles here.

Fanconi Anaemia. If you said it fast, it sounded like an

Italian tenor or a Tuscan hill town. But the charming musicality of the words disguised their lethal message. Lurking in the DNA of both Luke's parents were recessive genes that had combined to create a rare condition that would condemn their son to a short and painful life. At some point between the ages of three and twelve, he was almost certain to develop aplastic anaemia, a breakdown of the bone marrow that would ultimately kill him unless a suitable donor could be found. The stark verdict was that without a successful bone marrow transplant, Luke would be lucky to make it into his twenties.

That information had given her a mission. She soon learned that, without siblings, Luke's best chance of a viable bone marrow transplant would come from a family member—what the doctors called a mismatched related transplant. At first, this had confused Misha. She'd read about bone marrow transplant registers and assumed their best hope was to find a perfect match there. But according to the consultant, a donation from a mismatched family member who shared some of Luke's genes had a lower risk of complications than a perfect match from a donor who wasn't part of their extended kith and kin.

Since then, Misha had been wading through the gene pool on both sides of the family, using persuasion, emotional blackmail, and even the offer of reward on distant cousins and elderly aunts. It had taken time, since it had been a solo mission. John had walled himself up behind a barrier of unrealistic optimism. There would be a medical breakthrough in stem cell research. Some doctor somewhere would discover a treatment whose success didn't rely on shared genes. A perfectly matched donor would turn up on a register somewhere. John collected good stories and happy endings. He trawled the Internet for cases that had proved the doctors wrong. He came up with medical miracles and apparently inexplicable cures on a weekly basis. And he drew his hope from this. He couldn't see the point of Misha's constant pursuit. He knew somehow it would be all right. His capacity for denial was Olympic.

It made her want to kill him.

Instead, she'd continued to clamber through the branches of their family trees in search of the perfect candidate. She'd come to her final dead end only a week or so before today's terrible judgement. There was only one possibility left. And it was the one possibility she had prayed she wouldn't have to consider.

Before her thoughts could go any further down that particular path, a shadow fell over her. She looked up, ready to be sharp with whoever wanted to intrude on her. "John," she said wearily.

"I thought I'd find you hereabouts. This is the third place I tried," he said, sliding into the booth, awkwardly shunting himself round till he was at right angles to her, close enough to touch if either of them had a mind to.

"I wasn't ready to face an empty flat."

"No, I can see that. What did they have to say?" His craggy face screwed up in anxiety. Not, she thought, over the consultant's verdict. He still believed his precious son was somehow invincible. What made John anxious was her reaction.

She reached for his hand, wanting contact as much as consolation. "It's time. Six months tops without the transplant." Her voice sounded cold even to her. But she couldn't afford warmth. Warmth would melt her frozen state, and this wasn't the place for an outpouring of grief or love.

John clasped her fingers tight inside his. "It's maybe not too late," he said. "Maybe they'll—"

"Please, John. Not now."

His shoulders squared inside his suit jacket, his body tensing as he held his dissent close. "So," he said, an outbreath that was more sigh than anything else. "I suppose that means you're going looking for the bastard?"

Wednesday, 27th June 2007; Glenrothes

Karen scratched her head with her pen. *Why do I get all the good ones?* "Why did you leave it so long to try to trace your father?"

She caught a fleeting expression of irritation round Misha's mouth and eyes. "Because I'd been brought up thinking my father was a selfish blackleg bastard. What he did cast my mother adrift from her own community. It got me bullied in the play park and later on at school. I didn't think a man who dumped his family in the shit like that would be bothered about his grandson."

"He sent money," Karen said.

"A few quid here, a few quid there. Blood money," Misha said. "Like I said, my mum wouldn't touch it. She gave it away. I never saw the benefit of it."

"Maybe he tried to make it up to your mum. Parents don't always tell us the uncomfortable truths."

Misha shook her head. "You don't know my mum. Even with Luke's life at stake, she wasn't comfortable with me trying to track down my dad."

To Karen, it seemed a thin reason for avoiding a man who might provide the key to a boy's future. But she knew how deep feelings ran in the old mining communities, so she let it lie. "You say he wasn't where he was supposed to be. What happened when you went looking for him?"

Thursday, 21st June 2007; Newton of Wemyss

Jenny Prentice pulled a bag of potatoes out of the vegetable rack and set about peeling them, her body bowed over the sink, her back turned to her daughter. Misha's question hung unanswered between them, reminding them both of the barrier her father's absence had put between them from the beginning. Misha tried again. "I said—"

"I heard you fine. There's nothing the matter with my hearing," Jenny said. "And the answer is, I've no bloody idea. How would I know where to start looking for that selfish scabbing sack of shite? We've managed fine without him the last twenty-two years. There's been no cause to go looking for him."

"Well, there's cause now." Misha stared at her mother's rounded shoulders. The weak light that spilled in through the small kitchen window accentuated the silver in her undyed hair. She was barely fifty, but she seemed to have bypassed middle age, heading straight for the vulnerable stoop of the little old lady. It was as if she knew this attack would arrive one day and had chosen to defend herself by becoming piteous.

"He'll not help," Jenny scoffed. "He showed what he thought of us when he left us to face the music. He was always out for number one."

"Maybe so. But I've still got to try for Luke's sake," Misha said. "Was there never a return address on the envelopes the money came in?"

Jenny cut a peeled potato in half and dropped it in a pan of salted water. "No. He couldn't even be bothered to put a wee letter in the envelope. Just a bundle of dirty notes, that's all."

"What about the guys he went with?"

Jenny cast a quick contemptuous glance at Misha. "What about them? They don't show their faces round here."

"But some of them have still got family here or in East Wemyss. Brothers, cousins. They might know something about my dad."

Jenny shook her head firmly. "I've never heard tell of him since the day he walked out. Not a whisper, good or bad. The other men he went with, they were no friends of his. The only reason he took a lift with them was he had no money to make his own way south. He'll have used them like he used us and then he'll have gone his own sweet way once he got where he wanted to be." She dropped another potato in the pan and said without enthusiasm, "Are you staying for your dinner?"

"No, I've got things to see to," Misha said, impatient at her mother's refusal to take her quest seriously. "There must be somebody he's kept in touch with. Who would he have talked to? Who would he have told what he was planning?"

Jenny straightened up and put the pan on the old-fashioned gas cooker. Misha and John offered to replace the chipped and battered stove every time they sat down to the production number that was Sunday dinner, but Jenny always refused with the air of frustrating martyrdom she brought to every offer of kindness. "You're out of luck there too." She eased herself on to one of the two chairs that flanked the tiny table in the cramped kitchen. "He only had one real pal. Andy Kerr. He was a red-hot Commie, was Andy. I tell you, by 1984, there weren't many still keeping the red flag flying, but Andy was one of them. He'd been a union official well before the strike. Him and your father, they'd been best pals since school." Her face softened for a moment and Misha could almost make out the young woman she'd been. "They were always up to something, those two."

"So where do I find this Andy Kerr?" Misha sat down opposite her mother, her desire to be gone temporarily abandoned.

Her mother's face twisted into a wry grimace. "Poor soul. If you can find Andy, you'll be quite the detective." She leaned across and patted Misha's hand. "He's another one of your father's victims."

"How do you mean?"

"Andy adored your father. He thought the sun shone out of his backside. Poor Andy. The strike put him under terrible pressure. He believed in the strike, he believed in the struggle. But it broke his heart to see the hardship his men were going through. He was on the edge of a nervous breakdown, and the local executive forced him to go on the sick not long before your father shot the craw. Nobody saw him after that. He lived out in the middle of nowhere, so nobody noticed he was away." She gave a long, weary sigh. "He sent a postcard to your dad from some place up north. But of course, he was blacklegging by then, so he never got it. Later, when Andy came back, he left a note for his sister, saying he couldn't take any more. Killed himself, the poor soul."

"What's that got to do with my dad?" Misha demanded.

"I always thought your dad going scabbing was the straw that broke the camel's back." Jenny's expression was pious shading into smug. "That was what drove Andy over the edge."

"You can't know that." Misha pulled away in disgust.

"I'm not the only one around here that thinks the same thing. If your father had confided in anybody, it would have been Andy. And that would have been one burden too many for that fragile wee soul. He took his own life, knowing that his one real friend had betrayed everything he stood for." On that melodramatic note, Jenny got to her feet and lifted a bag of carrots from the vegetable rack. It was clear she had shot her bolt on the subject of Mick Prentice.

Wednesday, 27th June 2007; Glenrothes

Karen sneaked a look at her watch. Whatever fine qualities Misha Gibson might possess, brevity was not one of them. "So Andy Kerr turned out to be literally a dead end?"

"My mother thinks so. But apparently they never found his body. Maybe he didn't kill himself after all," Misha said.

"They don't always turn up," Karen said. "Sometimes the sea claims them. Or else the wilderness. There's still a lot of empty space in this country." Resignation took possession of Misha's face. She was, Karen thought, a woman inclined to believe what she was told. If anyone knew that, it would be her mother. Perhaps things weren't quite as clear cut as Jenny Prentice wanted her daughter to think.

"That's true," Misha said. "And my mother did say that he left a note. Will the police still have the note?"

Karen shook her head. "I doubt it. If we ever had it, it will have been given back to his family."

"Would there not have been an inquest? Would they not have needed it for that?"

"You mean a Fatal Accident Inquiry," Karen said. "Not without a body, no. If there's a file at all, it'll be a missing-person case."

"But he's not missing. His sister had him declared dead. Their parents both died in the Zeebrugge ferry disaster, but apparently their dad had always refused to believe Andy was dead so he hadn't changed his will to leave the house to the sister. She had to go to court to get Andy pronounced dead so she would inherit. That's what my mother said, anyway." Not a flicker of doubt disturbed Misha's expression.

Karen made a note, *Andy Kerr's sister,* and added a little asterisk to it. "So if Andy killed himself, we're back with scabbing as the only reasonable explanation of your dad's disappearance. Have you made any attempts to contact the guys he's supposed to have gone away with?"

Monday, 25th June 2007; Edinburgh

Ten past nine on a Monday morning, and already Misha felt exhausted. She should be at the Sick Kids' by now, focusing on Luke. Playing with him, reading to him, cajoling therapists into expanding their regimes, discussing treatment plans with medical staff, using all her energy to fill them with her conviction that her son could be saved. And if he could be saved, they all owed it to him to shovel every scrap of therapeutic intervention his way.

But instead, she was sitting on the floor, back to the wall, knees bent, phone cradled in her lap, notepad at her side. She told herself she was summoning the courage to make a phone call, but she knew in a corner of her mind exhaustion was the real reason for her inactivity.

Other families used the weekends to relax, to recharge their batteries. But not the Gibsons. For a start, fewer staff were on duty at the hospital, so Misha and John felt obliged to pile even more energy than usual into Luke. There was no respite when they came home either. Misha's acceptance that the last best hope for their son lay in finding her father had simply escalated the conflict between her missionary ardour and John's passive optimism.

This weekend had been harder going than usual. Having a time limit put on Luke's life imbued each moment they shared with more value and more poignancy. It was hard to avoid a kind of melodramatic sentimentality. As soon as they'd left the hospital on Saturday Misha had picked up the refrain she'd been delivering since she'd seen her mother. "I need to go to Nottingham, John. You know I do."

He shoved his hands into the pockets of his rain jacket, thrusting his head forward as if he was butting against a high wind. "Just phone the guy," he said. "If he's got anything to tell you, he'll tell you on the phone."

"Maybe not." She took a couple of steps at a trot to keep pace with him. "People always tell you more face to face. He could maybe put me on to the other guys that went down with him. They might know something."

John snorted. "And how come your mother can only remember one guy's name? How come she can't put you on to the other guys?"

"I told you. She's put everything out of her mind about that time. I really had to push her before she came up with Logan Laidlaw's name."

"And you don't think it's amazing that the only guy whose name she can remember has no family in the area? No obvious way to track him down?"

Misha pushed her arm through his, partly to make him slow down. "But I did track him down, didn't I? You're too suspicious."

"No, I'm not. Your mother doesn't understand the power of the Internet. She doesn't know about things like online electoral rolls or 192.com. She thinks if there's no human being to ask, you're screwed. She didn't think she was giving you anything you could use. She doesn't want you poking about in this, she's not going to help you."

"That makes two of you then." Misha pulled her arm free and strode out ahead of him.

John caught up with her on the corner of their street. "That's not fair," he said. "I just don't want you getting hurt unnecessarily."

"You think watching my boy die and not doing anything that might save him isn't hurting me?" Misha felt the heat of anger in her cheeks, knew the hot tears of rage were lurking close to the surface. She turned her face away from him, blinking desperately at the tall sandstone tenements.

"We'll find a donor. Or they'll find a treatment. All this stem cell research, it's moving really fast."

"Not fast enough for Luke," Misha said, the familiar sensation of weight in her stomach slowing her steps. "John, please. I need to go to Nottingham. I need you to take a couple of days off work, cover for me with Luke."

"You don't need to go. You can talk to the guy on the phone."

"It's not the same. You know that. When you're dealing with clients, you don't do it over the phone. Not for anything important. You go out and see them. You want to see the whites of their eyes. All I'm asking is for you to take a couple of days off, to spend time with your son."

His eyes flashed dangerously and she knew she'd gone too far. John shook his head stubbornly. "Just make the phone call, Misha."

And that was that. Long experience with her husband had taught her that when John took a position he believed was right, going over the same ground only gave him the opportunity to build stronger fortifications. She had no fresh arguments that could challenge his decision. So here she was, sitting on the floor, trying to shape sentences in her head that would persuade Logan Laidlaw to tell her what had happened to her father since he'd walked out on her more than twenty-two years earlier.

Her mother hadn't given her much to base a strategy on. Laidlaw was a waster, a womanizer, a man who, at thirty, had still acted like a teenager. He'd been married and divorced by twenty-five, building the sour reputation of a man who was too handy with his fists around women. Misha's picture of her father was patchy and partial, but even with the bias imposed by her mother, Mick Prentice didn't sound like the sort of man who would have had much time for Logan Laidlaw. Still, hard times made for strange company.

At last, Misha picked up the phone and keyed in the number she'd tracked down via Internet searches and directory enquiries. He'd probably be out at work, she thought on the fourth ring. Or asleep.

The sixth ring cut off abruptly. A deep voice grunted an approximate hello.

"Is that Logan Laidlaw?" Misha said, working to keep her voice level.

"I've got a kitchen and I don't want any insurance." The Fife accent was still strong, the words bumping into each other with the familiar rise and fall.

"I'm not trying to sell you anything, Mr. Laidlaw. I just want to talk to you."

"Aye, right. And I'm the prime minister."

She could sense he was on the point of ending the call. "I'm Mick Prentice's daughter," she blurted out, strategy hopelessly holed beneath the waterline. Across the distance, she could hear the liquid wheeze of his breathing. "Mick Prentice from Newton of Wemyss," she tried.

"I know where Mick Prentice is from. What I don't know is what Mick Prentice has to do with me."

"Look, I realize the two of you might not see much of each other these days, but I'd really appreciate anything you could tell me. I really need to find him." Misha's own accent slipped a few gears till she was matching his own broad tongue.

A pause. Then, with a baffled note, "Why are you talking to me? I haven't seen Mick Prentice since I left Newton of Wemyss way back in 1984."

"OK, but even if you split up as soon as you got to Nottingham, you must have some idea of where he ended up, where he was heading for?"

"Listen, hen, I don't have a clue what you're on about. What do you mean, split up as soon as we got to Nottingham?" He sounded irritated, what little patience he had evaporating in the heat of her demands.

Misha gulped a deep breath, then spoke slowly. "I just want to know what happened to my dad after you got to Nottingham. I need to find him."

"Are you wrong in the head or something, lassie? I've no idea what happened to your dad after I came to Nottingham, and here's for why. I was in Nottingham and he was in Newton of Wemyss. And even when we were both in the same place, we weren't what you would call pals."

The words hit like a splash of cold water. Was there something wrong with Logan Laidlaw's memory? Was he losing his grip on the past? "No, that's not right," she said. "He came to Nottingham with you."

A bark of laughter, then a gravel cough. "Somebody's been winding you up, lassie," he wheezed. "Trotsky would have crossed a picket line before the Mick Prentice I knew. What makes you think he came to Nottingham?"

"It's not just me. Everybody thinks he went to Nottingham with you and the other men."

"That's mental. Why would anybody think that? Do you not know your own family history?"

"What do you mean?"

"Christ, lassie, your great-grandfather. Your father's granddad. Do you not know about him?"

Misha had no idea where this was going, but at least he hadn't hung up on her as she'd earlier feared he would. "He was dead before I was even born. I don't know anything about him, except that he was a miner too."

"Jackie Prentice," Laidlaw said with something approaching relish. "He was a strike breaker back in 1926. After it was settled, he had to be moved to a job on the surface. When your life depends on the men in your team, you don't want to be a scab underground. Not unless everybody else is in the same boat, like with us. Christ knows why Jackie stayed in the village. He had to take the bus to Dysart to get a drink. There wasn't a bar in any of the Wemyss villages that would serve him. So your dad and your granddad had to work twice as hard as anybody else to be accepted down the pit. No way would Mick Prentice throw that respect away. He'd sooner starve. Aye, and see you starve with him. Wherever you got your info, they don't know what the hell they're talking about."

"My mother told me. It's what everybody says in the Newton." The impact of his words left her feeling as if all the air had been sucked from her.

"Well, they're wrong. Why would anybody think that?"

"Because the night you went to Nottingham was the last night anyone in the Newton saw him or heard from him. And because my mother occasionally gets money in the post with a Nottingham postmark."

Laidlaw breathed heavily, a concertina wheeze in her ear. "By Christ, that's wild. Well, sweetheart, I'm sorry to disappoint you. There was five of us left Newton of Wemyss that December night. But your dad wasn't among us."

Wednesday, 27th June 2007; Glenrothes

Karen stopped at the canteen for a chicken salad sandwich on the way back to her desk. Criminals and witnesses could seldom fool Karen, but when it came to food, she could fool herself seventeen ways before breakfast. The sandwich, for example. Wholegrain bread, a swatch of wilted lettuce, a couple of slices of tomato and cucumber, and it became a health food. Never mind the butter and the mayo. In her head, the calories were cancelled by the benefits. She tucked her notebook under her arm and ripped open the plastic sandwich box as she walked.

Phil Parhatka looked up as she flopped into her chair. Not for the first time, the angle of his head reminded her that he looked like a darker, skinnier version of Matt Damon. There was the same jut of nose and jaw, the straight brows, *The Bourne Identity* haircut, the expression that could swing from open to guarded in a heartbeat. Just the colouring was different. Phil's Polish ancestry was responsible for his dark hair, brown eyes, and thick pale skin; his personality had contributed the tiny hole in his left earlobe, a piercing that generally accommodated a diamond stud when he was off duty. "How was it for you?" he said.

"More interesting than I expected," she admitted, getting up again to fetch herself a Diet Coke. Between bites and swallows, she gave him a concise précis of Misha Gibson's story.

"And she believes what this old geezer in Nottingham told her?" he said, leaning back in his chair and linking his fingers behind his head.

"I think she's the sort of woman who generally believes what people tell her," Karen said.

"She'd make a lousy copper, then. So, I take it you'll be passing it across to Central Division to get on with?"

Karen took a chunk out of her sandwich and chewed vigorously, the muscles of her jaw and temple bulging and contracting like a stress ball under pressure. She swallowed before she'd finished chewing properly, then washed the mouthful down with a swig of Diet Coke. "Not sure," she said. "It's kind of interesting."

Phil gave her a wary look. "Karen, it's not a cold case. It's not ours to play with."

"If I pass it over to Central, it'll wither on the vine. Nobody over there's going to bother with a case where the trail went cold twenty-two years ago." She refused to meet his disapproving eye. "You know that as well as I do. And according to Misha Gibson, her kid's drinking in the last-chance saloon."

"That still doesn't make it a cold case."

"Just because it wasn't opened in 1984 doesn't mean it's not cold now." Karen waved the remains of her sandwich at the files on her desk. "And none of this lot are going anywhere any time soon. Darren Anderson—nothing I can do till the cops in the Canaries get their fingers out and find which bar his ex-girlfriend's working in. Ishbel Mackindoe—waiting for the lab to tell me if they can get any viable DNA from the anonymous letters. Patsy Millar—can't get any further with that till the Met finish digging up the garden in Haringey and do the forensics."

"There's witnesses in the Patsy Millar case that we could talk to again."

Karen shrugged. She knew she could pull rank on Phil and shut him up that way, but she needed the ease between them too much. "They'll keep. Or else you can take one of the DCs and give them some on-the-job training."

"If you think they need on-the-job training, you should give them this stone-cold missing person case. You're a DI now,

Karen. You're not supposed to be chasing about on stuff like this." He waved a hand towards the two DCs sitting at their computers. "That's for the likes of them. What this is about is that you're bored." Karen tried to protest but Phil carried on regardless. "I said when you took this promotion that flying a desk would drive you mental. And now look at you. Sneaking cases out from under the woolly suits at Central. Next thing, you'll be going off to do your own interviews."

"So?" Karen screwed up the sandwich container with more force than was strictly necessary and tossed it in the bin. "It's good to keep my hand in. And I'll make sure it's all above board. I'll take DC Murray with me."

"The Mint?" The tone in Phil's voice was incredulous, the look on his face offended. "You'd take the Mint over me?"

Karen smiled sweetly. "You're a sergeant now, Phil. A sergeant with ambitions. Staying in the office and keeping my seat warm will help your aspirations become a reality. Besides, the Mint's not as bad as you make out. He does what he's told."

"So does a collie dog. But a dog would show more initiative."

"There's a kid's life at stake, Phil. I've got more than enough initiative for both of us. This needs to be done right and I'm going to make sure it is." She turned to her computer with an air of having finished with the conversation.

Phil opened his mouth to say more, then thought better of it when he saw the repressive glance Karen flashed in his direction. They'd been drawn to each other from the start of their careers, each recognizing nonconformist tendencies in the other. Having come up the ranks together had left the pair of them with a friendship that had survived the challenge of altered status. But he knew there were limits to how far he could push Karen, and he had a feeling he'd just butted up against them. "I'll cover for you here, then," he said.

"Works for me," Karen said, her fingers flying over the keys. "Book me out for tomorrow morning. I've a feeling Jenny Prentice might be a wee bit more forthcoming to a pair of polis than she was to her daughter."

THURSDAY, 28TH JUNE 2007; EDINBURGH

Learning to wait was one of the lessons that courses in journalism didn't teach. When Bel Richmond had had a full-time job on a Sunday paper, she had always maintained that she was paid not for a forty-hour week but for the five minutes when she talked her way across a doorstep that nobody else had managed to cross. That left a lot of time for waiting. Waiting for someone to return a call. Waiting for the next stage of the story to break. Waiting for a contact to turn into a source. Bel had done a lot of waiting and, while she'd become skilled at it, she had never learned to love it.

She had to admit she'd passed the time in surroundings that were a lot less salubrious than this. Here, she had the physical comforts of coffee, cookies, and newspapers. And the room she'd been left in commanded the panoramic view that had graced a million shortbread tins. Running the length of Princes Street, it featured a clutch of keynote tourist sights—the castle, the Scott Monument, the National Gallery, and Princes Street Gardens. Bel spotted other significant architectural eye candy, but she didn't know enough about the city to identify it. She'd visited the Scottish capital only a few times, and conducting this meeting here hadn't been her choice. She'd wanted it in London, but her reluctance to show her hand in advance had turfed her out of the driving seat and into the role of supplicant.

Unusually for a freelance journalist, she had a temporary research assistant. Jonathan was a journalism student at City University, and he'd asked his tutor to assign him to Bel for his work experience assignment. Apparently he liked her style. She'd been mildly gratified by the compliment and delighted at the prospect of having eight weeks free from drudgery. And so it was Jonathan who had made the first contact with Maclennan Grant Enterprises. The message he'd returned with was simple. If Ms. Richmond was not prepared to state her reason for wanting a meeting with Sir Broderick Maclennan Grant, Sir Broderick was not prepared to meet her. Sir Broderick did not give interviews. Further arm's-length negotiations had led to this compromise.

And now Bel was, she thought, being put in her place. Being forced to cool her heels in a hotel meeting room. Being made to understand that someone as important as the personal assistant to the chairman and principal shareholder of the country's twelfth most valuable company had more pressing calls on her time than dancing attendance on some London hack.

She wanted to get up and pace, but she didn't want to reveal any lack of composure. Giving up the high ground was not something that had ever come naturally to her. Instead she straightened her jacket, made sure her shirt was tucked in properly, and picked a stray piece of grit from her emerald suede shoes.

At last, precisely fifteen minutes after the agreed time, the door opened. The woman who entered in a flurry of tweed and cashmere resembled a school mistress of indeterminate age but one accustomed to exerting discipline over her pupils. For one crazy moment, Bel nearly jumped to her feet in a Pavlovian response to her own teenage memories of terrorist nuns. But she managed to restrain herself and stood up in a more leisurely manner.

"Susan Charleson," the woman said, extending a hand. "Sorry to keep you waiting. As Harold Macmillan once said, 'Events, dear boy. Events.' "

Bel decided not to point out that Harold Macmillan had been referring to the job of prime minister, not wet nurse to a captain of industry. She took the warm dry fingers in her own. A moment's sharp grip, then she was released. "Annabel Richmond."

Susan Charleson ignored the armchair opposite Bel and headed instead for the table by the window. Wrong-footed, Bel scooped up her bag and the leather portfolio beside it and followed. The women sat down opposite each other and Susan smiled, her teeth like a line of chalky toothpaste between the dark pink lipstick. "You wanted to see Sir Broderick," she said. No preamble, no small talk about the view. Just straight to the chase. It was a technique Bel had used herself on occasion, but that didn't mean she enjoyed the tables being turned.

"That's right."

Susan shook her head. "Sir Broderick does not speak to the press. I fear you've had a wasted journey. I did explain all that to your assistant, but he wouldn't take no for an answer."

It was Bel's turn to produce a smile without warmth. "Good for him. I've obviously got him well trained. But there seems to be a misunderstanding. I'm not here to beg for an interview. I'm here because I think I have something Sir Broderick will be interested in." She lifted the portfolio on to the table and unzipped it. From inside, she took a single A3 sheet of heavyweight paper, face down. It was smeared with dirt and gave off a faint smell, a curious blend of dust, urine, and lavender. Bel couldn't resist a quick teasing look at Susan Charleson. "Would you like to see?" she said, flipping the paper.

Susan took a leather case from the pocket of her skirt and extracted a pair of tortoiseshell glasses. She perched them on her nose, taking her time about it, but her eyes never left the stark black-and-white images before her. The silence between the women seemed to expand, and Bel felt almost breathless as she waited for a response. "Where did you come by this?" Susan said, her tone as prim as a Latin mistress.

Monday, 18th June 2007; Campora, Tuscany, Italy

At seven in the morning, it was almost possible to believe that the baking heat of the previous ten days might not show up for work. Pearly daylight shimmered through the canopy of oak and chestnut leaves, making visible the motes of dust that spiralled upwards from Bel's feet. She was moving slowly enough to notice because the unpaved track that wound down through the woods was rutted and pitted, the jagged stones scattered over it enough to make any jogger conscious of the fragility of ankles.

Only two more of these cherished early-morning runs before she'd have to head back to the suffocating streets of London. The thought provoked a tiny tug of regret. Bel loved slipping out of the villa while everyone else was still asleep. She could walk barefoot over cool marble floors, pretending she was chatelaine of the whole place, not just another holiday tenant carving off a slice of borrowed Tuscan elegance.

She'd been coming on holiday with the same group of five friends since they'd shared a house in their final year at Durham. That first time, they'd all been cramming for their finals. One set of parents had a cottage in Cornwall that they'd colonized for a week. They'd called it a study break, but in truth, it had been more of a holiday that had refreshed and relaxed them, leaving them better placed to sit exams than if they'd huddled over books and articles. And although they were modern young women not given to superstition, they'd all felt that their week together had somehow been responsible for their good degrees. Since then, they'd gathered together every June for a reunion, committed to pleasure.

Over the years, their drinking had grown more discerning, their eating more epicurean, and their conversation more outrageous. The locations had become progressively more luxurious. Lovers were never invited to share the girls' week. Occasionally, one of their number had a little wobble, claiming pressure of work or family obligations, but they were generally whipped back into line without too much effort.

For Bel, it was a significant component of her life. These women were all successful, all private sources she could count on to smooth her path from time to time. But still, that wasn't the main reason this holiday was so important to her. Partners had come and gone, but these friends had been constant. In a world where you were measured by your last headline, it felt good to have a refuge where none of that mattered. Where she was appreciated simply because the group enjoyed themselves more with her than without her. They'd all known each other long enough to forgive each other's faults, to accept each other's politics, and to say what would be unsayable in any other company. This holiday formed part of the bulwark she constantly shored up against her own insecurities. Besides, it was the only holiday she took these days that was about what she wanted. For the past half-dozen years, she'd been bound to her widowed sister Vivianne and her son Harry. The sudden death of Vivianne's husband from a heart attack had left her emotionally stranded and practically struggling. Bel had barely hesitated before throwing her lot in with her sister and her nephew. On balance it had been a good decision, but even so she still treasured this annual work-free break from a family life she hadn't expected to be living. Especially now that Harry was teetering on the edge of teenage existential angst. So this year, even more than in the past, the holiday had to be special, to outdo what had gone before.

It was hard to imagine how they could improve on this, she thought as she emerged from the trees and turned into a field of sunflowers preparing to burst into bloom. She speeded up a little as she made her way along the margin, her nose twitching at the aromatic perfume of the greenery. There was nothing she'd change about the villa, no fault she could find with the informal gardens and fruit trees that surrounded the loggia and the pool. The view across the Val d'Elsa was stunning, with Volterra and San Gimignano on the distant skyline.

And there was the added bonus of Grazia's cooking. When they'd discovered that the "local chef" trumpeted on the website was the wife of the pig farmer down the hill, they'd been wary of taking up the option of having her come to the villa and prepare a typically Tuscan meal. But on the third afternoon, they'd all been too stunned by the heat to be bothered with cooking so they'd summoned Grazia. Her husband Maurizio had delivered her to the villa in a battered Fiat Panda that appeared to be held together with string and faith.

He'd also unloaded boxes of food covered in muslin cloths. In fractured English, Grazia had thrown them out of the kitchen and told them to relax with a drink on the loggia.

The meal had been a revelation—nutty salamis and prosciutto from the rare Cinta di Siena pigs Maurizio bred, coupled with fragrant black figs from their own tree; spaghetti with pesto made from tarragon and basil; quails roasted with Maurizio's vegetables, and long fingers of potatoes flavoured with rosemary and garlic; cheeses from local farms, and finally, a rich cake heavy with limoncello and almonds.

The women never cooked dinner again.

Grazia's cooking made Bel's morning runs all the more necessary. As forty approached, she struggled harder to maintain what she thought of as her fighting weight. This morning, her stomach still felt like a tight round ball after the meltingly delicious *melanzane alla parmigiana* that had provoked her into an excessive second helping. She'd go a little farther than usual, she decided. Instead of making a circuit of the sunflower field and climbing back up to their villa, she would take a track that ran from the far corner through the overgrown grounds of a ruined *casa colonica* she'd noticed from the car. Ever since she'd spotted it on their first morning, she'd indulged a fantasy of buying the ruin and transforming it into the ultimate Tuscan retreat, complete with swimming pool and olive grove. And of course, Grazia on hand to cook. Bel had few qualms about poaching, neither in fantasy nor reality.

But she knew herself well enough to understand it would never be more than a pipe dream. Having a retreat implied a willingness that was alien to her, to step away from the world of work. Maybe when she was ready to retire she could contemplate devoting herself to such a restoration project. Except that she recognized that as another daydream. Journalists never really retired. There was always another story on the horizon, another target to pursue. Not to mention the terror of being forgotten. All reasons why past relationships had failed to stay the course, all reasons why the future probably held the same imperfections. Still, it would be fun to take a closer look at the old house, to see just how bad a state it was in. When she'd mentioned it to Grazia, she'd pulled a face and called it *rovina*. Bel, whose Italian was fluent, had translated it for the others: "ruin." Time to find out whether Grazia was telling the truth or just trying to divert the interest of the rich English women.

The path through the long grass was still surprisingly clear, bare soil packed hard by years of foot traffic. Bel took the opportunity to pick up speed, then slowed as she reached the edge of the gated courtyard in front of the old farmhouse. The gates were dilapidated, hanging drunkenly from hinges that were barely attached to the tall stone posts. A heavy chain and padlock held them fastened. Beyond, the courtyard's broken paving was demarcated with tufts of creeping thyme, chamomile, and coarse weeds. Bel shook the gates without much expectation. But that was enough to reveal that the bottom corner of the right-hand gate had parted company completely with its support. It could readily be pulled clear enough to allow an adult through the gap. Bel slipped through and let go. The gate creaked faintly as it settled back into place, returning to apparent closure.

Close up, she could understand Grazia's description. Anyone taking this project on would be in thrall to the builders for a very long time. The house surrounded the courtyard on three sides, a central wing flanked by a matching pair of arms. There were two storeys, with a loggia running round the whole of the upper floor, doors and windows giving on to it, providing the bedrooms with easy access to fresh air and common space. But the loggia floor sagged, what doors remained were skewed, and the lintels above the windows were cracked and oddly angled. The window panes on both floors were filthy, cracked, or missing. But still the solid lines of the attractive vernacular architecture were obvious and the rough stones glowed warm in the morning sun.

Bel couldn't have explained why, but the house drew her closer. It had the raddled charm of a former beauty sufficiently self-assured to let herself go without a fight. Unpruned bougainvillea straggled up the peeling ochre stucco and over the low wall of the loggia. If nobody chose to fall in love with this place soon, it was going to be overwhelmed by vegetation. In a couple of generations, it would be nothing more than an inexplicable mound on the hillside. But for now, it still had the power to bewitch.

She picked her way across the crumbling courtyard, passing cracked terracotta pots lying askew, the herbs they'd contained sprawling and springing free, spicing the air with their fragrances. She pushed against a heavy door made of wooden planks hanging from a single hinge. The wood screeched against an uneven floor of herringbone brick, but it opened wide enough for Bel to enter a large room without squeezing. Her first impression was of grime and neglect. Cobwebs were strung in a maze from wall to wall. The windows were mottled with dirt. A distant scurrying had Bel peering around in panic. She had no fear of news editors, but four-legged rats filled her with revulsion.

As she grew accustomed to the gloom, Bel realized the room wasn't completely empty. A long table stood against one wall. Opposite was a sagging sofa. Judging by the rest of the place, it should have been rotten and filthy, but the dark red upholstery was still relatively clean. She filed the oddity for further consideration.

Bel hesitated for a moment. None of her friends, she was sure, would be urging her to penetrate deeper into this strange deserted house. But she had built her career on a reputation for fearlessness. Only she knew how often the image had concealed levels of anxiety and uncertainty that had reduced her to throwing up in gutters and strange toilets. Given what she'd faced down in her determination to secure a story, how scary could an abandoned ruin be?

A doorway in the far corner led to a cramped hallway with a worn stone staircase climbing up to the loggia. Beyond, she could see another dark and grubby room. She peered in, surprised to see a thin cord strung across one corner from which half a dozen metal coat hangers dangled. A knitted scarf was slung round the neck of one of the hangers. Beneath it, she could see a crumpled pile of camouflage material. It looked like one of the shooting jackets on sale at the van that occupied the turnout opposite the café on the main Colle Val d'Elsa road. The women had been laughing about it just the other day, wondering when exactly it had become fashionable for Italian men of all ages to look as if they'd just walked in from a tour of duty in the Balkans. *Weird,* she thought. Bel cautiously climbed the stairs to the loggia, expecting the same sense of long-abandoned habitation.

But as soon as she emerged from the stairwell, she realized she'd stepped into something very different. When she turned to her left and glanced in the first door, she understood this house was not what it seemed. The rancid mustiness of the lower floor was only a faint note here, the air almost as fresh as it was outside. The room had obviously been a bedroom, and fairly recently at that. A mattress lay on the floor, a bedspread flung back casually across the bottom third. It was dusty but had none of the ingrained grime the lower floor had led Bel to expect. Again, a cord was strung across the corner. There were a dozen empty hangers, but the final three held slightly crumpled shirts. Even from a distance, she could see they were past their best, fade lines across the sleeves and collars.

A pair of tomato crates acted as bedside tables. One held a stump of candle in a saucer. A yellowed copy of the *Frankfurter Allgemeine Zeitung* lay on the floor next to the bed. Bel picked it up, noting that the date was less than four months ago. So that gave her an idea of when this place had been last abandoned. She lifted one of the shirtsleeves and pressed it to her nose. Rosemary and marijuana. Faint but unmistakable.

She went back to the loggia and checked out the other rooms. The pattern was similar. Three more bedrooms containing a handful of leftovers—a couple of T-shirts, paperbacks and magazines in English, Italian, and German, half a bottle of wine, the stub of a lipstick, a leather sandal whose sole had parted company with its upper—the sort of things you would leave behind if you were moving out with no thought of who might come after. In one, a bunch of flowers stuck in an olive jar had dried to fragility.

The final room on the west side was the biggest so far. Its windows had been cleaned more recently than any of the others, its shutters renovated and its walls whitewashed. Standing in the middle of the floor was a silk-screen printing frame. Trestle tables set against one wall contained plastic cups stained inside with dried pigments, and brushes stiff with neglect. A scatter of spots and blots marked the floor. Bel was intrigued, her curiosity overcoming any lingering nervousness at being alone in this peculiar place. Whoever had been here must have cleared out in a hurry. Leaving a substantial silk-screen frame behind wasn't what you would do if your departure was planned.

She backed out of the studio and made her way along the loggia to the wing opposite. She was careful to stay close to the wall, not trusting the undulating brick floor with her weight. She passed the bedroom doors, feeling like a trespasser on the *Mary Celeste*. A silence unbroken even by birdsong accentuated the impression. The last room before the corner was a bathroom whose nauseating mix of odours still hung in the air. A coil of hosepipe lay on the floor, its tail end disappearing through a hole in the masonry near the window. So they had improvised some sort of running water, though not enough to make the toilet anything less than disgusting. She wrinkled her nose and backed away.

Bel rounded the corner just as the sun cleared the corner of the woods, flooding her in sudden warmth. It made her entry into the final room all the more chilling. Shivering at the dank air, she ventured inside. The shutters were pulled tight, making the interior almost too dim to discern anything. But as her eyes adjusted, she gained a sense of the room. It was the twin of the studio in scale, but its function was quite different. She crossed to the nearest window and struggled with the shutter, finally managing to haul it halfway open. It was enough to confirm her first impression; this had been the heart of the occupation of the *casa rovina*. A battered old cooking range connected to a gas cylinder stood by a stone sink. The dining table was scarred and stripped to the bare wood, but it was solid and had beautifully carved legs. Seven unmatched chairs sat around it, an eighth overturned a few feet away. A rocking chair and a couple of sofas lined the walls. Odd bits of crockery and cutlery lay scattered around, as if the inhabitants couldn't be bothered collecting them when they'd left.

As Bel walked back from the window, a rickety table caught her eye. Standing behind the door, it was easy to miss. An untidy scatter of what appeared to be posters lay across it. Fascinated, she moved towards it. Two strides and she stopped short, her sharp gasp echoing in the dusty air.

Before her on the limestone flags was an irregular stain, perhaps three feet by eighteen inches. Rusty brown, its edges were rounded and smooth, as if it had flowed and pooled rather than spilled. It was thick enough to obscure the flags beneath. One section on the farthest edge looked smudged and thinned, as if someone had tried to scrub it clean and soon given up. Bel had covered enough stories of domestic violence and sexual homicide to recognize a serious bloodstain when she saw it.

Startled, she stepped back, head swivelling from side to side, heart thudding so hard she thought it might choke her. What the hell had happened here? She looked around wildly, noticing other dark stains marking the floor beyond the table. *Time to get out of here,* the sensible part of her mind was screaming. But the devil of curiosity muttered in her ear. *There's been nobody here for months. Look at the dust. They're long gone. They're not going to be back any time soon. Whatever happened here was good reason for them to clear out. Check out the posters . . .*

Bel skirted the stain, giving it as wide a berth as she could without touching any of the furniture. All at once, she felt a taint in the air. Knew it was imagination, but still it seemed real. Back to the room, face to the door, she crab-walked to the table and looked down at the posters strewn across it.

The second shock was almost more powerful than the first.

Bel knew she was pushing too hard up the hill, but she couldn't pace herself. She could feel the sweat from her hand coating the good-quality paper of the rolled-up poster. At last the track emerged from the trees and became less treacherous as it approached their holiday villa. The road sloped down almost imperceptibly, but gravity was enough to give her tired legs an extra boost, and she was still moving fast when she rounded the corner of the house to find Lisa Martyn stretched out on the shady terrace in a pool chair with Friday's *Guardian* for company. Bel felt relief. She needed to talk to someone and, of all her companions, Lisa was least likely to turn her revelations into dinner party gossip. A human rights lawyer whose compassion and feminism seemed as ineluctable as every breath she took, Lisa would understand the potential of the discovery Bel thought she had made. And her right to handle it as she saw fit.

Lisa dragged her eyes away from the newspaper, distracted by the unfamiliar heave of Bel's breath. "My God," she said. "You look like you're about to stroke out."

Bel put the poster down on a chair and leaned over, hands on knees, dragging breath into her lungs, regretting those secret, stolen cigarettes. "I'll be—OK in—a minute."

Lisa struggled ungainly out of the chair and hurried into the kitchen, returning with a towel and bottle of water. Bel stood straight, took the water, and poured half over her head, snorting as she breathed it in by accident. Then she rubbed her head with the towel and slumped into a chair. She swallowed a long draught of water while Lisa returned to her pool chair. "What was all that about?" Lisa said. "You're the most dignified jogger I know. Never seen an out-of-breath Bel before. What's got you into such a state?"

"I found something," Bel said. Her chest was still struggling, but she could manage short bursts of speech. "At least, I think I found something. And if I'm right, it's the story of my career." She reached for the poster. "I was kind of hoping you might be able to tell me whether I've completely lost the plot."

Intrigued, Lisa tossed the paper to the ground and sat up. "So, what is it, this thing that might be something?"

Bel unrolled the heavy paper, weighing it down at the corners with a pepper grinder, a coffee mug, and a couple of dirty ashtrays. The image on the A3 sheet was striking. It had been designed to look like a stark black-and-white woodcut in the German Expressionist style. At the top of the page, a bearded man with an angular shock of hair leaned over a screen, his hands holding wooden crosses from which three marionettes dangled. But these were no ordinary marionettes. One was a skeleton, the second a goat, and the third a representation of Death with his hooded robe and scythe. There was something indisputably sinister about the image. Across the bottom, enclosed by a funereal black border, was a blank area about three inches deep. It was the sort of space where a small bill might be posted announcing a performance.

"Fuck me," Lisa said. At last, she looked up. "Catriona Maclennan Grant," she said. There was wonder in her voice. "Bel . . . where the hell did you find this?"

Thursday, 28th June 2007; Edinburgh

Bel smiled. "Before I answer that, I want to clarify a few things."

Susan Charleson rolled her eyes. "You can't imagine you're the first person who's walked through the door with a faked-up copy of the ransom poster. I'll tell you what I've told them. The reward is contingent on finding Sir Broderick's grandson alive or demonstrating conclusively that he is dead. Not to mention bringing Catriona Maclennan Grant's killers to justice."

"You misunderstand me," Bel said, smile mischievous but not giving an inch. "Ms. Charleson, I'm really not interested in Sir Broderick's money. But I do have one condition."

"You're making a mistake here." Susan Charleson's voice had acquired an edge. "This is a police matter. You're in no position to be imposing conditions."

Bel placed a hand firmly on the poster. "I can walk out the door now with this poster and forget I ever saw it. I'd have little difficulty in lying to the police. I'm a journalist, after all." She was beginning to enjoy herself far more than she'd anticipated. "Your word against mine, Ms. Charleson. And I know you don't want me to walk out on you. One of the skills a successful journalist has to learn is how to read people. And I saw the way you reacted when you looked at this. You know this is the real thing, not some faked-up copy."

"You've a very aggressive attitude." Susan Charleson sounded almost nonchalant.

"I like to think of it as assertive. I didn't come here to fall out with you, Ms. Charleson. I want to help. But not for free. In my experience, the rich don't appreciate anything they don't have to pay for."

"You said you weren't interested in money."

"That's true. And I'm not. I am, however, interested in reputation. And my reputation is built on being not just first with the story but with getting to the story behind the story. I think there are areas where I can help unravel this story more effectively than official channels. I'm sure you'll agree once I've explained where this poster came from. All I'm asking is that you don't obstruct me looking into the case. And beyond that, that you and your boss cooperate when it comes to sharing information about what was going on around the time Catriona was kidnapped."

"That's quite a significant request. Sir Broderick is not a man who compromises his privacy readily. You'll appreciate I don't have the authority to grant what you are asking."

Bel shrugged one shoulder delicately. "Then we can meet again when you have an answer." She slid the poster across the table, opening the portfolio to replace it there.

Susan Charleson stood up. "If you can spare me a few more minutes, I might be able to give you an answer now."

Bel knew at that point that she had won. Susan Charleson wanted this too badly. She would persuade her boss to accept the deal. Bel hadn't been this excited in years. This wasn't just a slew of news stories and features, though there wasn't a paper in the world that wouldn't be interested. Especially after the Madeleine McCann case. With access to the mysterious Brodie Grant plus the chance of discovering the fate of his grandson, this was potentially a bestseller. *In Cold Blood* for the new millennium. It would be her ticket for the gravy train.

Bel gave a little snort of laughter. Maybe she could use the proceeds to buy the *casa rovina* and bring things full circle. It was hard to imagine what could be neater.

Thursday, 28th June 2007; Newton of Wemyss

It had been a few years since Karen had last taken the single-track road to Newton of Wemyss. But it was obvious that the hamlet had undergone the same transformation as its sister villages on the main road. Commuters had fallen ravenous upon all four of the Wemyss villages, seeing rustic possibilities in what had been grim little miners' rows. One-bedroom hovels had been knocked through to make lavish cottages, back yards transformed by conservatories that poured light into gloomy living-kitchens. Villages that had shrivelled and died following the Michael pit disaster in '67 and the closures that followed the 1984 strike had found a new incarnation as dormitories whose entire idea of community was a pub quiz night. In the village shops you could buy a scented candle but not a pint of milk. The only way you could tell there had ever been a mining community was the scale model of pit winding gear that straddled the point where the private steam railway had once crossed the main road laden with open trucks of coal bound for the railhead at Thornton Junction. Now, the whitewashed miners' rows looked like an architect's deliberate choice of what a vernacular village ought to look like. Their history had been overwhelmed by a designer present.

Since her last visit, Newton of Wemyss had spruced itself up. The modest war memorial stood on a triangle of shaven grass in the centre. Wooden troughs of flowers stood around it at perfect intervals. Immaculate single-storey cottages lined the village green, the only break in the low skyline the imposing bulk of the local pub, the Laird o' Wemyss. It had once been owned collectively by the local community under the Gothenburg system, but the hard times of the eighties had forced it to close. Now it was a destination restaurant, its "Scottish Fusion" cuisine drawing visitors from as far afield as Dundee and Edinburgh and its prices lifting it well out of her budget. Karen wondered how far Mick Prentice would have had to travel for a simple pint of heavy if he'd stayed put in Newton.

She consulted the Mapquest directions she'd printed out and pointed to a road at the apex of the triangle to her driver, DC Jason "the Mint" Murray. "You want to go down the lane there," she said. "Towards the sea. Where the pit used to be."

They left the village centre behind immediately. Shaggy hedgerows fringed a field of lush green wheat on the right. "All this rain, it's making everything grow like the clappers," the Mint said. It had taken him the full twenty-five-minute journey from the office to summon up a comment.

Karen couldn't be bothered with a conversation about the weather. What was there to say? It had rained all bloody summer so far. Just because it wasn't raining right this minute didn't mean it wouldn't be wet by the end of the day. She looked over to her left where the colliery buildings had once stood. She had a vague memory of offices, pithead baths, a canteen. Now it had been razed to its concrete foundation, weeds forcing through jagged cracks as they reclaimed it. Marooned beyond it was a single untouched miners' row; eight raddled houses stranded in the middle of nowhere by the demolition of the buildings that had provided the reason for their existence. Beyond them was a thick stand of tall sycamores and beeches, a dense windbreak between the houses and the edge of the cliff that plunged down thirty feet to the coastal path below. "That's where the Lady Charlotte used to be," she said.

"Eh?" The Mint sounded startled.

"The pit, Jason."

"Oh. Right. Aye. Before my time." He peered through the windscreen, making her wonder uneasily if he needed glasses. "Which house is it, guv?"

She pointed to the one second from the end. The Mint eased the car round the potholes as carefully as if it had been his own and came to a halt at the end of Jenny Prentice's path.

In spite of Karen's phone call setting up the meeting, Jenny took her time answering the door, which gave them plenty of opportunity to examine the cracked concrete flags and the depressing patch of weedy gravel in front of the house. "If this was mine . . . ," the Mint began, then trailed off, as if it was all too much to contemplate.

The woman who answered the door had the air of someone who had spent her days lying down so life could more easily trample over her. Her lank greying hair was tied back haphazardly, strands escaping at both sides. Her skin was lined and puckered, with broken veins mapping her cheeks. She wore a nylon overall that came to mid-thigh over cheap black trousers whose material had gone bobbly. The overall was a shade of lavender found nowhere in nature. Karen's parents still lived in a street populated by ex-miners and their kin in unfashionable Methil, but even the most dysfunctional of their neighbours would have taken more trouble with their appearance when they knew they were in for any kind of official visit. Karen didn't even bother trying to avoid judging Jenny Prentice on her appearance. "Good morning, Mrs. Prentice," she said briskly. "I'm DI Pirie. We spoke on the phone. And this is DC Murray."

Jenny nodded and sniffed. "You'd better come in."

The living room was cramped but clean. The furniture, like the carpet, was unfashionable but not at all shabby. A room for special occasions, Karen thought, and a life where there were few of those.

Jenny waved them towards the sofa and perched on the edge of an armchair opposite. She was clearly not going to offer them any sort of refreshment. "So. You're here because of our Misha. I thought you lot would have something better to do, all the awful things I keep reading about in the newspapers."

"A missing husband and father is a pretty awful thing, wouldn't you say?" Karen said.

Jenny's lips tightened, as if she'd felt the burn of indigestion. "Depends on the man, Inspector. The kind of guy you run into doing your job, I don't imagine too many of their wives and kids are that bothered when they get taken away."

"You'd be surprised. A lot of their families are pretty devastated. And at least they know where their man is. They don't have to live with uncertainty."

"I didn't think I was living with uncertainty. I thought I knew damn fine where Mick was until our Misha started raking about trying to find him."

Karen nodded. "You thought he was in Nottingham."

"Aye. I thought he'd went scabbing. To be honest, I wasn't that sorry to see the back of him. But I was bloody livid that he put that label round our necks. I'd rather he was dead than a blackleg, if you really want to know." She pointed at Karen. "You sound like you're from round here. You must know what it's like to get tarred with that brush."

Karen tipped her head in acknowledgement. "All the more galling now that it looks like he didn't go scabbing after all."

Jenny looked away. "I don't know that. All I know is that he didn't go to Nottingham that night with that particular bunch of scabs."

"Well, we're here to try to establish what really happened. My colleague here is going to take some notes, just to make sure I don't misremember anything you tell me." The Mint hastily took out his notebook and flipped it open in a nervous flurry of pages. Maybe Phil had been right about his deficiencies, Karen thought. "Now, I need his full name and date of birth."

"Michael James Prentice. Born 20th January 1955."

"And you were all living here at the time? You and Mick and Misha?"

"Aye. I've lived here all my married life. Never really had a choice in the matter."

"Have you got a photo of Mick you could let us have? I know it's a long time ago, but it could be helpful."

"You can put it on the computer and make it older, can't you?" Jenny went to the sideboard and opened a drawer.

"Sometimes it's possible." But too expensive unless there's a more pressing reason than your grandson's leukaemia.

Jenny took out an immaculate black leather album and brought it back to the chair. When she opened it, the covers creaked. Even upside down and from the other side of the room, Karen could see it was a wedding album. Jenny quickly turned past the formal wedding shots to a pocket at the back, thickly stuffed with snaps. She pulled out a bundle and flicked through them. She paused at a couple, then finally settled on one. She handed Karen a rectangular picture. It showed the heads and shoulders of two young men grinning at the camera, corners of the beer glasses in shot as they toasted the photographer. "That's Mick on the left," Jenny said. "The good-looking one."

She wasn't lying. Mick Prentice had tousled dark blond hair, cut in the approximation of a mullet that George Michael had boasted in his Wham! period. Mick had blue eyes, ridiculously long eyelashes, and a dangerous smile. The sickle crescent of a coal tattoo sliced through his right eyebrow, saving him from being too pretty. Karen could see exactly why Jenny Prentice had fallen for her husband. "Thanks," she said. "Who's the other guy?" A raggedy mop of brown hair, long, bony face, a few faint acne scars pitting the sunken cheeks, lively eyes, a triangular grin like the Joker in the Batman comics. Not a looker like his pal, but something engaging about him all the same.

"His best pal. Andy Kerr."

The best pal who killed himself, according to Misha. "Misha told me your husband went missing on Friday the fourteenth of December 1984. Is that your recollection?"

"That's right. He went out in the morning with his bloody paints and said he'd be back for his tea. That was the last I saw him."

"Paints? He was doing a bit of work on the side?"

Jenny made a sound of disdain. "As if. Not that we couldn't have used the money. No, Mick painted watercolours. Can you credit it? Can you imagine anything more bloody useless in the 1984 strike than a miner painting watercolours."

"Could he not have sold them?" the Mint chipped in, leaning forward and looking keen.

"Who to? Everybody round here was skint and there was no money for him to go someplace else on the off chance." Jenny gestured at the wall behind them. "He'd have been lucky to get a couple of pounds apiece."

Karen swivelled round and looked at the three cheaply framed paintings on the wall. West Wemyss, Macduff Castle, and the Lady's Rock. To her untutored eye, they looked vivid and lively. She'd have happily given them house room, though she didn't know how much she'd have been willing to pay for the privilege back in 1984. "So, how did he get into that?" Karen asked, turning back to face Jenny.

"He did a class at the Miners' Welfare the year Misha was born. The teacher said he had a gift for it. Me, I think she said the same to every one of them that was halfway good looking."

"But he kept it up?"

"It got him out of the house. Away from the dirty nappies and the noise." Bitterness seemed to come off Jenny Prentice in waves. Curious but heartening that it didn't seem to have infected her daughter. Maybe that had something to do with the stepfather she'd spoken about. Karen reminded herself to ask about the other man in Jenny's life, another who seemed notable for his absence.

"Did he paint much during the strike?"

"Every day it was fair he was out with his kitbag and his easel. And if it was raining, he was down the caves with his pals from the Preservation Society."

"The Wemyss caves, do you mean?" Karen knew the caves that ran back from the shore deep into the sandstone cliffs between East Wemyss and Buckhaven. She'd played in them a few times as a child, oblivious to their historical significance as a major Pictish site. The local kids had treated them as indoor play areas, which was one of the reasons why the Preservation Society had been set up. Now there were railings closing off the deeper and more dangerous sections of the cave network, and amateur historians and archaeologists had preserved them as a playground for adults. "Mick was involved with the caves?"

"Mick was involved in everything. He played football, he painted his pictures, he messed about in the caves, he was up to his eyes in the union. Anything and everything was more important than spending time with his family." Jenny crossed one leg over the other and folded her arms across her chest. "He said it kept him sane during the strike. I think it just kept him out the road of his responsibilities."

Karen knew this was fertile soil for her inquiries, but she could afford to leave it for later. Jenny's suppressed anger had stayed put for twenty-two years. It wasn't about to go anywhere now. Something much more immediate interested her. "So, during the strike, where did Mick get the money for paints? I don't know much about art, but I know it costs a few bob for proper paper and paint." She couldn't imagine any striking miner spending money on art supplies when there was no money for food or heating.

"I don't want to get anybody into trouble," Jenny said.

Yeah, right. "It was twenty-three years ago," Karen said flatly. "I'm really not interested in small-scale contra from the time of the miners' strike."

"One of the art teachers from the high school lived up at Coaltown. He was a wee cripple guy. One leg shorter than the other and a humphy back. Mick used to do his garden for him. The guy paid him in paints." She gave a little snort. "I said could he not pay him in money or food. But apparently the guy was paying out all his wages to the ex-wife. The paints he could nick from the school." She refolded her arms. "He's dead now anyway."

Karen tried to tamp down her dislike of this woman, so different from the daughter who had beguiled her into this case. "So what was it like between you, before Mick disappeared?"

"I blame the strike. OK, we had our ups and downs. But it was the strike that drove a wedge between us. And I'm not the only woman in this part of the world who could say the same thing."

Karen knew the truth of that. The terrible privations of the strike had scarred just about every couple she had known back then. Domestic violence had erupted in improbable places; suicide rates had risen; marriages had shattered in the face of implacable poverty. She hadn't understood it at the time, but she did now. "Maybe so. But everybody's story's different. I'd like to hear yours."

Friday, 14th December 1984; Newton of Wemyss

"I'll be back for my tea," Mick Prentice said, slinging the big canvas bag across his body and grabbing the slender package of his folded easel.

"Tea? What tea? There's nothing in the house to eat. You need to be out there finding food for your family, not messing about painting the bloody sea for the umpteenth time," Jenny shouted, trying to force him to halt on his way out the door.

He turned back, his gaunt face twisted in shame and pain. "You think I don't know that? You think we're the only ones? You think if I had any idea how to make this better I wouldn't be doing it? Nobody has any fucking food. Nobody has any fucking money." His voice caught in his throat like a sob. He closed his eyes and took a deep breath. "Down the Welfare last night, Sam Thomson said there was talk of a food delivery from the Women Against Pit Closures. If you get yourself down there, they're supposed to be here about two o'clock." It was so cold in the kitchen that his words formed a cloud in front of his lips.

"More handouts. I can't remember the last time I actually chose what I was going to cook for the tea." Jenny suddenly sat down on one of the kitchen chairs. She looked up at him. "Are we ever going to get to the other side of this?"

"We've just got to hold out a bit longer. We've come this far. We can win this." He sounded as if he was trying to convince himself as much as her.

"They're going back, Mick. All the time, they're going back. It was on the news the other night. More than a quarter of the pits are back working. Whatever Arthur Scargill and the rest of the union executives might say, there's no way we can win. It's just a question of how bloody that bitch Thatcher will make the losing."

He shook his head vehemently. "Don't say that, Jenny. Just because there are a few pockets down south where they've caved in. Up here, we're rock solid. So's Yorkshire. And South Wales. And we're the ones that matter." His words sounded hollow, and there was no conviction in his face. They were, she thought, all beaten. They just didn't know when to lie down.

"If you say so," she muttered, turning away. She waited till she heard the door close behind him, then slowly got up and put her coat on. She picked up a heavy-duty plastic sack and left the freezing chill of the kitchen for the damp cold of the morning. This was her routine these days. Get up and walk Misha to school. At the school gate, the bairn would be given an apple or an orange, a bag of chips, and a chocolate cookie by the Friends of the Lady Charlotte, a ragtag and bobtail bunch of students and public sector workers from Kirkcaldy who made sure none of the kids started the day on an empty stomach. At least, not on school mornings.

Then back to the house. They'd given up taking milk in their tea, when they could get tea. Some mornings, a cup of hot water was all Jenny and Mick had to start the day. That hadn't happened often, but once was enough to remind you how easy it would be just to fall off the edge.

After a hot drink, Jenny would take her sack into the woods and try to collect enough firewood to give them a few hours of heat in the evening. Between the union executives always calling them "comrade" and the wood gathering, she felt like a Siberian peasant. At least they were lucky to live right by a source of fuel. It was, she knew, a lot harder for other folk. It was their good fortune that they'd kept their open fireplace. The miners' perk of cheap coal had seen to that.

She went about her task mechanically, paying little attention to her surroundings, turning over the latest spat between her and Mick. It sometimes seemed it was only the hardship that kept them together, only the need for warmth that kept them in the same bed. The strike had brought some couples closer together, but plenty had split like a log under an axe after those first few months, once their reserves had been bled dry.

It hadn't been so bad at the start. Since the last wave of strikes in the seventies, the miners had earned good money. They were the kings of the trade union movement—well paid, well organized, and well confident. After all, they'd brought down Ted Heath's government back then. They were untouchable. And they had the cash to prove it.

Some spent up to the hilt—foreign holidays where they could expose their milk-white skin and coal tattoos to the sun, flash cars with expensive stereos, new houses that looked great when they moved in but started to scuff round the edges almost at once. But most of them, made cautious by history, had a bit put by. Enough to cover the rent or the mortgage, enough to feed the family and pay the fuel bills for a couple of months. What had been horrifying was how quickly those scant savings had disappeared. Early on, the union had paid decent money to the men who piled into cars and vans and minibuses to join flying pickets to working pits, power stations, and coking plants. But the police had grown increasingly heavy-handed in making sure the flyers never made it to their destinations, and there was little enthusiasm for paying men for failing to reach their objectives. Besides, these days the union bosses were too busy trying to hide their millions from the government's sequestrators to be bothered wasting money in a fight they had to know in their hearts was doomed. So even that trickle of cash had run dry, and the only thing left for the mining communities to swallow had been their pride.

Jenny had swallowed plenty of that over the past nine months. It had started right at the beginning when she'd heard the Scottish miners would support the Yorkshire coalfield in the call for a national strike not from Mick but from

Arthur Scargill, president of the National Union of Mineworkers. Not personally, of course. Just his yapping harangue on the TV news. Instead of coming straight back from the Miners' Welfare meeting to tell her, Mick had been hanging out with Andy and his other union pals, drinking at the bar like money was never going to be a problem. Celebrating King Arthur's battle-cry in the time-honoured way. *The miners united will never be defeated.*

The wives knew the hopelessness of it all, right from the start. You go into a coal strike at the beginning of winter, when the demand from the power stations is at its highest. Not in the spring, when everybody's looking to turn off their heating. And when you go for major industrial action against a bitch like Margaret Thatcher, you cover your back. You follow the labour laws. You follow your own rules. You stage a national ballot. You don't rely on a dubious interpretation of a resolution passed three years before for a different purpose. Oh yes, the wives had known it was futile. But they'd kept their mouths shut and, for the first time ever, they'd built their own organization to support their men. Loyalty, that was what counted in the pit villages and mining communities.

And so Mick and Jenny were still hanging together. Jenny sometimes wondered if the only reason Mick was still with her and Misha was because he had nowhere else to go. Parents dead, no brothers or sisters, there was no obvious refuge. She'd asked him once and he'd frozen like a statue for a long moment. Then he'd scoffed at her, denying he wanted to be gone, reminding her that Andy would always put him up in his cottage if he wanted to be away. So, no reason why she should have imagined that Friday was different from any other.

Thursday, 28th June 2007; Newton of Wemyss

"So this wasn't the first time he'd gone off with his paints for the day?" Karen said. Whatever was going on in Jenny Prentice's head, it was clearly a lot more than the bare bones she was giving up.

"Four or five times a week, by the end."

"What about you? What did you do for the rest of the day?"

"I went up the woods for some kindling, then I came back and watched the news on the telly. It was quite the day, that Friday. King Arthur was in court for police obstruction at the Battle of Orgreave. And Band Aid got to number one. I tell you, I could have spat in their faces. All that effort for bairns thousands of miles away when there were hungry kids on their own doorsteps. Where was Bono and Bob Geldof when our kids were waking up on Christmas morning with bugger all in their stockings?"

"It must have been hard to take," Karen said.

"It felt like a slap in the face. Nothing glamorous about helping the miners, was there?" A bitter little smile lit up her face. "Could have been worse, though. We could have had to put up with that sanctimonious shite Sting. Not to mention his bloody lute."

"Right enough." Karen couldn't hide her amusement. Gallows humour was never far from the surface in these mining communities. "So, what did you do after the TV news?"

"I went down the Welfare. Mick had said something about a food handout. I got in the queue and came home with a packet of pasta, a tin of tomatoes, and two onions. And a pack of dried Scotch broth mix. I mind I felt pretty pleased with myself. I collected Misha from the school and I thought it might cheer us up if we put up the Christmas decorations, so that's what we did."

"When did you realize it was late for Mick to be back?"

Jenny paused, one hand fiddling with a button on her overall. "That time of year, it's early dark. Usually, he'd be back not long after me and Misha. But with us doing the decorations, I didn't really notice the time passing."

She was lying, Karen thought. But why? And about what?

Friday, 14th December 1984; Newton of Wemyss

Jenny had been one of the first in the queue at the Miners' Welfare, and she'd hurried home with her pitiful bounty, determined to get a pot of soup going so there would be something tasty for the tea. She rounded the pithead baths building, noticing all her neighbours' houses were in darkness. These days, nobody left a welcoming light on when they went out. Every penny counted when the fuel bills came in.

When she turned in at her gate, she nearly jumped out of her skin. A shadowy figure rose from the darkness, looming huge in her imagination. She made a noise halfway between a gasp and a moan.

"Jenny, Jenny, calm down. It's me. Tom. Tom Campbell. I'm sorry, I didn't mean to scare you." The shape took form and she recognized the big man standing by her front door.

"Christ, Tom, you gave me the fright of my life," she complained, moving past him and opening the front door. Conscious of the breathtaking chill of the house, she led the way into the kitchen. Without hesitation, she filled her soup pan with water and put it on the stove, the gas ring giving out a tiny wedge of heat. Then she turned to face him in the dimness of the afternoon light. "How are you doing?"

Tom Campbell shrugged his big shoulders and gave a half-hearted smile. "Up and down," he said. "It's ironic. The one time in my life I really needed my pals and this strike happens."

"At least you've got me and Mick," Jenny said, waving him to a chair.

"Well, I've got you, anyway. I don't think I'd be on Mick's Christmas card list, always supposing anybody was sending any this year. Not after October. He's not spoken to me since then."

"He'll get over it," she said without a shred of conviction. Mick had always had his reservations about the wider ripples of the schoolgirl friendship between Jenny and Tom's wife Moira. The women had been best pals forever, Moira standing chief bridesmaid at Jenny and Mick's wedding. When it came time to return the favour, Jenny had been pregnant with Misha. Mick had pointed out that her increasing size was the perfect excuse to turn Moira down, what with having to buy the bridesmaid's dress in advance. It wasn't a suggestion, more an injunction. For although Tom Campbell was by all accounts a decent man and a handsome man and an honest man, he was not a miner. True, he worked at the Lady Charlotte. He went underground in the stomach-juddering cage. He sometimes even got his hands dirty. But he was not a miner. He was a pit deputy. A member of a different union. A management man there to see that the health and safety rules were followed and that the lads did what they were supposed to. The miners had a term for the easiest part of any task—"the deputy's end." It sounded innocuous enough, but in an environment where every member of a gang knew his life depended on his colleagues, it expressed a world of contempt. And so Mick Prentice had always held something in reserve when it came to his dealings with Tom Campbell.

Mick had resented the invitations to dinner at their detached house in West Wemyss. He'd mistrusted Tom's invitations to join him at the football. He'd even begrudged the hours Jenny spent at Moira's bedside during her undignified but swift death from cancer a couple of years before. And when Tom's union had dithered and swithered over joining the strike a couple of months before, Mick had raged like a toddler when they'd finally come down on the side of the bosses.

Jenny suspected part of the reason for his anger was the kindness Tom had shown them since the strike had started to bite. He'd taken to stopping by with little gifts—a bag of apples, a sack of potatoes, a soft toy for Misha. They'd always come with plausible excuses—a neighbour's tree with a glut, more potatoes in his allotment than he could possibly need, a raffle prize from the bowling club. Mick had always grumbled afterwards. "Patronizing shite," he'd said.

"He's trying to help us without shaming us," Jenny said. It didn't hurt that Tom's presence reminded her of happier times. Somehow, when he was there, she felt a sense of possibility again. She saw herself reflected in his eyes, and it was as a younger woman, a woman who had ambitions for her life to be different. So although she knew it would annoy Mick, Jenny was happy for Tom to sit at her kitchen table and talk.

He drew a limp but heavy parcel from his pocket. "Can you use a couple of pounds of bacon?" he said, his brow creasing in anxiety. "My sister-in-law, she brought it over from her family's farm in Ireland. But it's smoked, see, and I can't be doing with smoked bacon. It gives me the scunners. So I thought, rather than it go to waste . . . " He held it out to her.

Jenny took the package without a second's hesitation. She gave a little snort of self-deprecation. "Look at me. My heart's all a flutter over a couple of pounds of bacon. That's what Margaret Thatcher and Arthur Scargill have done between them." She shook her head. "Thank you, Tom. You're a good man."

He looked away, unsure what to say or do. His eyes fixed on the clock. "Do you not need to pick up the bairn? I'm sorry, I wasn't thinking about the time when I was waiting, I just wanted to . . ." He got to his feet, his face pink. "I'll come again."

She heard the stumble of his boots in the hall then the click of the latch. She tossed the bacon on to the counter and turned off the pan of water. It would be a different soup now.

Moira had always been the lucky one.

Thursday, 28th June 2007; Newton of Wemyss

Jenny's eyes came off the middle distance and focused on Karen. "I suppose it was about seven o'clock when it dawned on me that Mick hadn't come home. I was angry, because I'd actually got a half-decent tea to put on the table. So I got the bairn to her bed, then I got her next door to sit in so I could run down the Welfare and see if Mick was there." She shook her head, still surprised after all these years. "And of course, he wasn't."

"Had anybody seen him?"

"Apparently not."

"You must have been worried," Karen said.

Jenny shrugged one shoulder. "Not really. Like I said, we hadn't exactly parted on the best of terms. I just thought he'd taken the huff and gone over to Andy's."

"The guy in the photo?"

"Aye. Andy Kerr. He was a union official. But he was on the sick from his work. Stress, they said. And they were right. He'd killed himself within the month. I often thought Mick going scabbing was the last straw for Andy. He worshipped Mick. It would have broken his heart."

"So that's where you assumed he was?" Karen prompted her.

"That's right. He had a cottage out in the woods, in the middle of nowhere. He said he liked the peace and quiet. Mick took me out there one time. It gave me the heebie jeebies. It was like the witch's house in one of Misha's fairy stories—there was no sign of it till suddenly you were there, right in front of it. You wouldn't catch me living there."

"Could you not have phoned to check?" the Mint butted in. Both women stared at him with a mixture of amusement and indulgence.

"Our phone had been cut off months before, son," Jenny said, exchanging a look with Karen. "And this was long before mobiles."

By now, Karen was gagging for a cup of tea, but she was damned if she was going to put herself in Jenny Prentice's debt. She cleared her throat and continued. "When did you start to worry?"

"When the bairn woke me up in the morning and he still wasn't home. He'd never done that before. It wasn't as if we'd had a proper row on the Friday. Just a few cross words. We'd had worse, believe me. When he wasn't there in the morning, I really started to think there was something badly wrong."

"What did you do?"

"I got Misha fed and dressed and took her down to her pal Lauren's house. Then walked out through the woods to Andy's place. But there was nobody there. And then I remembered Mick had said that now he was on the sick, Andy was maybe going to go off up to the Highlands for a few days. Get away from it all. Get his head straight. So of course he wasn't there. And by then, I was really starting to get scared. What if there had been an accident? What if he'd been taken ill?" The memory still had the power to disturb Jenny. Her fingers picked endlessly at the hem of her overall.

"I went up to the Welfare to see the union reps. I figured if anybody knew where Mick was, it would be them. Or at least they'd know where to start looking." She stared down at the floor, her hands clasped tight in her lap. "That's when the wheels really started to come off my life."

Saturday, 15th December 1984; Newton of Wemyss

Even in the morning, without the press of bodies to raise the temperature, the Miners' Welfare Institute was warmer than her house, Jenny noticed as she walked in. Not by much, but enough to be perceptible. It wasn't the sort of thing that usually caught her attention, but today she was trying to think of anything except the absence of her husband. She stood hesitant for a moment in the entrance hall, trying to decide where to go. The NUM strike offices were upstairs, she vaguely remembered, so she made for the ornately carved staircase. On the first-floor landing, it all became much easier. All she had to do was to follow the low mutter of voices and the high thin layer of cigarette smoke.

A few yards down the hall, a door was cracked ajar, the source of the sound and the smell. Jenny tapped nervously and the room went quiet. At last, a cautious voice said, "Come in."

She slid round the door like a church mouse. The room was dominated by a U-shaped table covered in tartan oil-coth. Half a dozen men were slouched around it in varying states of despondency. Jenny faltered when she realized the man at the top corner was someone she recognized but did not know. Mick McGahey, former Communist, leader of the Scottish miners. The only man, it was said, who could stand up to King Arthur and make his voice heard. The man who had been deliberately kept from the top spot by his predecessor. If Jenny had a pound for every time she'd heard someone say how different it would have been if McGahey had been in charge, her family would have been the best-fed and best-dressed in Newton of Wemyss. "I'm sorry," she stuttered. "I just wanted a word . . ." Her eyes flickered round the room, wondering which of the men she knew would be best to focus on.

"It's all right, Jenny," Ben Reekie said. "We were just having a wee meeting. We're pretty much done here, eh, lads?" There was a discontented murmur of agreement. But Reekie, the local secretary, was good at taking the temperature of a meeting and moving things along. "So, Jenny, how can we help you?"

She wished they were alone but didn't have the nerve to ask for it. The women had learned a lot in the process of supporting their men, but face to face their assertiveness still tended to melt away. But it would be all right, she told herself. She'd lived in this cocooned world all her adult life, a world that centred on the pit and the Welfare, where there were no secrets and the union was your mother and your father. "I'm worried about Mick," she said. No point in beating about the bush. "He went out yesterday morning and never came back. I was wondering if maybe . . . ?"

Reekie rested his forehead on his fingers, rubbing it so hard he left alternating patches of white and red across the centre. "Jesus Christ," he hissed from between clenched teeth.

"And you expect us to believe you don't know where he is?" The accusation came from Ezra Macafferty, the village's last survivor of the lock-outs and strikes of the 1920s.

"Of course I don't know where he is." Jenny's voice was plaintive, but a dark fear had begun to spread its chill across her chest. "I thought maybe he'd been in here. I thought somebody might know."

"That makes six," McGahey said. She recognized the rough deep rumble of his voice from TV interviews and open-air rallies. It felt strange to be in the same room with it.

"I don't understand," she said. "Six what? What's going on?" Their eyes were all on her, boring into her. She could feel their contempt but didn't understand what it was for. "Has something happened to Mick? Has there been an accident?"

"Something's happened, all right," McGahey said. "It looks like your man's away scabbing to Nottingham."

His words seemed to suck the air from her lungs. She stopped breathing, letting a bubble form round her so the words would bounce off. It couldn't be right. Not Mick. Dumb, she shook her head hard. The words started to seep back in but they still made no sense. "Knew about the five . . . thought there might be more . . . always a traitor in the ranks . . . disappointed . . . always a union man."

"No," she said. "He wouldn't do that."

"How else do you explain him not being here?" Reekie said. "You're the one that came to us looking for him. We know a van load went down last night. And at least one of them is a pal of your Mick. Where the hell else is he going to be?"

Thursday, 28th June 2007; Newton of Wemyss

"I couldn't have felt worse if they'd accused me of being a whore," Jenny said. "I suppose, in their eyes, that's exactly what I was. My man away scabbing, it would be no time at all before I'd be living on immoral earnings."

"You never doubted that they were right?"

Jenny pushed her hair back from her face, momentarily stripping away some of the years and the docility. "Not really. Mick was pals with Iain Maclean, one of the ones that went to Nottingham. I couldn't argue with that. And don't forget what it was like back then. The men ran the game and the union ran the men. When the women wanted to take part in the strike, the first battle we had to fight was against the union. We had to beg them to let us join in. They wanted us where we'd always been—in the back room, keeping the home fires burning. Not standing by the braziers on the picket lines. But even though we got Women Against Pit Closures off the ground, we still knew our place. You'd have to be bloody strong or bloody stupid to try and blow against the wind round here."

It wasn't the first time Karen had heard a version of this truth. She wondered whether she'd have done any better in the same position. It felt good to think she'd stand by her man a bit more sturdily. But in the face of the community hostility Jenny Prentice must have faced, Karen reckoned she'd probably have caved in too. "Fair enough," she said. "But now that it looks like Mick might not have gone scabbing after all, have you got any idea what might have happened to him?"

Jenny shook her head. "Not a scooby. Even though I couldn't believe it, the scabbing kind of made sense. So I never thought about any other possibility."

"Do you think he'd just had enough? Just upped and left?"

She frowned. "See, that wouldn't be like Mick. To leave without the last word? I don't think so. He'd have made sure I knew it was all my fault." She gave a bitter laugh.

"You don't think he might have gone without a word as a way of making you suffer even more?"

Jenny's head reared back. "That's sick," she protested. "You make him sound like some kind of a sadist. He wasn't a cruel man, Inspector. Just thoughtless and selfish like the rest of them."

Karen paused for a moment. This was always the hardest part when interviewing the relatives of the missing. "Had he fallen out with anybody? Did he have any enemies, Jenny?"

Jenny looked as if Karen had suddenly switched into Urdu. "Enemies? You mean, like somebody that would kill him?"

"Maybe not mean to kill him. Maybe just fight him?"

This time, Jenny's laugh had genuine warmth. "By Christ, that's funny coming from you." She shook her head. "The only physical fights Mick ever got into in all the years we were married were with your lot. On the picket lines. At the demonstrations. Did he have enemies? Aye, the thin blue line. But this isn't South America, and I don't recall any talk about the disappeared of the miners' strike. So the answer to your question is no, he didn't have the kind of enemies that he'd get into a fight with."

Karen studied the carpet for a long moment. The gung-ho violence of the police against the strikers had poisoned community relations for a generation or more. Never mind that the worst offenders came from outside forces, bused in to make up the numbers and paid obscene amounts of overtime to oppress their fellow citizens in ways most people chose to avoid knowing about. The fallout from their ignorance and arrogance affected every officer in every coalfield force. Still did, Karen reckoned. She took a deep breath and looked up. "I'm sorry," she said. "The way they treated the miners, it was inexcusable. I like to think we wouldn't act like that now, but I'm probably wrong. Are you sure there wasn't anybody he'd had a run-in with?"

Jenny didn't even pause for thought. "Not that I knew about. He wasn't a troublemaker. He had his principles, but he didn't use them as excuses to pick fights. He stood up for what he believed in, but he was a talker, not a fighter."

"What if the talking didn't work? Would he back down?"

"I'm not sure I follow you."

Karen spoke slowly, feeling her way into the idea. "I'm wondering if he bumped into this Iain Maclean that day and tried to talk him out of going to Nottingham. And if Iain wouldn't change his mind, and maybe had his pals there to back him up . . . Would Mick have got into a fight with them, maybe?"

Jenny shook her head firmly. "No way. He'd have said his piece and, if that didn't work, he'd have walked away."

Karen felt frustrated. Even after the passage of so much time, cold cases usually provided one or two loose ends to pick away at. But so far, there seemed to be nothing to reach for here. One last question, then she was out of this place. "Do you have any idea at all where Mick might have gone painting that day?"

"He never said. The only thing I can tell you is that in the winter he often went along the shore to East Wemyss. That way, if it came on rain, he could go down to the caves and shelter there. The preservation group, they had a wee bothy at the back of one of the caves with a camping stove where they could brew up. He had keys, he could make himself right at home," she added, the acid back in her voice. "But I've no idea whether he was there that day or not. He could have been anywhere between Dysart and Buckhaven." She looked at her watch. "That's all I know."

Karen got to her feet. "I appreciate your time, Mrs. Prentice. We will be continuing our inquiries and I'll keep you informed." The Mint scrambled to his feet and followed her and Jenny to the front door.

"I'm not bothered for myself, you understand," Jenny said when they were halfway down the path. "But see if you can find him for the bairn's sake."

It was, Karen thought, the first sign of emotion she'd shown all morning. "Get your notebook out," she said to the Mint as they got into the car. "Follow-ups. Talk to the neighbour. See if she remembers anything about the day Mick Prentice disappeared. Talk to somebody from the cave group, see who's still there from 1984. Get another picture of what Mick Prentice was really like. Check in the files for anything about this Andy Kerr, NUM official, supposedly committed suicide around the time Mick disappeared. What's the story there? And we need to track down these five scabs and get Nottingham to have a chat with them." She opened the passenger door again as the Mint finished scribbling. "And since we're here already, let's have a crack at the neighbour."

She was barely two steps from the car when her phone rang. "Phil," she said.

No pleasantries, just straight to the point. "You need to get back here right now."

"Why?"

"The Macaroon is on the warpath. Wants to know why the hell you're not at your desk."

Simon Lees, Assistant Chief Constable (Crime), was temperamentally different from Karen. She was convinced his bedtime reading consisted of the Police, Public Order and Criminal Justice (Scotland) Act 2006. She knew he was married with two teenage children, but she had no idea how that could have happened to a man so obsessively organized. It was sod's law that on the first morning in months when she was doing something off the books the Macaroon should come looking for her. He seemed to believe that it was his divine right to know the whereabouts of any of the officers under his command, whether on or off duty. Karen wondered how close he'd come to stroking out on discovering she was not occupying the desk where he expected to find her. Not close enough, by the sounds of it. "What did you tell him?"

"I said you were having a meeting with the evidence store team to discuss streamlining their cataloguing procedures," Phil said. "He liked the idea, but not the fact that it wasn't listed in your electronic appointments list."

"I'm on my way," Karen said, confusing the Mint by getting back into the car. "Did he say why he was looking for me?"

"To me? A mere sergeant? Gimme a break, Karen. He just said it was 'of the first importance.' Somebody probably stole his digestive biscuits."

Karen gestured impatiently at the Mint. "Home, James, and don't spare the horses." He looked at her as if she was mad, but he did start the car and drive off. "I'm coming in," she said. "Get the kettle on."

Glenrothes

The double helix of frustration and irritation twisted in Simon Lees's gut. He shifted in his chair and rearranged the family photos on his desk. What was wrong with these people? When he'd gone looking for DI Pirie and failed to find her where she should be, DS Parhatka had acted as if that were perfectly fine. There was something fundamentally lackadaisical about the detectives in Fife. He'd realized that within days of arriving from Glasgow. It amazed him that they'd ever managed to put anyone behind bars before he'd arrived with his analytical methods, streamlined investigations, sophisticated crime linkage, and the inevitable rise in the detection rate.

What riled him even more was the fact that they seemed to have no gratitude for the modern methods he'd brought to the job. He even had the suspicion that they were laughing at him. Take his nickname. Everybody in the building seemed to have a nickname, most of which could be construed as mildly affectionate. But not him. He'd discovered early on that he'd been dubbed the Macaroon because he shared the surname of a confectionary firm whose most famous product had become notorious because of an ancient advertising jingle; its cheerful racism would provoke rioting in the streets if it were to be aired in twenty-first-century Scotland. He blamed Karen Pirie; it was no coincidence that the nickname had surfaced after his first run-in with her. It had been typical of most of their encounters. He wasn't quite sure how it happened, but she always seemed to wrong-foot him.

Lees still smarted at that early memory. He'd barely got his feet under the table but he'd started as he meant to go on, instigating a series of training days. Not the usual macho posturing or tedious revision of the rules of engagement, but fresh approaches to issues of modern policing. The first tranche of officers had assembled in the training suite, and Lees had started his preamble, explaining how they would spend the day developing strategies for policing a multicultural society. His audience had looked mutinous, and Karen Pirie had led the charge. "Sir, can I make a point?"

"Of course, Detective Inspector Pirie." His smile had been genial, hiding his annoyance at being interrupted before he'd even revealed the agenda.

"Well, sir, Fife's not really what you'd call multicultural. We don't have many people here who are not indigenous Brits. Apart from the Italians and the Poles, that is, and they've been here so long we've forgotten they're not from here."

"So racism's all right by you, is it, Inspector?" Maybe not the best reply, but he'd been driven to it by the apparently Neanderthal attitude she'd expressed. Not to mention that bland pudding face she presented whenever she said anything that might be construed as inflammatory.

"Not at all, sir." She'd smiled, almost pityingly. "What I would say is that, given we have a limited training budget, it might make more sense to deal first with the sort of situations we're more likely to encounter day to day."

"Such as? How hard to hit people when we arrest them?"

"I was thinking more of strategies to deal with domestic violence. It's a common call-out and it can easily escalate. Too many people are still dying every year because a domestic has got out of hand. And we don't always know how to deal with it without inflaming the situation. I'd say that was my number one priority right now, sir."

And with that short speech, she'd cut the ground from under his feet. There was no way back for him. He could carry on with the planned training, knowing that everyone in the room was laughing at him. Or he could postpone till he could put together a programme to deal with DI Pirie's suggestion and lose face completely. In the end, he'd told them to spend the rest of the day researching the subject of domestic violence in preparation for another training day.

Two days later, he'd overheard himself referred to as the Macaroon. Oh yes, he knew who to blame. But as with everything she did to undermine him, there was nothing he could pin directly on her. She'd stand there, looking as shaggy, stolid, and inscrutable as a Highland cow, never saying or doing anything that he could complain about. And she set the style for the rest of them, even though she was stranded on the fringes in the Cold Case Review Team where she should be able to wield no influence whatsoever. But somehow, thanks to Pirie, dealing with the detectives of all three divisions was like herding cats.

He tried to avoid her, tried to sideline her via his operational directives. Until today, he'd thought it was working. Then the phone had rung. "Assistant Chief Constable Lees," he'd announced as he picked up the phone. "How may I be of assistance?"

"Good morning, ACC Lees. My name is Susan Charleson. I'm personal assistant to Sir Broderick Maclennan Grant. My boss would like to talk to you. Is this a good time?"

Lees straightened up in his chair, squaring his shoulders. Sir Broderick Maclennan Grant was notorious for three things—his wealth, his misanthropic reclusiveness, and the kidnap and murder of his daughter Catriona twenty-odd years before. Unlikely though it seemed, his PA calling the ACC Crime could mean only that there had been some sort of development in the case. "Yes, of course, perfect time, couldn't be better." He dredged his memory for details, only half listening to the woman on the phone. Daughter and grandson kidnapped, that was it. Daughter killed in a botched ransom handover, grandson never seen again. And now it looked as if he was going to be the one to have the chance finally to solve the case. He tuned in to the woman's voice again.

"If you'll bear with me, I'll put you through now," she said.

The hollow sound of dead air, then a dark, heavy voice said, "This is Brodie Maclennan Grant. And you're the assistant chief constable?"

"That's right, Sir Broderick. ACC Lees. Simon Lees."

"Are you aware of the unsolved murder of my daughter Catriona? And the kidnapping of my grandson Adam?"

"Of course, naturally, there's not an officer in the land who—"

"We believe some new evidence has come to light. I'd be obliged if you'd arrange for Detective Inspector Pirie to come to the house tomorrow morning to discuss it with me."

Lees actually held the phone away from his face and stared at it. Was this some kind of elaborate practical joke? "DI Pirie? I don't quite . . . I could come," he gabbled.

"You're a desk man. I don't need a desk man." Brodie Grant's voice was dismissive. "DI Pirie is a detective. I liked the way she handled that Lawson business."

"But . . . but it should be a more senior officer who deals with this," Lees protested.

"Isn't DI Pirie in charge of your Cold Case Review Team?" Grant was beginning to sound impatient. "That's senior enough for me. I don't care about rank, I care about effectiveness. That's why I want DI Pirie at my house at ten tomorrow morning. That should give her enough time to acquaint herself with the basic facts of the case. Good day, Mr. Lees." The line went dead, and Simon Lees was left alone with his rising blood pressure and his bad mood.

Much as it grieved him, he had no choice but to find DI Pirie and brief her. At least he could make it sound as though sending her was his idea. But in spite of there being no appointment in the electronic diary system he had instituted for his senior detectives, she hadn't been at her desk. It was all very well, officers doing things on their own initiative, but they had to learn to leave a record of their movements.

He was on the point of marching back down to the CCRT squad room to find out why DI Pirie hadn't appeared yet when a sharp rap on the door was followed without any interval by the entrance of DI Pirie. "Did I invite you to come in?" Lees said, glowering across the room at her.

"I thought it was urgent, sir." She kept walking and sat down in the visitor's chair across the desk from him. "DS Parhatka gave me the impression that whatever it is you wanted me for, it couldn't wait."

What an advert for the service, he thought crossly. Shaggy brown hair flopping into her eyes, the merest smudge of make-up, teeth that really could have done with some serious orthodontics. He supposed she was probably a lesbian, given her penchant for trouser suits that really were a mistake given the breadth of her hips. Not that he had anything against lesbians, his internal governor reminded him. He just thought it gave people the wrong impression about today's police service. "Sir Broderick Maclennan Grant called me earlier this morning," he said. The only sign of interest was a slight parting of her lips. "You know who Sir Broderick Maclennan Grant is, I take it?"

Karen looked puzzled by the question. She leaned back in her seat and recited, "Third richest man in Scotland, owns half of the profitable parts of the Highlands. Made his money building roads and houses and running the transport systems that serve them. Owns a Hebridean island but lives mostly in Rotheswell Castle near Falkland. Most of the land between there and the sea belongs either to him or to the Wemyss estate. His daughter Cat and her baby son Adam were kidnapped by an anarchist group in 1985. Cat was shot dead when the ransom handover went wrong. Nobody knows what happened to Adam. Grant's wife committed suicide a couple of years later. He remarried about ten years ago. He has a wee boy who must be about five or six." She grinned. "How did I do?"

"It's not a contest, Inspector." Lees felt his hands closing into fists and lowered them below the desk. "It appears that there may be some fresh evidence. And since you are in charge of cold cases, I thought you should deal with it."

"What sort of evidence?" She leaned on the arm of her chair. It was almost a slouch.

"I thought it best that you confer directly with Sir Broderick. That way there can be no possibility of confusion."

"So he didn't actually tell you?"

Lees could have sworn she was enjoying this. "I've arranged for you to meet him at Rotheswell Castle tomorrow morning at ten. I need hardly remind you how important it is that we are seen to be taking this seriously. I want Sir Broderick to understand this matter will have our full attention."

Karen stood up abruptly, her eyes suddenly cold. "He'll get exactly the same attention as every other bereaved parent I deal with. I don't make distinctions among the dead, sir. Now, if that's all, I've got a case file to assimilate before morning." She didn't wait for a dismissal. She just turned on her heel and walked out, leaving Lees feeling that she didn't make many distinctions among the living either.

Yet again, Karen Pirie had left him feeling like an idiot.

Rotheswell Castle

Bel Richmond took a last quick look through her file on Catriona Maclennan Grant, double-checking that her list of questions covered all the angles. Broderick Maclennan Grant's inability to suffer fools was as notorious as his dislike of publicity. Bel suspected that he would pounce on the first sign of unpreparedness on her part and use that as an excuse to break the deal she had brokered with Susan Charleson.

Truth to tell, she was still amazed that she had pulled it off. She stood up, closing her laptop and pausing to check her look in the mirror. *Tits and teeth. You don't get a second chance to make a first impression.* Country house weekend, that was the look she'd gone for. She'd always been good at camouflage. Another of the many reasons she was so good at what she did. Blending in, becoming "one of us," whoever the "us" happened to be, was a necessary evil. So if she was sleeping under Brodie Grant's baronial roof, she needed to look the part. She straightened the Black Watch tartan dress she'd borrowed from Vivianne, checked her kitten heels for scuffs, pushed her crow-black hair behind one ear, and parted her scarlet lips in a smile. A glance at her watch confirmed it was time to head downstairs and discover what the formidable Susan Charleson had lined up.

As she turned the corner of the wide staircase, she had to jink to one side to avoid a small boy careering up. He brought his flailing limbs under control on the half-landing, gasped, "Sorry," then hurtled on upwards. Bel blinked and raised her eyebrows. It had been a couple of years since she'd last had a similar small boy encounter, and she hadn't missed it a bit. She carried on down, but before she reached the bottom, a woman wearing cords the colour of butter and a dark red shirt swung round the newel post then stopped dead, taken by surprise. "Oh, sorry, I didn't mean to startle you," she said. "You haven't seen a small boy go past, have you?"

Bel gestured over her shoulder with her thumb. "He went thataway."

The woman nodded. Now she was nearer, Bel could see she was a good ten years older than she'd first thought; late thirties, at least. Good skin, thick chestnut hair, and a trim build gave the illusion a helping hand. "Monster," the woman said. They met a couple of steps from the bottom. "You must be Annabel Richmond," she said, extending a slender hand that was chilly in spite of the comfortable warmth trapped inside the thick walls of the castle. "I'm Judith. Brodie's wife."

Of course she was. How could Bel have imagined a nanny so perfectly groomed? "Lady Grant," she said, wincing inside.

"Judith, please. Even after all these years married to Brodie, I still want to look over my shoulder when someone calls me Lady Grant." She sounded as though she wasn't just saying it out of fake humility.

"And I'm Bel, apart from my by-line."

Lady Grant smiled, her eyes already scanning the stairs above. "Bel it is. Look, I can't stop now, I have to capture the monster. I'll see you at dinner." And she was off, taking the stairs two at a time.

Feeling overdressed in comparison with the chatelaine of Rotheswell, Bel made her way back down the stone-flagged hallways to Susan Charleson's office. The door was open and Susan, who was talking on the phone, beckoned her in. "Fine. Thank you for organizing that, Mr. Lees." She replaced the phone and came round the desk, ushering Bel back towards the door. "Perfect timing," she said. "He likes punctuality. Is your room to your liking? Do you have everything you need? Is the wireless access working?"

"It's all perfect," Bel said. "Lovely view too." Feeling as if she'd wandered into a BBC2 drama scripted by Stephen Poliakoff, she allowed herself to be led back through the maze of corridors whose walls were lined with poster-sized photographs of the Scottish landscape printed on canvas to resemble paintings. She was surprised by how cosy it felt. But then, this wasn't quite her idea of a castle. She'd expected something like Windsor or Alnwick. Instead, Rotheswell was more like a fortified manor with turrets. The interior resembled a country house rather than a medieval banqueting hall. Substantial but not as intimidating as she'd feared.

By the time they stopped in front of a pair of tall arched mahogany doors, she was beginning to regret not having thought of breadcrumbs.

"Here we are," Susan said, opening one of the doors and leading Bel into a billiard room panelled in dark wood with shutters over the windows. The only light came from an array of lamps above the full-size table. As they walked in, Sir Broderick Maclennan Grant looked up from sighting down his cue. A thick shock of startling silver hair falling boyishly over a broad forehead, eyebrows a pair of silver bulwarks over eyes so deep set their colour was guesswork, a parrot's bill of a nose, and a long thin mouth over a square chin made him instantly recognizable; the lighting made him a dramatic figure.

Bel knew what to expect from photographs, but she was startled by the crackle of electricity she felt in his presence. She'd been in the company of powerful men and women before, but she'd felt this instant charisma only a handful of times. She understood at once how Brodie Grant had built his empire from the ground up.

He straightened up and leaned on his cue. "Miss Richmond, I take it?" His voice was deep and almost grudging, as if he hadn't used it enough.

"That's right, Sir Broderick." Bel wasn't sure whether to advance or stay put.

"Thank you, Susan," Grant said. As the door closed behind her, he waved towards a pair of well-worn leather armchairs flanking a carved marble fireplace. "Sit yourself down. I can play and talk at the same time." He returned to study his shot while Bel shifted one of the chairs so she could watch him more directly.

She waited while he played a couple of shots, the silence rising between them like a drowning tide. "This is a beautiful house," she said finally.

He grunted. "I don't do small talk, Miss Richmond." He cued swiftly and two balls collided with a crack like a gunshot. He chalked his cue and studied her for a long moment. "You're probably wondering how on earth you managed this. Direct access to a man notorious for his loathing of the media spotlight. Quite an achievement, eh? Well, I'm sorry to disappoint you, but you just got lucky." He walked round the table, frowning at the position of the balls, moving like a man twenty years younger.

"That's how I've got some of my best stories," Bel said calmly. "It's a big part of what successful journalism is about, the knack of being in the right place at the right time. I don't have a problem with luck."

"Just as well." He studied the balls, cocking his head for a different angle. "So, are you not wondering why I've chosen to break my silence after all these years?"

"Yes, of course I am. But to be honest, I don't think your reasons for talking now will have much to do with what I end up writing. So it's more personal curiosity than professional."

He stopped halfway through his preparation for a shot and straightened up, staring at her with an expression she couldn't read. He was either furious or curious. "You're not what I expected," he said. "You're tougher. That's good."

Bel was accustomed to being underestimated by the men in her world. She was less used to them admitting their mistake. "Damn right, I'm tough. I don't rely on anybody else to fight my battles."

He turned to face her, leaning on the table and folding his arms over his cue. "I don't like being in the public eye," he said. "But I'm a realist. Back in 1985, it was possible for someone like me to exert a degree of influence over the media. When Catriona and Adam were kidnapped, to a large extent we controlled what was printed and broadcast. The police cooperated with us too." He sighed and shook his head. "For all the good it did us." He leaned the cue on the table and came to sit opposite Bel.

He sat in the classic alpha male pose: knees spread wide, hands on his thighs, shoulders back. "The world is a different place now," he said. "I've seen what you people do to parents who have lost children. Mohamed Al Fayed, made to look like a paranoid buffoon. Kate McCann, turned into a modern-day Medea. Put one foot wrong and they bury you. Well, I'm not about to let that happen. I'm a very successful man, Miss Richmond. And I got that way by accepting that there are things I don't know, and understanding that the way to overcome that is to employ experts and listen to them. As far as this business goes, you are my hired gun. Once the word gets out that there is new evidence, the media will go wild. But I will not be talking to anyone but you. Everything goes through you. So whatever image reaches the public will be the one you generate. This place was built to withstand a siege, and my security is state of the art. None of the reptiles gets near me or Judith or Alec."

Bel felt a smile tugging at the corners of her mouth. Exclusive access was every hack's wet dream. Usually she had to work her arse off to get it. But here it was, on a plate and for free. Still, let him keep on thinking that she was the one doing him a favour. "And what's in it for me? Apart from becoming the journalist that all the others love to hate?"

The thin line of Grant's lips compressed further, and his chest rose as he breathed deeply. "I will talk to you." The words came out as if they'd been ground between a pair of millstones. It was clearly meant to be a moment reminiscent of Moses descending from Mount Sinai.

Bel was determined not to be impressed. "Excellent. Shall we make a start then?" She reached into her bag and produced a digital recorder. "I know this is not going to be easy for you, but I need you to tell me about Catriona. We'll get to the kidnapping and its consequences, but we're going to have to go back before that. I want to have a sense of what she was like and what her life was like."

He stared into the middle distance, and for the first time Bel saw a man who looked his seventy-two years. "I'm not sure I'm the best person for that," he said. "We were too alike. It was always head to head with me and Catriona." He pushed himself out of the armchair and went back to the billiard table. "She was always volatile, even when she was wee. She had toddler tantrums that could shake the walls of this place. She grew out of the tantrums but not out of the tempers. Still, she could always charm her way right back into your good graces. When she put her mind to it." He glanced up at Bel and smiled. "She knew her own mind. And you couldn't shift her once she was set on something."

Grant moved round the table, studying the balls, lining up his next shot. "And she had talent. When she was a child, you never saw her without a pencil or a paintbrush in her hand. Drawing, painting, modelling with clay. She never stopped. She didn't grow out of it like most kids do. She just got better at it. And then she discovered glass." He bent over the table and stunned the cue ball into the red, slotting it into the middle pocket. He respotted the red and studied the angles.

"You said you were always head to head with each other. What were the flashpoints?" Bel said when he showed no sign of continuing his reminiscences.

Grant gave a little snort of laughter. "Anything and everything. Politics. Religion. Whether Italian food was better than Indian. Whether Mozart was better than Beethoven. Whether abstract art had any meaning. Whether we should plant beech or birch or Scots pine in the Check Bar wood." He straightened up slowly. "Why she didn't want to take over the company. That was a big one. I didn't have a son then. And I've never had a problem with women in business. I saw no reason why she shouldn't take over MGE once she'd learned how it all works. She said she'd rather stick needles in her eyes."

"She didn't approve of MGE?" Bel asked.

"No, it wasn't anything to do with the company or its policies. What she wanted was to be an artist in glass. Sculpting, blowing, casting—anything you could do with glass, she wanted to be the best. And that didn't leave any room for building roads or houses."

"That must have been a disappointment."

"Broke my heart." Grant cleared his throat. "I did everything I could to talk her out of it. But she wouldn't be talked out of it. She went behind my back, applied for a place at Goldsmiths in London. And she got it." He shook his head. "I was all for cutting her adrift without a penny, but Mary—my wife, Cat's mother—she shamed me into agreeing to support her.

She pointed out that, for somebody who hated being in the public eye, I'd be throwing a hell of a bone to the tabloids. So I let myself be talked into it." He gave a wry smile. "Almost reconciled myself to it too. And then I found out what was really going on."

Wednesday, 13th December 1978; Rotheswell Castle

Brodie Grant swung the Land Rover into a gravel-scattering turn and ground to a halt yards from the kitchen door of Rotheswell Castle. He stamped into the house, a chocolate Lab at his heels. He strode through the kitchen, leaving a swirl of freezing air in his wake, barking at the dog to stay. He moved through the house with the speed and certainty of a man who knows precisely where he is going.

At last he burst into the prettily decorated room where his wife indulged her passion for quilting. "Did you know about this?" he said. Mary looked up, startled. She could hear the rush of his breathing from across the room.

"About what, Brodie?" she said. She'd been married to a force of nature long enough not to be ruffled by a grand entrance.

"You talked me into this." He threw himself into a low armchair, struggling to untangle his legs. "'It's what she wants, Brodie. She'll never forgive you if you stand in her way, Brodie. You followed your dreams, Brodie. Let her follow hers.' That's what you said. So I did. Against my better judgement, I said I would back her up. Finance her bloody degree. Keep my mouth shut about what a bloody waste of time it is. Stop reminding her how few artists ever make any kind of a living from their self-indulgent bloody carry-on. Not till they're dead, anyway." He banged his fist on the arm of the chair.

Mary continued piecing her fabric and smiled. "You did, Brodie. And I'm very proud of you for it."

"And now look where it's got us. Look what's really going on."

"Brodie, I've no idea what you're talking about. Do you think you could explain? And with due consideration for your blood pressure?" She'd always had the gift of gently teasing him out of his extreme positions. But today, it wasn't working well. Brodie's dander was up, and it was going to take more than an application of sweet reason to restore him to his normal humour.

"I've been out with Sinclair. Checking the drives for the shoot on Friday."

"And how were the drives?"

"Perfectly fine. They're always fine. He's a good keeper. But that's not the point, Mary." His voice rose again, incongruous in the cosy room with its stacked riot of fabrics on the shelves.

"No, Brodie. I realize that. What is the point, exactly?"

"Fergus bloody Sinclair, that's what. I told Sinclair. Back in the summer, when his bloody son was sniffing round Cat. I told him to keep the boy away from my daughter, and I thought he'd listened to me. But now this." He waved his hands as if he was throwing a pile of hay in the air.

Mary finally put down her work. "What's the matter, Brodie? What's happened?"

"It's what's *going* to happen. You know how we breathed a sigh of relief when he signed up for his bloody estate management degree at Edinburgh? Well, it turns out that wasn't the only iron in his bloody fire. He's only gone and accepted a place at London University. He's going to be in the same bloody city as our daughter. He'll be all over her like a rash.

Bloody gold-digging peasant." He scowled and smacked his fist down on the chair again. "I'm going to settle his hash, you see if I don't."

To his astonishment, Mary was laughing, rocking back and forward at her piecing table, tears glistening at the corners of her eyes. "Oh, Brodie," she gasped. "I can't tell you how funny this is."

"Funny?" he howled. "That bloody boy's going to ruin Cat and you think it's funny?"

Mary jumped to her feet and crossed the room to her husband. Ignoring his protests, she sat on his lap and ran her fingers through his thick hair. "It's all right, Brodie. Everything's going to be fine."

"I don't see how." He jerked away from her hand.

"Me and Cat, we've been trying to figure out how to tell you for the past week."

"Tell me what, woman?"

"She's not going to London, Brodie."

He straightened up, almost toppling Mary on to the floor. "What do you mean, not going to London? Is she giving up this daftness? Is she coming to work with me?"

Mary sighed. "Don't be silly. You know in your heart she's doing what she should be doing. No, she's been offered a scholarship. It's a combination of academic study and working in a designer glass factory. Brodie, it's absolutely the best training in the world. And they want our Catriona."

For a long moment, he allowed himself to be torn between pride and fear. "Where about?" he said at last.

"It's not so far, Brodie." Mary ran the back of her hand down his cheek. "It's only Sweden."

"Sweden? Bloody Sweden? Jesus Christ, Mary. Sweden?"

"You make it sound like the ends of the earth. You can fly there from Edinburgh, you know. It takes less than two hours.

Honestly, Brodie. Listen to yourself. This is wonderful. It's the best possible start for her. And you won't have to worry about Fergus being in the same place. He's not likely to turn up in a small town between Stockholm and Uppsala, is he?"

Grant put his arms round his wife and rested his chin on her head. "Trust you to find the silver lining." His mouth curled in a cruel smile. "It's certainly going to put Fergus bloody Sinclair's gas at a peep."

THURSDAY, 28TH JUNE 2007; ROTHESWELL CASTLE

"So you argued with Cat about boyfriends as well?" Bel said. "Was it all of them, or just Fergus Sinclair in particular?"

"She didn't have that many boyfriends. She was too focused on her work. She went out for a few months with one of the sculptors at the glass factory. I met him a couple of times. Swedish, but a sensible enough lad all the same. I could see she wasn't serious, though, so there was no need to argue about him. But Fergus Sinclair was a different kettle of fish." He paced the perimeter of the table, the anger obvious. "The police never took him seriously as a suspect, but I wondered at the time whether he might have been behind what happened to Cat and Adam. He certainly couldn't accept it when she finally cut the ties between them. And he couldn't accept that she wouldn't acknowledge him as Adam's father. At the time, I thought it was possible he took the law into his own hands. Though it's hard to see him having the wit to put something that complicated together."

"But Cat continued her relationship with Fergus after she went to Sweden?"

Tiredness seemed suddenly to hit Grant and he dropped back into the chair opposite Bel. "They were very close. They'd run about together when they were kids. I should have put a stop to it but it never crossed my mind that it would ever come to anything. They were so different. Cat with her art and Sinclair with no more ambition than to follow his father into keepering. Different class, different aspirations. The only thing that I could see pulling them together was that life had landed them in the same place. So yes, when she came back in the holidays and he was around, they got back together again. She made no secret of it, even though she knew how I felt about Sinclair. I kept hoping she'd meet someone she deserved but it never happened. She kept going back to Sinclair."

"And yet you didn't sack his father? Move him off the estate?"

Grant looked shocked. "Good God, no. Have you any idea how hard it is to find a keeper as good as Willie Sinclair? You could interview a hundred men before you'd find one with his instincts for the birds and the land. A decent man, too. He knew his son wasn't in Cat's league. He was ashamed that he couldn't stop Fergus chasing Cat. He wanted to bar him from the family home, but his wife wouldn't have it." He shrugged. "I can't say I blame her. Women are always soft with their sons."

Bel tried to hide her surprise. She'd assumed Grant would stop at nothing to have his own way where his daughter was concerned. He was apparently more complex than she'd given him credit for. "What happened after she came back from Sweden?"

Grant rubbed his face with his hands. "It wasn't pretty. She wanted to move out. Set up a studio where she could work and sell things from, somewhere with living quarters attached. She had her eye on a couple of properties on the estate. I said the price of my support was that she stop seeing Sinclair." For the first time, Bel saw sadness seeping round the edges of the simmering anger. "It was stupid of me. Mary said so at the time, and she was right. They were both furious with me, but I wouldn't give in. So Cat went her own way. She spoke to the Wemyss estate and rented a property from them. An old gatehouse with what had been a logging shed, set back from the main road. Perfect for attracting customers. A parking area in front of the old gates, studio and display space, and living quarters tucked away behind the walls. All the privacy you could want. And everybody knew. Catriona Maclennan Grant had gone to the Wemyss estate to spite her old man."

"If she needed your support, how did she pay for it all?" Bel asked.

"Her mother equipped the studio, paid the first year's rent, and stocked the kitchen till Cat started selling pieces." He couldn't suppress a smile. "Which didn't take long. She was good, you know. Very good. And her mother saw to it that all her friends went there for wedding presents and birthday gifts. I was never angrier with Mary than I was then. I was outraged. I felt thwarted and disrespected and it really did not help when bloody Sinclair came back from university and picked up where he'd left off."

"Were they living together?"

"No. Cat had more sense than that. I look back at it now and I sometimes think she only went on seeing him to spite me. It didn't last that long after she'd set the studio up. It was pretty much over about eighteen months before . . . before she died."

Bel did her mental arithmetic and came up with the wrong answer. "But Adam was only six months old when they were kidnapped. So how could Fergus Sinclair be his father if he split up with Cat eighteen months earlier?"

Grant sighed. "According to Mary, it wasn't a clean break. Cat kept telling Sinclair it was over but he wouldn't take no for an answer. These days, you'd call it harassment. Apparently he kept turning up with a pathetic puppy face and Cat didn't always have the strength to send him away. And then she got pregnant." He stared at the floor. "I'd always imagined what it would be like to be a grandfather. To see the family line continue. But when Cat told us, all I felt was anger. That bastard Sinclair had wrecked her future. Saddled her with his child, ruined her chances of the career she'd dreamed of. The one good thing she did was refuse to have anything more to do with him. She wouldn't acknowledge him as the father, she wouldn't see him or talk to him. She made it plain that, this time, it really was over and done."

"How did he take that?"

"Again, I got it secondhand. This time from Willie Sinclair. He said the boy was devastated. But all I cared about was that he'd finally got the message that he was never going to be part of this family. Willie advised the boy to put some distance between himself and Cat, and for once, he listened. Within a few weeks, he'd got a job in Austria, working on some hunting estate near Salzburg. And he's worked in Europe ever since."

"And now? You still think he might have been responsible for what happened?"

Grant made a face. "If I'm honest, no. Not really. I don't think he had the brains to come up with such a complicated plot. I'm sure he'd have loved to get his hands on his son and take his revenge on Cat at the same time, but it's much more likely that it was some politically motivated bastards who thought it would be clever to get me to fund their revolution."

Wearily, he got to his feet. "I'm tired now. The police are coming tomorrow morning and we'll be going through all the other stuff then. We'll see you at dinner, Miss Richmond." He walked out of the room, leaving Bel with plenty to ponder. And to transcribe. When Brodie Grant had said he would talk to her, she hadn't imagined for a moment he would provide her with this rich seam of information. She was going to have to consider very carefully how to present him to the world's media. One foot wrong and she knew the mine would be closed down. And now she'd had a taste of what lay within, that was definitely the last thing she wanted.

GLENROTHES

The Mint was staring at the computer screen as if it was an artefact from outer space when Karen got back to her office. "What have you got for me?" she asked. "Have you tracked down the five scabs yet?"

"None of them's got a criminal record," he said.

"And?"

"I wasn't sure where else to look."

Karen rolled her eyes. Her conviction that the Mint had been dumped on her as a form of sabotage by the Macaroon intensified daily. "Google. Electoral rolls. 192.com. Vehicle licensing. Make a start there, Jason. And then fix me up a site meeting with the cave preservation person. Better leave tomorrow clear, see if you can get him to meet me on Saturday morning."

"We don't work Saturdays usually," the Mint said.

"Speak for yourself," Karen muttered, making a note to

herself to ask Phil to come with her. Scots law's insistence on corroboration for all evidence made it hard to be a complete maverick.

She woke her computer from hibernation and tracked down the contact details of her opposite number in Nottingham. To her relief, DCI Des Mottram was at his desk, receptive to her request. "I think it's probably a dead end, but it's one that needs to be checked out," she said.

"And you don't fancy a trip down to the Costa del Trent," he said, amused resignation in his voice.

"It's not that. I've just had a major case reopen today and there's no way I can spare a couple of bodies on something that probably won't take us any further forward except in a negative way."

"Don't worry about it. I know how it goes. It's your lucky day, though, Karen. We got two new CID aides on Monday and this is exactly the kind of thing I can use to break them in. Nothing too complicated, nothing too dodgy."

Karen gave him the names of the men. "I've got one of my lads looking for last known addresses. Soon as he's got anything, I'll get him to e-mail you." A few more details, and she was done. Right on cue, Phil Parhatka walked back into the room, a bacon roll transmitting a message straight to the pleasure centres of Karen's brain. "Mmm," she groaned. "Christ, that smells glorious."

"If I'd known you were back, I'd have got you one. Here, we'll go halves." He took a knife out of his drawer and cut the roll in half, tomato sauce squirting over his fingers. He handed over her share, then licked his fingers. What more, Karen wondered, could a woman ask for in a man?

"What did the Macaroon want?" Phil said.

Karen bit into the roll and spoke through a mouthful of

soft sweet dough and salty bacon. "New development in the Catriona Maclennan Grant case."

"Really? What's happened?"

Karen grinned. "I don't know. King Brodie didn't bother to tell the Macaroon. He just told him to send me round tomorrow morning. So I need to get myself up to speed smartish. I've already sent for the records, but I'm going to check it out online first. Listen . . ." She drew him to one side. "The Mick Prentice business. I need to talk to somebody on Saturday and obviously the Mint doesn't do Saturdays. Any chance I can talk you into coming along with me?"

"Coming along where?"

"The Wemyss caves."

"Really?" Phil perked up. "We get to go behind the railings?"

"I expect so," Karen said. "I didn't know you were into the caves."

"Karen, I used to be a wee boy."

She rolled her eyes. "Right enough."

"Besides, the caves have got really cool stuff. Pictish inscriptions and drawings. Iron Age carvings. I like the idea of being a secret squirrel and taking a look at the things you don't usually get to see. Sure, I'll come with you. Have you logged the case yet?"

Karen looked embarrassed. "I want to see where it goes. It was a hard time round here. If something bad happened to Mick Prentice, I want to get to the bottom of it. And you know how the media are always poking around in what we're doing in CCRT. I've a feeling this is one where we've got a better chance of finding out what happened if we can keep the lid on it a bit."

Phil finished his roll and wiped his mouth with the back

of his hand. "Fair enough. You're the boss. Just make sure the Macaroon can't use it as a stick to beat you with."

"I'll watch my back. Listen, are you busy right now?"

He tossed the empty paper bag in the bin with an overhead action, preening himself when it landed right in the middle. "Nothing I can't put to one side."

"See what you can dig up on a guy called Andy Kerr. He was an NUM official during the strike. Lived in a cottage in the middle of Wemyss woods. He was on the sick with depression around the time Mick went missing. Supposedly topped himself, but the body was never recovered."

Phil nodded. "I'll see what I can find."

As he returned to his own desk, Karen was Googling Catriona Maclennan Grant. The first hit took her to a two-year-old broadsheet newspaper feature published to mark the twentieth anniversary of the young sculptor's death. Three paragraphs in, Karen felt a physical jolt in the middle of her chest. "It's amazing how few people are available to talk about this case," she read. "Cat Grant's father has never spoken to the press about what happened. Her mother killed herself two years after the death of her daughter. Her ex-boyfriend, Fergus Sinclair, refuses to be interviewed. And the officer in charge of the case is also beyond our reach—he is himself serving life for murder."

"Oh Christ," she groaned. She hadn't even seen the case file but already this was turning into the assignment from hell.

Kirkcaldy

It was after ten when Karen walked through her front door with a bundle of files and a fish supper. The notion that she was playing at keeping house had never deserted her. Maybe it was something to do with the house itself, an identikit box on a 1960s warren development to the north of Kirkcaldy. The sort of place people started out in, clinging to the hope it wasn't going to be where they ended up. Low-crime suburbia, a place where you could let kids play out in the street so long as you didn't live on one of the through roads. Traffic accidents, not abductions, were what parents feared here. Karen could never quite remember why she'd bought it, though it had seemed like a good idea at the time. She suspected the appeal had been that it came completely refurbished, probably by somebody who'd got the idea from a TV property development programme. She'd bought the furniture with the house, right down to the pictures on the walls. She didn't care that she hadn't chosen the stuff she lived among. It was the kind of thing she'd probably have picked anyway and it had saved her the hassle of a Sunday in IKEA. And nobody could deny that it was a million times nicer than the faded floral clutter her parents inhabited. Her mother kept waiting for her to revert to type, but it wasn't going to happen. When she had a weekend off, Karen wanted nothing more than a curry with her pals and a significant amount of time on the sofa watching football and old films. Not homemaking.

She dumped everything on the dining table and went in search of a plate and cutlery. She still had some standards, for God's sake. She tossed her coat over a chair and sat down to her meal, flipping a folder open and reading as she ate. She'd worked her way through the Grant case files earlier and made a note of the questions she wanted answers to. Now finally she had the chance to look over the material Phil had gathered for her.

As she'd expected, the original missing persons report could hardly have been more sketchy. Back then, the disappearance of an unmarried, childless adult male with a history of clinical depression barely dented the police consciousness. It was nothing to do with the fact that the miners' strike had stretched the force's staffing levels almost to breaking point and everything to do with the fact that, back then, missing persons were not a priority. Not unless they were small children or attractive young women. Even these days, only the fact of Andy Kerr's medical problems would have guaranteed him mild interest.

He'd been reported missing by his sister Angie on Christmas Eve. He'd failed to show up at their parents' home for the traditional family celebration. Angie, home from teacher training college for the holidays, had left a couple of messages on his answering machine in the previous week, trying to arrange meeting up for a drink. Andy hadn't responded, but that wasn't unusual. He'd always been dedicated to his job, but since the strike had begun, he'd become workaholic.

Then on the afternoon of Christmas Eve, Mrs. Kerr had admitted that Andy was on sick leave for depression. Angie had persuaded her father to drive her over to Andy's cottage in the Wemyss woods. The place had been cold and deserted, the fridge empty of fresh food. A note was propped up against the sugar bowl on the kitchen table. Amazingly, it had been bagged and included in the file. *If you're reading this, it's probably because you're worried about me. Don't be. I've had enough. It's just one thing after another and I can't take it any more. I've gone away to try and get my head straight. Andy.*

It wasn't exactly a suicide note, but if you found a body near a message like that, you wouldn't be expecting a murder victim. And the sister had said Andy liked to go mountain walking. She could see why the uniform who'd checked out the cottage and the surrounding woodland had recommended no further action aside from circulating the information to other forces in Scotland. A comment on the file in a different hand noted that Angie Kerr had applied to have her brother declared dead in 1992 and the application had been granted.

The last page was in Phil's familiar writing. "The Kerr parents died in the Zeebrugge ferry disaster in 1987. Angie couldn't claim their estate till she could have Andy declared dead. When she finally got probate in 1993, she sold up and emigrated to New Zealand. She teaches piano in Nelson on the South Island, works from home." Angie Kerr's full address and phone number followed.

She'd had a rough time of it, Karen thought. Losing her brother and both parents in the space of a couple of years was tough enough, without having to go through the process of having Andy formally declared dead. No wonder she'd wanted to move to the other side of the world. Where, she noted, it would now be half past eleven in the morning. A perfectly civilized time to call someone.

One of the few things Karen had bought for her home was an answering machine that allowed her to make digital recordings of her phone calls, recordings which she could then transfer via a USB connection to her computer. She'd tried to persuade the Macaroon to acquire some for the office, but he'd seemed unimpressed. Probably because it hadn't been his idea. Karen wouldn't have minded betting something similar would turn up in the main CID office before long, the brainchild of ACC Lees himself. Never mind. At least she could use the system at home and reclaim the cost of the calls.

A woman answered on the third ring, the Scots accent obvious even in the two syllables of "Hello?"

Karen introduced herself then said, "Is this Angie Kerr?"

"Kerr as was. Mackenzie as is. Is this about my brother? Have you found him?" She sounded excited, pleased almost.

"I'm afraid not, no."

"He didn't kill himself, you know. I've always thought he had an accident. Came off a mountain somewhere. No matter how depressed he was, Andy would never have killed himself. He wasn't a coward." Defiance travelled well.

"I'm sorry," Karen said. "I really have no answers for you. But we are looking again at events around the time he went missing. We're investigating the disappearance of Mick Prentice, and your brother's name came up."

"Mick Prentice." Angie sounded disgusted. "Some friend he turned out to be."

"What do you mean?"

"I don't think it's any coincidence that he went scabbing just before Andy took off."

"Why do you say that?"

A short pause, then Angie said, "Because it would feel like the worst betrayal. Those guys had been friends since the first day at school. Mick becoming a scab would have broken Andy's heart. And I think he saw it coming."

"What makes you say that?"

"The last time I saw him, he knew there was something going on with Mick."

SUNDAY, 2ND DECEMBER 1984; WEMYSS WOODS

A visit home was never complete for Angie without time spent with her brother. She tried to get back at least once a term, but although the bus ride from Edinburgh was only an hour, it sometimes seemed too big an undertaking. She knew the problem was the different kind of distance that was growing between her and her parents as she moved more freely through a world that was alien to theirs: lectures, student societies, parties where drugs were as common as drink, and a conversational range that outstripped anything she'd ever encountered back in Fife. Not that there weren't opportunities for broadening one's intellectual horizons there. But the reading rooms and WEA courses and Burns Clubs were for the men. Women had never had the access or the time. The men did their shifts underground, then their time was their own. But the women's work truly was never done, especially for those whose landlords were the old coal companies or the nationalized coal board. Angie's own grandmother hadn't had running hot water or a bath in her home until she'd been in her sixties. So the men didn't easily take to women with an education.

Andy was one of the exceptions. His move from the coal face to working for the union had exposed him to the wider equality policies pursued by the trade union movement. There might not be women working in the pits, but contact with other unions had persuaded Andy that the world would not end if you treated women as fellow members of the human race. And so brother and sister had grown closer, replacing their childhood squabbling with genuine debate. Now Angie looked forward to Sunday afternoons spent with her brother, tramping through the woods or nursing mugs of hot chocolate by the fire.

That afternoon, Andy had met her off the bus at the end of the track that led deep into the woods to his cottage. They'd planned to skirt the woods and walk down to the shore, but the sky threatened rain so they opted to head back for the cottage. "I've got the fire on for you coming," Andy had said as they set off. "I feel guilty about having the money for the coal, so I don't usually bother. I just put another sweater on."

"That's daft. Nobody blames you for still getting a wage."

Andy shook his head. "That's where you're wrong. There's plenty think we should be kicking back our wages into the union pot."

"And who does that help? You're doing a job. You're supporting the men on strike. You deserve to be paid." She linked her arm with his, understanding how embattled he felt.

"Aye, and a lot of the strikers think they should be getting something from the union too. I've heard a few of them down the Welfare saying that if the union had been paying strike pay, they wouldn't be having to work so hard to keep the funds out of the hands of the sequestrators. They wonder what the union funds are for, if not to support the members when there's a strike on." He sighed, head down as if he was walking into a high wind. "And they've got a point, you know?"

"I suppose so. But if you've willingly handed over the decision-making to your leaders, which they've done by agreeing to strike without a national ballot, then you can't really start to complain when they make decisions you're not so keen on." Angie looked closely at her brother, seeing how the lines of strain round his eyes had deepened since she'd last seen him. His skin looked waxy and unhealthy, like that of a man who has spent too long indoors without vitamin supplements. "And it doesn't help anybody if you let them wind you up about it."

"I don't feel like I'm much help to anybody right now," he said, so quietly it was almost lost in the scuffle of dead leaves beneath their feet.

"That's just silly," Angie protested, knowing it wasn't enough but not knowing what else to say.

"No, it's the truth. The men I represent, their lives are falling apart. They're losing their homes because they can't pay the mortgage. Their wives have sold their wedding rings. Their kids go to school hungry. They've got holes in their shoes. It's like a bloody Third World country here, only we don't have charities raising money to help us with our disaster. And I can't do anything about it. How do you think that makes me feel?"

"Pretty shitty," Angie said, hugging his arm tighter to her. There was no resistance; it was like embracing the stuffed draught excluder their mother used to keep the living room as stifling as she could manage. "But you can only do the best you can. Nobody expects you to solve all the problems of the strike."

"I know." He sighed. "But I used to feel part of this community. I've belonged here all my life. These days, it feels like the guys on strike are on one side of the fence and everybody else is on the other side. Union officials, pit deputies, managers, fucking Tory government—we're all the enemy."

"Now you're really talking rubbish. There's no way you're on the same side as the Tories. Everybody knows that." They walked on in silence, quickening their pace as the promise of rain became a reality. It sheeted down in cold hard drops. The bare branches above their heads offered little protection against the penetrating downpour. Angie let go his arm and began to run. "Come on, I'll race you," she said, exhilarated somehow by the drenching cold. She didn't check to see whether he was following her. She just hurtled pell-mell through the trees, jinking and swerving to stay with the winding path. As always, emerging into the clearing where the cottage hunkered down seemed impossibly sudden. It sat there like something out of the Brothers Grimm, a low squat building with no charm except its isolation. The slate roof, grey harling, black door and window frames would easily have qualified it as the home of the wicked witch in the eyes of any passing child. A wooden lean-to sheltered a coal box, a wood pile, and Andy's motorbike and sidecar.

Angie ran to the porch and turned round, panting. There was no sign of Andy. A couple of minutes passed before he trudged out of the trees, light brown hair plastered dark to his head. Angie felt deflated at the failure of her attempt to lighten his spirits. He said nothing as he led the way into the cottage, as neat and spartan as a barracks. The only decoration was a series of wildlife posters that had been given away free with one of the Scottish Sunday papers. One set of shelves was crammed with books on natural history and politics; another with LPs. It couldn't have been less like the rooms she frequented in Edinburgh, but Angie liked it better than any of them. She shook her head like a dog to shed the raindrops from her dark blond hair, tossed her coat over a chair, and curled up in one of the secondhand armchairs that flanked the fire. Andy went straight through to the scullery to make the hot chocolate.

As she waited for him to come through, Angie fretted over how she might lift his mood. Usually she made him laugh with tales of her fellow students and their antics, but she sensed that wasn't going to work today. It would feel too much like insensitive tales of the over-privileged. Maybe the answer was to remind him of the people who still believed in him.

He came back with two steaming mugs on a tray. Usually they had cookies, but clearly anything that smacked of luxury was off the menu today. "I've been giving most of my wages to the hardship fund," he said, noticing her noticing. "Just keeping enough for the rent and the basics."

They sat facing each other, nursing their hot drinks to let the warmth seep back into their cold hands. Angie spoke first. "You shouldn't pay attention to them. The people who really know you don't think you're one of the enemy. You should listen to people like Mick who know who you are. What you are."

"You think?" His mouth twisted in a bitter expression. "How can the likes of Mick know who I am when I don't know who they are any more?"

"What do you mean, you don't know who Mick is any more? The two of you have been best pals for twenty-odd years. I don't believe the strike has changed either of you that much."

"You'd think so, wouldn't you?" Andy stared into the fire, his eyes dull and his shoulders sagging. "Men round here, we're not supposed to talk about our feelings. We live in this atmosphere of comradeship and loyalty and mutual dependence, but we never talk about what's going on inside us. But me and Mick, we weren't like that. We used to tell each other everything. There was nothing we couldn't talk about." He pushed his damp hair back from his high narrow forehead. "But lately something's changed. I feel like he's holding back. Like there's something really important that he can't bring himself to talk about."

"But that could be anything," Angie said. "Something between him and Jenny, maybe. Something it wouldn't be right to talk to you about."

Andy snorted. "You think he doesn't talk about Jenny? I know all about that marriage, trust me. I could draw you a map of the fault lines between that pair. No, it's not Jenny. The only thing I can think is that he agrees with the rest of them. That I'm neither use nor ornament to them right now."

"You sure you're not imagining things? It doesn't sound like Mick."

"I wish I was. But I'm not. Even my best pal thinks I'm not fit to be trusted any more. I just don't know how long I can go on doing my work, feeling like this."

Now Angie was starting to feel genuinely worried. Andy's

despair was clearly far beyond anything she knew how to deal with. "Andy, don't take me wrong, but you need to go and see the doctor."

He made a noise like a laugh strangled at birth. "What? Aspirin and Disprin, the painkilling twins? You think I'm losing my marbles? You think that pair would know what to do about it if I was? You think I need temazepam like half the bloody women round here? Happy pills to make it not matter?"

"I want to help you, Andy. And I don't have the skills. You need to talk to somebody that knows what they're doing, and the doctor's a good place to start. Even Aspirin and Disprin know more than I do about depression. I think you're depressed, Andy. Like, clinically depressed, not just miserable."

He looked as if he was going to cry. "You know the worst thing about what you just said? I think you might be right."

THURSDAY, 28TH JUNE 2007; KIRKCALDY

It sounded plausible. Andy Kerr had sensed Mick Prentice was keeping something from him. When it appeared Mick had joined the scabs and gone to Nottingham, it might have been enough to push someone in a fragile state over the edge. But it looked as if Mick Prentice hadn't gone to Nottingham at all. The question, Karen thought, was whether Andy Kerr knew what had really happened to his best friend. And whether he was involved in his disappearance. "And you never spoke to Andy after that Sunday?" she asked.

"No. I tried to ring him a couple of times, but I just got the answering machine. And I didn't have a phone where I was living so he couldn't call me back. Mum told me the doctor had signed him off his work with depression, but that was all I knew."

"Do you think it's possible he and Mick went off somewhere together?"

"What? You mean, just turned their back on everybody and waltzed off into the sunset like Butch Cassidy and the Sundance Kid?"

Karen winced. "Not that, exactly. More like they'd both had enough and couldn't see any other way out. No question that Andy was having his problems. And you suggested Mick and Jenny weren't getting along too well. Maybe they just decided on a clean break?"

She could hear Angie breathing on the other side of the world. "Andy wouldn't do that to us. He would never have hurt us like that."

"Could Mick have talked him into it? You said they'd been pals since school. Who was the leader? Who was the follower? There's always one who leads and one who follows. You know that, Angie. Was Mick the leader?" No one pushed more gently but firmly than Karen on a roll.

"I suppose so. Mick was the extrovert, Andy was much quieter. But they were a team. They were always in trouble, but not in a bad way. Not with the police. Just always in trouble at school. They'd booby-trap chemistry experiments with fireworks. Glue teachers' desks shut. Andy was good with words and Mick was artistic, so they'd print up posters with fake school announcements. Or Mick would forge notes from teachers letting the pair of them off classes they didn't like. Or they'd mess about in the library, swapping the dust jackets on the books. I'd have had a breakdown if I'd ever had pupils like them. But they grew out of it. By the time of the strike, they'd both settled down into their lives." There was more than a hint of regret in her voice. "So yes, theoretically Mick might have talked Andy into doing a runner. But it wouldn't have lasted. They'd have come back. They couldn't stay away. Their roots were too deep."

"You tore yours up," Karen observed.

"I fell in love with a New Zealander, and all my family were dead," Angie said flatly. "I wasn't leaving anybody behind to grieve."

"Fair enough. Can we go back to Mick? You said Andy had implied there were problems in his marriage?"

"She trapped him into that marriage, you know. Andy always thought she got pregnant on purpose. She was supposed to be on the pill, but amazingly it didn't work and the next thing was Misha was on the way. She knew Mick came from a decent family, the kind of people who don't run away from their responsibilities. So of course he married her." There was a bitter edge in her tone that made Karen wonder whether Angie had carried a torch for Mick Prentice before her New Zealander came along.

"Not the best of starts, then."

"They seemed happy enough to begin with." Angie's grudging admission came out slowly. "Mick treated her like a little princess and she lapped it up. But she didn't like it one little bit when the hard times hit. I thought at the time that she'd pushed him into scabbing because she'd had enough of being skint."

"But she really suffered after he went," Karen said. "It was a terrible stigma, being the wife of a scab. She wouldn't have let him leave her behind to face that on her own."

Angie made a dismissive noise in the back of her throat. "She had no idea what it would be like until it hit her. She didn't get it. She wasn't one of us, you know. People talk about the working class as if it's just one big lump, but the demarcation lines are just as well defined as they are among any other class. She was born and bred in East Wemyss, but she wasn't one of us. Her dad didn't get his hands dirty. He worked in the Co-operative. He served behind the counter in the store. He wore a collar and tie to his work. I bet he never voted Labour in his life. So I'm not sure how clearly she understood what would happen to her if Mick went on the black."

It made sense. Karen understood viscerally what Angie was saying. She knew people like that from her own community. People who didn't fit anywhere, who had a deep groove across their backsides from a lifetime of sitting on the fence. It lent weight to the idea that Mick Prentice might have gone scabbing. Except that he hadn't. "The thing is, Angie, it looks like Mick didn't go scabbing that night. Our preliminary inquiries indicate that he didn't join the five men who went to Nottingham."

A shocked silence. Then Angie said, "He could have gone somewhere else on his own."

"He had no money. No means of transport. He didn't take anything with him when he went out that morning except his painting gear. Whatever happened to him, I don't think he went scabbing."

"So what did happen to him?"

"I don't know that yet," Karen said. "But I plan to find out. And here's the question I have to start asking. Let's assume Mick didn't go scabbing. Who might have had a reason for wanting him out of the way?"

FRIDAY, 29TH JUNE 2007; NOTTINGHAM

Femi Otitoju entered the fourth address into Google Earth and studied the result. "Come on, Fem," Mark Hall muttered. "The DCI's got his eye on us. He's wondering what the hell you're doing, playing around on the computer after he's given us an assignment."

"I'm working out the most efficient order to do the interviews in, so we don't waste half the day backtracking." She looked at the four names and addresses supplied by some DC in Fife and numbered them according to her logic. "And I've told you. Don't call me Fem." She printed the list and folded it neatly into her unscuffed handbag. "My name is Femi."

Mark rolled his eyes and followed her out of the Cold Case Review office, flashing a nervous smile at DCI Mottram as they went. He'd been gagging for his temporary transfer to CID, but if he'd been warned that it would mean working with Femi Otitoju, he might have had second thoughts. The word round the station when they were both still in uniform was that, in Otitoju's case, PC stood for Personal Computer. Her uniform had always been immaculate, her shoes polished to a military sheen. Her plain clothes followed the same pattern. Neatly pressed anonymous grey suit, blinding white shirt, impeccable hair. And shoes still polished like mirrors. Everything she did was by the book; everything was precise. Not that Mark had anything against doing things properly. But he'd always believed there was a place for spontaneity, especially in an interview. If the person you were talking to veered off at a tangent, it didn't hurt to follow for a while. Sometimes it was among the tangents that the truth was hiding. "So these four were all miners from Fife who broke the strike to go down the pits here?" he said.

"That's right. There were originally five of them, but one of them, Stuart McAdam, died two years ago of lung cancer."

How did she remember that stuff? And why did she bother? "And who are we going to see first?"

"William John Fraser. Known as Billy. Fifty-three years old, married with two grown-up children, one at Leeds University, the other at Loughborough. He's a self-employed electrician now." She hitched her bag higher on her shoulder. "I'll drive, I know where we're going."

They emerged in the windy parking lot behind the station and headed for an unmarked CID pool car. It would, Mark knew, be full of someone else's rubbish. CID and cars were like dogs and lampposts, he'd discovered. "Won't he be at work now?" He opened the passenger door to find the footwell held plastic sandwich containers, empty Coke cans, and five Snickers bar wrappers. Something white snapped at the corner of his peripheral vision. Otitoju was waving an empty carrier bag at him. "There you go," she said. "Stick the rubbish in there and I'll take it to the bin."

Mark reminded himself that she did have her uses after all. They hit the main ring road, still busy even after the worst of the morning rush, and headed west. The road was flanked with dirty red-brick houses and the sort of businesses that managed to hang on by a fingernail in the teeth of classier opposition elsewhere. Convenience stores, nail studios, hardware shops, launderettes, fast-food outlets, and hairdressers. It was depressing driving past it. Mark was grateful for his city-centre flat in a converted lace mill. It might be small, but he didn't have to deal with this crap in his personal life. And there was a great Chinese just round the corner that delivered.

Fifteen minutes round the ring road and they turned off into a pleasant enclave of semi-detached brick cottages. They looked as if they'd been built in the 1930s; solid, unpretentious, and nicely proportioned. Billy Fraser's house was on a corner plot, with a substantial, well-established garden. "I've lived in this city all my life and I didn't even know this place existed," Mark said.

He followed Otitoju up the path. The door was answered by a woman who couldn't have been much over five feet. She had the look of someone just past her best; silver strands in her light brown bob, jawline starting to soften, a few more pounds than was comfortable. Mark thought she was in pretty good nick for her age. He dived straight in before Otitoju could scare her. "Mrs. Fraser?"

The woman nodded, looking anxious. "Yes, that's me." Local accent, Mark noted. So he hadn't brought a wife from Fife. "And you are . . . ?"

"I'm Mark Hall and this is my colleague Femi Otitoju. We're police officers and we need to have a word with Billy. It's nothing to worry about," he added hastily, seeing the look of panic on Mrs. Fraser's face. "Someone he used to know back in Fife has been reported missing and we need to ask Billy a few questions."

The woman shook her head. "You'll be wasting your time, duck. Billy's not kept in touch with anyone from Fife except the lads he came down here with. And that was more than twenty years ago."

"The man we're interested in went missing more than twenty years ago," Otitoju said bluntly. "So we do need to speak to your husband. Is he at home?" Mark felt like kicking her as he watched Mrs. Fraser's face close down on them. Otitoju had definitely been behind the door when sisterhood got handed out.

"He's at work."

"Can you tell us where he's working, flower?" Mark said, trying to get back on a conversational keel.

He could practically see the mental debate on the woman's face. "Wait a minute," she said at last. She returned with a large-format diary open at that day's date. She turned it to face him. "There."

Otitoju was already scribbling the address down on her precious sheet of paper. Mrs. Fraser caught sight of the names. "You're in luck," she said. "Johnny Ferguson's working with him today. You'll be able to kill two birds with one stone." From the expression on her face, she wasn't convinced that was a metaphor.

The two ex-miners were working a scant five-minute drive away, refitting a shop on the main drag. "From kebab shop to picture framing in one easy move," Mark said, reading the clues. Fraser and Ferguson were hard at work, Fraser chiselling out a channel for cables, Ferguson demolishing the bench seat running along one wall for the takeaway's customers. They both stopped what they were doing when the two police officers entered, eyeing them warily. It was funny, Mark thought, how some people always recognized a cop instantly, while others seemed oblivious to whatever signals he and his kind gave off. It was nothing to do with guilt or innocence, as he'd naïvely thought at first. Just an instinct for the hunter.

Otitoju introduced them and explained why they were there. Fraser and Ferguson both looked bemused. "Why would anybody think he'd have come with us?" Ferguson said.

"More to the point, why would anybody think we'd have taken him?" Billy Fraser wiped the back of his hand across his mouth in a gesture of disgust. "Mick Prentice thought the likes of us were beneath him. Even before we went scabbing, he looked down on other folk. Thought he was better than us."

"Why would he think that?" Mark asked.

Fraser pulled a packet of Bensons out of his overalls. Before he could get the cigarette out of the packet, Otitoju had placed her smooth hand over the rough one. "That's against the law now, Mr. Fraser. This is a place of work. You can't smoke in here."

"Aw, for fuck's sake," Fraser complained, turning away as he shoved his smokes back in his pocket.

"Why would Mick Prentice think he was better than you?" Mark said again.

Ferguson took up the challenge. "Some men went on strike because the union told them to. And some went on strike because they were convinced they were right and they knew what was best for the rest of us. Mick Prentice was one of the ones who thought they knew best."

"Aye," Fraser said bitterly. "And he had his pals in the union taking care of him." He rubbed fingers and thumb together in the universal representation of money.

"I don't understand," Mark said. "I'm sorry, mate, I'm too young to remember the strike. But I thought one of the big problems was that you didn't get strike pay?"

"You're right, son," Fraser said. "But for a while, the lads that went on the flying pickets got cash in hand. So when there was any picketing duty available, it was always the same ones that got the nod. And if your face didn't fit, there was nothing for you. But Mick's face fit better than most. His best pal was an NUM official, see?"

"It was harder for some of us than others," Ferguson added. "I expect Prentice's pal slipped him the odd fiver or bag of food when the picketing money ran out. Most of us weren't that lucky. So no, Mick Prentice didn't come with us. And Billy's right. We wouldn't have had him if he'd asked."

Otitoju was prowling round the room, scrutinizing their

work as if she were a building inspector. "The day you left. Did you see Mick Prentice at all?"

The two men exchanged a look that seemed furtive to Mark. Ferguson quickly shook his head. "Not really," he said.

"How can you 'not really' see somebody?" Otitoju demanded, turning back towards them.

Friday, 14th December 1984; Newton of Wemyss

Johnny Ferguson stood in the dark at the bedroom window where he could see the main road through the village. The room wasn't cold, but he was shivering slightly, the hand cupping his rollie trembling, interrupting the smooth rise of the smoke. "Come on, Stuart," he muttered under his breath. He took another drag off his cigarette and looked again at the cheap watch on his wrist. Ten minutes late. His right foot began tapping involuntarily.

Nothing was stirring. It was barely nine o'clock, but there was hardly a light showing. People couldn't afford the electricity. They went down the Welfare for a bit of light and heat or they went to bed, hoping they might sleep long enough for the nightmare to be over when they woke. For once, though, the quiet of the streets didn't bother Ferguson. The fewer people the better to witness what was happening tonight. He knew exactly what he was about to do and it scared the living shit out of him.

Suddenly, a pair of headlights swung into sight round the corner of Main Street. Against the dim street lights, Ferguson could make out the shape of a transit van. The old shape, not the new one that the police used as troop carriers in their operations against the miners. As the van drew closer, he could see it was dark in colour. Finally, Stuart was here.

Ferguson pinched out his cigarette. He took a last look round the bedroom where he'd slept for the last three years, ever since he'd taken the tenancy on the tiny house. It was too gloomy to see much, but then there wasn't much to be seen. What couldn't be sold had been broken up for firewood. Now there was just the mattress on the floor with an ashtray and a tattered Sven Hassel paperback beside it. Nothing left to regret. Helen was long gone, so he might as well turn his back on the fucking lot of them.

He clattered downstairs and opened the door just as Stuart was about to knock. "Ready?" Stuart said.

A deep breath. "As ready as I'll ever be." He pushed a holdall towards Stuart with a foot and grabbed another holdall and a black trash bag. Ten fucking years at the coal face, and that was all he had to show for it.

They took two steps of the four that would bring them to the van and suddenly they weren't alone. A figure came hustling round the corner like a man on a mission. A couple of yards closer and the shape resolved itself into Mick Prentice. Ferguson felt a cold hand clutch his chest. Christ, that was all they needed. Prentice ripping into them, shouting the odds and doors opening all the way down the street.

Stuart threw his holdall into the back of the van, where Billy Fraser was already settled on a pile of bags. He turned to face Prentice, ready to make something of it if he had to.

But the rage they expected wasn't raining down on them. Instead, Prentice just stood there, looking like he was going to burst into tears. He looked at them and shook his head. "No, lads. No. Dinnae do it," he said. He kept on saying it. Ferguson could hardly believe this was the same man who'd chivvied them and rallied them and goaded them into staying loyal to the union. It was, he thought, a measure of how this strike had broken them.

Ferguson pushed past Prentice, stowed his bags, and climbed in beside Fraser, who pulled the doors closed behind him. "Fucking amazing," Fraser said.

"He looked like he just took a punch to the gut," Ferguson said. "The guy's lost it."

"Just be grateful," Fraser said. "Last thing we needed was him going off like a fucking rocket, bringing the place down about us." He raised his voice as the engine roared into life. "Let's go, Stu. The new life starts here."

Friday, 29th June 2007

"Were there any witnesses to this encounter?" Otitoju said.

"Stuart's dead now, so I'm the only witness left," Fraser said. "I was in the van. The back door was open and I saw the whole thing. Johnny's right. Prentice looked gutted. Like it was a personal affront, what we were doing."

"It might have been a different story if it had been Iain in the van and not you," Ferguson said.

"Why might that have made a difference?" Mark said.

"Iain and him were pals. Prentice might have felt the need to try and talk him out of it. But Iain was the last pick-up, so I guess we were off the hook. And that was the last time we saw Prentice," Ferguson said. "I've still got family up there. I heard he'd taken off, but I just assumed he'd gone off with that pal of his, the union guy. I can't remember his name—"

"Andy something," Fraser said. "Aye, when you told me they were both on the missing list, I thought they'd decided to bugger off and make a fresh start somewhere else. You have to understand, people's lives were falling apart by then. Men did things you'd never have thought they were capable of." He turned away and walked to the door, stepping outside and taking out his cigarettes.

"He's right," Ferguson said. "And mostly we didn't want to think too much about it. Come to that, we still don't want to. So unless there's anything else, we'll say good day to you." He picked up his crowbar and returned to his task.

Unable to think of anything else to ask, Mark started for the door. Otitoju hesitated briefly before following him to the car. They sat in silence for a moment, then Mark said, "It must have been bloody awful."

"It doesn't excuse their lawlessness," Otitoju said. "The miners' strike drove a wedge between us and the people we serve. They made us look brutal even though we were provoked. They say even the Queen was shocked by the battle of Orgreave, but what did people expect? We're supposed to keep her peace. If people don't consent to be policed, what else can we do?"

Mark stared at her. "You scare me," he said.

She looked surprised. "I sometimes wonder if you're in the right job," she said.

Mark looked away. "You and me both, flower."

Rotheswell Castle

In spite of her determination to deal with Sir Broderick Maclennan Grant on precisely the same terms as she would anyone else, Karen had to admit her stomach was off message. Anxiety always affected her digestive tract, putting her off her food and precipitating urgent dashes to the toilet. "If I had more interviews like this, I wouldn't need to think about going on a diet," she said as she and Phil set off for Rotheswell Castle.

"Ach, dieting's overrated," said Phil from the comfortable vantage point of a man whose weight hadn't wavered since he'd turned eighteen, no matter what he ate or drank. "You're fine just the way you are."

Karen wanted to believe him, but she couldn't. Nobody could find her chunky figure appealing, not unless they were a lot more hard up for female company than Phil need be. "Aye, right." She opened her briefcase and ran through the key points of the case file for Phil's benefit. She'd barely reached the end of her summary when they turned into the gateway of Rotheswell. They could see the castle in the distance beyond the bare branches of a stand of trees, but before they could approach their identities had to be verified. They both had to get out of the car and hold their warrant cards up to the CCTV camera. Eventually, the solid wooden gates swung open, allowing the car access to a sort of security airlock. Phil drove forward, Karen walking beside the car. The wooden gates swung shut behind them, leaving them contained as if in a giant cattle pen. Two security men emerged from a guardhouse and inspected the exterior and interior of the car, Karen's briefcase, and the pockets of Phil's duffel coat.

"He's got better security than the prime minister," Karen said as they finally drove up the drive.

"Easier to get a new prime minister than a new Brodie Grant," Phil said.

"I bet that's what he thinks, anyway."

As they approached the house, an elderly man in a waterproof jacket and a tweed cap rounded the nearest turret and waved them towards the far side of the gravel apron in front of the house. By the time they'd parked, he'd vanished, leaving them no option but to approach the massive studded wooden doors in the middle of the frontage. "Where's Mel Gibson when you need him?" Karen muttered, raising a hefty iron door knocker and letting it fall with a satisfying bang. "It's like a very bad film."

"And we still don't know why we're here." Phil looked glum. "Hard to see what could live up to this build-up."

Before Karen could reply, the door swung open on silent hinges. A woman who reminded her of her primary school teacher said, "Welcome to Rotheswell. I'm Susan Charleson, Sir Broderick's personal assistant. Come on in."

They filed into an entrance hall that, provided the grand staircase had been removed, could comfortably have accommodated Karen's house. She had no chance to take much in other than a general atmosphere of rich colour and warmth before they were hustled a short distance down a wide corridor. "You're DI Pirie, I presume," Susan Charleson said. "But I'm not familiar with your colleague's name and rank."

"Detective Sergeant Phil Parhatka," he said with as much pomp as he could muster in the teeth of her formality.

"Good, now I can introduce you," she said, stepping to one side and opening a door. She waved them into a drawing room where CID could comfortably have staged their annual Burns' Supper. They'd have had to push some of the furniture back to the walls to make room for the country dancing, but still, it wouldn't have been much of a squeeze.

There were three people in the room, but Karen was instantly focused on the one who radiated the charisma. Brodie Grant might be knocking at the wrong side of seventy, but he was still more glamorous than either of the women who flanked him. He stood to one side of the substantial carved stone mantel, left hand cupping his right elbow, right hand casually holding a slim cigar, face as still and striking as the magazine cover shot she'd found on Google Images. He wore a grey-and-white tweed jacket whose weight suggested cashmere and silk rather than Harris or Donegal, a black turtleneck, matching trousers, and the sort of shoes Karen had only ever seen on the feet of rich Americans. She thought they were called tasselled oxfords or something. They looked like something a kiltie doll would wear rather than a captain of industry. She was so busy studying his weird footwear that she almost missed the introductions.

She looked up in time to catch the faintest twitch of a smile on the mouth of Lady Grant, elegant in a heather mixture suit with the classic velveteen collar that somehow always spoke of money and class to Karen. But the smile felt strangely complicit.

Susan Charleson introduced the other woman. "This is Annabel Richmond, a freelance journalist." Wary now, Karen nodded an acknowledgement. What the hell was a journalist doing here? If she knew one thing about Brodie Grant, it was that he was so allergic to the media he should be going into anaphylactic shock any moment now.

Brodie Grant stepped forward and indicated with a wave of his cigar that they should sit on a sofa within loudhailing distance of the fireplace. Karen perched on the edge, conscious that it was the type of seat that would swallow her, making anything other than a clumsy exit impossible. "Miss Richmond is here at my request for two reasons," Grant said. "One, I'll come to in a moment. The other is that she'll be acting as liaison between the media and the family. I will not be giving press conferences or making sentimental televised appeals. So she is your first port of call if you're looking for something to feed the reptiles."

Karen inclined her head. "That's your prerogative," she said, trying to sound as if she was making a concession out of the goodness of her heart. Anything to claw back some control. "I understand from Mr. Lees that you believe some new evidence has emerged relating to the kidnap of your daughter and grandson?"

"It's new evidence all right. No doubt of that. Susan?" He glanced expectantly at her. Smart enough to anticipate her boss's demands, she was already advancing towards them with a plastic-covered sheet of plywood. As she drew near, she turned it round to face Karen and Phil.

Karen felt a shimmer of disappointment. "This isn't the first time we've seen something like this," she said, studying the monochrome print of the puppeteer and his sinister marionettes. "I came across three or four instances in the files."

"Five, actually," Grant said. "But none like this. The previous ones were all dismissed because they diverged in some way from the originals. The reproductions DCI Lawson distributed to the media at the time were subtly altered so we could weed out any copycats. All the ones that have turned up since were copies of the altered versions."

"And this one's different?" Karen said.

Grant nodded his approval. "Spot on, Inspector. It's identical in every respect. I'm well aware that the reward I've offered is a temptation to some people. I kept my own copy of the original so I could compare anything that was brought directly to me. As this was." He gave a wan smile. "Not that I needed a copy. I'll never forget a single detail. The first time I clapped eyes on it, it burned itself on to my memory."

Saturday, 19th January 1985

Mary Grant poured her husband a second cup of coffee before he noticed he'd finished his first. She'd been doing it for so many years it still surprised him that his cup needed so many refills when he stayed in hotels. He turned the page of his newspaper and grunted. "Some good news at last. Lord Wolfenden's shuffled off this mortal coil."

Mary's expression was one of weary resignation rather than shock. "That's a horrible thing to say, Brodie."

Without lifting his eyes, he said, "The man made the world a more horrible place, Mary. So I'm not sorry he's gone."

Years of marriage had knocked most of the combativeness out of Mary Grant. But even if she'd intended to say anything, she wouldn't have had the chance. To the surprise of both Grants, the door to the breakfast room burst open without a knock and Susan Charleson practically ran in. Brodie dropped his paper on to his scrambled eggs, taking in her pink cheeks and shortness of breath.

"I'm sorry," she gabbled. "But you have to see this." She thrust a large manila envelope at him. On the front was his name and address, with the words "Private" and "Confidential" written in thick black marker above and below.

"What in the name of God is it that can't wait till after breakfast?" he said, poking two fingers into the envelope to reveal a thick piece of paper folded into quarters.

"This," Susan said, pointing to the envelope. "I put it back in the envelope because I didn't want anybody else to get a look at it."

Making an impatient noise, Grant pulled out the paper and unfolded it. It looked like an advertising poster for a macabre puppet show. In stark black and white, a puppeteer leaned over the set, manipulating a group of marionettes that included a skeleton and a goat. It reminded him of the kind of prints he'd once seen on a TV programme about the art Hitler hated. Even while he was thinking this, his eyes were scanning the bottom section of the poster. Where one would expect to find details of the puppet show performance there was a very different message.

> YOUR GREEDY EXPLOITATIVE CAPITALISM IS ABOUT TO BE PUNISHED. WE HAVE YOUR DAUGHTER AND YOUR GRANDSON. DO AS WE TELL YOU IF YOU WANT TO SEE THEM AGAIN. NO POLICE. JUST GO ABOUT YOUR BUSINESS AS USUAL. WE ARE WATCHING YOU. WE WILL CONTACT YOU AGAIN SOON. THE ANARCHIST COVENANT OF SCOTLAND.

"Is this some kind of sick joke?" Grant said, throwing it down on the table and pushing his chair back. As he stood up Mary snatched the poster, then dropped it as if it had burned her fingers.

"Oh my God," she breathed. "Brodie?"

"It's a trick," he said. "Some sick bastard trying to give us a bit of a fright."

"No," Susan said. "There's more." She picked up the envelope where it had fallen to the floor and shook out a Polaroid photo. Silently she handed it to Grant.

He saw his only daughter tied to a chair. A slash of packing tape covered her mouth. Her hair was a mess; a smudge of dirt or a bruise marked her left cheek. Between her and the camera, a gloved hand held enough of the front page of the previous day's *Daily Record* to leave no room for doubt. He felt his legs give way and he collapsed back into his chair, his eyelids fluttering as he tried to regain control of himself. Mary reached for the photograph, but he shook his head and held it tight against his chest. "No," he said. "No, Mary."

There was a long silence, then Susan said, "What do you need me to do?"

Grant couldn't form words. He didn't know what he thought, what he felt, or what he wanted to say. It was an experience as alien and as unlikely as taking recreational drugs. He was always in charge of himself and most of what happened around him. To be powerless was something that hadn't happened for so long he had forgotten how to cope with it.

"Do you want me to call the chief constable?" Susan said.

"It says not to," Mary said. "We can't take risks with Catriona and Adam."

"To hell with that," Grant said in a pale approximation of his normal voice. "I'm not being pushed around by a bunch of bloody anarchists." He forced himself upright, sheer will overcoming the fear that was already eating him from the inside out. "Susan, call the chief constable. Explain the situation. Tell him I want the best officer he has who doesn't look like a policeman. I want him at the office in an hour. And now I'm going to the office. Going about my business as usual, if they really are watching."

"Brodie, how can you?" White-faced, Mary looked stricken. "We have to do what they tell us."

"No, we don't. We just have to look as if we are." His voice was stronger now. Having fixed on the bare beginnings of a plan gave him strength to recover himself. He could deal with the fear if he could make himself believe he was doing something to resolve the situation. "Susan, get things moving." He went to Mary and patted her on the shoulder. "It'll be all right, Mary. I promise you." If he couldn't see her face, he didn't have to deal with her doubt or terror. He had enough to worry about without that extra burden.

DYSART, FIFE

Other men might have paced the floor waiting for the police to arrive. Brodie Grant had never been one to waste his energy on pointless activity. He sat in his office chair, swivelled away from the desk so he faced the spectacular view across the Forth estuary to Berwick Law, Edinburgh, and the Pentlands. He stared out over the stippled grey water, ordering his thoughts to avoid any waste of time once the police arrived. He hated to squander anything, even that which could be readily replaced.

Susan, who had followed him to work at the usual time, came through the door that separated her office from his. "The police are here," she said. "Shall I bring them in?"

Grant swung round in his chair. "Yes. Then leave us." He registered the look of surprise on her face. She was accustomed to being privy to all his secrets, to knowing more than Mary ever cared to. But this time, he wanted the circle to be as small as possible. Even Susan was one person too many.

She ushered in two men in painters' overalls, then pointedly closed the door behind her. Grant was pleased with the ruse. "Thank you for coming so promptly. And so discreetly," he said, studying the pair of them. They looked too young for so important a task. The elder, lean and dark, was probably in his early to mid-thirties, the other, fair and ruddy, his late twenties.

The dark one spoke first. To Grant's surprise, his introduction went straight to the heart of his own reservations. "I'm Detective Inspector James Lawson," he said. "And this is Detective Constable Rennie. We've been personally briefed by the chief constable. I know you're probably thinking I'm on the young side to be running an operation like this, but I've been chosen because of my experience. Last year the wife of one of the East Fife players was abducted. We managed to resolve the matter without anybody getting hurt."

"I don't remember hearing anything about that," Grant said.

"We managed to keep the lid on very successfully," Lawson said, the briefest of proud smiles flitting across his face.

"Wasn't there a trial? How could you keep that out of the papers?"

Lawson shrugged. "The kidnapper pleaded guilty. It was over and done with before the press even noticed. We're pretty good at news management here in Fife." His quick smile flashed again. "So you see, sir, I'm the man with the relevant experience."

Grant gave him a long appraising stare. "I'm glad to hear it." He took a pair of tweezers from his drawer and delicately shifted the blank sheet of paper that he'd placed over the ransom poster. "This is what arrived in the post this morning. Accompanied by this—" Carefully lifting it by its edges, he turned over the Polaroid.

Lawson moved closer and studied them intently. "And you're sure this is your daughter?"

For the first time, Grant's grip on his self-control slipped a fraction. "You think I don't know my own daughter?"

"No, sir. But for the record, I have to be sure you're sure."

"I'm sure."

"In that case, there's not much room for doubt," Lawson said. "When did you last see or hear from your daughter?"

Grant made an impatient gesture with his hand. "I don't know. I suppose I saw her last about two weeks ago. She'd brought Adam over to visit. Her mother will have spoken to her or seen her since then. You know how women are." The sudden guilt he felt was not so much a twinge as a slow pulse. He didn't regret anything he'd said or done; he regretted only that it had caused a rift between him and Cat.

"We'll talk to your wife," Lawson said. "It would be helpful for us to get an idea of when this happened."

"Catriona has her own business. Presumably if the gallery was closed, someone will have noticed. There must be hundreds, thousands of people who drive past every day. She was scrupulous about the open and closed sign." He gave a tight, wintry smile. "She had a good head for business." He pulled a pad towards him and scribbled down the address and directions to Catriona's gallery.

"Of course," Lawson said. "But I thought you didn't want the kidnappers to know you had come to us?"

Grant was taken aback by his own stupidity. "I'm sorry. You're right. I'm not thinking straight. I . . ."

"That's my job, not yours." There was kindness in Lawson's tone. "You can rest assured that we'll make no inquiries that raise suspicion. If we can't find something out in an apparently natural way, we leave it alone. The safety of Catriona and Adam is paramount. I promise you that."

"That's a promise I expect you to keep. Now, what's the next step?" Grant was back in command of himself but unnerved by the emotions that kept throwing him off balance.

"We'll be putting a tap and a trace on your phone lines in case they try to contact you that way. And I'm going to need you to go to Catriona's home. It's what the kidnappers would expect. You have to be my eyes inside her house. Anything out of place, anything unusual, you need to make a note of it. You'll have to carry a briefcase or something, so if for example there's two mugs on the table, you can bring them out to us. We'll also need something of Catriona's so that we can get her prints. A hairbrush would be ideal, then we get her hair too." Lawson sounded eager.

Grant shook his head. "You'll have to get my wife to do that. I'm not very observant." He wasn't about to admit he'd crossed the threshold only once, and that reluctantly.

"She'll be happy to have something to do. To feel useful."

"Fine, we'll see to that." Lawson tapped the poster with a pen. "On the surface, this looks like a political act rather than a personal one. And we'll be checking out intelligence on any group that might have the resources and the determination to pull off something like this. I need to ask you, though—have you had any run-ins with any special interest group? Some organization that might have a few hotheads on the fringes who would think this was a good idea?"

Grant had already asked himself the same question while he'd been waiting for the police. "The only thing I can think of is a problem we had a year or so ago with one of those 'save the whale' outfits. We had a development on the Black Isle that they claimed would adversely affect the habitat of some bunch of dolphins in the Moray Firth. All nonsense, of course. They tried to stop our construction crew—the usual stunt, lying in front of the JCBs. One of them got hurt. Their own stupid fault, which was how the authorities saw it. But that was the end of it. They went off with their tail between their legs and we got on with the development. And the dolphins are perfectly fine, by the way."

Lawson had visibly perked up at Grant's information. "Nevertheless, we'll have to check it out," he said.

"Mrs. Charleson will have all the files. She'll be able to tell you what you need to know."

"Thanks. I also have to ask you if there's anyone you can think of who has a personal grievance against you. Or anyone in your family."

Grant shook his head. "I've tramped on a lot of toes in my time. But I can't think of anything I've done that would provoke someone into doing this. Surely this is about money, not spite? Everybody knows I'm one of the richest men in

Scotland. It's not a secret. To me, that's the obvious motive here. Some bastard wants to get their hands on my hard-earned cash. And they think this is the way to do it."

"It's possible," Lawson agreed.

"It's more than possible. It's the most likely scenario. And I'm damned if they're going to get away with it. I want my family back, and I want them back without giving an inch to these bastards." Grant slammed the flat of his hand down on the desk. The two policemen jumped at the sudden crack.

"That's why we're here," Lawson said. "We'll do everything possible to produce the outcome you're looking for."

Back then, Grant's confidence was still intact. "I expect nothing less," he said.

Friday, 29th June 2007; Rotheswell Castle

Listening to Grant's account of that first morning after the world had changed, what struck Karen was everybody's assumption that this had all been about Brodie Grant. Nobody seemed to have considered that the person being punished here was not Grant himself but his daughter. "Did Catriona have any enemies?"

Grant gave her an impatient frown. "Catriona? How could she have enemies? She was a single parent and an artist in glass. She didn't live the sort of life that generated personal animosity." He sighed and pursed his lips.

Karen told herself not to be daunted by his attitude. "Sorry. I expressed myself badly. I should have asked if you knew of anyone she'd upset."

Grant gave her a small nod of satisfaction, as if she'd passed a test she hadn't even known about. "The father of her child. He was upset, all right. But I never really thought he had it in him, and your colleagues could never find any evidence to connect him to the crime."

"Are you talking about Fergus Sinclair?" Karen asked.

"Who else? I thought you'd brought yourself up to speed with the background?" Grant demanded.

Karen was beginning to feel sorry for everyone obliged to put up with Brodie Grant's level of irritation. She suspected it wasn't reserved for her. "There's only one mention of Sinclair in the file," she said. "In the notes of an interview with Lady Grant, Sinclair is mentioned as Adam's putative father."

Grant snorted. "Putative? Of course he was the boy's father. They'd been seeing each other on and off for years. But what do you mean, there's only one reference to Sinclair? There must be more. They went to Austria to interview him."

"Austria?"

"He worked over there. He's a qualified estate manager. He's worked in France and Switzerland since, but he went back to Austria about four years ago. Susan can give you all the details."

"You've kept tabs on him?" It wasn't surprising, Karen thought.

"No, Inspector. I told you: I never thought Sinclair had the gumption to pull this off. So why would I keep tabs on him? The only reason I know where Sinclair's living is that his father is still my head keeper." Grant shook his head. "I can't believe this isn't all in the file."

Karen was thinking the same thing, but she didn't want to admit it. "And as far as you know, was there anybody else Catriona had upset?"

Grant's face was as wintry as his hair. "Only me, Inspector. Look, it's obvious from where this new evidence has turned up that this had nothing to do with Cat personally. It's obviously political. Which makes it about what I stand for, not whose heart Cat had broken."

"So where did this poster turn up?" Phil said. Karen was grateful for the interruption. He was good at jumping in and steering interviews in more productive directions when she was in danger of getting bogged down.

"In a ruined farmhouse in Tuscany. Apparently the place had been squatted." He extended his arm towards the journalist. "This is the other reason Miss Richmond is here. She's the person who found it. Doubtless you'll want to talk to her." He pointed to the poster. "You'll want to take that with you, too. I expect there will be tests you need to do on it. And, Inspector . . . ?"

Karen recovered her breath in the face of his high-handedness. "Yes?"

"I don't want to read about this in the paper tomorrow morning." He glared at her as if defying her to respond.

Karen held her fire for a moment, trying to compose a reply that encompassed what she wanted to say and left out anything that might be misconstrued. Grant's expression changed to a prompt. "Whatever we release to the media and the timing of any release will be an operational decision," she said at last. "It will be made by me and, where appropriate, my superior officers. I fully understand how painful all this is for you, but I'm sorry, sir. We have to base our decisions on what we think is most likely to produce the best outcome. You might not always agree with that, but I'm afraid you don't get a veto." She waited for the explosion, but none came. She supposed he'd save that for the Macaroon or his bosses.

Instead, Grant nodded mildly to Karen. "I have confidence in you, Inspector. All I ask is that you communicate with Miss Richmond here in advance, so we're forearmed against the mob." He ran a hand through his thick silver hair in a gesture that looked well practised. "I have high hopes that this time the police will get to the truth. With all the advances in forensic science, you should have a head start on Inspector Lawson." He turned away in what was clearly a dismissal.

"I expect I'll have some further questions for you," Karen said, determined not to cede all control of the encounter. "If Catriona didn't have any enemies, maybe you could think of the names of some of her friends who might be able to help us. Sergeant Parhatka will let you know when I want to talk to you again. In the meantime—Miss Richmond?"

The woman inclined her head and smiled. "I'm at your disposal, Inspector."

At least someone round here had a vague notion of how things were supposed to work. "I'd like to see you in my office this afternoon. Shall we make it four o'clock?"

"What's wrong with interviewing Miss Richmond here? And now?" Grant said.

"This is my investigation," Karen said. "I'll conduct my interviews where it suits me. And because of other ongoing inquiries, it suits me to be in my office this afternoon. Now, if you'll excuse us?" She got to her feet, registering Lady Grant's guarded amusement and Susan Charleson's prim disapproval. Grant himself was still as a statue.

"It's all right, Susan, I'll see the officers out," Lady Grant said, jumping to her feet and heading for the door before the other woman gathered her self-possession.

As they followed her down the hallway, Karen said, "This must be hard for you."

Lady Grant half-turned, walking backwards with the assurance of someone who knows every inch of her territory. "Why do you say that?"

"Watching your husband revisit such a terrible time. I wouldn't want to see someone I cared about going through all that."

Lady Grant looked puzzled. "He lives with it every day, Inspector. He may not give that impression, but he dwells on it. Sometimes I catch him looking at our son Alec, and I know he's thinking about what might have been, with Adam. About what he's lost. Having something fresh to focus on is almost a relief for him." She swivelled on her toes and turned her back to them again. As they followed her, Karen caught Phil's eye and was surprised by the anger she saw there.

"Still, you wouldn't be human if a part of you wasn't hoping we won't find Adam alive and well," Phil said, the lightness of his tone a contrast to the darkness of his expression.

Lady Grant stopped in her tracks and whirled round, eyebrows drawn down. A blush of pink spread up her neck. "What the hell do you mean by that?"

"I think you know exactly what I mean, Lady Grant. We find Adam and suddenly your boy Alec isn't Brodie's only heir," Phil said. It took guts, Karen thought, to assume the role of the investigation's lightning rod.

For a moment Lady Grant looked as if she might slap his face. Karen could see her chest rising and falling with the effort of holding herself in check. Finally, she forced herself to assume the familiar pose of civility. "Actually," she said, her words clipped and tight, "you're looking at this from precisely the wrong angle. Brodie's absolute commitment to uncovering his grandson's fate fills me with confidence about Alec's future. A man so bound by obligation to his own flesh and blood is never going to let our son down. Believe it or not, Sergeant, Brodie's quest for the truth gives me hope. Not fear." She turned on her heel and marched to the front door, where she pointedly held it open for them.

Once the door had closed behind them, Karen said, "Jeez, Phil, why not tell us what you really think? What brought that on?"

"I'm sorry." He opened the passenger door for her, a small courtesy he seldom bothered to extend. "I'd had enough of playing at Miss Marple. All that country house murder bollocks. Bloodless and civilized. I just wanted to see if I could provoke an honest reaction."

Karen grinned. "I think it's safe to say you did that. I just hope we don't get buried in the fallout."

Phil snorted. "You're not exactly behind the door when it comes to being a hardarse. 'This is my investigation,'" he mimicked, not unkindly.

She settled herself in the car. "Aye, well. The illusion of being in charge. It was nice while it lasted."

Nottingham

The beauties of the Nottingham Arboretum were not so much diminished as rendered invisible by the sheets of rain that blinded DC Mark Hall as he followed Femi Otitoju up the path that led to the Chinese Bell Tower. She'd finally shown some emotion, but it wasn't exactly what Mark had been hoping for.

Logan Laidlaw had been even less pleased than Ferguson and Fraser to see them. Not only had he refused to let them across the threshold of his flat, he'd told them he had no intention of repeating what he'd told Mick Prentice's daughter. "Life's too bloody short to waste my energy going over that stuff twice," he'd said, then slammed the door shut in their faces.

Otitoju had turned the deep purple of pickled beet, breathing heavily through her nose. Her hands had bunched into fists and she'd actually drawn her foot back as if she was going to kick the door. Pretty wild, considering there wasn't that much of her. Mark had put a hand on her arm. "Leave it, Femi. He's within his rights. He doesn't have to talk to us."

Otitoju had swung round, her whole body compressed in anger. "It shouldn't be allowed," she said. "They should have to talk to us. It should be against the law for people to refuse to answer our questions. It should be an offence."

"He's a witness, not a criminal," Mark said, alarmed by his vehemence. "It's what they told us when we were doing our induction. Police by consent, not coercion."

"It's not right," Otitoju said, storming back to the car. "They expect us to solve crimes, but they don't give us the tools to do the job. Who the hell does he think he is?"

"He's somebody whose opinion of the police was set in stone back in 1984. Have you never seen the news reports from back then? Mounted police rode into the pickets, like they were Cossacks or something. If we used our batons like that, we'd be up on a charge. It wasn't our finest hour. So it's not really surprising that Mr. Laidlaw doesn't feel like talking to us."

She shook her head. "It just makes me wonder what he has to hide."

The drive across town from Iain Maclean's house to the Arboretum hadn't done much to improve her temper. Mark caught up with her. "Leave this to me, OK?" he said.

"You think I can't conduct an interview?"

"No, I don't think that. But I know enough about ex-miners to know they're a pretty macho bunch. You saw back there with Ferguson and Fraser—they didn't take kindly to you asking questions."

Otitoju stopped abruptly and threw her head back, letting the rain course down her face like cold tears. She straightened up and sighed. "Fine. Let's pander to their prejudices. You do the chat." Then she set off again, this time at a more measured pace.

They arrived at the Chinese Bell Tower to find two middle-aged men in council overalls sheltering from the downpour. The narrow pillars that supported the elegant roof offered little protection from the scatterings of rain thrown around by the gusty wind, but it was better than being completely out in the open. "I'm looking for Iain Maclean," Mark said, glancing from one to the other.

"That would be me," the shorter of the two said, bright blue eyes sparkling in a tanned face. "And who are you?"

Mark identified them both. "Is there somewhere we can go and get a cup of tea?"

The two men looked at each other. "We're supposed to be tidying up the borders, but we were just about to give up and go back to the greenhouses," Maclean said. "There's no café here, but you could come back with us and we could brew up there."

Ten minutes later, they were squashed into a corner at the back of a large plastic-covered tunnel, out of the way of the other gardeners, whose curious stares quickly subsided once they realized there was no drama happening. The smell of humus hung heavy in the air, reminding Mark of his granddad's allotment shed. Iain Maclean wrapped his large hands round a mug of tea and waited for them to speak. He'd shown no surprise at their arrival, nor had he asked them why they were there. Mark suspected Fraser or Ferguson had warned him.

"We wanted to talk to you about Mick Prentice," he began.

"What about Mick? I've not seen him since we moved south," Maclean said.

"Neither has anybody else," Mark said. "Everybody assumed he'd gone south with you, but that's not what we've been hearing today."

Maclean scratched the silver bristles that covered his head in a neat crew cut. "Aye well. I'd heard folk thought that back in the Newton. It just shows you how willing they are to think the worst. There's no way Mick would have joined us. I don't see how anybody who knew him could think that."

"You never contradicted them?"

"What would be the point? As far as they're concerned I'm a dirty blackleg miner. Nothing I have to say in anybody's defence would carry any weight in the Newton."

"To be fair, it's not just a matter of jumping to conclusions. His wife's had money sent to her on and off since he left. The postmark was Nottingham. That's one of the main reasons everybody thought he'd done the unthinkable."

"I can't explain that. But I'm telling you this: Mick Prentice could no more go scabbing than fly to the moon."

"That's what everybody keeps telling us," Mark said. "But people do things that seem out of character when they're desperate. And by all accounts, Mick Prentice was desperate."

"Not that desperate."

"You did it."

Maclean stared into his coffee. "I did. And I've never been so ashamed all my days. But my wife was pregnant with our third. I knew there was no way we could bring another bairn into that life. So I did what I did. I talked about it with Mick beforehand." He flashed a swift glance at Mark. "We were pals, me and him. We were at the school together. I wanted to explain to him why I was doing it." He sighed. "He said he understood why I was set on going. That he felt like getting out too. But scabbing wasn't for him. I don't know where he went, but I knew for sure it wasn't down another pit."

"When did you know he'd gone missing?"

He screwed his face up as he thought. "It's hard to say. I think it was maybe when the wife came down to join me. So that would make it round about the February. But it might have been after that. The wife, she's still got family back in the Wemyss. We don't go back there. We wouldn't be welcome. Folk have got long memories, you know? But we stay in touch and sometimes they come here for a visit." A pale apology of a smile crossed his face. "The wife's nephew, he's a student at the university down here. Just finishing his second year. He comes round for his dinner now and again. So aye, I heard Mick had gone on the missing list, but I couldn't tell you for sure when I knew."

"Where do you think he went? What do you think happened?" In his eagerness, Mark forgot the cardinal rule of asking only one question at a time. Maclean ignored both of them.

"How come you're interested in Mick all of a sudden?" he said. "Nobody's come looking for him all these years. What's the big deal now?"

Mark explained why Misha Gibson had finally reported her father missing. Maclean shifted awkwardly in his seat, his coffee slopping over his fingers. "That's hellish. I mind when Misha was just a wee lassie herself. I wish I could help. But I don't know where he went," he said. "Like I said, I've not seen hide nor hair of him since I left the Newton."

"Have you heard from him?" Otitoju chipped in.

Maclean gave her a flat hard look. On his weatherbeaten face, it rested as impassive as Mount Rushmore. "Don't get smart with me, hen. No, I haven't heard from him. As far as I'm concerned, Mick Prentice fell off Planet Iain the day I came down here. And that's exactly what I expected."

Mark tried to rebuild the rapport, injecting sympathy into

his voice. "I understand that," he said. "But what do you think happened to Mick? You were his pal. If anyone can come up with an answer, it would be you."

Maclean shook his head. "I really don't know."

"If you had to hazard a guess?"

Again he scratched his head. "I tell you what. I thought him and Andy had taken off together. I thought they'd both had enough, that they'd buggered off somewhere else to start all over again. Clean sheet, and that."

Mark remembered Prentice's friend's name from the briefing document. But there had been no mention of them leaving together. "Where would they go? How could they just disappear without a trace?"

Maclean tapped the side of his nose. "Andy was a Commie, you know. And that was when Lech Wałesa and Solidarity was a big deal in Poland. I always thought the pair of them had buggered off there. Plenty of pits in Poland, and that wouldn't have felt like scabbing. No way, no how."

"Poland?" Mark felt as if he needed a crash course in twentieth-century political history.

"They were trying to overthrow totalitarian Communism," Otitoju said crisply. "To replace it with a sort of workers' socialism."

Maclean nodded. "That would have been right up Andy's street. I figured he'd talked Mick into going with him. That would explain how nobody heard from them. Stuck digging coal behind the Iron Curtain."

"It's been in mothballs for a while now, the Iron Curtain," Mark said.

"Aye, but who knows what kind of life they made for themselves over there? Could be married with kids, could have put the past right behind them. If Mick had a new family, he wouldn't be wanting the old one emerging from the woodwork, would he?"

Suddenly Mark had one of those revelatory moments where he could see the wood hidden among the trees. "It was you that sent the money, wasn't it? You put cash in an envelope and sent it to Jenny Prentice because you thought Mick wouldn't be sending her any money from Poland."

Maclean seemed to shrink back against the translucent polythene wall. His face screwed up so tight it was hard to see his bright blue eyes. "I was only trying to help. I've done OK since I came down here. I always felt sorry for Jenny. Seemed like she'd ended up with the sticky end because Mick didn't have the courage of his convictions."

It seemed an odd way to put it, Mark thought. He could have left it at that; it wasn't his case, after all, and he could do without the aggravation pulling at a loose thread might bring. But on the other hand, he wanted to make the most of this posting. He wanted to parlay the position of CID aide into a permanent transfer to the detective division. So going the extra mile was definitely part of the plan. "Is there something you're not telling us, Iain?" he said. "Some other reason Mick had for taking off the way he did, without a word to anyone?"

Maclean drained his coffee and put the mug down. His hands, disproportionately large from a lifetime of hard manual work, clasped and unclasped themselves. He looked like a man uncomfortable with the contents of his own head. He took a deep breath and said, "I suppose it makes no odds now. You can't make somebody pay when they're the wrong side of the grave."

Otitoju was about to break Maclean's silence, but Mark gripped her arm in warning. She subsided, her mouth a compressed line, and they waited.

At last, Maclean spoke. "I've never told anybody this. For all the good keeping schtum's done. You have to understand, Mick was a big union man. And of course, Andy was a full-time NUM official. Feet under the table, well in there with the top men. I don't doubt Andy told Mick a lot of things he maybe shouldn't have." He gave a wan smile. "He was always trying to impress Mick, to be his best pal. We were all in the same class at school. The three of us used to hang about together. But you know how it is with threesomes. There's always the leader and the other two trying to keep in with him, trying to edge out the other one. That's how it was with us. Mick in the middle, trying to keep the peace. He was good at it too, clever at finding ways to keep the pair of us happy. Never letting either one of us get the upper hand. Well, not for long anyway."

Mark could see Maclean relaxing as he remembered the relative ease of those early days. "I know just what you mean," he said quietly.

"Anyway, we all stayed pals. Me and the wife, we'd go out in a foursome with Mick and Jenny. Him and Andy would play football together. Like I said, he was good at finding things that made the both of us feel like we had a wee bit of something special. So anyway, a couple of weeks before I came away down here, we spent the day together. We walked along to Dysart harbour. He set up his easel and painted, and I fished. I told him what I had planned and he tried to talk me out of it. But I could tell his heart wasn't really in it. So I asked him what was bothering him." He stopped again, his strong fingers working against each other.

"And what was it?" Mark said, leaning forward to close Otitoju's stiff presence out of the circle, to make it a male environment.

"He said he thought one of the full-time officials had his hand in the till." Then he locked eyes with Mark, who could sense the terrible betrayal that lay behind Maclean's words. "We were all skint and starving, and one of the guys who was supposed to be on our side was lining his own pockets. It might not sound like a big deal now, but back then, it shook me to the very core."

Thursday, 30th November 1984; Dysart

A mackerel was tugging at his line, but Iain Maclean paid it no mind. "You're fucking joking," he said. "Nobody would do that."

Mick Prentice shrugged, never taking his eyes off the cartridge paper pinned to his easel. "You don't have to believe me. But I know what I know."

"You must have misunderstood. No union official would steal from us. Not here. Not now." Maclean looked as if he was going to burst into tears.

"Look, I'll tell you what I know." Mick swept his brush across the paper, leaving a blur of colour along the horizon. "I was in the office last Tuesday. Andy had asked me to come in and help him with the welfare requests, so I was going through the letters we'd had in. I tell you, it would break your heart, reading what folk are going through." He cleaned his brush and mixed a greenish grey colour on his pocket-sized palette. "So I'm going through this stuff in the wee cubbyhole off the main office, and this official is out front. Anyway, some woman came in from Lundin Links. Tweed suit, stupid mohair beret. You know the kind—Lady Bountiful, looking out for the peasants. She said they'd had a coffee morning at the golf club and they'd raised two hundred and thirty-two pounds to help the poor families of the striking miners."

"Good for them," Maclean said. "Better going to us than Thatcher's bloody crew."

"Right enough. So he thanks her and off she goes. Now, I didn't actually see where the money went, but I can tell you it didn't go in the safe."

"Aw, come on, Mick. That proves nothing. Your guy might have been taking it straight to the branch. Or the bank."

"Aye, right." Mick gave a humourless laugh. "Like we put money in the bank these days when the sequestrators are breathing down our neck."

"All the same," Maclean said, feeling offended somehow.

"Look, if that was all, I wouldn't be bothered. But there's more. One of Andy's jobs is to keep a tally of money that comes in from donations and the like. All that money's supposed to be passed through to the branch. I don't know what happens to it then, whether it comes back to us as handouts or whether it ends up at the court of King Arthur, salted away in some bloody Swiss bank account. But everybody that collects any money is supposed to tell Andy and he writes it up in a wee book."

Maclean nodded. "I remember having to tell him what we made when we were doing the street collections back in the summer."

Mick paused briefly, staring out at the point where the sea met the land. "I was at Andy's the other night. The book was sitting on the table. When he went to the toilet, I took a wee look. And the donation from Lundin Links wasn't there."

Maclean jerked so roughly on his line that he lost the fish. "Fuck," he said, reeling in furiously. "Maybe Andy wasn't up to date."

"I wish it was that simple. But that's not it. The last entries in Andy's book were four days after that money was handed in."

Maclean threw his rod on the stone flags at his feet. He could feel tears pricking his eyes. "That's a fucking disgrace. And you expect me to feel guilty about going to Nottingham? At least that's an honest day's work for an honest day's pay, not stealing. I can't believe that."

"I couldn't believe it either. But how else can you explain it?" Mick shook his head. "And this is a guy who's still on a wage."

"Who is it?"

"I shouldn't tell you. Not till I've decided what I'm going to do about it."

"It's obvious what you've got to do. You've got to tell Andy. If there's an innocent explanation, he'll know what it is."

"I can't tell Andy," Mick protested. "Christ, sometimes I feel like walking away from the whole fucking mess. Drawing a line and starting again someplace else." He shook his head. "I can't tell Andy, Iain. He's already depressed. I tell him this, it could send him over the edge."

"Well, tell somebody else. Somebody from the branch. You've got to nail the bastard. Who is it? Tell me. A couple of weeks, I'm going to be out of here. Who am I going to tell?" Maclean felt the need to know burning inside him. It was one more thing that could help him believe he was doing the right thing. "Tell me, Mick."

The wind whipped Mick's hair into his eyes, saving him from the desperation in Maclean's face. But the need to share his burden was too heavy to ignore. He pushed his hair back and looked his friend in the eye. "Ben Reekie."

Friday, 29th June 2007; Glenrothes

Karen had to admit she was impressed. Not only had the Nottingham team done a great job, but DC Femi Otitoju had typed up her report and e-mailed it in record time. Mind you, Karen thought, she'd probably have done the same in her shoes. Given the quality of the information she and her partner had been able to extract, any officer on CID trial would be desperate to make the most of it.

And there was something here to make the most of. DC Otitoju and her oppos had found out who had been muddying the waters by sending money to Jenny Prentice from Nottingham. And crucially, she'd also given the first possible answer to the question of who might be happy to see the back of Mick Prentice. Feelings were running high by then, the union growing in unpopularity in many quarters. Violence had erupted more times than anyone could count, and not always between police and strikers. Mick Prentice could have found himself consumed by the fire he was playing with. If he'd confronted Ben Reekie with what he knew; if Ben Reekie was guilty as charged; and if Andy Kerr had been dragged into the affair because of his connection to the other two, then there was motive for getting rid of both of the men who had gone missing around the same time. Maybe Angie Kerr had been right about her brother. Maybe he hadn't killed himself. Maybe Mick Prentice and Andy Kerr were both victims of a killer—or killers—desperate to protect the reputation of a crooked union official.

Karen shuddered. "Too much imagination," she said out loud.

"What's that?" Phil dragged his eyes from the computer screen to frown at her.

"Sorry. Just giving myself a telling off for being melodramatic. I tell you, though, if this Femi Otitoju ever fancies a move north, I'd swap her for the Mint so fast it would make his eyes water."

"Not that that's saying much," Phil said. "By the way, what are you doing here? Shouldn't you be talking to the lovely Miss Richmond?"

"She left a message." Karen glanced at her watch. "She'll be here in a wee while."

"What's the hold-up been?"

"Apparently she had to talk to some newspaper lawyer about an article she wrote."

Phil tutted. "Just like Brodie Grant. Still think we're the servant class, that lot. Maybe you should keep her waiting."

"I can't be bothered getting into stupid game playing. Here, have a look at this. The paragraph I've highlighted." She passed Otitoju's report over to Phil and waited for him to read it. As soon as he lifted his eyes from the page, she spoke. "That's a sighting of Mick Prentice a good twelve hours after he walked out of the house. And it sounds like he wasn't himself."

"It's weird. If he was taking off, why was he still hanging around at that time of night? Where had he been? Where was he going? What was he waiting for?" Phil scratched his chin. "Makes no sense to me."

"Me neither. But we're going to have to try and find out. I'll add it to my list." She sighed. "Somewhere below having a proper conversation with the Italian police."

"I thought you'd spoken to them?"

She nodded. "An officer at their headquarters in Siena, some guy called Di Stefano that Pete Spinks in Child Protection dealt with a couple of years back. He speaks pretty good English, but he needs more info."

"So you'll be looking at Monday now?"

Karen nodded. "Aye. He said not to expect anybody in their office after two o'clock on a Friday."

"Nice work if you can get it," Phil said. "Speaking of which, do you fancy a quick drink after you're finished talking to Annabel Richmond? I've got to go round to my brother's for dinner, but I've time for a swift half."

Karen was torn. The prospect of a drink with Phil was always enticing, but her absence from the office meant that her admin load had gone unattended for too long. And she couldn't catch up tomorrow because they were off to the caves. She toyed with the idea of slipping out for a quick drink, then coming back to the office. But she knew herself well enough to know that once she'd escaped from her desk she would find any excuse to avoid returning to the paperwork. "Sorry," she said. "I need to clear the decks."

"Maybe tomorrow, then? We could treat ourselves to lunch at the Laird o' Wemyss."

Karen laughed. "Have you won the pools? Do you know what that place costs?"

Phil winked. "I know they have a special deal for lunch on the last Saturday of the month. Which would be tomorrow."

"And I thought I was the detective round here. OK, you've got a deal." Karen turned her attention back to her notes, making sure she knew exactly what to ask Annabel Richmond.

Karen's phone rang five minutes before the agreed time. The journalist was in the building. She asked a uniform to show Richmond to the interview room where she'd met Misha Gibson, then gathered her papers together and headed downstairs. She walked in to find her witness leaning on the window sill and staring out at the thin strands of cloud stretched across the sky. "Thanks for coming in, Miss Richmond," Karen said.

She turned, her smile apparently genuine. "It's Bel, please," she said. "I should be thanking you for being so accommodating. I appreciate your flexibility." She crossed to the table and sat down, fingers intertwined, seeming relaxed. "I hope I'm not keeping you late."

Karen wondered when she'd last been home at five on a Friday and couldn't come up with an answer. "I wish," she said.

Bel's laugh was warm and conspiratorial. "Tell me about it. I suspect your work culture is scarily similar to mine. I must say, by the way, that I'm impressed."

Karen knew it was a ploy but rose to the bait anyway. "Impressed by what?"

"Brodie Grant's pulling power. I didn't imagine I'd be dealing with the woman who put Jimmy Lawson behind bars."

Karen felt the blush rising up her neck, knew she'd be looking blotchy and ugly, and wanted to kick the furniture. "I don't talk about that," she said.

Again that mellow, inviting laugh. "I don't imagine it's a popular topic of conversation between you and your colleagues. It must make them watch their backs, knowing you were responsible for pinning three murders on your boss."

She made it sound as though Karen had fitted Lawson up. In truth, once she'd been invited to think the unthinkable, the evidence had been there for the finding. One twenty-five-year-old rape and murder, two fresh kills to cover that past misdemeanour. Not nailing Lawson would have been the fit-up. It was tempting to tell Bel Richmond just that. But Karen knew that responding would start a conversation that could only go places she didn't want to revisit. "Like I said, I don't talk about it." Bel cocked her head, gave a smile that Karen read as rueful but confident. Not a defeat but a delay. Karen's smile was inward, knowing the journalist was wrong on that score.

"So, how do you want to do this, Inspector Pirie?" Bel said.

Stolidly refusing to be seduced by Bel's charm, Karen kept her voice official. "What I need right now is for you to be my eyes and ears and take me through what happened, step by step. How you found it, where you found it. The whole story. All the details you can remember."

"It started with my morning run," Bel began. Karen listened carefully as she told the story of her discovery again. She took notes, jotting down questions to ask afterwards. Bel appeared to be candid and comprehensive in her account, and Karen knew better than to break the flow of a helpful witness on a roll. The only sounds she made were wordless murmurs of encouragement.

At last Bel came to the end of her story. "To be honest, I'm surprised you recognized the poster right away," Karen said. "I'm not sure I would have."

Bel shrugged. "I'm a hack, Inspector. It was a huge story at the time. I had just reached the age where I thought I might like to be a journalist. I'd started paying proper attention to newspapers and news bulletins. More than the average person. I guess the image lodged in the deep recesses of my brain."

"I can see how that would happen. But, given that you understood the significance of it, I'm surprised you didn't bring it straight to us rather than Sir Broderick." Karen let the unspoken accusation lie in the air between them.

Bel's answer came smoothly. "Two reasons, really. First, I had no idea who to contact. I thought if I just walked into my local police station it might not be treated very seriously. And second, the last thing I wanted to do was to waste police time. For all I knew, this was some sick copy. I reckoned Sir Broderick and his people would know at once whether this was something that ought to be taken seriously."

Slick answer, Karen thought. Not that she expected Bel Richmond to admit any interest in the substantial reward Brodie Grant still offered. Nor in the prospect of gaining unrivalled access to the ultimate source. "Fair enough," she said. "Now, you said you had the impression that whoever had been living there had cleared out in a hurry. And you told me about what looked like a bloodstain in the kitchen. Did it seem to you that the two things were connected?"

A moment's silence, then Bel said, "I'm not sure how I would be able to make a judgement about that."

"If the stain on the floor was old, or it wasn't blood, it could be part of the landscape. Chairs sitting on it, that sort of thing."

"Oh, right. Yes, I hadn't thought of it in those terms. No, I don't think it was part of the scenery. There was a chair overturned near it." She spoke slowly, obviously summoning the scene in her mind. "One section looked like someone had tried to clean it up then realized it was pointless. The floor's made of stone slabs, not glazed tiles. So the stone soaked up the blood."

"Were there any other posters or printed material?"

"Not that I saw. But I didn't search the place. To be honest, the poster freaked me out so much I couldn't wait to get out." She gave a little laugh. "Not really the image of the intrepid investigative hack, am I?"

Karen couldn't be bothered bolstering her ego. "The poster freaked you out? Not the blood?"

Again a pause for thought. "You know something? That hadn't occurred to me till now. You're right. It *was* the poster, not the blood. And I don't really know why."

Saturday, 30th June 2007; East Wemyss

The sea wall was new since Karen had last visited East Wemyss. She'd deliberately arrived early so she could take a walk around the lower part of the village. They'd sometimes walked along the foreshore between there and Buckhaven when she'd been a kid. She remembered a run-down fag-end of a place, shabby and forlorn. Now it was spruced up and smart, old houses recently harled white or sandstone red and new ones looking fresh out of the box. The deconsecrated church of St. Mary's-by-the-Sea had been saved from dilapidation and turned into a private home. Thanks to the EU, a sea wall had been built with sturdy blocks of local stone to hold the Firth of Forth at bay. She walked along the Back Dykes, trying to get her bearings. The woodland behind the manse was gone, replaced by new houses. Same with the old factory buildings. And the skyline ahead of her was transformed now the pit winding gear and the bing were gone. If she hadn't known it was the same place, she'd have been hard pressed to recognize it.

She had to admit it was an improvement, though. It was easy to be sentimental about the old days and forget the appalling conditions so many people were forced to live in. They were economic slaves too, trapped by poverty into shopping only at the local establishments. Even the Co-operative, supposedly run for the benefit of its members, was pricey compared to the shops in Kirkcaldy High Street. It had been a hard way of life, the community spirit its only real compensation. The loss of that small offset must have been a killer blow for Jenny Prentice.

Karen turned back towards the parking lot, looking along the seashore to the striated red sandstone bluff that marked the start of the string of deep caves huddled along the base of the cliff. In her memory, they were quite separate from the village, but now a row of houses butted right up against the outside edge of the Court Cave. And there were information boards for the tourists, telling them about the caves' five-thousand-year history of habitation. The Picts had lived there. The Scots had used them as smithies and glassworks. The back wall of the Doo Cave was pocked with dozens of literal pigeonholes. Down through time, the caves had been used by the locals for purposes as diverse as clandestine political meetings, family picnics on rainy days, and romantic trysts. Karen had never dropped her knickers there, but she knew girls who had and thought none the worse of them for it.

Walking back, she saw Phil's car draw up where tarmac gave way to the coastal path. Time to explore a different conjunction of past and present. By the time she reached the parking lot, Phil had been joined by a tall, stooped man with a gleaming bald head, dressed in the kind of jacket and trousers that the middle classes had to buy before they could attempt any walk more challenging than a stroll to the local pub. All zippers and pockets and high-tech materials. Nobody Karen had grown up with had special clothes or boots for walking. You just went out for a walk in your street clothes, maybe adding an extra layer in the winter. Didn't stop them doing eight or nine miles before dinner.

Karen mentally shook herself as she approached the two men. Sometimes she freaked herself out, thinking like her granny. Phil introduced her to the other man, Arnold Haigh. "I've been secretary of the Wemyss Caves Preservation Society since 1981," he said proudly in an accent that had its roots a few hundred miles south of Fife. He had a long thin face with an incongruous snub nose and teeth that gleamed an unnatural white against weatherbeaten skin.

"That's real dedication," Karen said.

"Not really." Haigh chuckled. "No one else has ever wanted the job. What exactly is it you wanted to talk to me about? I mean, I know it's Mick Prentice, but I haven't even thought of him in years."

"Why don't we take a look at the caves and we can talk as we go?" Karen suggested.

"Surely," Haigh said graciously. "We can stop off in the Court Cave and the Doo Cave, then have a cup of coffee in the Thane's Cave."

"A cup of coffee?" Phil sounded bemused. "They've got a café down here?"

Haigh chuckled again. "Sorry, Sergeant. Nothing so grand. The Thane's Cave was closed to the public after the rock fall of 1985, but the society has keys to the railings. We thought it was appropriate to maintain the tradition of the caves having a useful function, so we set up a little clubhouse area in a safe part of the cave. It's all very ad hoc, but we enjoy it." He strode off towards the first cave, not seeing the look of mock horror Phil gave Karen.

The first sign that the cliffs were less than solid was a hole in the sandstone that had been bricked up years before. Some of the bricks were missing, revealing darkness within. "Now, that opening and the passage behind it is man-made," Haigh said, pointing to the brickwork. "As you can see, the Court Cave juts out further than the others. Back in the nineteenth century, high tide reached the cave mouth, cutting off East Wemyss from Buckhaven. The lasses who gutted the herring couldn't get between the two villages at high tide, so a passage was cut through the west side of the cave, which allowed them to pass along the shore safely. Now, if you'll follow me, we'll go in by the east entrance."

When she'd said "talk as we go," this hadn't been quite what Karen had in mind. Still, since they were doing this in their own time, for once there was no hurry and, if it settled Haigh down, it could work to their advantage. Glad that she'd chosen jeans and sneakers, she followed the men round the front of the cave and up a path by a low fence. Near the cave the fence had been trampled down, and they stepped over the bent wires and made their way into the cave, where the beaten-earth floor was surprisingly dry, given the amount of rain there had been in recent weeks. The fact that the roof was supported by a brick column with a sign warning DANGER: NO ENTRY was less reassuring.

"Some people believe the cave got its name from King James the Fifth, who liked to go among his people in disguise," Haigh said, switching on a powerful flashlight and shining it up into the roof. "He was said to have held court here among the Gypsies who lived here at the time. But I think it's more likely that this was where the baronial courts were held in the Middle Ages."

Phil was roaming around, his face eager as a schoolboy's on the best-ever day trip. "How far back does it go?"

"After about twenty metres, the floor rises to the roof. There used to be a passage that ran three miles inland to Kennoway, but a roof fall closed the opening at this end, so the Kennoway entrance was sealed up for safety's sake. Makes you wonder, doesn't it? What were they up to here that they needed a secret passage to Kennoway?" Haigh chuckled again. Karen could only imagine how irritated this little tic would make her by the time they'd finished their interview.

She left the two men exploring the cave and walked back into the fresh air. The sky was dappled grey with the promise of rain. The sea reflected the sky and came up with a few more shades of its own. She turned back to the lush green summer growth and the brilliant colours of the sandstone, both still vibrant in spite of the gloominess of the weather. Before long, Phil emerged, Haigh still talking at his back. He gave Karen a rueful grin; she returned a stony face.

Next came the Doo Cave and a lecture on the historical necessity of keeping pigeons for fresh meat in winter. Karen listened with half an ear; then when Haigh paused for a moment she said, "The colours are amazing in here. Did Mick paint inside the caves?"

Haigh looked startled by the question. "Yes, as a matter of fact he did. Some of his watercolours are on display at the cave information centre. It's the various mineral salts in the rock that create the vivid colours."

Before he could get into his stride on that subject, Karen asked another question. "Was he here a lot during the strike?"

"Not really. He was helping with the flying pickets to start with, I believe. But we didn't see him any more than usual. Less, if anything, as autumn and winter wore on."

"Did he say why that was?"

Haigh looked blank. "No. Never occurred to me to ask him. We're all volunteers, we all do what we can manage."

"Shall we get that cup of coffee now?" Phil said, his struggle between duty and pleasure obvious to Karen though not, thankfully, to Haigh.

"Good idea," Karen said, leading them back into daylight. Getting to the Thane's Cave was harder work, involving a clamber over the rocks and concrete that acted as a rough breakwater between the sea and the foot of the cliffs. Karen remembered the beach being lower, the sea less close, and she said so.

Haigh agreed, explaining that over the years the level of the beach had risen, partly because of the spoil from the coal mines. "I've heard some of the older residents talk about golden sands along here when they were children. Hard to credit now," he said, waving a hand at the grainy black of the tiny smooth fragments of coal that filled the spaces between the rocks and pebbles.

They emerged on to a grassy semi-circle. Perched on the cliff above them was the sole remaining tower of Macduff Castle—something else Karen remembered from her childhood. There had been more ruins around the tower, but they'd been removed by the council on the grounds of health and safety some years before. She remembered her father complaining about it at the time.

In the base of the cliff were several openings. Haigh headed for a sturdy metal grille protecting a narrow entrance a mere five feet tall. He unlocked the padlock and asked them to wait. He went inside, disappearing round a turn in the narrow passage. He returned almost immediately with three hard hats. Feeling like an idiot, Karen put one on and followed him inside. The first few yards were a tight fit, and she heard Phil cursing behind her as he banged an elbow against the wall. But soon it opened out into a wide chamber whose ceiling disappeared into darkness.

Haigh groped in a niche in the wall and suddenly the pale yellow of battery-operated lights cast a soft glow round the cave. Half a dozen rickety wooden chairs sat round a Formica-topped table. On a deep ledge about three feet above the ground sat a camping stove, half a dozen litre bottles of water, and mugs. The makings for tea and coffee were enclosed in plastic boxes. Karen looked around and just knew that the mainstays of the cave preservation group were all men. "Very cosy," she said.

"Supposedly there was a secret passage from this cave to the castle above," Haigh said. "Legend has it that was how

Macduff escaped when he came home to find his wife and children slain and Macbeth in possession." He gestured to the chairs. "Take a seat, please," he said, fiddling with stove and kettle. "So, why the interest in Mick after all this time?"

"His daughter has only just got round to reporting him missing," Phil said.

Haigh half-turned, puzzled. "But he's not missing, surely? I thought he'd gone off to Nottingham with another bunch of lads? Good luck to them, I thought. There was nothing here but misery back then."

"You didn't disapprove of the blackleg miners, then?" Karen asked, trying not to make it sound too sharp.

Haigh's chuckle echoed spookily. "Don't get me wrong. I've got nothing against trade unions. Working people deserve to be treated decently by their employers. But the miners were betrayed by that self-serving egomaniac Arthur Scargill. A true case of lions led by a jackass. I watched this community fall apart. I saw terrible suffering. And all for nothing." He spooned coffee into mugs, shaking his head. "I felt sorry for the men, and their families. I did what I could—I was the regional manager for a specialist food importer, and I brought as many samples as I could back to the village. But it was just a drop in the ocean. I totally understood why Mick and his friends did what they did."

"You didn't think there was something selfish about him leaving his wife and child behind? Not knowing what had happened to him?"

Haigh shrugged, his back to them. "To be honest, I didn't know much about his personal circumstances. He didn't discuss his home life."

"What did he talk about?" Karen asked.

Haigh brought over two plastic tubs, one containing sachets of sugar pilfered from motorway service stations and hotel bedrooms, the other little pots of non-dairy creamer from the same sources. "I don't really recall, so it was probably the usual. Football. TV. Projects to raise money for work on the caves. Theories about what the various carvings meant." Again the chuckle. "I suspect we're a bit dull to outsiders, Inspector. Most hobbyists are."

Karen thought about lying but couldn't be bothered. "I'm just trying to get an impression of what Mick Prentice was like."

"I always thought he was a decent, straightforward sort of bloke." Haigh brought the coffees over, taking almost exaggerated care not to spill any. "To be honest, apart from the caves, we didn't have a great deal in common. I thought he was a talented painter, though. We all encouraged him to paint the caves, inside and out. It seemed appropriate to have a creative record, since the main fame of the caves rests on their Pictish carvings. Some of the best are here in the Thane's Cave." He picked up his flashlight and targeted it at a precise spot on the wall. He didn't have to think about it. In the direct line of the beam, they could see the unmistakable shape of a fish, tail down, carved in the rock. In turn, he revealed a running horse and something that could have been a dog or a deer. "We lost some of the cupping designs in the fall of '85, but luckily Mick had done some paintings of them not long before."

"Where was the fall?" Phil said, peering towards the back of the cave.

Haigh led them to the furthest corner, where a jumble of rocks were piled almost to the roof. "There was a small second chamber linked by a short passage." Phil stepped forward to take a closer look, but Haigh grabbed his arm and yanked him back. "Careful," he said. "Where there's been a recent fall, we can never be sure how secure the roof is."

"Is it unusual to have cave-ins?" Karen said.

"Big ones like this? They used to happen quite regularly when the Michael pit was still working. But it closed in 1967 after—"

"I know about the Michael disaster," Karen interrupted. "I grew up in Methil."

"Of course." Haigh looked suitably rebuked. "Well, since they stopped working underground, there hasn't been much movement in the caves. We haven't had a major fall since this one, in fact."

Karen felt the twitch of her copper's instinct. "When exactly was the fall?" she said slowly.

Haigh seemed surprised at her line of questioning, giving Phil a glance of what felt like male complicity. "Well, we can't be precise about it. To be honest, from mid-December to mid-January is pretty much a dead time for us. Christmas and New Year and all that. People are busy, people are away. All we can say with any certainty is that the passage was clear on 7th December. One of our members was here that day, taking detailed measurements for a grant proposal. As far as we know, I was the next person in the cave. It's my wife's birthday on 24th January and we had some friends visiting from England. I brought them along to see the caves and that's when I discovered the fall. It was quite a shock. Of course, I cleared them out at once and called the council when we got back."

"So, some time between 7th December 1984 and 24th January 1985, the roof fell in?" Karen wanted to be sure she had it right. Two and two were coming together in her head, and she was pretty sure they weren't making five.

"That's right. Though I think myself it was earlier rather than later," Haigh said. "The air was clear in the cave. And that takes longer than you might think. You could say the dust had well and truly settled."

Newton of Wemyss

Phil looked at Karen with concern. In front of her was a perfectly presented pithivier of pigeon breast, surrounded by tiny new potatoes and a tower of roasted baby carrots and courgettes. The Laird o' Wemyss was more than living up to its reputation. But the plate had been sitting before Karen for at least a minute and she hadn't even lifted her cutlery. Instead of tucking in, she was staring at her plate, a frown line between her eyebrows. "Are you all right?" he said cautiously. Sometimes women behaved in strange and unpredictable ways around food.

"Pigeons," she said. "Caves. I can't get my mind off that fall."

"What about it? Cave falls happen. That's why they've got signs up warning people. And padlocked railings to keep them out. Health and safety, that's the bosses' mantra these days." He cut off a piece of his crispy fillet of sea bass and loaded it on his fork with the sesame hoisin vegetables.

"But you heard that guy. This is the only significant roof fall in any of the caves since the pit closed back in '67. What if it wasn't an accident?"

Phil shook his head, chewing and swallowing hastily. "You're doing that melodrama thing again. This is not Indiana Jones and the Wemyss Caves, Karen. It's a guy who went on the missing list when his life was shite."

"Not one guy, Phil. Two of them. Mick and Andy. Best pals. Not the kind to go scabbing. Not the kind to leave loved ones behind without a word."

Phil put down his fork and knife. "Did it ever occur to you that they might have been an item? Mick and his best pal Andy with the isolated cottage deep in the heart of the woods? Being gay in a place like Newton of Wemyss back in the early eighties can't have been the easiest thing in the world."

"Of course it occurred to me," Karen said. "But you can't just run with theories that have absolutely nothing to back them up. Nobody we've spoken to has even hinted at it. And believe me, if Fife has one thing in common with Brokeback Mountain, it's that folk talk. Don't get me wrong. I'm not dismissing it. But until I have something to base it on, I've got to file it right at the back of my mind."

"Fair enough," Phil said, starting in on his food again. "But you've got no more foundation for your notion that there's somebody buried under an unnatural cave fall."

"I never said anybody was buried," Karen said.

He grinned. "I know you, Karen. There's no other reason you'd be interested in a pile of rock."

"Maybe so," she said without a trace of defensiveness. "But I'm not just punting wild ideas. If there's one group of people who know all about shot-firing to bring down rock precisely where they want it, it's miners. And the shot-firers also had access to explosives. If I was looking for someone to blow up a cave, the first person I would go to would be a miner."

Phil blinked. "I think you need to eat. I think you've got low blood sugar."

Karen glowered at him for a moment, then she picked up her knife and fork and attacked the food with her usual gusto. Once she'd demolished a few mouthfuls, she said, "That takes care of the low blood sugar. And I still think I'm on to something. If Mick Prentice didn't go on the missing list of his own free will, he disappeared because somebody wanted him out of the way. Lo and behold, we have somebody that wanted him out of the way. What did Iain Maclean tell us?"

"That Prentice discovered Ben Reekie had his hand in the union's till," Phil said.

"Exactly. Pocketing money that was supposed to go to the branch. From all we've heard about Mick, he wouldn't have let that pass. And it's hard to see how he could pursue it without Andy being involved, since he was the one keeping the records. I don't think it was in their natures to do nothing about it. And if it had become common knowledge, Reekie would have been lynched, and you know it. That's a very tasty motive, Phil."

"Maybe so. But if it was two against one, how did Reekie kill the pair of them? How did he get the bodies in the cave? How did he get his hands on explosive charges in the middle of a strike?"

Karen's grin had always managed to disarm him. "I don't know yet. But, if I'm right, sooner or later I will know. I promise you that, Phil. And try this for starters: we know when Mick went missing, but we don't have an exact date for Andy's disappearance. It's entirely possible they were killed separately. They could have been killed in the cave. And as for getting hold of explosives—Ben Reekie was a union official. All sorts of people will have owed him favours. Don't pretend you don't know that."

Phil finished his fish and pushed his plate away from him. He raised his hands, palms towards Karen, indicating surrender. "So what do we do now?"

"Clear those rocks and see what's behind them," she said, as if the answer was obvious.

"And how are we going to do that? As far as the Macaroon's concerned, you're not even investigating this. And even if it was official, there's no way he'd stretch his precious budget to cover an archaeological dig for a pair of bodies that probably aren't there."

Karen paused with a forkful of pigeon breast halfway to her mouth. "What did you just say?"

"There's no budget."

"No, no. You said 'an archaeological dig.' Phil, if it wasn't for this pigeon coming between us, I could kiss you. You are a genius."

Phil's heart sank. It was hard to avoid the feeling that this was another fine mess he'd got himself into.

Kirkcaldy

Sometimes it was more sensible to make work calls from home. Until she'd actually got things under way and had her pitch firmly in place, Karen didn't want the Macaroon to get a sniff of what she was up to. Phil's words had set off a chain reaction in her brain. She wanted that rock fall cleared. The dates Arnold Haigh had given her offered the promise of being able to sneak it past the Macaroon under the pretext of a possible connection to the Grant case, but the cheaper she could make it, the less likely he would be to ask too many questions.

She settled herself down at the dining table with phone, notepad, and contacts book. Comfortable though she was with new technology, Karen still maintained a physical record of names, addresses, and phone numbers. She reasoned that if the world ever went into electronic meltdown she would still be able to find the people she needed. It had naturally occurred to her that, in that event, there would be no functioning telephones and the transport network would also be in meltdown, but nevertheless her contacts book felt like a security blanket. And if it ever came to it, much easier to destroy without trace than any electronic memory.

She flicked it open at the appropriate page and ran her finger down the list till she came to Dr. River Wilde. The forensic anthropologist had been one of the mentors on a course Karen had attended aimed at improving the scientific awareness of detectives with responsibility at crime scenes. On the face of it, it would have been hard to find much common ground between the two women, but they had formed an instant if unlikely bond. Although neither of them would ever have explained it thus, it was something to do with the way they both appeared to play the game while subtly undermining the authority of those who had failed to earn their respect.

Karen liked the way River never tried to blind her audience with science. Whether lecturing to a group of cops whose scientific education had ended in their teens or sharing an anecdote in the bar, she managed to convey complicated information in terms that a lay person could understand and appreciate. Some of her stories were horrifying; others reduced her listeners to helpless laughter; still others gave them pause.

The other thing that made River a great potential ally was that the man in her life was a cop. Karen hadn't met him, but from everything River had said, he sounded like her kind of cop. No bullshit, just a driven desire to get to the heart of things the straight way. So she'd come away from the forensics course with a greater understanding of her job but also with what felt like a new friendship. And that was rare enough to be worth nurturing. Since then, the women had met up a couple of times in Glasgow, the mid-point between Fife and River's base in the Lake District. They'd enjoyed their nights out, occasions that had cemented what their first encounter had started. Now Karen would find out if River had been serious when she'd offered her students as a cut-price team for exploratory work that couldn't really justify a big-budget spend.

River answered her mobile on the second ring. "Rescue me," she said.

"From what?"

"I'm sitting on the verandah of a wooden hut watching Ewan's terrible cricket team and praying for rain. The things we do for love."

Chance would be a fine thing. "At least you're not making the teas."

River snorted. "No way. I made that clear right from the start. No washing of sports kit, no slaving away in primitive kitchens. I get the hard stare from a lot of the other WAGs, but if they think I'm bothered, they're confusing me with someone who gives a shit. So how's tricks with you?"

"Complicated."

"So, nothing new there, then. We need to get together, have a night out. Uncomplicate yourself."

"Sounds good to me. And we might just manage it sooner than you think."

"Ah-hah. You've got something brewing?"

"You could say that. Listen, you remember you once said that you had a small army of students at your disposal if I ever needed help on the cheap?"

"Sure," River said easily. "You trying to get something done off the books?"

"Sort of." Karen explained the bare bones of the scenario. River made small noises of encouragement as she spoke.

"OK," she said when Karen had finished. "So we need forensic archaeologists first, preferably the big strong ones who can hump rocks. Can't use the final-year students because they're still doing exams. But it's nearly the end of term and I can press-gang the first- and second-years. Plus any of the anthros I can get my hands on. I can call it a field trip, make them think there's Brownie points to be had. When do you need us?"

"How about tomorrow?"

There was a long silence. Then River said, "Morning or afternoon?"

The phone call with River left Karen feeling all revved up with nowhere to go. She used some of her sudden excess of energy to arrange accommodation for the students at the campsite on the links at nearby Leven. She tried to watch a DVD of *Sex and the City* but it only irritated her. It was always like this when she was in the middle of a case. No appetite for anything but the hunt. Hating being stalled because it was the weekend, or tests took time, or nothing could be done till the next bit of information fell into place.

She tried to distract herself by cleaning. Trouble was, she never spent long enough in the house to make much mess. After an hour's blitzing, there was nothing left that warranted attention.

"To hell with it," she muttered, grabbing her car keys and making for the door. Strictly speaking, the laws of evidence required that she shouldn't be flying solo when she was talking to witnesses. But Karen told herself she was only colouring in the background, not actually taking evidence. And if she stumbled across something that might be relevant later in court, she could always send a couple of officers back another day to take a formal statement.

The drive back to Newton of Wemyss took less than twenty minutes. There was no sign of life in the isolated enclave where Jenny Prentice lived. No children played; nobody sat in their garden to enjoy the late afternoon sunshine. The short terrace of houses had assumed a dispirited air that would take more than a bit of summer weather to disperse.

This time, Karen approached the house next door to Jenny Prentice. She was still on a quest to get a sense of what Mick

Prentice had really been like. Someone who was close enough to the family to be entrusted with the care of Misha must have had some dealings with her father.

Karen knocked and waited. She was just about to give up and head back to her car when the door cracked open on the chain. A tiny wizened face peered out at her from beneath a mass of heavy grey curls.

"Mrs. McGillivray?"

"I don't know you," the old woman said.

"No." Karen took out her official ID and held it up in front of the smeared lenses of the big glasses that made faded blue eyes swim large behind them. "I'm a police officer."

"I didn't call the police," the woman said, cocking her head and frowning at Karen's warrant card.

"No, I know that. I just wanted to have a wee word with you about the man who used to live next door." Karen gestured with her thumb towards Jenny's house.

"Tom? He's been dead years."

Tom? Who was Tom? Oh shit, she'd forgotten to ask Jenny Prentice about Misha's stepdad. "Not Tom, no. Mick Prentice."

"Mick? You want to talk about Mick? What are the police doing with Mick? Has he done something wrong?" She sounded confused, which filled Karen with foreboding. She'd spent enough time trying to get coherent information out of old people to know that it could be an uphill struggle with dubious results.

"Nothing like that, Mrs. McGillivray," Karen reassured her. "We're just trying to find out what happened to him all those years ago."

"He let us all down, that's what happened," the old woman said primly.

"Right enough. But I just need to clear up some of the details. I wonder if I could come in and have a wee chat with you?"

The woman exhaled heavily. "Are you sure you've got the right house? Jenny's the one you want. There's nothing I can tell you."

"To be honest, Mrs. McGillivray, I'm trying to get an idea of what Mick was really like." Karen switched on her best smile. "Jenny's a wee bit biased, if you get my drift?"

The old woman chuckled. "She's a besom, Jenny. Not a good word to say about him, has she? Well, lassie, you'd better come through." A rattle as the chain came off, then Karen was admitted to a stuffy interior. There was an overwhelming smell of lavender, with bass notes of stale fat and cheap cigarettes. She followed Mrs. McGillivray's bent figure through to the back room, which had been knocked through to make a kitchen diner. It looked like the work had been done in the seventies and nothing had been changed since, including the wallpaper. The various fades and stains bore witness to sunlight, cooking, and smoking. The low sun streamed in, slanting a gold light across the worn furniture.

A caged budgie chattered alarmingly as they walked in. "Quiet now, Jocky. This is a nice police lady come to talk to us." The budgie let out a stream of chirrups which sounded as if it was swearing at them, then subsided. "Sit yourself down. I'll get the kettle on."

Karen didn't really want a cup of tea but knew the conversation would go better if she let the old woman fuss around her. They ended up facing each other across a surprisingly well-scrubbed table, a pot of tea and a plate of obviously home-made cookies between them. The sun lit Mrs. McGillivray like stage lighting, revealing details of make-up that had clearly been applied without the benefit of her glasses. "He was a lovely lad, Mick. A braw-looking fella, with that blond hair and big shoulders. He always had a smile and a cheery word for me," she confided as she poured the tea into china cups so fine you could see the sunlight in the tea. "I've been a widow thirty-two years now, and never had a better neighbour than young Mick Prentice. He'd always turn his hand to any wee job that I couldn't manage. It was never a trouble to him. A lovely laddie, right enough."

"It must have been hard on them, the strike." Karen helped herself to one of the proffered bourbon creams.

"It was hard on everybody. But that's not why Mick went away scabbing."

"No?" *Keep it casual, don't show you're particularly interested.*

"She drove him to it. Keeping company with that Tom Campbell right under his nose. No man would put up with that, and Mick had his pride."

"Tom Campbell?"

"He was never away from the door. Jenny had been a pal of his wife. She helped nurse the poor soul when she had the cancer. But after she died, it was like he couldn't stay away from Jenny. You had to wonder what had been going on all along." Mrs. McGillivray winked conspiratorially.

"You're saying Jenny was having an affair with Tom Campbell?" Karen bit her tongue on the questions she wanted to ask but knew she'd be better leaving till later. *Who was Tom Campbell? Where is he now? Why did Jenny not mention him?*

"I won't say what I can't swear to. All I know is that there was hardly a day went by when he didn't come calling. And always when Mick was out of the house. He never came empty-handed either. Wee parcels of this, packets of that. During the strike, Mick used to say his Jenny could make a pound go further than any other woman in the Newton. I never told him the reason why."

"How come Tom Campbell had stuff to hand out? Was he not a miner, then?"

Mrs. McGillivray looked like the tea she'd just drunk had turned to vinegar. "He was a deputy." Karen suspected she'd have accorded more respect to the word "paedophile."

"And you think Mick found out what was going on between them?"

She nodded emphatically. "Everybody else in the Newton knew what was what. It's the usual story. The other half is always the last to know. And if anybody had their doubts, Tom Campbell was in there fast enough after Mick took his leave."

Too late, Karen remembered she hadn't followed up the subject of Misha's stepfather. "He moved in with Jenny?"

"A few months went by before he moved in. Keeping up appearances, for what it was worth. Then he had his feet right under Mick's table."

"Did he not have a house of his own? On a deputy's money, I'd have thought . . ."

"Oh aye, he had a braw house along at West Wemyss. But Jenny wouldn't move. She said it was for the bairn's sake. That Mick going had been upheaval enough for Misha without being uprooted from her own home." Mrs. McGillivray pursed her lips and shook her head. "But you know, I've often wondered. I don't think she ever loved Tom Campbell the way she loved Mick. She liked what he could give her, but I think her heart aye belonged to Mick. For all her carrying on, I never quite believed that Jenny stopped loving Mick. I think she stayed put because deep down she believes Mick'll come back one day. And she wants to be sure he knows where to find her."

It was, Karen thought, a theory based on soap opera sentimentality. But it did have the merit of making sense of what seemed otherwise inexplicable. "So what happened with her and Tom?"

"He rented out his own house and moved in next door. I never had much to do with him. He didn't have Mick's easy way with folk. And things were never easy between the Lady Charlotte boys and the deputies, especially after the pit was closed in 1987." The old woman shook her head, jiggling the lank grey curls. "But Jenny got her come-uppance." Her smile was gleeful.

"How come?"

"He died. Took a massive heart attack on the golf course at Lundin Links. It must be getting on for ten years ago. And when the will was read, Jenny got a hell of a shock. He'd left everything in trust for Misha. She got the lot when she was twenty-five, and Jenny never saw a penny." Mrs. McGillivray raised her teacup in a toast. "Served her right, if you ask me."

Karen couldn't find it in her heart to disagree. She drained her cup and pushed back her chair. "You've been very helpful," she said.

"He was round here the very day Mick went to Nottingham," Mrs. McGillivray said. It was the verbal equivalent of grabbing someone by the arm to prevent them leaving.

"Tom Campbell?"

"The very same."

"When did he show up?" Karen asked.

"It must have been round about three o'clock. I like to listen to the afternoon play on the radio in the front room. I saw him coming up the path then hanging about waiting for Jenny to get back. I think she'd been down the Welfare—she'd got some packets and tins, one of the handouts they picked up there."

"You seem to remember it very clearly."

"I mind it so well because that morning was the last time I ever saw Mick. It stuck in my mind." She poured herself another cup of tea.

"How long did he stay? Tom Campbell, I mean."

Mrs. McGillivray shook her head. "Now there I can't help you. After the play was finished, I went down to the green to catch the bus for Kirkcaldy. I'm not able for it now, but I used to like to go to the big Tesco down by the bus station. I'd get the bus in and a taxi back. So I don't know how long he stayed." She took a long drink of her tea. "I sometimes wondered, you know."

"Wondered what?"

The old woman looked away. Reached into the pocket of her saggy cardigan and pulled out a packet of Benson & Hedges. Extracted a cigarette and took her time lighting it. "I wondered if he paid Mick off."

"You mean, paid him to leave town?" Karen couldn't hide her incredulity.

"It's not such a daft idea. Like I said, Mick had his pride. He wouldn't have stayed where he thought he wasn't wanted. So if he was set on going anyway, maybe he took Tom Campbell's money."

"Surely he'd have had too much self-respect for that?"

Mrs. McGillivray breathed out a thin stream of smoke. "It would be dirty money either way. Maybe Tom Campbell's money felt a wee bit cleaner than the coal board's? And besides, when he left that morning, it didn't look like he was going any further than the shore, to do his painting. If Tom Campbell paid him, he wouldn't have needed to come back for his clothes or anything, would he?"

"You're sure he didn't come back for his stuff later?"

"I'm sure. Trust me, there's no secrets in this row."

Karen's eyes were on the old woman but her mind was racing. She didn't believe for a minute that Mick Prentice had sold his place in the marital bed to Tom Campbell. But maybe Tom Campbell had wanted to take that place badly enough to come up with a different scenario to dispose of his rival.

So much for picking up a bit of character background. Karen bit back a sigh and said, "I'd like to send a couple of officers round to see you on Monday morning. Maybe you could tell them what you've just told me?"

Mrs. McGillivray perked up. "That would be lovely. I could bake some scones."

Rotheswell Castle

Just because she was stuck at Rotheswell like a self-immured Rapunzel didn't mean Bel Richmond could turn her back on the rest of her work. Even if she was deprived of access to Grant, she didn't have to twiddle her thumbs. She'd spent most of the day writing up an interview for a *Guardian* feature. It was almost done, but she needed a bit of distance before the final polish. A visit to the pool house concealed in a nearby stand of pine trees would do the trick, she thought, pulling her swimsuit from her bag. Halfway across the room, the house phone rang.

Susan Charleson's voice was crisp and clear. "Are you busy?"

"I was just going for a swim."

"Sir Broderick has an hour free. He'd like to continue your background briefing."

There was clearly no room for discussion. "Fine." Bel sighed. "Where'll I find him?"

"He'll see you downstairs in the Land Rover. He thought you might like to see where Catriona lived."

She couldn't complain about that. Anything that added colour to the story was well worth her time. "Five minutes," she said.

"Thank you."

Quickly, Bel changed into jeans and her weatherproof jacket, thanking the fashionista gods that stylized construction boots had come into vogue, allowing her to look vaguely as if she was ready for country life. She grabbed her recorder and hurried downstairs. A shiny Land Rover Defender sat outside the front door, engine running. Brodie Grant sat behind the wheel. Even from a distance, she could see his gloved fingers drumming on the steering wheel.

Bel climbed aboard and gave him her best smile. She hadn't seen him since the bizarre interview with the cops the day before. She'd eaten a working lunch alone in her room, and he'd been missing from the dinner table. Judith had said he was at some men-only charity boxing dinner, and she sounded relieved to be missing it. Their conversation had been anodyne; either Judith herself or the ever-present Susan had steered it sideways whenever it threatened to become in any way revealing. Bel had felt frustrated and exploited.

But now she was alone with him again she could forgive all that. She considered asking him if he really thought he could control Karen Pirie like the lord of the manor in a 1930s crime drama, but thought better of it. Best to use the time to beef up her background on the case. "Thanks for taking me to see Cat's place," she said.

"We won't be able to go inside," he said, releasing the

handbrake and setting off round the back of the house and down a track that led through the pine trees. "It's had several sets of tenants since, so you're not really missing anything. So, what did you think of Inspector Pirie?"

There was no clue in his face or voice to what he wanted to hear, so Bel settled on the truth. "I think she's one of those people it's easy to underestimate," she said. "I suspect she's a smart operator."

"She is," Grant said. "I expect you know that she's the reason the former assistant chief constable of this county is serving life in prison. A man who was apparently beyond suspicion. But she was capable of questioning his probity. And once she started, she didn't stop till she'd established beyond doubt that he was a cold-blooded killer. Which is why I want her on this. Back when Catriona died, we were all guilty of thinking along the traditional tramlines. And look where that got us. If we're going to have a second bite at the cherry, I want someone who will think outside the box."

"Makes sense," Bel said.

"So what do you want to talk about next?" he said as they emerged from the trees into a clearing that ended with a high wall and another of the airlock-style gates like the one Bel had entered by when she first arrived. Clearly nobody got into the grounds of Rotheswell unless they were welcome. Grant slowed enough to let the security guards be sure who was behind the wheel, then accelerated on to the main road.

"What happened next?" she said, switching on her recorder and holding it out between them. "You got the first demand and started working with the police. How did things go after that?"

He stared ahead resolutely, showing no signs of emotion. As they rolled past chequered fields of ripening grain and grazing, the sun slipping in and out of louring grey clouds, his words spilled out in an unsettling flow. It was hard for Bel to keep any kind of professional distance. Living with her nephew Harry had given her insight enough to readily imagine the anguish of a parent in Brodie Grant's situation. That understanding generated enough sympathy to absolve him from almost any criticism. "We waited," he said. "I've never known time to drag like it did then."

Monday, 21st January 1985; Rotheswell Castle

For a man who didn't have the patience to let a pint of Guinness settle, waiting to hear from the Anarchist Covenant of Scotland was exquisite torture. Grant roamed Rotheswell like a pinball, almost literally bouncing off walls and doorways in his efforts to stop himself imploding. There was no sense or logic to his movements, and when he and his wife crossed paths, he could barely find the words to respond to her anxious enquiries.

Mary seemed to be much more in control, and he came close to resenting her for it. She had been to Cat's cottage and reported to both him and Lawson that, apart from an overturned chair in the kitchen, nothing seemed out of place. The sell-by date on the milk had been Sunday, indicating she hadn't been gone more than a few days at most.

The nights were worse than the days. He didn't sleep so much as collapse when physical exhaustion overcame him. Then he'd wake with a start, disorientated and unrefreshed. As soon as consciousness reasserted itself, he wished he was unconscious again. He knew he was supposed to be behaving normally, but that was beyond him. Susan cancelled all his engagements and he holed up inside the walls at Rotheswell.

By Monday morning, he was as close to a wreck as he'd ever felt. The face he saw in the mirror looked as if it belonged in a prisoner-of-war camp, not a rich man's castle. He didn't even care that those around him could see his vulnerability. All he wanted was for the post to arrive, to bring with it something concrete, something that could liberate him from impotence and give him a task. Even if it was only raising whatever ransom the bastards wanted. If it had been up to him, he would have staked out the sorting office in Kirkcaldy, stopping his postie like an old-fashioned highwayman and demanding his mail. But he accepted the madness of that. Instead he paced to and fro behind the letterbox where the castle's mail would drop to the mat at some point between half past eight and nine o'clock.

Lawson and Rennie were already on the spot. They'd arrived in a plumber's van wearing tradesmen's overalls via the back drive at eight. Now they sat stolidly in the hall, waiting for the post. Mary, stunned with the Valium he'd insisted she take, sat on the bottom step in her pyjamas and dressing gown, arms wrapped around her calves, chin on her knees. Susan moved among them with teas and coffees, her normal composure hiding God alone knew what. Grant certainly had no idea how she had held everything together over the past couple of days.

Lawson's radio crackled an incomprehensible message and moments later there was a rustle and a clatter of the letterbox. The day's bundle of mail cascaded to the floor, Grant falling on it like a starving man on the promise of food. Lawson was almost as fast, grabbing the big manila envelope seconds after Grant's fingers closed on it. "I'll take that," he said.

Grant yanked it from him. "No, you bloody won't. It's addressed to me and you'll see it in good time." He clasped it to his chest and stood up, backing away from Lawson and Rennie.

"OK, OK," Lawson said. "Just take it easy, sir. Why don't you sit down next to your wife?"

To his own surprise Grant did as Lawson suggested, subsiding on the stairs beside Mary. He stared at the envelope, suddenly unwilling to discover what demands were about to be made of him. Then Mary laid her hand on his arm and it felt like an unexpected transfusion of strength. He ripped back the flap and pulled out a thick wad of paper. Unfolding it, he saw that this time there were two copies of the puppeteer poster. Before he could take in the words written inside the box at the foot of each, he spotted the Polaroid. He went to cover it, but Mary was too fast for him, reaching across and grabbing it.

This time, Cat's mouth wasn't taped up. Her expression was angry and defiant. She was bound to a chair with loops of parcel tape, the wall behind her a white blank. A gloved hand held the previous day's *Sunday Mail* in the foreground of the picture.

"Where's Adam?" Mary demanded.

"We have to assume he's there. It's a bit harder to get a baby to pose," Lawson said.

"But there's no proof. He could be dead for all you know." Mary put her hand to her mouth as if trying to push the treacherous words back.

"Don't be silly," Grant said, putting his arm round her and injecting spurious warmth into his voice. "You know what Catriona's like. There's no way she'd be this cooperative if they'd done anything to Adam. She'd be screaming like a banshee and throwing herself to the floor, not sitting there all meek and still." He squeezed her shoulders. "It's going to be all right, Mary."

Lawson waited for a moment, then said, "Can we take a look at the message?"

Grant's eyelids flickered and he nodded. He spread the top poster open on his knees and read its message, written in the same thick black marker as the previous one.

> WE WANT A MILLION. £200,000 IN USED, NON-SEQUENTIAL £20 NOTES, IN A HOLD-ALL. THE REST IN UNCUT DIAMONDS. THE HANDOVER WILL BE ON WEDNESDAY EVENING. WHEN YOU HAND OVER THE RANSOM, YOU WILL GET ONE OF THEM BACK. YOU GET TO CHOOSE WHICH ONE.

"Jesus Christ," Grant said. He passed the poster to Lawson, who had gloved up in anticipation. The second sheet offered no more cheer.

> WHEN WE AUTHENTICATE THE DIAMONDS AND KNOW THE MONEY IS SAFE, WE WILL RELEASE THE OTHER HOSTAGE. REMEMBER, NO POLICE. DO NOT FUCK WITH US. WE KNOW WHAT WE ARE DOING AND WE ARE NOT AFRAID TO SPILL BLOOD FOR THE CAUSE. THE ANARCHIST COVENANT OF SCOTLAND.

"What have you done to track these people down?" Grant demanded. "How close are you to finding my family?"

Lawson held a hand up while he studied the second poster. He passed it to Rennie and said, "We're doing everything we can. We've spoken to Special Branch and MI5, but neither of them has any knowledge of an activist group called the Anarchist Covenant of Scotland. We managed to get a fingerprint man and an evidence officer into Catriona's cottage under cover of darkness on Saturday night. So far we've no direct leads from that, but we're working on it. Also, we had an officer posing as a customer asking around to see if anyone knew when Catriona's workshop would be open. We've established that she was definitely working on Wednesday but nobody can confirm they saw any sign of her after that. We've had no reports of anything untoward in the area. No suspicious vehicles or behaviour. We—"

"What you're saying is that you have nothing and you know nothing," Grant interrupted brutally.

Lawson didn't even flinch. "That's often the way in kidnap cases. Unless the snatch happens in a public place, there's little to go on. And where there's a small child involved, it's very easy to control the adult, so you don't even get the sort of struggle that generates forensic evidence. Generally, the handover is the point where we can make real progress."

"But you can't do anything then. Can't you read, man? They're going to hold on to one of them till they're sure we haven't double-crossed them," Grant said.

"Brodie, they're both going to be there at the handover," Mary said. "Look, it says we get to choose one of them."

Grant snorted. "And which one are we going to choose? It's bloody obvious that we'd go for Adam. The most vulnerable one. The one who can't look out for himself. Nobody in their right mind would leave a six-month-old baby with some bunch of anarchist terrorists if they had any choice. They'll bring Adam and leave Catriona behind wherever they're keeping them. That's what I'd do if it was me." He looked to Lawson for confirmation.

The policeman refused to meet his eyes. "That's certainly one possibility," he said. "But whatever they do, we have options. We can try to follow them. We can put a tracking device in the holdall and another among the diamonds."

"And if that doesn't work? What's to stop them coming back for more?" Grant said.

"Nothing. It's entirely possible they'll ask for a second ransom." Lawson looked deeply uncomfortable.

"Then we'll pay," Mary said calmly. "I want my daughter and my grandson back safely. Brodie and I will do whatever it takes to achieve that. Won't we, Brodie?"

Grant felt cornered. He knew what the answer was supposed to be, but he was surprised by his ambivalence. He cleared his throat. "Of course we will, Mary." This time Lawson's eyes locked on his, and Grant understood that he might have given a little too much away. He needed to remind the cop that he had something at stake too. "And so will Mr. Lawson, Mary. I promise you that."

Lawson folded the posters together and slid them back into the envelope. "We're all a hundred per cent committed to getting Catriona and Adam back safely," he said. "And the first thing on the agenda is that you have to start making arrangements with your bank."

"My bank? You mean, we're giving them the real thing?" Grant felt incredulous. If he'd ever thought about anything like this, he'd assumed the police had a stash of marked counterfeit ready for such contingencies.

"It would be very dangerous at this point to do anything else," Lawson said. He stared at the carpet, the very picture of embarrassment. "I take it you do have the money?"

Saturday, 30th June 2007; Newton of Wemyss

"Cheeky bastard tried to look like he was embarrassed to ask, but I could tell he was actually enjoying putting me on the spot," Grant said, stepping on the gas as they left Coaltown of Wemyss behind them. "Don't get me wrong. Lawson never put a foot out of place in the whole investigation. I've no reason to suspect he was anything other than totally committed to catching the bastards who took Catriona and Adam. But I could tell there was a part of him that was secretly enjoying watching me get my come-uppance."

"Why was that, do you think?"

Grant slowed as a gap appeared in the high wall they were driving alongside. "Envy, pure and simple. Doesn't matter what label you put on it—class warfare, machismo, chip on the shoulder. It comes down to the same thing. There's a lot of people out there who resent what I have." He pulled off the road into a large turnout. The wall angled inwards on both sides, giving way in the middle to tall gates made of a thick lattice of wood painted black, built to resemble a medieval portcullis. Set into the wall on one side was the frontage of a two-storey house, built from the same blocks of local red sandstone as the wall itself. Net curtains blanked the windows, none of them twitching at the sound of the Land Rover's engine. "And those same people resented Catriona too. It's ironic, isn't it? People assumed Catriona got such a great start in her professional life because of me. They never realized it was in spite of me."

He cut the engine and got out, slamming the door behind him. Bel followed, intrigued by the insights he was giving her, the unwitting as much as the witting. "And you? Is their envy of you ironic too?"

Grant swung round on his heel and glowered at her. "I thought you'd done your research?"

"I have. I know you started out in a miner's row in Kelty. That you built your business from nothing. But a couple of places in the cuttings there's a big hint that your marriage didn't exactly hurt your meteoric rise." Bel knew she was playing with fire here, but if she was going to capitalize on this unique access and parlay it into something career-changing, she needed to get beneath the surface to the material nobody else had even suspected, never mind reached down into.

Grant's heavy brows drew together in a glare, and for a moment she thought she was going to experience the withering blast of his temper. But something shifted in his expression. She could see the effort it took, but he managed a twisted little smile and shrugged. "Yes, Mary's father did have power and influence in areas that were crucial to the building of my business." He spread his arms in a gesture of helplessness. "And yes, marrying her did me nothing but good in a professional sense. But here's the thing, Bel. My Mary was smart enough to know she'd be miserable if she married a man who didn't love her. And that's why she chose me." His smile slowly faded. "I never had a choice in the matter. And I never had a choice when she chose to leave me behind." Abruptly he turned away and strode towards the heavy gates.

FRIDAY, 23RD JANUARY 1987; EILEAN DEARG

They spent so little time together these days. The thought had plagued Grant at every meal he'd eaten at Rotheswell all week. Breakfast without her. Lunch without her. Dinner without her.

There had been guests; business associates, politicians, and of course, Susan. But none of them had been Mary. The time without her had reached critical mass this week. He couldn't go on with this distance between them. He needed her now as much as he ever had. Nothing made Cat's death easier, but Mary made it bearable. And now her absence, today of all days, was entirely unbearable.

She'd left on Monday, saying she needed to be on her own. On the island, she would have the peace she wanted. There were no staff there. It took only twenty minutes to walk round, but a couple of miles out to sea felt a long way from anywhere and anyone. Grant liked to go there for the thinking as much as the fishing. Mary mostly left him to it, joining him only occasionally. He couldn't remember her ever going there alone. But she'd been adamant.

Of course there was no phone line. She had a car phone, but the car would be in the hotel parking lot on Mull, half a mile from the jetty. And besides, there would be no signal for a car phone in the wilderness of the Hebridean chain. He hadn't even heard her voice since she'd said goodbye on Monday.

And now he'd had enough of the silence. Two years to the day since his daughter had died and his grandson had disappeared, Grant did not want to be alone with his pain. He tried not to be too harsh on himself over what had gone wrong, but guilt had still scarred his heart. He sometimes wondered if Mary blamed him too, if that was why she absented herself so often. He had tried to tell her the only people who should carry responsibility for Catriona's death were the men who had kidnapped her, but he could barely convince himself, never mind her.

He'd set off after an early breakfast, phoning ahead to the hotel to make sure someone would be available to take him over to his island. He'd had to pull off the road a couple of times when the grief clogging his throat threatened to overwhelm him. He'd arrived while there was still a faint smudge of daylight in the sky, but by the time they'd crossed the water, dusk was well advanced. But the path to the lodge was broad and well tended, so he had no fear of straying.

As Grant grew near, he was surprised to see no lights showing. When she was quilting, Mary had an array of lights that would shame a theatre rig. Maybe she wasn't quilting. Maybe she was sitting in the sun room at the back of the house, watching the last threads of light across the western sky. Grant quickened his step, refusing to acknowledge the ragged claws of fear dragging across his chest.

The door wasn't locked. It swung open on oiled hinges. He reached for the light and the hall sprung into sharp relief. "Mary," he called. "It's me." The dead air seemed to absorb his words, preventing them from carrying any distance.

Grant strode down the hall, throwing doors open as he went, calling his wife's name, panic tightening his scalp and making him tearful. Where the hell was she? She wouldn't be outside. Not this late. Not when it was this cold.

He found her in the sun room. But she wasn't watching the sunset. Mary Grant would never watch the sunset again. A scatter of pills and an empty vodka bottle broke the secret of her silence. Her skin was already cool.

SATURDAY, 30TH JUNE 2007; NEWTON OF WEMYSS

Bel caught up with Grant by the heavy beams of the gate. Close up, she could see there was a smaller entrance cut into one of the gates, big enough to take a small van or a large car. On the other side was a rutted track leading deep into thick woodland.

"She left a note," he said. "I have it by heart still. 'I'm so sorry, Brodie. I can't do this any more. You deserve better and I can't get better. I can't bear to see your pain and I can't bear my own. Please, try to love again. I pray you can.' " His face twisted in a bitter smile. "Judith and Alec. That's me doing what she told me. Have you heard of the Iditarod race?"

Startled by the abrupt change in subject, Bel could only stutter, "Yes. In Alaska. Dog sleds."

"One of the biggest hazards they face is something called drum ice. What happens is that the water recedes from under the ice, leaving a thin skin over an air pocket. From above, it looks just like the rest of the ice field. But you put any weight on it and you fall through. And you can't get out because the sides are sheer ice. That's what losing Catriona and Adam and Mary feels like sometimes. I don't know when the ground under my feet is going to stop supporting me." He cleared his throat and pointed at a small wooden barn just visible on the edge of the trees. "That was Catriona's workshop and showroom. It was in better nick back then. When she was open for business, she had a couple of A-boards by the roadside. She'd leave the inner gate ajar, enough for people to walk in and out but not wide enough for cars. There was plenty of room for people to park out here." He waved his hand at the ample space where he'd left the Land Rover. The subject of his first wife was clearly closed. But he'd given her a wonderful gift with the image of the drum ice. Bel knew she could make something remarkable out of that.

She surveyed the scene. "But, theoretically, whoever kidnapped her could have opened the gate wide enough to drive through? Then they'd have been pretty much invisible from the road."

"That was what the police thought initially, but the only tyre tracks they found belonged to Catriona's own car. They must have parked out here, where it's hard standing. Anyone driving past could have seen them. They were taking a hell of a risk."

Bel shrugged. "Yes and no. If they physically had hold of Adam, Cat would have done what she was told."

Grant nodded. "Even a woman as bloody-minded as my daughter would have put her son first. I've no doubts about that." He turned away. "I still blame myself."

It seemed an extreme reaction, even for a control freak. "How do you mean?" Bel asked.

"I relied too heavily on the police. I should have taken more responsibility for the way things played out. I tried. Just not hard enough."

WEDNESDAY, 23RD JANUARY 1985; ROTHESWELL CASTLE

"We know what we're doing," Lawson said. He was beginning to sound tetchy, which didn't fill Grant with confidence. "We can end this tonight."

"You should have the area under surveillance," Grant said. "They could already be in place."

"I imagine they know roughly when the mail is delivered," Lawson said. "If they wanted to get the jump on us, they would have dug in before we even got the message with the arrangements. So it makes no odds, really."

Grant stared down at that morning's Polaroid. This time, Cat was lying on her side on a bed, Adam leaning wide-eyed against her. Again, the *Daily Record* provided proof of life. At least, proof of life for the previous day. "Why there?" he said. "It's such an odd place. It's not like you can make a quick getaway."

"Maybe that's why they chose it. If they can't get away quickly, you can't either. They're still going to have one hostage. They can use her as a bargaining chip to make you keep your distance until they can get to their vehicle," Lawson said. He spread out the large-scale map Rennie had brought in. The site for the handover was circled in red. "The Lady's Rock. It's about halfway between the old pithead at East Wemyss and the eastern edge of West Wemyss. The nearest points they can drive to are here, at the start of the woods . . ." Lawson tapped the map. "Or here. In the parking lot at West Wemyss. If I was them, I wouldn't choose West Wemyss. It's further from the main road. It takes a crucial few minutes longer to get on to the grid."

"More options when you do get there, though," Grant pointed out. "Towards Dysart or the Boreland, towards Coaltown, or down the Check Bar Road to the Standing Stone, and then more or less anywhere."

"We'll have all the options covered," Lawson said.

"You can't take any chances," Grant said. "They'll have the ransom. They might sacrifice Cat for the sake of their getaway."

"What do you mean?"

"If I was a kidnapper who had my hands on the ransom and I realized your men were on my tail, I'd throw my hostage out of the car," Grant said, sounding much cooler than he felt. "You'd stop for her because you are civilized. They know that. They can afford to gamble on it."

"We won't take any risks," Lawson said.

Grant threw his hands up in frustration. "That's not the right answer either. You can't play safety first in a situation like this. You have to be willing to take calculated risks. You have to go with the moment. You can't be rigid. You have to be flexible. I didn't get to the top of the tree by not taking any risks."

Lawson gave him a measured stare. "And if I take a risk that I think is necessary, and it backfires? Will you be the one shouting loudest for my head on the block?"

Grant closed his eyes for a moment. "Of course I bloody will," he said. "Now, I've got two lives and a million pounds riding on this. You need to convince me you know what you're doing. Can we run through this again?"

SATURDAY, 30TH JUNE 2007; NEWTON OF WEMYSS

"I knew I'd let her down. Right then, I knew it." Grant sighed heavily. "Still, I kept believing that if it all went to hell, someone would come forward. That someone must have seen something."

"It didn't happen." It was a flat statement.

"No. It didn't happen." He turned and looked at Bel. His expression was perplexed. "Nobody ever came forward. Not about the actual kidnap itself. Not about where they were held. Nobody ever gave the police a single piece of credible eye-witness testimony. Oh, there were the usual nutters. And people calling in good faith. But after they were investigated, every single report was dismissed."

"That seems odd," Bel said. "Usually there's something. Even if it's only a falling out among thieves."

"I think so too. The police never seemed to think it was peculiar. But I've always wondered how they managed it without there being a single witness to any of it."

Bel looked pensive. "Maybe there wasn't a falling out among thieves because they weren't thieves."

"What do you mean?"

"I'm not quite sure," she said slowly.

Grant looked frustrated. "That's the trouble with this case." He set off towards the Land Rover. "Nobody's ever been sure about bloody anything. The only thing that's certain is that my daughter is dead."

Sunday, 1st July 2007; East Wemyss

Karen had never had a particularly high opinion of students. It was one reason why she'd opted to join the police straight from school, in spite of her teachers' attempts to persuade her to go to university. She didn't see the point of building up four years of debt when she could be earning good money and doing a proper job. Nothing she'd seen of the lives of her former schoolmates had made her feel she'd made a mistake.

But River Wilde's crew was forcing her to admit that maybe students weren't all self-indulgent slackers. They'd arrived just before eleven; they'd unloaded their gear and set up their tarpaulins and floodlights by noon; and they'd organized a pizza run, bolted their food, and begun the difficult but delicate task of shifting tons of rock and rubble by hand. Once they had established a rhythm with picks, trowels, sieves, and brushes, River left them to it and joined Karen where she sat at the cave society's table, feeling pretty much redundant.

"Very impressive," Karen said.

"They don't get out much," River said. "Well, not in a professional sense, anyway. They're raring to go."

"How long do you think it'll take to clear the obstruction?"

River shrugged. "Depends how far back it goes. It's impossible to guess. One of my postgrads has his first degree in earth sciences, and he says that sandstone is notoriously unpredictable when it starts to move. Once we get some clearance up at the top, we can stick a drill probe in. That should give us an idea of how far back it goes. If we hit clear air, we can shove a fibre-optic camera down. Then we'll have a much better sense of what we're dealing with."

"I really appreciate this," Karen said. "I'm taking a bit of a flyer here."

"So I gathered. You want to fill me in? Or is it better if I don't know?"

Karen grinned. "You're doing me the favour. Better you know what the score is." She took River through the key points of her investigation, elaborating where River asked for more detail. "What do you think?" she said at last. "You think I can finesse it?"

River held out a hand, waggling it from side to side to indicate it could go either way. "How smart is your boss?" she asked.

"He's a numpty," Karen said. "All the insight of a shag-pile carpet."

"In that case, you might get lucky."

Before Karen could reply, a familiar shape emerged from the gloom of the cave entry. "Are you lassies not one short?" Phil said, coming into the light and pulling up a chair.

"What're you on about?" Karen said.

"Hubble bubble, toil and trouble," he said. "Trick of the light. Sorry, boss." He thrust out a hand. "You must be Dr. Wilde. I have to say, I thought Karen was a one-off, but apparently I was wrong."

"He means that in a nice way," Karen said, rolling her eyes. "Phil, you have to learn to play nice with strange women. Especially ones who know seventeen different undetectable ways to kill you."

"Excuse me," River said, apparently offended. "I know a hell of a lot more than seventeen ways."

Ice broken, Phil had River explain what her team were hoping to achieve. He listened carefully, and when she had finished, he stared across at the students. They'd already made a visible dent in the top corner where fallen rocks met the roof. "No offence," he said, "but I hope this all turns out to be a waste of time."

"You still hoping Mick Prentice is alive and well and digging holes in Poland, like Iain Maclean suggested?" Karen said, pity withering her tone.

"I'd rather that than find him under those rocks."

"And I'd rather my numbers had come up on the lottery last night," Karen said.

"Nothing wrong with a bit of optimism," River said kindly. She got to her feet. "I'd better do some leading by example. I'll call you if anything comes up."

There was no difficulty in finding two parking places in Jenny Prentice's terraced street. Phil followed Karen up the path, muttering under his breath that the Macaroon was going to throw a fit when he found out about River's big dig.

"It's all under control," Karen said. "Don't worry." The door opened abruptly and Jenny Prentice glared at them. "Good afternoon, Mrs. Prentice. We'd like to have a wee chat with you." Steel in the eyes and the voice.

"Aye well, I don't want to have any kind of chat with you just now. It's not convenient."

"It is for us," Phil said. "Do you want to do it here where the neighbours can tune in? We could come in, if you'd rather do it that way?"

Another figure appeared behind Jenny. Karen couldn't help being pleased when she recognized Misha Gibson. "Who is it, Mum?" she said, then realized. "Inspector Pirie—have you got news?" The hope that sprang into her eyes felt like a reproach.

"Nothing concrete," Karen said. "But you were right. Your dad didn't go to Nottingham with the scabs. Whatever happened to him, it wasn't that."

"So if you've not come with news, why are you here?"

"We've one or two questions we need to ask your mum," Phil said.

"Nothing that can't wait for tomorrow," Jenny said, folding her arms across her chest.

"All the same, no reason not to get them out of the way today," Karen said, smiling at Misha.

"I don't see my daughter that often," Jenny said. "I don't want to waste the time we've got talking to you."

"It won't take long," Karen said. "And it does concern Misha too."

"Come on, Mum. They've come all the way out here, the least we can do is invite them in," Misha said, steering her mother away from her position on the threshold. The look Jenny gave them would have shrivelled smaller souls, but she conceded and swung away from them, back into the front room they'd spoken in last time.

Karen refused the tea Misha offered, barely allowing mother and daughter to settle before she went straight to the point. "When we last spoke, you never mentioned Tom Campbell."

"Why should I?" Jenny couldn't keep the hostility from her voice.

"Because he was here the day your husband disappeared. And not for the first time, either."

"Why shouldn't he be here? He was a friend of the family. He was very generous to us during the strike." Jenny's mouth clamped tight as a mousetrap.

"What are you suggesting, Inspector?" Misha sounded genuinely puzzled.

"I'm not suggesting anything. I'm asking Jenny why she's never mentioned that Campbell was here that day."

"Because it was irrelevant," Jenny said.

"How long was it after Mick disappeared that you and Tom started having a relationship?" The question hung alongside the dust motes that inhabited the air.

"You've got a very nasty mind," Jenny said.

Karen shrugged. "It's a matter of record that he moved in here. That you lived together as a family. That his will left everything to Misha. All I'm asking was how much time elapsed between Mick vanishing and Tom getting his feet under the table."

Jenny flashed an unreadable look at her daughter. "Tom was a good man. You've got no right to come here with your innuendos and slanders. The man wasn't long widowed. His wife was my best pal. He needed friends about him. And he was a deputy, so most of the men didn't want to know."

"I'm not disputing any of that," Karen said. "I'm just trying to get the facts straight. It doesn't help me find Mick, you not telling me the whole story. So how long was it before Tom and you moved from friendship to something more?"

Misha made an impatient noise. "Tell her what she wants to know, Mum. She'll just get it from somebody else otherwise. It's got to be better coming from you than the local sweetie wives."

Jenny stared at her feet, studying battered slippers nearly through at the toes as if the answer was written there and she didn't have the right glasses on. "We were both lonely. We'd both been abandoned, it felt like. And he was good to us, very good to us." There was a long pause, then Misha put out her hand to cover her mother's clenched fist. "I asked him to my bed six weeks to the day after Mick walked out on us. We'd have starved if it hadn't been for Tom. We were both looking for comfort."

"Nothing wrong with that." The gentle words came, surprisingly, from Phil. "We're not here to make judgements."

Jenny gave the barest of nods. "He moved in with us in May."

"And he was a great stepdad," Misha said. "He couldn't have done a better job if he'd been my real dad. I loved Tom."

"We both did," Jenny said. Karen couldn't help thinking she was trying to convince herself as much as them. She remembered Mrs. McGillivray's contention that Jenny Prentice's heart had only ever belonged to Mick.

"Did you ever wonder whether Tom had anything to do with Mick leaving?"

Jenny's head snapped back, her eyes blazing at Karen. "What the hell is that supposed to mean? You think Tom did something to Mick? You think he did away with Mick?"

"You tell me. Did he?" Karen was as implacable as Jenny was roused.

"You're barking up the wrong tree," Misha said, her voice loud and defiant. "Tom wouldn't hurt a fly."

"I didn't say anything about Campbell causing Mick any harm. I find it extremely interesting that you both leapt to the assumption that that's what I meant," Karen said. Jenny looked baffled, Misha furious. "What I was wondering was whether Mick realized there was some bond between you and Tom. By all accounts, he was a proud man. Maybe he decided it would be best for everybody if he left the field clear for a man you seemed to prefer."

"You're talking pure shite," Jenny hissed. "There was nothing going on between me and Tom back then."

"No? Well, maybe Tom thought there might be if he could take Mick out of the picture. He had plenty of money. Maybe he bought Mick off." It was an outrageous suggestion, she knew. But outrage often precipitated interesting outcomes.

Jenny pulled her hand away from Misha and shifted away from her daughter. "This is your fault," she shouted at her daughter. "I don't have to listen to this. In my own home, she dares to slander the man that gave you everything. What have you brought down on us, Michelle? What have you done?" Tears spilled down her cheeks as she drew her hand back and slapped Misha hard across the face.

Karen was on her feet and moving. But she wasn't fast enough. Jenny had made it out of the room before anyone could stop her. Stunned, Misha pressed a hand to her scarlet cheek. "Leave her," she shouted. "You've done enough damage for one day." She caught her breath, then collected herself. "I think you should leave," she said.

"I'm sorry things got out of hand," Karen said. "But that's the trouble with taking the lid off the box. You never know what's going to pop out."

Monday, 2nd July 2007; Glenrothes

ACC Simon Lees stared at the piece of paper Karen Pirie had placed in front of him. He'd read it three times and still it made no sense. He knew he was going to have to ask her for an explanation and that somehow he would end up on the back foot. It felt so unfair. First thing on Monday morning, and the sanctuary of his office was already breached. "I'm not entirely clear why we're paying for this"—he checked the paper again, trying to shake the suspicion that Pirie was indulging in a twisted practical joke—"Dr. River Wilde to lead a team of students in a 'forensic dig' in a cave at East Wemyss."

"Because it's going to cost us about a tenth of what the forensic science service would charge us. And I know how you like us to get value for money," Karen said.

Lees thought she knew full well that wasn't what he had meant. "I'm not referring to the budget implications," he said peevishly. "What I'm trying to understand is why this"—he cast his hands upwards in a gesture of frustration—"this circus is happening at all."

"I thought I was to leave no stone unturned in my investigation of Catriona Maclennan Grant's kidnap," Karen said sweetly.

Was she making fun of him? Or did she really not understand what she'd just said? "I didn't mean that literally, Inspector. What the hell is all this in aid of?" He waved the budget requisition form at her.

"It came to my notice in the course of my inquiries that there had been a somewhat unusual roof fall in one of the Wemyss caves in January 1985. I say unusual, because since the Michael pit closed in 1967, the ground has settled and there have been no other major falls." Karen savoured the look of bafflement on Lees's face. "When I looked into this further, I found out that the fall had been discovered on Thursday, 24th January."

"And?" Lees looked uncomprehending.

"That's the day after Catriona was killed, sir."

"I know that, Inspector. I am familiar with the case. But I still fail to see what a roof fall in an obscure cave has to do with anything." He fiddled with the photograph frame on his desk.

"Well, sir, it's like this." Karen leaned back in her chair. "As far as the locals are concerned, the caves aren't really obscure. Everybody knows about them. Most folk have played in them at least once when they were wee. Now, one of the things that we never found out back then was where Catriona and Adam were being held. We never had any witness reports that tied them in to any particular location. And I got to thinking. That time of year, the caves are pretty well deserted. It's too cold for kids to be playing outside, and there's never enough bright daylight to tempt passersby beyond the first few feet of any of the caves."

Lees felt himself drawn into her narrative in spite of himself. She didn't deliver reports the way his other officers did. Mostly it drove him slightly crazy, but sometimes, like today, he couldn't resist the shape of her storytelling. "You're saying the caves could have been a potential hiding place for the kidnappers? Isn't that a bit Enid Blyton?" he said, trying to reassert himself.

"Very popular, Enid Blyton, sir. Maybe she could even be called inspirational. Anyway, the cave in question, the Thane's Cave, has a gated railing along the front to keep people out these days. But back then, there was just a fence across the access passageway. It wasn't meant to be impregnable. The cave society used the Thane's Cave as a kind of clubhouse. Still do, as a matter of fact. The railing was just there to discourage the casual explorer. So it wouldn't have been difficult for anyone to gain access."

"But they'd have been like rats in a trap if they'd been found," Lees protested.

"Well, that's the thing. We can't be entirely sure about that. There's always been a story that there was a passageway down from Macduff Castle to the cave."

"Oh for heaven's sake, Inspector. Have you been taking drugs? This is insane."

"With respect, sir. It makes a kind of sense. We know the kidnappers escaped from the scene in a boat. Police witnesses said at the time it sounded like a small outboard. But by the time they scrambled the chopper and got the spotlight on the sweep, there was no sign of any wee boats anywhere in range of the Lady's Rock. Now, it was a high tide that night. What if they just shot a couple of miles up the shore and hid the boat in the cave? They'd have got an inflatable in, no bother. They dump it with the rest of their make-shift camp, then get out, bringing the roof down behind them."

Lees shook his head. "It sounds like a cross between *The Dangerous Book for Boys* and *Die Hard*. How exactly do you think they went about"—he paused to do that thing with two fingers that indicated quotation marks and also for some reason irritated his wife out of all proportion to the offence—"bringing the roof down behind them?"

Karen smiled far too brightly for his liking. "I've no idea, sir. Hopefully Dr. Wilde's team will be able to tell us. I'm pretty sure we'll find something behind that rock fall that will justify all this expense."

Lees held his head in his hands. "I think you've lost your mind, Inspector."

"Never mind," she said, getting to her feet. "It's the Brodie Grant case. You can spend pretty much what you like, sir. This is one time when nobody's going to question the budget."

Lees could feel the blood pounding in his ears. "Are you taking the piss?"

Immediately he regretted swearing, not least because she looked as if she thought it was definitely an improvement. "No, sir," Karen said soberly. "I'm taking this case very seriously."

"You've got a funny way of showing it." Lees slammed his palms down on the desk. "I want to see some proper police work here, not a day trip to Kirrin Island. It's time you did some digging into the past. It's time you went to talk to Lawson." That would teach her who was boss.

But somehow she'd already defused his little bomb. "I'm glad you think so, sir. I've arranged an appointment for"—she consulted her watch—"three hours' time. So if you don't mind, I'm away to put the pedal to the metal and head for the Blue Toon."

"Pardon?" Why could these Fifers not speak plain English?

Karen sighed. "I've to drive to Peterhead." She headed for the door. "I keep forgetting you're not from here." She cast a quick look over her shoulder. "You don't really get us, do you, sir?"

But before he could respond, she was gone, the door left wide open. Like a barn door behind a cow, he thought bitterly, getting up to slam it shut. What had he done to deserve this bloody woman? And how the hell was he going to come out of the Brodie Grant case smelling of roses when he was forced to rely on the investigative skills of a woman who thought it might be interesting to dig up a bloody cave?

Campora, Tuscany

With a sense of relief, Bel Richmond turned off the SS2, the treacherous divided highway that corkscrews down Tuscany from Florence to Siena. As usual, the Italian drivers had scared the living shit out of her, driving too fast and too close, wing mirrors almost touching as they shot past her in tight bends that seemed to make the narrow lanes even smaller. The fact that she was in a hire car only magnified the unpleasantness.

Bel thought of herself as a pretty good driver, but Italy never failed to shred her nerves. And thanks to this latest assignment, she was feeling sufficiently shredded, thank you very much.

On Sunday evening, she'd eaten dinner off a tray in her room. Her choice; she'd been invited to join the Grants in the dining room, but she'd pleaded the demands of work. The reality was more prosaic, but its selfishness made it impossible to admit to. In truth, Bel craved her own company. She wanted to hang out of the window smoking the red Marlboros Vivianne had nagged her into supposedly giving up months before. She wanted to watch some crap TV, and she wanted to gossip on the phone with any of the women friends whose connection made her feel better. She wanted to run away home and play some shoot-'em-up Playstation game with Harry. It was always the same when she found herself living at close quarters with the subjects of her journalism. There was only so much intimacy she could take.

But her pleasure in her own company had been short-lived. She'd barely started watching the first episode of a new U.S. cop show when there was a knock at the door. Bel muted the TV, put down her glass of wine, and got up from the sofa. She opened the door to find Susan Charleson, a thin plastic folder in her hand. "I'm sorry to interrupt," she said. "But I'm afraid this is rather urgent."

Disguising the ill grace she felt, Bel stepped back and waved her in. "Come in," she sighed.

"May I?" Susan gestured to the sofa.

"Make yourself at home." Bel sat down at the opposite end, leaving as much space between them as possible. She hadn't taken to Susan Charleson. Behind the chilly efficiency, there was nothing to latch on to, no glimmer of sisterly warmth to build the conspiracy of friendship on. "How can I help you?"

Susan cocked her head to one side and gave a wry little smile. "You'll have realized that Sir Broderick is given to quick decisions that he expects everyone else to turn into realities."

"That's one way of putting it," Bel said. *Used to getting his own way* might have been a better one. "So what has he decided he needs from me?"

"You're pretty quick off the mark yourself," Susan said. "That's probably why he likes you." She gave Bel a measured look. "He doesn't like many people. When he does, he rewards us very well."

Flattery and bribery, the twisted twins. Thank heavens she'd reached a point in her career where she could feed and clothe herself without having to cave in to their poisoned gifts. "I do things because they interest me. If they don't interest me, I don't do them well, so there's not much point, really."

"Fair enough. He'd like you to go to Italy."

Whatever she'd been expecting, it hadn't been that. "Why?"

"Because he thinks the Italian police have no investment in this case so they won't be working it very hard. If DI Pirie goes out there, or sends one of her team, she'll be hampered by the language and by being an outsider. He thinks you might do better, given that you speak Italian. Not to mention the fact that you're just back from there and presumably have some recent acquaintance with the locals. Not the police, obviously. But the locals who might actually know something of what's been going on at that ruined villa." Susan smiled at her. "If nothing else, you get an expenses-paid trip back to Tuscany."

Bel didn't have to think about it for long. This was probably the only chance she'd have to get the jump on the police in terms of new information. "How do you know I speak Italian?" She stalled, not wanting to look too much of a pushover.

A wintry smile. "It's not just journalists who know how to do research."

I asked for that. "When does he want me to go?"

Susan held out the folder. "There's a flight to Pisa at six tomorrow morning. You're booked on it, and there's a hire car arranged at the airport. I didn't reserve accommodation—I thought you'd rather sort out your own. You will, of course, be reimbursed."

Bel was taken aback. "Six in the morning?"

"It's the only direct flight. I've checked you in. You'll be driven to the airport. It only takes forty minutes at that time of the morning—"

"Yes, fine," Bel said impatiently. "You were very sure I'd agree."

Susan put the folder on the sofa between them and stood up. "It was a pretty safe bet."

So here she was, bouncing down a dirt road in the Val d'Elsa past fields of sunflowers just bursting into dramatic flower, the hot beat of excitement pulsing in her throat. She didn't know if Brodie Grant's name would open doors in Italy as easily as it did in Scotland, but she had a sneaking suspicion that he'd know exactly how to manipulate the bone-deep corruption that underpinned everything here. There was nothing in Italy these days that couldn't be reduced to a transaction.

Except friendship, of course. And thanks to that, at least she had a roof over her head. The villa, of course, was out of the question. Not because of the cost—she was pretty sure she could have made Brodie Grant spring for it—but because it was high season in Tuscany. But she'd been lucky. Grazia and Maurizio had converted one of their old barns into holiday apartments, and the smallest, a studio with a tiny terrace, had been available. When she'd called from the airport, Grazia had tried to offer it to her for free. It had taken Bel almost ten minutes to explain that someone was paying her expenses so Grazia should overcharge as much as she liked.

Bel turned off the track on to a narrower rutted lane that wound up through a forest of oaks and chestnuts. After a mile or so, she emerged on a small plateau with an olive grove and a field of maize. At the far end was a tight cluster of houses beyond a hand-painted sign that read BOSCOLATA. Bel negotiated the tight turns and carried on, back into the trees. As she rounded the second bend after Boscolata, she slowed and peered through the undergrowth at the ruined villa where this trail had started. There was nothing to show it was of any interest, other than a piece of red-and-white tape tied half-heartedly to the gate. So much for the Italian police investigation.

Another five minutes' tortuous driving and Bel pulled into Grazia's farmyard. A tan hound with droopy ears and a pink nose danced at the end of his chain, barking with all the bravado of a dog who knows nobody is going to come close enough to bite. Before Bel could open her door, Grazia appeared on the steps leading down from the loggia, wiping her hands on her apron, her face crinkling in a broad smile.

Extravagant greetings and the settling of Bel into the beautifully appointed studio took half an hour and had the advantage of helping Bel recover the rhythms of the language. Then the two women settled down with a cup of coffee in Grazia's dim kitchen, the thick stone walls keeping the summer heat at bay as they had done for hundreds of years. "And now, you have to tell me why you are back so soon," Grazia said. "You said it was something to do with work?"

"Sort of," Bel said, wrestling her Italian back into shape. "Tell me, have you noticed anything going on down at the ruined villa recently?"

Grazia gave her a suspicious look. "How do you know about that? The carabinieri were there on Friday. They took a look around, then they went to talk to the people in Boscolata. But what has this got to do with you?"

"When we were here on holiday, I went exploring in the old villa. I found something there that connects to an unsolved crime back in England. A case from twenty years ago."

"What kind of crime?" Grazia looked anxious. The swollen joints of her hands moved restlessly on the table.

"A woman and her baby son were kidnapped. But something went wrong when the ransom was being handed over. The woman was killed, and they never found out what happened to the child." Bel spread her hands and shrugged. Somehow, such gestures came more naturally when she was speaking Italian.

"And you found something here connected to that?"

"Yes. The kidnappers called themselves anarchists and they delivered their demands in the form of a poster. I found a poster just like it down at the villa."

Grazia shook her head in amazement. "The world is getting smaller and smaller. So when did you go to the carabinieri?"

"I didn't. I didn't think they'd believe me. Or if they did, they wouldn't be interested in something that happened back in the UK twenty-odd years ago. I waited till I got home, then I went to the woman's father. He's a very rich man, a powerful man. The sort of person who makes things happen."

Grazia gave a grim little laugh. "It would take a man like that to make the carabinieri get off their backsides and come all the way out here from Siena. That explains why they were so interested in who had been living in the villa."

"Yes. I thought it looked as if squatters had been living there."

Grazia nodded. "The villa belonged to Paolo Totti. He died, maybe a dozen years ago. A silly man, very vain. He'd spent all his money buying a big house to impress everyone, but he didn't have enough left over to look after the place like it deserved. And then he died without a will. His family have been fighting over the villa ever since. It drags on through the courts and every year the villa falls down a little bit more. Nobody from the family does anything to repair it in case they end up with nothing to show. They stopped coming near it years ago. So sometimes people move in for a while. They stay for summer then they go. The last lot, they stayed longer." Grazia finished her coffee and stood up. "All I know is gossip, but we'll go down to Boscolata and talk to my friends there. They'll tell you a damn sight more than they told those bossy carabinieri."

PETERHEAD, SCOTLAND

Karen studied James Lawson as he approached. No more ramrod bearing, head high and back straight. His shoulders were slumped, his steps small and tight. Three years in jail had put ten years on him. He lowered himself into the chair across the table from her, fidgeting and fussing till at last he settled. A small attempt at controlling some part of the interview, she thought.

Then he looked up. He still had the flat, hard cop stare, his eyes burning, his face stony. "Karen," he said, acknowledging her with a tiny nod. His lips, pale and bluish, compressed in a tight line.

She couldn't see any point in small talk. There was nothing to be said that wouldn't lead straight to recrimination and bitterness. "I need your help," she said.

Lawson's mouth relaxed into a sneer. "Who do you think you are? Clarice Starling? You'd need to lose a few pounds before you could give Jodie Foster a run for her money."

Karen reminded herself that Lawson had attended the same interrogation courses she had. He knew all about probing for your opponent's weaknesses. But then, so did she. "It might be worth going on a diet for Hannibal Lecter," she said. "But not for a disgraced cop that's pulled his last trout out of Loch Leven."

Lawson raised his eyebrows. "Did they send you on a smart-arse course before you took your inspector's exam? If you're supposed to be buttering me up, you're not exactly going about it the right way."

Karen gave a resigned shake of the head. "I haven't got the time or the energy for this. I'm not here to flatter your ego. We both know how these things play out. You help me, your life inside these four walls gets a wee bit less horrible for a while. You walk away from me, who knows what shitty little stunt is going to make your life that wee bit more miserable? Up to you, Jimmy."

"It's Mr. Lawson to you."

She shook her head. "That would imply more respect than you deserve. And you know it." Her point made, she'd refrain from calling him anything. She could hear him breathing hard through his nose, a faint wheeze at the end of each exhalation.

"You think you could make my life any more miserable?" He glared at her. "You have no bloody idea. They keep me in isolation because I'm an ex-cop. You're the first visitor I've had this year. I'm too old and too ugly to interest anybody else. I don't smoke and I don't need any more phone cards." He gave a faint snort of laughter, phlegm bubbling in his throat. "How much worse do you think you can make it?"

She stared back at him, unflinching. She knew what he'd done and there was no place for pity or compassion in her heart for him. She didn't care if they spat in his food. Or worse. He had betrayed her and everyone else who had worked with him. Most of the cops Karen knew were in the job for decent motives. They made sacrifices for the job, they cared that it was done properly. Discovering that a man whose orders they'd followed without flinching was a triple killer had shattered morale in the CID. The fractures were still healing. Some people still blamed Karen, arguing that it would have been better to let sleeping dogs lie. She didn't know how they could sleep at night.

"They tell me you use the library a lot," she said. His eyes flinched. She knew she had him. "It's important to keep your mind active, isn't it? Otherwise you really do go stir crazy. I hear you can download books and music on a wee MP3 player from the library these days. Listen any time you've a mind to."

He looked away, folding and unfolding his fingers. "You still on cold cases?" The concession of the words seemed to take energy he could ill spare.

"It's my department now. Robin Maclennan retired." Karen kept her voice neutral and her face impassive.

Lawson looked over her shoulder at the blank wall behind her. "I was a good cop. I didn't leave many loose ends for you carrion crows to pick over," he said.

Karen gave him a measured stare. He'd killed three people and tried to frame a vulnerable man for two murders, and yet he still thought of himself as a good cop. The capacity of criminals for self-delusion never ceased to amaze her. She wondered that he could sit there with a straight face after the laws he'd broken, the lies he'd told, and the lives he'd shattered. "You cleared a lot of cases," was the best she could manage. "But I've got what looks like new evidence on one that's still open."

Lawson's expression didn't change, but she sensed a flicker of interest as he shifted slightly in his chair. "Catriona Maclennan Grant," he said, allowing himself a self-satisfied smirk. "For you to come yourself, it has to be murder. And that's the only unsolved murder where I was SIO."

"Nothing wrong with your deductive skills," Karen said.

"So, what? You finally got something to nail the bastard, after all this time?"

"What bastard?"

"The ex-boyfriend, of course . . ." Lawson's grey skin furrowed as he dredged his memory for details. "Fergus Sinclair. Gamekeeper. She'd given him the push, wouldn't let him be a father to his kid."

"You think Fergus Sinclair kidnapped her and the baby? Why would he do that?"

"To get his hands on his kid and enough money to keep the pair of them in high style," Lawson said, as if he were instructing a small child in the obvious. "Then he killed her during the handover so she couldn't finger him. We all knew he'd done it, we just couldn't prove it."

Karen leaned forward. "There's nothing about that in the file," she said.

"Of course there isn't." Lawson made a derisive noise in his throat. "Christ, Karen, do you think we were stupid back then?"

"You didn't have to disclose everything to the defence in 1985," she pointed out. "No operational reason why you shouldn't have left a wee pointer for anyone coming after you."

"All the same, we didn't put anything on paper that we couldn't back up with solid evidence."

"Fair enough. But there's nothing in the file to suggest you even looked at him. No interview notes or tapes, no statements. The only mention in the file is in a statement from Lady Grant saying she believed Sinclair was the father of Catriona's son but that her daughter had always refused to confirm that."

Lawson looked away. "Brodie Maclennan Grant's a powerful man. We all agreed, right up to chief constable level. Nothing went in the file that we couldn't back up a hundred and ten per cent." He cleared his throat. "Even though we thought Sinclair was the obvious suspect, we didn't want to sign his death warrant."

Karen's mouth opened and closed. Her eyes widened. "You thought Brodie Grant would have Sinclair killed?"

"You didn't see the pain he was in after Cat died. I wouldn't have put it past him." His mouth snapped shut and he glared at her defiantly.

She'd thought Brodie Grant was a harsh, driven man. But it had never crossed Karen's mind to consider him a potential commissioner of death. "You were wrong about that," she said. "Sinclair was always safe. Grant doesn't think he had it in him."

Lawson snorted. "He might be saying that now. But at the time, you could feel the hatred coming off him for that lad."

"And you looked close at Sinclair?"

Lawson nodded. "He seemed promising. He had no alibi. He was working abroad. Austria, I think it was. Estate management, that's his line." He frowned again, scratching his clean-shaven chin. He started speaking slowly, speeding up as memory took shape. "We sent a team over to talk to him. They didn't find anything that let him off the hook. He'd been off work on holiday for the crucial time—kidnap, ransom notes, handover, getaway. And the guy we consulted at the art school said the poster was in the German Expressionist style, which kind of tied in with where he was living."

He shrugged. "But Sinclair said he'd been on a skiing holiday. Moving from one resort to the next. Sleeping in his Land Rover to save money. He had ski-lift passes for all the relevant dates, paid for with cash. We couldn't prove he hadn't been where he said he'd been. More to the point, we couldn't prove he was where we thought he was. It was the only real lead we had, and it took us nowhere."

Monday, 21st January 1985; Kirkcaldy

Lawson flicked through the folder again, as if he might find something he'd missed on his previous pass. It was still painfully thin. Without raising his head, he called across the office to DC Pete Rennie. "Has nothing come in from the crime scene lads yet?"

"I just spoke to them. They're working as fast as they can, but they're not optimistic. They said it looks like they're dealing with people who are smart enough not to leave traces." Rennie sounded both apologetic and anxious, as if he knew this was somehow going to be his fault.

"Useless wankers," Lawson muttered. After the initial flash of excitement provoked by the second note from the kidnappers, it had been a day of mounting frustration. He'd had to accompany Grant to the bank, where they'd had a difficult meeting with a senior official who had mounted his high horse, announcing the bank had a policy of non-cooperation with kidnappers. And that was without either of them saying a word about the reason for Grant's request. They'd ended up having to speak to a director of the bank before they'd made any headway.

Then Grant had taken him to some fancy gentleman's club in Edinburgh and sat him down with a large whisky in spite of his protestations about being on duty. When the waiter put his drink in front of him, he ignored it and waited for Grant to say what was on his mind. This was one investigation where Lawson knew better than to appear to be in the driving seat.

"I've got kidnap insurance, you know," Grant had said without preamble.

Lawson had wanted to ask how that worked, but he didn't want to look like some provincial numpty who didn't know what he was doing. "Have you spoken to them?"

"Not so far." Grant swirled the malt round inside the crystal tumbler. The heavy phenolic smell of the whisky rose in a miasma that made Lawson feel faintly sick.

"Can I ask why not?"

Grant took out a cigar and started the fiddly process of trimming and lighting. "You know how it is. They'll want to come in mob-handed. The price of the ransom will be them running the show."

"Is that a problem?" Lawson was feeling a little out of his depth. He took a sip of whisky and nearly spat it out. It tasted like the kind of cough medicine his grandmother had sworn by. It didn't seem to belong to the same family as the dram of Famous Grouse he enjoyed by his own fireside.

"I'm worried it will get out of hand. They've got two hostages. If they get so much as a sniff that we've set them up, who knows what they're capable of?" He lit the cigar and screwed up his eyes to peer at Lawson through the smoke. "What I need to know is whether you're confident you can bring this to a successful conclusion. Do I need to take a chance on outsiders? Or can you get my daughter and grandson back to me?"

Lawson tasted the sweet, cloying smoke in his throat. "I

believe I can," he said, wondering if his own career was about to go the same way as the cigar.

And that was how they'd left it. So here he was now, still at his desk while the evening crept inexorably towards night. Nothing was happening, except that his words seemed more and more foolhardy. He glared at Rennie. "Have you managed to track down Fergus Sinclair yet?"

Rennie's shoulders hunched and he squirmed in his seat. "Yes and no," he said. "I found out where he's working and I spoke to his boss. But he's not around. Sinclair, I mean. He's away on holiday. Skiing, apparently. And nobody knows where."

"Skiing?"

"He went off in his Land Rover with his skiing gear," Rennie said defensively, as if he'd personally packed up Sinclair's stuff.

"So he could be anywhere?"

"I suppose so."

"Including here? In Fife?"

"There's no evidence of that." Rennie's mouth seemed to slip sideways, as if his jaw had just realized it was on thin ice.

"Have you been on to the airlines? Airports? Channel ports? Have you made them go through their passenger lists?"

Rennie looked away. "I'll get on to it right away."

Lawson pinched the bridge of his nose between his thumb and forefinger. "And get on to the passport office. I want to know if Fergus Sinclair has ever applied for a passport for his son."

Monday, 2nd July 2007; Peterhead

"I was always convinced that Sinclair was involved somehow. It's not as if there were that many people who knew her routine well enough to do the snatch," Lawson said, a touch of defensiveness in his voice now.

Karen felt perplexed. "But what about the baby? If he did all that to get his hands on his son, where's Adam now?"

Lawson shrugged. "That's your million-dollar question, isn't it? Maybe Adam didn't survive the shootout. Maybe Sinclair had some woman lined up to take care of the kid for him. If I was you, I'd take a look at his life now. See if there's some lad in it the right age." He sat back, folding his hands in his lap. "So you've not come up with anything significant? This just a fishing expedition?"

She reached for the rolled-up poster she'd propped against her chair and slipped it free from its elastic band. She let it uncurl facing Lawson. He started to reach for it then stopped, giving her an interrogative look. "Go ahead," she said. "It's a copy."

Lawson carefully unfurled the paper. He studied the stark black-and-white artwork, running a finger over the puppeteer and his marionettes; the skeleton, Death, and the goat. "That's the poster the kidnappers used to communicate with Brodie Maclennan Grant." He pointed to the blank area at the bottom of the poster. "There, where you'd paste on the details of the show, that's where the messages would be written." He gave her a look of resignation. "But you know all that already. Where did this come from?"

"It turned up in an abandoned house in Tuscany. The place is falling down, been empty for years. According to the locals, it had been squatted on and off. The last lot cleared out overnight. No warning, no goodbyes. They left a lot of gear behind. Half a dozen of these posters included."

Lawson shook his head. "Pretty meaningless. We've had a few posters like this turn up over the years. Because Sinclair faked it up to look like some anarchist group hitting on Brodie Maclennan Grant, every now and again you'd get wankers using the poster to promote some direct action or festival or whatever. We checked them out every time, and there was never a connection to what happened to Catriona." He waved a hand dismissively.

Karen smiled. "You think I didn't know that? At least that much made it into the files. But this is different. None of the copies that turned up before was exact. There were differences in the detail, the way there would be if you were copying it off old newspaper cuttings. But this one's different. It's exactly the same. Forensics say it's identical. That it came off the same silk screen."

Lawson's eyes brightened, the spark of interest suddenly obvious in him. "You're kidding?"

"They've had all weekend to make their minds up. They say there's no doubt. But why would you keep the screen all these years? It's the one piece of evidence that ties the kidnappers into the crime."

Lawson smirked. "Maybe they didn't keep the screen. Maybe they just hung on to the posters."

Karen shook her head. "Not according to the document examiner. Neither the paper nor the ink had been developed in 1985. This was produced recently. On the original screen."

"It doesn't make sense."

"Like so many other things about this case," Karen muttered. Without realizing, she had slipped into her historic relationship with the man opposite. She was the junior officer, pricking him into making sense of the scraps she laid at his feet.

Unconsciously, Lawson responded, relaxing into the conversation for the first time. "What other things?" he said. "Once we'd fixed on Sinclair, it all came together."

"I don't see it. Why would Fergus Sinclair kill Cat at the handover?"

"Because she could identify him."

The impatience in his voice stung Karen, reminding her of their present roles. "I understand that. But why kill her then? Why not kill her beforehand? With her alive at the handover, he was setting up a really complicated situation. He had to control Cat and the baby, get his hands on the ransom, then shoot Cat and get away with the baby in the resulting confusion. He couldn't even be sure that he'd kill her. Not in the dark, with everybody milling around. It would have made life a lot simpler for him to have killed her before the ransom handover. Why didn't he kill her earlier?"

"Proof of life," Lawson said with the satisfaction of a man trumping an ace. "Brodie required proof of life before he'd go ahead."

"No, that doesn't fly," Karen said. "The kidnapper still had the bairn. He could use Adam for proof of life. You're not telling me Brodie Grant would refuse to pay the ransom if he didn't have proof of life for Cat too."

"No . . . He'd have paid whether Cat was alive or dead." Lawson frowned. "I hadn't thought of it like that. You're right. It doesn't make sense."

"Of course, if it wasn't Sinclair, she might not have had to die." Karen's eyes went dreamy as she tried the idea on for size. "It might have been a stranger. She might not have been able to identify him. Maybe it was an accident?"

Lawson cocked his head to one side and gave her a speculative look. Karen felt as if her fitness for purpose were being assessed. He did a little drum roll with his fingers on the edge of the chipped table. "Sinclair could have been the kidnapper, Karen. But not necessarily the killer. You see, there's something else that wasn't in the report."

Wednesday, 23rd January 1985; Newton of Wemyss

The tension was excruciating. The bulk of the Lady's Rock took a bite out of the starry sky, blocking out the shoreline beyond. The cold nibbled at Lawson's nose and ears and around the narrow bracelet between his leather gloves and the cuffs of his sweater. The air held the acrid tang of coal smoke and salt. The nearby sea was only a faint rumble and whisper on this windless night. The waning moon gave just enough light for him to see the taut features of Brodie Maclennan Grant a few yards away, just clear of the trees that sheltered Lawson himself. One hand held the holdall with the cash, the diamonds, and the tracking transmitters, the other grasped his wife's elbow tightly. Lawson imagined the pain radiating from that pincer grip and was glad he wasn't on the receiving end of it. Mary Maclennan Grant's face was in shadow, her head bowed. Lawson imagined she was shivering inside her fur coat, and not from the cold.

What he couldn't see were the half-dozen men he had stationed among the trees. That was just as well. If he couldn't see them, neither could the kidnappers. He'd hand-picked them, choosing the ones he believed to be both clever and brave, two qualities that coincided less often than he liked to admit. A couple of them were firearms trained, one with a handgun, the other on top of the Lady's Rock with an assault rifle, complete with night sights. They were under orders not to shoot except on his direct order. Lawson sincerely hoped he was overreacting by having them there.

He'd managed to pry some other uniforms from their routine duties guarding the pitheads and the power stations. Their buddies had resented their detachment, all the more since Lawson hadn't been in a position to explain the reason for their temporary secondment to his command. These extra officers were stationed at the rough ground at either end of the wood, the nearest points to the rendezvous where vehicles could be parked. Between them, they should be able to prevent a getaway if Lawson and his immediate team bungled the take-down at the handover.

Which was more than a possibility. This was a nightmare of a set-up. He'd tried to persuade Grant to say no, to insist on another place for the handover. Anything but a bloody beach in the middle of the night. He might as well have saved his breath. As far as Grant was concerned, Lawson and his men were there as a sort of private security force. He acted as if he was doing them enough of a favour by inviting them along against the express instructions of whoever had taken his daughter and grandson. In spite of what he'd said about the kidnap insurers' team, he didn't seem to appreciate how much could go wrong. It really didn't bear thinking about.

Lawson snatched a look at the luminous dial of his watch. Three minutes to go. It was so still, he'd have expected to hear their car engine in the distance. But acoustics were always unpredictable in the open. He'd noticed when he walked the path during his earlier reconnaissance how the looming bulk of the Lady's Rock acted as a baffle, cutting off the sound of the sea as effectively as a set of ear protectors. God alone knew how the woodland would distort the sound of an approaching vehicle.

Then without warning a brilliant burst of white light from the direction of the rock wiped out his night vision. All Lawson could make out was the mesmerizing circle of light. Without conscious thought, he stepped further back into the trees, afraid his cover was blown.

"Jesus Christ," Brodie Grant yelped, letting go of his wife and taking a couple of steps forward.

"Stay where you are." A disembodied shout from beyond the light. Lawson tried to place the accent, but there was nothing distinctive about it other than its Scottishness.

Lawson could make out Grant's profile, all colour stripped from his skin by the bleaching white light. His lips were stretched back over his teeth in a snarl. Unease squirmed in Lawson's stomach like acid indigestion. How the hell had the kidnappers got into position at the side of the rock without him seeing them? The moonlight had been enough to illuminate the path in both directions. He'd expected a vehicle. They had two hostages, after all. They could hardly march them a mile up the beach from West Wemyss or East Wemyss. The steep cliff behind him ruled out Newton of Wemyss.

The kidnapper shouted again. "OK, let's do it. Just like we said. Mrs. Grant, you walk towards us with the money."

"Not without proof of life," Grant bellowed.

The words were barely out of his mouth when a figure stumbled out in front of the light, a stark marionette that reminded Lawson of the posters the kidnappers had used to deliver their demands. As his eyes adjusted, he could see it was Cat. "It's me, Daddy," she called, her voice hoarse. "Mummy, bring me the money."

"What about Adam?" Grant shouted, grabbing his wife by the shoulder as she reached for the holdall. Mary nearly tripped and fell, but her husband had no eyes for her. "Where's my grandson, you bastards?"

"He's all right. As soon as they have the money and the diamonds, they'll hand him over," Cat shouted, desperation obvious in her voice. "Please, Mummy, bring the money like you're supposed to."

"Damn it," Grant said. He thrust the holdall at his wife. "Go on, do what she says."

This was out of control, Lawson knew it. To hell with the radio silence he'd called for. He reached for his radio and spoke as clearly as he dared. "Tango One and Tango Two. This is Tango Lima. Despatch officers to shore side of Lady's Rock. Do it now. Do not reply. Just deploy. Do it now."

As he spoke, he could see Mary walking uncertainly towards her daughter, shoulders hunched. He estimated there was about thirty-five yards between them. It seemed to him that Mary was covering more of the distance than her daughter. As they came within touching distance, he could see Cat reaching for the bag.

To his surprise, that was the moment Mary chose to cast aside the conditioning of thirty years' marriage to Brodie Grant. Instead of doing what she'd been told, first by the kidnappers' note and second by her husband, Mary clung on to the holdall in spite of Cat's efforts to pull it from her. He could hear Cat's exasperation as she said, "For Christ's sake, Mother, give me the bloody thing. You don't know what you're dealing with here."

"Give her the bloody bag, Mary," Grant yelled. Lawson could hear the man's breath rattling in his chest.

Then the kidnapper's voice rang out again. "Hand it over, Mrs. Grant. Or you won't see Adam again."

Lawson registered the horror on Cat's face as she looked desperately over her shoulder into the light. "No, wait," she shouted. "It's all going to be fine." She seemed to wrest the bag from her mother and take a step backwards.

Suddenly Grant sprang forward half a dozen paces, his hand disappearing inside his overcoat. "Damn it," he said. Then his voice rose. "I want my grandson and I want him now." His hand emerged, the dull sheen of an automatic pistol obvious in the glare of the light. "Nobody move. I've got a gun and I'm not afraid to use it. Bring Adam out now."

Later, Lawson would wonder at the collection of bad clichés that was Brodie Maclennan Grant. But at that moment, all he could feel was the weight of catastrophe as time seemed to slow. He started to run towards Grant as the businessman raised his arms in a two-handed shooter's stance. But before Lawson could take a second step, the light cut out, leaving him blind and helpless. He saw the flash of a muzzle near him, heard a shot, smelled cordite. Then a replay of the same sequence but this time from a distance. He tripped over a fallen branch and fell headlong. Heard a scream. A child crying. A high-pitched voice repeating, "Fuck." Then realized the voice was his.

A third shot rang out, this time from the woods. Lawson tried to stand, but hot spikes of pain spiralled up through his ankle. He rolled on his side, scrabbling for flashlight and radio. "Hold your fire," he yelled into the radio. "Hold your fire, that's an order." As he spoke, he could see flashlight beams criss-crossing the area as his men swarmed round the base of the rock.

"They've got a fucking boat," he heard somebody shout. Then a roar louder than the waves as the engine caught. Lawson closed his eyes momentarily. What a fiasco. He should have tried harder to make Grant refuse this set-up. It had been doomed from the start. He wondered what they'd managed to get away with. The kid, certainly. The money, probably. The daughter, maybe.

But he was wrong about Catriona Maclennan Grant. Terribly, horribly wrong.

MONDAY, 2ND JULY 2007; PETERHEAD

"Brodie Maclennan Grant had a gun?" Karen's voice rose to a squeak. "He fired a gun? And you kept that out of the report?"

"I had no choice. And it seemed like a good idea at the time," Lawson said with the cynical air of a man quoting his superiors.

"A good idea? Cat Grant died that night. In what sense was it a good idea?" Karen couldn't believe what she was hearing. The idea of such cavalier behaviour was completely alien to her.

Lawson sighed. "The world's changed, Karen. We didn't have a police complaints commissioner. We didn't have the kind of scrutiny you live with."

"Obviously," she said drily, remembering why he was where he was. "But still. You managed to cover up a civilian discharging a weapon in the middle of a police operation? Money talks, right enough."

Lawson shook his head impatiently. "It wasn't just money talking, Karen. The chief constable was thinking PR as well. Grant's only child was dead. His grandchild was missing. As far as the public was concerned, he was a victim. If we'd prosecuted him for the firearms offences, it would have looked like we were being vindictive—we can't catch the real villains, so we'll have you instead—that sort of thing. The view was that nobody's interests were served by revealing that Grant had been armed."

"Could it have been Grant's shot that killed Cat?" Karen demanded, forearms on the table, head thrusting like a rugby forward's.

Lawson shifted in his chair, leaning his weight to one side. "She was shot in the back. Work it out for yourself."

Karen leaned back in her chair, not liking the answer she came up with but knowing there would be nothing better coming from the man opposite her. "You were a right bunch of fucking cowboys in the old days, weren't you?" There was no admiration in her tone.

"We got the job done," Lawson said. "The public got what they wanted."

"The public didn't know the half of it, by all accounts." She sighed. "So we've got three gunshots, not the two that appear in the report?"

He nodded. "For all the difference it makes." He shifted again, angling his body towards the door.

"Is there anything else I should know about that didn't make it to the case file?" Karen said, reasserting herself as the person in control of the interview.

Lawson tilted his head back, eyeing the corner where the walls and ceiling met. He exhaled noisily, then pushed his lips out. "I think that's it," he finally said. He dragged his eyes back to meet her weary gaze. "We thought it was Fergus Sinclair at the time. And nothing's happened since to change my mind on that one."

Campora, Tuscany

The warmth of the Tuscan sun melted the stiffness in Bel's shoulders. She was sitting in the shade of a chestnut tree tucked away behind the cluster of houses at the tail end of Boscolata. If she craned her neck, she could see one corner of the terracotta tiled roof of Paolo Totti's ruined villa. Her more immediate view was, however, rather more appealing. On a low table in front of her was a jug of red wine, a bottle of water, and a bowl of figs. Around the table, her primary sources. Giulia, a young woman with a tumbled mane of black hair and skin marked with the angry puce scars of old acne, who made hand-painted toys for the tourist market in a converted pig sty; and Renata, a blond Dutch woman with a complexion the colour of Gouda, who worked part-time in the restoration department of the Pinoteca Nationale in nearby Siena. According to Grazia, who was leaning against the tree trunk shelling a sack of peas, the carabinieri had talked to both of the women already.

The social pleasantries had to be observed, and Bel contained herself while they chatted together. Eventually, Grazia moved them on. "Bel is also interested in what happened at the Totti villa," she said.

Renata nodded portentously. "I always thought someone would come asking about that," she said in perfectly enunciated Italian that sounded like computer-generated speech.

"Why?" Bel asked.

"They left so suddenly. One day they were here, the next day they were gone," Renata said.

"They went without a word," Giulia said, looking sulky. "I couldn't believe it. Dieter was supposed to be my boyfriend, but he didn't even say goodbye. I was the one who discovered they were gone. I went over to have coffee with Dieter that morning, just like I always did when they weren't setting off early for a show. And the place was deserted. As if they'd thrown everything they could grab hold of into the vans and just taken off. I haven't heard from that bastard Dieter since."

"When was this?" Bel asked.

"At the end of April. We had plans for the Mayday holiday,

but that all came to nothing." Giulia was clearly still pissed off.

"How many of them were there?" Bel said. Between them, Giulia and Renata counted them off on their fingers. Dieter, Maria, Rado, Sylvia, Matthias, Peter, Luka, Ursula, and Max. A mongrel mix from all over Europe. A motley crew that seemed on the face of it to have nothing to do with Cat Grant. "What were they doing there?" she asked.

Renata grinned. "I suppose you would say they were borrowing the place. They turned up last spring in two battered old camper vans and a flashy Winnebago and just moved in. They were very friendly, very sociable." She shrugged. "We're all a little alternative here in Boscolata. This place was a ruin back in the seventies when a few of us moved in illegally. Gradually we bought the properties and restored them to what you see now. So we were pretty sympathetic to our new neighbours."

"They became our friends," Giulia said. "The carabinieri are crazy, acting like they're criminals or something."

"So they just turned up without warning? How did they know the house was there?"

"Rado had a job at the cement works down in the valley a couple of years ago. He told me he used to go walking in the woods, and he came across the villa. So when they needed a place that was accessible to the main towns in this part of Tuscany, he remembered the villa and they came to stay," Giulia said.

"So what exactly did they do?" Bel asked, searching for some connection to the past at the heart of her inquiries.

Renata said, "They ran a puppet theatre." She seemed surprised that Bel hadn't known this. "Marionettes. Street theatre. During the tourist season, they had regular pitches. Firenze, Siena, Volterra, San Gimignano, Greve, Certaldo Alto. They did festivals too. Every little town in Tuscany has a festival of something—porcini mushrooms, antique salami-slicing machines, vintage tractors. So BurEst performed anywhere there was an audience."

"BurEst? How do I spell that?" Bel said.

Renata obliged. "It's short for Burattinaio Estemporaneo. They did a lot of improvisation."

"The poster from the villa—a black-and-white drawing of a puppeteer with some pretty strange marionettes—was that what they used for advertising?" Bel asked.

Renata shook her head. "Only for special performances. I only ever saw them use it when they did a performance in Colle Val d'Elsa for All Souls Day. Mostly, they used one with bright colours, sort of commedia dell'arte. A modern twist on the more traditional images of puppetry. It reflected their performance better than the monochrome poster."

"Were they popular?" Bel asked.

"I think they did OK," Giulia said. "They'd been in the south of France the summer before they came here. Dieter said Italy was a better place to work. He said the tourists were more open-minded and the locals were more tolerant of them. They didn't make a huge amount of money, but they did OK. They always had food on the table and plenty of wine. And they made everybody welcome."

"She's right," Renata said. "They weren't scroungers. If they ate dinner at your house, next time you ate with them." One corner of her mouth twitched downwards. "That's less usual than you'd think in these circles. They talk a lot about sharing and communality, but mostly they are even more selfish than the people they despise."

"Except for Ursula and Matthias," Giulia said. "They were more private. They didn't really socialize like the others did."

Renata snorted. "That's because Matthias thought he was in charge." She poured more wine for them all and continued. "It was Matthias who started the company, and he still liked everyone to treat him like he was the circus ringmaster. And Ursula, his woman, she bought into that whole thing. Matthias obviously took the lion's share of the income too. They had the best van, their clothes were always expensive hippy style. I think it was partly a generation thing—Matthias must be in his fifties, but most of the others were much younger. Twenties, early thirties at the very most."

It was all fascinating, but Bel was struggling to see what the link might be to Cat Grant's death and the disappearance of her son. This Matthias character sounded like the only one old enough to have had any connection to those distant events. "Does he have a son, Matthias?" she asked.

Both women looked at each other, puzzled. "There was no child with him," Renata said. "I never heard him speak of a son."

Giulia picked up a fig and bit into it, the purple flesh splitting and spilling seeds down her fingers. "He had a friend who came to visit sometimes. A British guy. He had a son."

Like all good reporters, Bel had an unquantifiable instinct for where the story lay. And that instinct told her she'd just hit gold. "How old was the son?"

Giulia licked her fingers clean while she considered. "Twenty? Maybe a bit older, but not much."

There were a dozen questions butting against each other inside Bel's head, but she knew better than to blurt them out in an urgent stream. She took a slow sip of her wine and said, "What else do you remember about him?"

Giulia shrugged. "I saw him a couple of times, but I only ever met him properly once. His name was Gabriel. He spoke perfect Italian. He said he'd grown up in Italy, he didn't remember ever living in England. He was studying, but I don't know where or what." She made an apologetic face. "Sorry, I wasn't that interested in him."

OK, it wasn't decisive. But it felt like a possibility. "What did he look like?"

Giulia looked more uncertain. "I don't know how to describe him. Tall, light brown hair. Quite good looking." She screwed her face up. "I'm not good at this kind of thing. What's so interesting about him anyway?"

Renata saved Bel from having to answer. "Was he at the New Year party?" she asked.

Giulia's face cleared. "Yes. He was there with his father."

"So he might be on a photograph," Renata said. She turned to Bel. "I had my camera with me. I took dozens of photographs that night. Let me get my laptop." She jumped up and headed back to her house.

"What about Gabriel's dad?" Bel asked. "You said he was British?"

"That's right."

"So how did he know Matthias? Was he British too?"

Giulia looked dubious. "I thought he was German. He and Ursula got together years ago in Germany. But he spoke Italian just like his friend. They sounded the same. So maybe he was British too. I don't know."

"What was Gabriel's dad called?"

Giulia sighed. "I'm not much use to you. I don't remember his name. I'm sorry. He was just another man my dad's age, you know? I was with Dieter, I wasn't interested in some old guy in his fifties."

Bel hid her disappointment. "Do you know what he does for a living? Gabriel's dad, I mean."

Giulia brightened, pleased that she knew the answer to something. "He's a painter. He paints landscapes for the tourists. He sells to a couple of galleries—one in San Gimignano and one in Siena. He also goes to the same sort of festivals that BurEst performed at, and sells his work there."

"Is that how he met Matthias?" Bel asked, trying not to feel disappointed that the mysterious Gabriel's father was not estate manager Fergus Sinclair. After all, an artist would fit right in with Cat's background. Maybe Adam's father was someone she knew from her student days. Or someone she'd met at a gallery or exhibition back in Scotland. There would be time to explore those possibilities later. Right now, she needed to pay attention to Giulia.

"I don't think so. I think they knew each other from way back."

As she spoke, Renata returned with her laptop. "Are you talking about Matthias and Gabriel's father? It's funny. It didn't seem as though they really liked each other that much. I don't know why I think that, but I do. It was more . . . you know how sometimes you stay in touch with someone because she's the only person left who shares the same past? You might not like them so much, but they give a connection back to something that was important. Sometimes it's family, sometimes it's a time of your life when important things happened. And you want to hold on to that link. That's how it seemed to me when I saw them together." As she spoke, her fingers were flying over the keyboard, summoning up a library of pictures. She placed the laptop where Giulia and Bel could see the screen, then came round behind them, leaning in so she could advance the shots.

It looked like half the parties Bel had ever been to. People sitting at tables drinking. People mugging at the camera.

People dancing. People getting more red in the face, more blurred around the eyes, and more uncoordinated as the evening wore on. Both of the Boscolata women giggled and exclaimed, but neither identified either Gabriel or his father.

Bel had almost given up hope when Giulia suddenly called out and pointed at the screen. "There. That's Gabriel in the corner." It wasn't the clearest of shots, but Bel didn't think she was seeing things. There were fifty years between them, but it wasn't hard to discern a resemblance between this boy and Brodie Grant. Cat's features had been a feminine translation of her father's striking looks. Unlikely though it was, a simulacrum of the original was staring out at her from a New Year party in an Italian squat. The same deep-set eyes, parrot nose, strong chin, and the distinctive thick shock of hair, only blond rather than silver. She dug in her handbag and pulled out a memory stick.

"Can I get a copy of that?" she asked.

Renata paused, looking thoughtful. "You didn't answer when Giulia asked why you are interested in this boy. Maybe you should answer now."

East Wemyss, Fife

River stripped off her heavy-duty gloves and straightened her back, trying not to groan. The trouble with working alongside her students was that she couldn't reveal any signs of weakness. Admittedly, they were a dozen or more years younger than her, but River was determined to demonstrate she was at least as fit as they were. So they might complain of aching arms and sore backs from shifting rock and rubble, but she had to maintain her Superwoman act. She suspected the only person she was kidding was herself, but that made no odds. The deception had to be maintained for the sake of her self-image.

She walked across the cave to where three of the students were sifting the dirt freed by the shifting of the rocks. So far, nothing of archaeological or forensic interest had turned up, but their enthusiasm seemed undiminished. River could remember her own earliest investigations; how the very fact of being involved in a real case was excitement enough to overcome the tedium of a repetitive, apparently fruitless task. She saw her own reactions mirrored in these students, and it made her happy to think that she had some responsibility for making sure the next generation of forensic investigators would bring that same commitment to speaking for the dead.

"Anything?" she said as she emerged from the shadows into the brilliance that illuminated their huddle.

Heads were shaken, negatives muttered. One of the archaeology postgrads looked up. "It'll get interesting when the labourers have finished clearing the rocks."

River grinned. "Don't let my anthropologists hear you calling them labourers." She glanced back at them affectionately. "With luck, they should have the bulk of the rocks out of the way by the end of the afternoon." They'd all been surprised by the discovery that the rock fall was only a few feet deep. In River's experience, cave falls tended to extend a long way back. A fault had to grow to a substantial size before it reached critical mass and brought a previously stable roof down. So when it collapsed, it took a lot of rock with it. But this was different. And that made it very interesting indeed.

Already, they'd removed the top seven or eight feet all the way back. A couple of the more intrepid among them had climbed up for a look when River had been off fetching lunchtime pies and sandwiches for everyone. They'd reported that it looked clear beyond the fall itself, apart from a few boulders that had rolled down from the main pile.

River walked outside to make a couple of phone calls, appreciating the salt air as a bonus. She'd barely finished speaking to her department secretary when one of the students burst out of the narrow entrance.

"Dr. Wilde," he shouted. "You need to come and see this."

CAMPORA, TUSCANY

Bel had pitched her story to provoke the maximum emotional response. From the stunned silence of Renata and Giulia, it looked as if she'd achieved her goal.

"That's so sad. I'd have been in bits if that had happened in my family," Giulia finally said, taking ownership of it in the style of a woman raised on soap operas and celebrity magazines. "That poor baby boy."

Renata was more objective. "And you think Gabriel might be that boy?"

Bel shrugged. "I have no idea. But that poster is the first definite lead there has been in over twenty years. And Gabriel looks incredibly like the missing boy's grandfather. It might be wishful thinking, but I wonder if we're on to something here."

Renata nodded. "So we must help in every way we can."

"I'm not talking to the carabinieri again," Giulia said. "Pigs."

"Hey," Grazia complained, rousing herself from her pea-shelling. "Don't you be insulting pigs. Our pigs are wonderful creatures. Intelligent. Useful. Not like the carabinieri."

Renata held her hand out. "Give me the memory stick. There's no point in talking to the carabinieri because they don't care about this case. Not like you do. Not like the family does. That's why we need to share everything with you." Expertly, she copied the picture on to Bel's memory stick. "Now we need to see if there are any more photos of Gabriel and his father."

By the end of the search, they had three shots where Gabriel appeared, though none of them was any clearer than the first. Renata had also found two images of his father—one in profile, one where half of his face was obscured by someone else's head. "Do you think anybody else has photos from that night?" Bel asked.

Both women looked dubious. "I don't remember anyone else taking pictures," Renata said. "But with mobile phones, who knows? I'll ask around."

"Thanks. And it would be helpful if you could ask if anyone else knew Gabriel or his father." Bel took the precious memory stick. As soon as she had the chance, she would send it to a colleague who specialized in enhancing dodgy photos of the great and the good doing things they shouldn't be doing with people they shouldn't be doing them with.

"I have a better idea," Grazia said. "Why don't I bring a pig down tonight? We can put it on the spit and you can meet everyone else. A nice bit of pork and a few glasses of wine and they'll be ready to tell you all they know about this Gabriel and his father."

Renata grinned and raised her glass in a toast. "I'll drink to that. But I'm warning you, Grazia, your pig might roast in vain. I don't think this guy was very sociable. I don't remember him joining in much with the party."

Grazia gathered her peapods together and stuffed them in a plastic bag. "Never mind. It's a good excuse to have some fun with my neighbours. Bel, are you staying down here or do you want a ride back up the hill?"

Now she had the prospect of gossiping with the whole community, Bel felt less urgency. "I'll come back now, and see you girls later," she said, draining her wine.

"Don't you want to know about the blood?" Giulia asked.

Caught halfway out of her chair, Bel nearly fell over. "The blood on the floor, you mean?" she said.

"Oh. You know about it." Giulia sounded disappointed.

"I know there's a bloodstain on the floor of the kitchen," Bel said. "But that's all I know."

"We went and had a look after the carabinieri left on Friday," Giulia said. "And the bloodstain was different from when I first saw it. The day after they left."

"Different how?"

"It's all brown and rusty now and soaked into the stone. But back then, it was still quite red and shiny. Like it was fresh."

"And you didn't call the cops?" Bel tried not to show her disbelief.

"It wasn't up to us," Renata said. "If the BurEst people had thought it was a police matter, they'd have made the call." She shrugged. "I know it seems strange to you, and if it had happened in Holland, I don't know that I would have done nothing. But things are different here. Nobody on the left trusts them. You saw how the Italian police reacted at the G8 in Genoa, the way they treated the protesters. Giulia asked a few of us whether she should call the police and we all agreed that the only thing that would achieve would be to give the cops an excuse to blame the puppeteers, no matter what happened."

"So you just blanked it?"

Renata shrugged. "It was in the kitchen. Who's to say it wasn't animal blood? It was none of our business."

Kirkcaldy

Karen crawled along the street, checking the house numbers. This was the first time she'd visited Phil Parhatka's new house in the centre of Kirkcaldy. He'd moved in three months before; kept promising a housewarming party but so far he hadn't delivered. Once upon a time, Karen had harboured dreams of them buying a place together some day. But she'd got past that. A guy like Phil was never going to be drawn to a dumpy wee thing like her, especially once her latest promotion set her in authority over him. Some men might like the idea of screwing the boss. Karen knew instinctively that wasn't part of Phil's fantasy life. So she'd chosen the maintenance of their friendship and close working relationship over what she classified as adolescent hankerings. If she was going to have to settle for being a career-driven spinster, she could at least make sure the career was as satisfying as it could be.

Part of the recipe for that job satisfaction was having someone to bounce ideas off. No individual detective was smart enough to see the whole picture of a complex investigation. Everyone needed a sounding board who saw things differently and was smart enough to articulate those differences. It was especially important in cold cases where, instead of leading a substantial team of officers, an SIO might have only one or two bodies at her disposal. And those foot soldiers usually didn't have the experience to make their input as valuable as she wanted. For Karen, Phil ticked all the boxes. And judging by the number of times he ran his cases past her, it was a two-way street.

Usually, they put their heads together in her office or in a quiet corner of a pub halfway between her house and his. But when she'd rung him on her way back from Peterhead, he'd already had a couple of glasses of wine. "I'm probably legal, but only just," he'd said. "Why don't you come round to my place? You can help me choose my living-room curtains."

Karen spotted the house number she was looking for and parked across Phil's driveway. She sat for a moment, wedded to the cop habit of checking out her surroundings before committing to leaving her vehicle. It was a quiet, unassuming street of stone semi-detached houses, square and solid, apparently as sound as when they'd first been built at the tail end of the nineteenth century. Gravel driveways and neat flowerbeds. Drawn curtains upstairs where children slept, shut off from the persistent daylight by heavy liners. She remembered how hard it had been to fall asleep on light summer evenings as a child. But her bedroom curtains had been thin. And her street had been noisy with music and conversations from the pub on the corner. Not like this. It was hard to believe the town centre was five minutes' walk away. It felt like the distant suburbs.

Alerted by the sound of her car, Phil had the door open before Karen was out of the driver's seat. Silhouetted against the light, he looked bigger. His pose contained the casual threat of the doorkeeper; one arm raised to lean on the door jamb, one leg crossed over the other, head cocked. But there was nothing threatening in his expression. His round, dark eyes twinkled in the light, and his smile crinkled his cheeks into creases. "Come away in," he greeted her, stepping back and gesturing for her to enter.

She stepped on to a perfect replica of a traditional Victorian tiled hallway, terracotta squares broken up with lozenges of white, blue, and claret. "Very nice," she said, noting the dado rail and the Lincrusta beneath it.

"My brother's girlfriend's an architectural historian. She's been through the place like a dose of salts. It's going to look like a bloody National Trust property before she's finished," he grumbled good-naturedly. "Turn right at the end of the hall."

Karen burst out laughing as she entered the room. "Christ, Phil," she giggled. "It was Colonel Mustard, in the Library, with the Lead Piping. You should be wearing a smoking jacket, not a Raith Rovers shirt."

He gave a rueful shrug. "You've got to see the funny side. Me, a cop, with the perfect body-in-the-library scenario." He waved a hand at the dark wooden bookshelves, the leather-topped desk, and the club chairs that flanked the elaborate fireplace. The room clearly hadn't been big to start with, but now it felt positively overstuffed. "She says this is what the master of the house would have had."

"In a house this size?" Karen said. "I think she's got delusions of grandeur. And somehow, I don't think he'd have gone for the tartan carpet."

The pink of embarrassment flushed his ears. "Apparently that's post-modern irony." He raised his eyebrows sceptically. "It's not all it seems, though," he said, brightening as he fiddled with one of the books. A section of shelving swung open to reveal a plasma screen TV.

"Thank God for that," Karen said. "I was beginning to wonder. Not much like the old place, is it?"

"I think I've outgrown the boy racer style of living," Phil said.

"Time to settle down?"

He shrugged, not meeting her eyes. "Maybe." He pointed to a chair and dropped into the one opposite. "So how was Lawson?"

"A changed man. And not in a good way. I've been thinking about it, driving back. He was always a tough bastard, but right up until we found out what he'd really been up to, I felt his motives were the right ones, you know? But the stuff he told me today . . . I don't know. It almost felt as if he was taking his chance to get his own back."

"What do you mean? What did he tell you?"

Karen held a hand up. "I'll get to that in a minute. I just want to let off steam, I suppose. I felt like he said what he did out of malice. Because he knew it would damage the reputation of the force, not because he wants to help us solve what happened to Cat and Adam Grant."

As she spoke, Phil reached for his pack of cigarillos and lit up. He hardly smoked in her company these days, she realized. There were so few places it was permissible. The familiar bittersweet aroma filled Karen's nostrils, strangely comforting after the day she'd had. "Does it matter what his motives are?" he said. "As long as what he's telling us is true?"

"Maybe not. And as it turns out, he did have something very interesting to tell us. Something that sheds a whole new light on what happened the night Cat Grant died. Apparently it wasn't just the cops and the kidnappers who were armed that night. Our pillar of society, Sir Broderick Maclennan Grant, had a gun with him. And he used it."

Phil's mouth hung open, smoke leaking into the air. "Grant had a shooter? You're kidding. How come we're only hearing about this now?"

"Lawson says the cover-up came from on high. Grant was a victim, nobody would be served by charging him. Bad PR, all that shit. But I think that decision completely altered the outcome." Karen pulled a file folder from her bag. She took out the drawing of the crime scene made by the forensic team at the time and spread it out between them. She pointed out where everyone had been standing. "Got that?" she asked.

Phil nodded.

"So what happened?" Karen said.

"The light went out, our guy fired high and wide, then there was another shot from behind Cat. The shot that killed her."

Karen shook her head. "Not according to Lawson. What he's saying now is that Cat and her mother were wrestling with the bag of money. Cat managed to get the bag and started to turn. Then Grant drew his firearm and demanded to see Adam. The light went out, Grant fired. There was a second shot, from beyond Cat. Then PC Armstrong fired wide."

Phil frowned, digesting what she'd said. "OK," he said slowly. "I don't quite see how that changes things."

"The bullet that killed Cat hit her in the back and exited through her chest. Into the sand. They never found the bullet. The wound wasn't consistent with Armstrong's weapon, so, given that Grant's gun was never mentioned, there was only one possible public explanation. The kidnappers killed Cat. Which made it a murder hunt."

"Oh, fuck," Phil groaned. "And of course, that's what totally puts the kybosh on any possibility of getting Adam back. These guys know they're going down for life, no question now that Cat's dead. They've got a bag of money and the kid. No way are they going to put themselves up for another confrontation with Grant. They're going to melt away into the night.

And Adam's just a liability now. He's worthless to them, alive or dead."

"Exactly. And we both know which side of the scales the weight comes down on. But there's more. The argument's always been that the nature of the wound plus the fact that Cat was shot in the back pointed inevitably to the kidnappers. But according to Lawson, Grant's gun could have inflicted the fatal wound. He says Cat had started to turn back towards the kidnappers when the light went out." She looked bleakly at Phil. "The chances are Grant killed his own daughter."

"And the cover-up cost him his grandson." Phil took a long drag on his cigarillo. "You going to talk to Brodie Grant about this?"

Karen sighed. "I don't see how I can avoid it."

"Maybe you should let the Macaroon deal with it?"

Karen laughed with genuine delight. "What a joy that would be. But we both know he'd throw himself off a tall building to dodge that bullet. No, I'm going to have to front him up myself. I'm just not sure of the best way to handle it. Maybe I'll wait till I see what the Italians have got for me. See if there's anything to sugar the pill." Before Phil could reply, Karen's phone rang. "Bloody thing," she muttered as she took it out. Then she read the screen and smiled. "Hello, River," she said. "How are you doing?"

"Never better." River's voice crackled and spat in her ear. "Listen, I think you need to get down here."

"What? Have you found something?"

"This is a crap connection, Karen. Better if you just come straight down."

"OK. Twenty minutes." She ended the call. "Get your slippers off, Sherlock. Bugger Brodie Grant. The good doctor has something for us."

Boscolata

Bel had to admit that Grazia knew how to create the perfect ambience for loosening tongues. As the sun slowly sank behind the distant hills and the lights of medieval hill towns scattered their dark slopes like handfuls of glitter, the inhabitants of Boscolata gorged on moist suckling pig accompanied by mounds of slow-roasted potatoes redolent with garlic and rosemary, and bowls of tomato salad pungent with basil and tarragon. Boscolata provided flagons of wine from their own vines, and Maurizio had added bottles of his home-made *vin santo* to the feast.

The knowledge that this unexpected celebration was in honour of Bel inclined them favourably towards her. She moved among them, chatting easily about all manner of things. But always, the conversation moved back to the puppeteers who had squatted Paolo Totti's villa. Gradually, she was able to conjure up a mental dossier of the people who had lived there. Rado and Sylvia, a Kosovan Serb and a Slovenian who had a gift for making puppets. Matthias, who had set up the company in the first place and now designed and built the sets. His woman, Ursula, responsible for organizing their schedule and greasing the wheels to make it possible. Maria and Peter from Austria, the principal puppeteers, and the three-year-old daughter they were determined to keep out of the formal school system. Dieter, a Swiss who was responsible for lighting and sound. Luka and Max, the second-string puppeteers who put up the posters, did most of the donkey work, and got to run their own show when a special presentation clashed with one of their regular pitches.

And then there were the visitors. Apparently, there had been plenty of those. Gabriel and his father hadn't stood out particularly, except that the father was clearly a friend of Matthias rather than a friend of the house. He kept himself to himself. Always polite but never actually open. Opinions varied as to his name. One thought it was David, another Daniel, a third Darren.

As the evening wore on, Bel began to wonder if there was any substance to her gut reaction to the photograph Renata had shown her. Everything else seemed so very insubstantial. Then, as she helped herself to a glass of *vin santo* and a handful of *cantuccini,* a teenage boy sidled up to her.

"You're the one who wants to know about BurEst, right?" he mumbled.

"That's right."

"And that lad, Gabe?"

"What do you know?" Bel said, moving closer to him, letting him feel they were in a conspiracy of two.

"He was there, the night they legged it."

"Gabriel, you mean?"

"That's right. I didn't say anything before, because I was supposed to be at school, only I wasn't, you know?"

Bel patted his arm. "Believe me, I know all about it. I didn't really get on with school either. Much more interesting things to be doing."

"Yeah, well. Anyway, I was in Siena, and I saw Matthias walking up from the station with Gabe. Matthias had been away for a couple of days. I didn't have anything better to do, so I followed them. They walked across town to the car park by the Porta Romana, and they came out in Matthias's van."

"Were they talking? Did they seem to be friendly?"

"They looked pretty fed up. They had their heads down, they weren't saying much. Not unfriendly, as such. Just like they were both pissed off about something."

"Did you see them again? Back here?"

The boy gave a jerky half-shrug. "I never saw them. But when I got back, Matthias's van was there. The others had gone off all the way to Grossetto to do a special performance. That's a good couple of hours' drive, so they'd gone by the time I got back. I just assumed Matthias and Gabe were in the villa." He gave a lairy grin. "Doing who knows what."

Judging by the blood on the floor, Bel thought, it wasn't anything like as much fun as this unimaginative young man was picturing. The real question was whose the blood was. Had BurEst fled because they'd come back to find their leader dead in a pool of his own blood? Or had they scattered because their leader had Gabriel's blood on his hands? "Thanks," she said, turning away and refilling a glass that had somehow become empty. She drifted away from the chattering crowd and walked along the fringe of the vineyard. Her informant had given her plenty to think about. Matthias had been gone for a few days. He came back with Gabriel. The two had been alone in the villa. By the middle of the following morning, the whole troupe had cleared out in a hurry, leaving the same posters once used by the Anarchist Covenant of Scotland and a large bloodstain on the floor.

You didn't have to be much of a detective to figure out that something had gone horribly wrong. But to whom? And maybe more important, why?

EAST WEMYSS

Summer in Scotland, Karen thought bitterly as she scrambled down the path to the Thane's Cave. Still daylight at nine o'clock, a thin drizzle soaking her, and the midges biting like there was no tomorrow. She could see them in a cloud round Phil's head as she followed him down to the beach. She was sure they were worse now than when she was a kid. Bloody global warming. The wee beasties got more vicious and the weather got worse.

As the path levelled out, she could see a couple of River's students huddled under an overhang, enjoying a fly fag. Maybe if she stood upwind, their smoke would see the midges off. Beyond them, River herself was pacing, phone to her ear, head down, long dark hair pulled back in a ponytail that stuck through the back of her baseball cap. What chilled Karen more than the rain was the gleam of the white paper overall River was wearing. The anthropologist turned, caught sight of them, and brought her call to an abrupt end. "Just telling Ewan not to expect me home for a few days," she said ruefully.

"So what have you got?" Karen asked, urgency stripping courtesy to the bone.

"Come on in and I'll show you."

They followed her into the cave, the working lights creating an abstract pattern of darkness and light that took a moment to adjust to. The clearing crew had stopped work and were sitting around eating sandwiches and drinking cans of soft drinks. Karen and Phil were magnets for their interest, and their eyes never left the cops.

River led the way to where the rock fall had blocked the passage leading back into the rock. Almost all of the boulders and small stones had been shifted, leaving a narrow opening. She played a powerful flashlight over the remaining rubble, showing that the actual fall was only about four feet deep. "We were surprised to find how shallow this fall was. We would have expected it to go back twenty feet or more. That made me suspicious right from the word go."

"What do you mean?" Phil asked.

"I'm not a geologist. But as I understand it from my colleagues in earth sciences, it takes a lot of pressure for a natural cave-in to happen. When they were mining underground around here, it produced a lot of stress in the rocks above, so you would get big fractures and falls. It's that scale of geological pressure that causes roof falls in old caves like this. They've been here for eight thousand years. They don't just collapse for no reason at all. But when they do go, it's like pulling the keystone out of a bridge. And you get a big fall." As she spoke, River kept moving the flashlight beam around, showing that the roof was surprisingly sound on either side of the fall. "On the other hand, if you know what you're doing, a small explosive charge will create a controlled fall that affects only a relatively small area." She raised her eyebrows at Karen. "The kind of thing that's done down mines all the time."

"You're saying this fall was created deliberately?" Karen said.

"You'd need an expert to give you a definitive yes or no, but based on what little I do know, I would say it looks that way to me." She swung round and shone the flashlight at a section of the cave wall about five feet above the ground. There was a roughly conical hole in the rock, black streaks staining the red sandstone. "That looks like a shot hole to me," River said.

"Shit," Karen said. "What now?"

"Well, when I saw this, I thought we needed to step very carefully once we'd cleared a path through. So I put on the J-suit and went through by myself. There's maybe three metres of passageway, then it opens out into quite a big chamber. Maybe five metres by four metres." River sighed. "It's going to be a bastard to process."

"And there's a reason to process it?" Phil asked.

"Oh yes. There's a reason." She shone the flashlight at their feet. "You can see the floor's just packed earth. Just inside the chamber, on the left, the earth is loose. It had been tramped down, but I could see it was different in texture from the rest of the floor. I set up some lights and a camera and started moving soil." River's voice had become cool and distant. "I didn't have to go far. About six inches down, I found a skull. I haven't moved it. I wanted you to see it in situ before we do anything further." She waved them back from the fall. "You'll need suits," she said, turning to the students. "Jackie, could you bring me over suits and bootees for DI Pirie and DS Parhatka?"

As they suited up, River ran through their options. It boiled down to either letting the students work on under River's close supervision or bringing in the force's own CSI team. "It's your decision," River said. "All I would say is that we're not only the budget option, we're the recently trained specialist option. I don't know what your level of expertise is in archaeology and anthropology, but I'm betting a small force like Fife is not going to have a team of leading-edge specialists on the payroll."

Karen gave her the look that reduced her DCs to childhood. "We've not had a case like this while I've been serving. Anything out of the usual run of things, we use outside experts all the time. The main issue is making sure the evidence will hold up in court. I know you're a qualified expert witness, but your students are not. I'm going to have to run this past the Macaroon, but I think we should continue with your crew. There have to be two video cameras running at all times, though, and you have to be on site whenever they're working." She fastened her suit, glad that Jackie had given her one big enough to accommodate her generous proportions. CSIs weren't always so considerate. She thought they sometimes did it on purpose, to make her feel uncomfortable in what they regarded as their domain. "Let's have a look at it, then."

River handed them each a flashlight. "I haven't taped off an approach route," she said, strapping on a head lamp. "Just stay as far to the left as you can."

They followed her bobbing light into the darkness. Karen gave a last look over her shoulder, but it was hard to see anything beyond Phil's silhouette. The quality of the air changed as they passed the remains of the rock fall, the saltiness replaced by a faint mustiness tinged with the acid of old bird and bat droppings. A dull glow ahead of them indicated the spotlight on the video camera that was still running.

River stopped as the walls fell back and broadened out into the chamber. Her flashlight augmented the camera light, revealing a small area of the earthen floor where the soil had been scraped back to create a shallow depression. Gleaming dull against the reddish brown earth was the unmistakable outline of a human skull.

"You were right," Phil said softly.

"You have no idea how much that pisses me off," Karen said heavily, taking in all the details. She turned away, gathering her thoughts. "Poor bastard, whoever you are."

Tuesday, 3rd July 2007; Glenrothes

Karen pulled into her parking space at headquarters and turned off the engine. She sat for a long moment, watching the rain reclaim her windscreen. This was not going to be the easiest morning of her career. She had a body, but technically it was the wrong body. She had to stop the Macaroon going off at half-cock and assuming this was one of Catriona Maclennan Grant's kidnappers. And to do that, she would have to admit she'd been working on something he didn't know about. Phil had been right. She shouldn't have indulged her desire for hands-on policing. It was small consolation that she'd made more headway in the case of Mick Prentice than the woolly suits would have done. Getting out of this without a formal reprimand would be a result.

Sighing, she grabbed her files and ran through the driving rain. She pushed the door open, head down, heading straight for the lifts. But Dave Cruickshank's voice made her break stride. "DI Pirie," he called. "There's a lady here to see you."

Karen turned as Jenny Prentice rose hesitantly from a chair in the reception area. She'd obviously made an effort. Her grey hair was neatly braided, and her outfit was clearly the one she kept for best. The dark red wool coat would normally have been insanely warm for July, but not this year. "Mrs. Prentice," Karen said, hoping the sinking of her heart wasn't as obvious on the outside.

"I need to speak to you," Jenny said. "It'll not take long," she added, seeing Karen glance at the wall clock.

"Good. Because I've not got long," Karen said. There was a small interview room off the foyer, and she led the way there. She dumped her folders on a chair in one corner, then sat opposite Jenny across a small table. She wasn't in the mood for coaxing. "I take it you've come to answer the questions I tried to ask you yesterday?"

"No," Jenny said, as mulish as Karen herself could be. "I've come to tell you to call it off."

"Call what off?"

"This so-called missing person hunt for Mick." Her eyes

locked defiantly with Karen's. "He's not missing. I know where he is."

It was the last thing Karen had expected to hear. "What do you mean, you know where he is?"

Jenny shrugged. "I don't know how else to put it. I've known for years where he was. And that he wanted nothing more to do with us."

"So why keep it a secret? Why am I only hearing this now? Don't you understand the concept of wasting police time?" Karen knew she was almost shouting, but she didn't care.

"I didn't want to upset Misha. How would you feel if somebody told you your father wanted nothing to do with you? I wanted to spare her."

Karen stared at her uncertainly. Jenny's voice and expression held conviction. But Karen couldn't afford to take her at face value. "What about Luke? Surely you want to do everything you can to save him? Doesn't Misha have the right to ask for his help?"

Jenny looked at her with contempt. "You think I haven't already asked him? I begged him. I sent him photos of wee Luke to try and change his mind. But he just said the boy was nothing to do with him." She looked away. "I think he's got a new family now. We don't matter to him. Men seem to manage that better than women."

"I'm going to need to talk to him," Karen said.

Jenny shook her head. "No way."

"Look, Mrs. Prentice," Karen said through mounting irritation, "a man has been reported missing. You say he's not but I have only your word for that. I need to confirm what you're telling me. I wouldn't be doing my job right if I didn't."

"And what happens then?" Jenny gripped the edge of the table. "What do you say when Misha asks you how the investigation's going? Do you lie to her? Is that part of your job? Do you lie to her and hope she never finds out the truth from some other polis somewhere down the line? Or do you tell the truth and let Mick break her heart all over again?"

"It's not my job to make those judgements. I'm supposed to find out the truth and then it's out of my hands. You need to tell me where Mick is, Mrs. Prentice." Karen knew she was hard to resist when she brought the full force of her personality to bear. But this defiant little woman was giving as good as she got.

"All I'm telling you is that you're wasting your time looking for a missing person that isn't missing. Call it off, Inspector. Just call it off."

Something about Jenny Prentice was striking a bum note. Karen couldn't identify what it was, but until she could, she wasn't giving an inch. She stood up and pointedly stepped away to pick up her folders. "I don't believe you. And anyway, you're too late, Jenny," she said, turning back to face her. "We've found a body."

She'd read about the colour draining from people's faces, but she'd never seen it before. "That can't be right." Jenny's voice was a whisper.

"It's right enough, Jenny. And the place we found it—thanks to you, we know it's a place where Mick used to hang about." Karen opened the door. "We'll be in touch." She waited pointedly while Jenny came to herself and shuffled out the door, a woman utterly reduced by words. For once, Karen had little sympathy. Whatever Jenny Prentice's motives for that little performance, Karen was certain now that a performance was what it had been. Jenny had no more idea of where Mick Prentice was than Karen herself.

All she had to do now was figure out why it was so important to Jenny that the police give up the hunt. Another encounter, another puzzle. They seemed to be walking hand in hand these days. Some weeks, you couldn't buy a straight answer.

"But that's fantastic news, Inspector." It wasn't often that Karen Pirie's reports brought Simon Lees satisfaction, far less delight. But he couldn't hide the fact that he was doubly pleased at what she had to tell him today. Not only had they uncovered a body that would progress a case dormant for over twenty years, but they'd also achieved it on a shoestring budget.

Then a horrible thought occurred to him. "It is an adult skeleton?" he said, apprehension tightening his chest.

"Yes, sir."

Why was she looking so miserable about it? She'd acted on a hunch and it had come good. In her shoes, he'd be like a dog with two tails. Well, actually, that was pretty much how he felt anyway. This was his operation ultimately; its results reflected credit on him as much as on his officers. For once, she'd brought him sunshine instead of shit. "Well done," he said briskly, pushing his chair back. "I think we should go straight over to Rotheswell and break the good news to Sir Broderick." Her pudding face ran through a series of different expressions, ending in what looked very like consternation. "What's wrong? You haven't told him already?"

"No, I haven't," she said slowly. "And that's because I'm really not convinced this has anything to do with Adam Grant's disappearance."

He understood the words, but it made no sense. She'd organized this whole operation on the basis that the cave fall had been discovered after the ransom disaster. She'd implied that one of the kidnappers could be lying underneath the rubble. He would never have authorized it otherwise. But now she seemed to be suggesting this body had nothing to do with the case she was supposed to be investigating. It was Alice-through-the-looking-glass stuff. "I don't understand," he said plaintively. "You told me you thought there might be a boat. Implied there might be a body. And you find a body. But instead of celebrating being right, you're telling me it's the wrong body."

"I couldn't have put it better myself," she said, daring to smile.

"But why?" He could hear himself almost howling, and he cleared his throat noisily. "Why?" he repeated, an octave lower.

She twisted in her seat and crossed her legs. "It's a bit difficult to explain."

"I don't care. Start somewhere. Preferably the beginning." Lees couldn't stop his hands clenching and unclenching. He wished he still had the stress ball his kids had given him one Christmas, the stress ball he'd thrown away because he was far too much in control to need something like that.

"We had a very unusual case come in the other day," she began. She sounded hesitant, a version of herself he'd never seen before. If this wasn't so infuriating, he'd almost have been able to enjoy that. "A man reported missing by his daughter."

"That's hardly unusual," he snapped.

"It is when the disappearance happened in 1984. At the height of the miners' strike," Karen shot straight back, all hesitancy gone. "I took a wee look at it, and discovered there were a couple of people who had good reason for wanting this guy out of the way. Both of them worked in the mining industry. Both of them knew about shot-firing rock. Neither of them would have been too hard-pressed to get their hands on explosives. And like I tried to explain to you before, sir, everybody round here knows about the caves." She paused momentarily and glared at him. It was a look that bordered on insubordination. "I knew you would never sanction digging out the rock fall on account of one striking miner on the missing list."

"So you lied?" Lees pounced. He wasn't taking this cavalier rebelliousness any longer.

"No, I didn't lie," she said calmly. "I was just a bit creative with the truth. That cave fall really was discovered after Catriona Maclennan Grant died. And the chopper couldn't find the boat the kidnappers escaped in. What I gave you was a reasonable hypothesis. But on the balance of probabilities, I'm saying this is more likely to be the body of Mick Prentice than some unknown kidnapper."

Lees could feel the blood pumping in his head. "Unbelievable."

"Actually, sir, I think you'd have to say we got a result. I mean, it's not like we spent all this money for nothing. At least we've got a body to show for it. OK, it maybe gives us more questions than answers. But you know, sir, we talk about it being our job to speak for the dead, to get justice for people who can't get it for themselves. If you look at it like that, this is an opportunity to serve."

Lees felt something snap inside his head. "An opportunity? What planet are you on? It's a bloody nightmare. You're supposed to be focusing all your resources on finding who killed Catriona Grant and what happened to her son, not farting around on some missing persons case from 1984. What am I supposed to say to Sir Broderick? 'We'll get round to your family once Inspector Pirie can be bothered.' You think you're a law unto yourself," he raged. "You just drive a coach and horses through protocol. You follow your hunches as if they were based on something more than a woman's intuition. You . . . you . . ."

"Careful, sir. You're bordering on sexism there," Karen said sweetly, her eyes wide with assumed innocence. "Men have intuition too. Only, you call it logic. Look on the bright side. If it is Mick Prentice, we've already put together a lot of information about what was going on around the time of his disappearance. We've got a head start on that murder inquiry. And it's not like we're ignoring the Grant case. I'm working closely with the Italian police, but these things take time. Of course, if I was to go out to Italy, it might speed things up . . . ?"

"You're going nowhere. Once this is all over you may not even be—" The phone rang across the end of his threat. He grabbed it. "I thought I said no calls, Emma? . . . Yes, I know who Dr. Wilde is . . ." He sighed harshly. "Fine. Send her in." He replaced the phone carefully and glared at Karen. "We will be revisiting this. But Dr. Wilde is here. Let's see what she has to say."

The woman who walked in was not what he'd expected. For a start, she looked like an adolescent still waiting for her growth spurt. Barely five feet tall, she was lean as a whippet. Dark hair pulled back from a face dominated by large grey eyes and a wide mouth accentuated the comparison. She wore construction boots, jeans, and a denim shirt faded almost white in places under a battered waxed waterproof jacket. Lees had never seen anyone who looked less like an academic. She held out a slim hand, saying, "You must be Simon Lees. It's a pleasure to meet you."

He looked at her hand, imagining the places it had been and the things it had touched. Trying not to shudder, he gripped her cool fingers briefly and gestured towards the other visitor's chair. "Thank you for your help," he said, attempting to put his anger at Karen back in its box for now.

"My pleasure," River said, sounding as if she meant it. "It's a great opportunity for me to work a live case with my students.

They get a lot of lab experience, but you can't compare that to the real thing. And they've done a terrific job."

"So it seems. Now, am I to assume you are here because you have something to report?" He knew he sounded stiff as one of her cadavers, but it was the only way he could keep himself under control. River exchanged a quick unreadable look with Karen, and he felt his temper rising again. "Or do you need access to more facilities? Is that it?"

"No. We have access to what we need. I just wanted to bring DI Pirie up to speed, and when DS Parhatka told me she was in a meeting with you, I thought I'd grab the chance to meet you. I hope I haven't interrupted anything?" River leaned forward, giving him the full benefit of a smile that reminded him of Julia Roberts'. It was hard to maintain anger in the teeth of a smile like that.

"Not at all," he said, feeling calmer by the second. "It's always good to put a face to the name."

"Even when it's such a stupid name," River said ruefully. "Hippy parents, before you ask. Now, you'll want to know what I've learned so far." She took out her pocket organizer and hit a couple of keys. "We worked late into the night to clear the skeleton and remove it from the shallow grave." She turned to Karen. "I've given Phil a copy of the video." Back to her organizer. "I did a preliminary examination early this morning and I can give you some information. Our skeleton is a male. He's over twenty and less than forty. There is some hair, but it's hard to tell what colour it was originally. It's taken up stain from the soil. He's had some dental work, so once you narrow down the possibilities we can follow up on that. And we'll be able to get DNA."

"When was he buried?" Lees asked.

River shrugged. "There are more extensive and expensive and time-consuming tests that we can do. But right now it's hard to be precise about how long he's been in the ground. However, I can say with a high degree of certainty that he was still alive for at least part of 1984."

"That's amazing," Lees exclaimed. "You people in forensics astonish me."

Karen gave him a cool stare. "Loose change in his pockets, was there?" she said to River.

"Actually, no pockets left to speak of," River said. "He was wearing cotton and wool so it's mostly gone. The coins were lying inside the pelvic girdle." She smiled at Lees again. "Sorry, not science this time. Just observation."

Lees cleared his throat, feeling foolish. "Is there anything else you can tell us at this stage?"

"Oh yes," River said. "He absolutely didn't die a natural death."

San Gimignano

As she drove round the parking lot for the third time in search of the elusive space, Bel cast her mind back to her memories of what San Gimignano had been like before it became a UNESCO World Heritage site. No question that it was worth the rating. The medieval inhabitants had used the soft grey limestone to build a huddled maze of streets around a central piazza with its ancient well. When it threatened to outgrow its massive city walls, they'd simply chosen to build tall rather than sprawl. Dozens of towers speared the skyline, giving a jagged, gap-toothed appearance from the plain below. Definitely unique. Definitely world heritage. And definitely ruined by its status.

Bel had first come to the spectacular Tuscan hill town in the early eighties when the streets were almost empty of tourists. There were proper shops back then—bakers, greengrocers, butchers, cobblers. Shops where you could buy washing powder or underpants or a comb. Locals actually drank coffee in the bars and cafés. Now, it had been transformed. The only opportunity to buy proper food and clothes was at the Thursday market. Apart from that, everything was targeted at tourists. Enotecas selling overpriced *vernaccia* and *chianti* that the locals wouldn't drink if you paid them. Leather stores, all selling identical factory-produced handbags and wallets. Souvenir shops and gelaterie. And of course, art galleries for those with more money than sense. Bel hoped it was the locals who were making the money, because they were the ones paying the highest price.

At least the streets wouldn't be too crowded so early in the day, ahead of the tour buses. Bel finally squeezed into a parking spot and headed for the vast stone portal that guarded the higher entry to the town. She had barely gone a hundred feet when she came to the first art gallery. The owner was just raising his shutters when she arrived. Bel checked him out; probably about her age, smooth skinned and dark haired, stylishly framed glasses that made his eyes look too small, a little too plump for the tight jeans and Ralph Lauren shirt. An appeal to his vanity would probably be the best approach. She waited patiently, then followed him inside. The walls were covered with prints and watercolours filled with the Tuscan clichés—cypress trees, sunflowers, rustic farmhouses, poppies. They were all well executed and pretty, but there wasn't one she would have hung on her walls. Production-line paintings for tour-bus punters ticking off the next place on the list. God, she'd become a snob in her old age.

The owner had settled himself behind a leather-topped desk, obviously meant to look antique. Probably about as old as his car, Bel thought. She approached, plastering her least predatory smile on her face. "Good morning," she said. "What a wonderful display of paintings. Anyone would be lucky to have these on their walls."

"We pride ourselves on the quality of our art works," he said without a flicker of irony.

"Amazing. They make the landscape come alive. I wonder if you can help me?"

He eyed her up from top to toe. She could see him pricing everything from her Harvey Nicks' sundress to her market stall straw bag before deciding how much wattage to put into his own smile. He must have liked what he saw; she got the full benefit of his cosmetic dentistry. "It will be my pleasure," he said. "What is it that you are looking for?" He stood up, adjusting his shirt to hide his extra pounds.

Apologetic smile. "I'm not actually looking for a painting," she said. "I'm looking for a painter. I'm a journalist." Bel took her business card from the pocket in her dress and handed it over, ignoring the wintry look that had replaced the previous warmth. "I'm looking for a British landscape painter who's been living over here, earning a living for the last twenty years or so. The difficult thing is that I don't know his name. It begins with a D—David, Darren, Daniel. Something like that. He has a son in his early twenties, Gabriel." She'd made printouts of Renata's photos and she took them out of her bag. "This is the son, and this is the painter I want to track down. My editor thinks there's a feature there." She shrugged. "I don't know. I need to talk to him, find out what his story is."

He glanced at the photos. "I don't know him," he said. "All my artists are Italian. Are you sure he's a professional? There are a lot of amateurs who sell stuff on the pavements. A lot of them are foreigners."

"Oh no, he's a professional all right. He's represented here and in Siena." She spread her hands to take in the stuff on the walls. "Obviously not good enough for you, though." She took the photos back. "Thanks for your time." He had already turned away, heading for his comfy chair surrounded by his soulless paintings. No sale, no more conversation.

There was, she knew, no shortage of galleries. Two more, then she'd have a coffee and a cigarette. Another three, then an ice-cream. Little treats to drag her through the work.

She didn't make it to the ice-cream. At the fifth gallery she tried, she hit gold. It was a light and airy space, paintings and sculptures spread out so they could be appreciated. Bel actually enjoyed walking through to the desk in the back. This time, it was a middle-aged woman behind a modern, functional desk piled with brochures and catalogues. She wore the crumpled linen uniform of the more relaxed class of Italian middle-class womanhood. She looked up from her computer and gave Bel a vague, slightly harassed look. "Can I help?" she said, her words running into each other.

Bel launched into her spiel. A few sentences in, the woman's hand flew to her mouth, her eyes widening in shock. "Oh my God," she said. "Daniel. You mean Daniel?"

Bel pulled the prints out and showed them to the woman. She looked as if she might burst into tears. "That's Daniel," she said. She reached out and touched Gabriel's head with her fingertips. "And Gabe. Poor sweet Gabe."

"I don't understand," Bel said. "Is there a problem?"

The woman took a deep, shuddering breath. "Daniel's dead." She spread her hands in a gesture of sorrow. "He died back in April."

Now it was Bel's turn to feel a jolt. "What happened?"

The woman leaned back in her chair and ran a hand through her curly black hair. "Pancreatic cancer. He was diagnosed just before Christmas. It was horrible." Tears sparkled in her eyes. "It shouldn't have happened to him. He was . . . he was such a lovely man. Very gentle, very reserved. And he loved his boy so much. Gabe's mother, she died giving birth. Daniel brought him up single-handed and he did a great job."

"I'm so sorry," Bel said. At least the blood on the floor of the villa Totti wasn't Daniel's. "I had no idea. I'd just heard about this terrific British artist who'd been making a living out here for years. I wanted to do a feature about him."

"Do you know his work?" The woman got up and beckoned Bel to follow her. They ended up in a small room at the back of the gallery. On the wall were a series of vibrant triptychs, abstract representations of landscape and seascape. "He did watercolours as well," the woman said. "The watercolours were more figurative. He could sell more of them. But these were what he loved."

"They're splendid," said Bel, meaning it. Really wishing she had met the man who had seen the world like this.

"Yes. They are. I hate that there will be no more of them." She reached out and brushed the textured acrylic paint with her fingertips. "I miss him. He was a friend as well as a client."

"I wonder if you can put me in touch with his son?" Bel said, not losing sight of why she was there. "Maybe I could still do that feature. A sort of tribute."

The woman smiled, a sad little curl of the lips. "Daniel always spurned publicity when he was alive. He had no interest in the cult of personality. He wanted his paintings to speak for him. But now . . . it would be good to see his work appreciated. Gabe might like it." She nodded slowly.

"Can you give me his phone number? Or address?" Bel said.

The woman looked slightly shocked. "Oh no, I couldn't do that. Daniel always insisted on privacy. Please, give me your card and I will contact Gabe. Ask him if he is willing to talk to you about his father."

"Is he still around, then?"

"Where else would he be? Tuscany is the only home he's ever known. His friends are all here. We're taking turns to make sure he has at least one decent meal a week."

As they walked back to the desk, it dawned on Bel that she hadn't discovered Daniel's surname. "Have you got a brochure or a catalogue of his work?" she asked.

The woman nodded. "I'll print it out for you."

Ten minutes later, Bel was back out on the street. At last she had something concrete to grab on to. The hunt was on.

Coaltown of Wemyss

The whitewashed cottages that lined the main street were spick and span, their porches supported by rustic tree trunks. They'd always been well maintained because they were what people saw when they travelled through the village. These days, the back streets looked just as smart. But Karen knew it hadn't always been like that. The hovels of Plantation Row had been a notorious slum, ignored by their landlord because what no eye from polite society ever saw was not worth bothering with. But even from the doorstep of this particular cottage, Karen suspected that somehow, if Effie Reekie had found herself in a hellhole, she'd have turned it into a little paradise. The front door looked as if it had been washed down that morning, there wasn't a dead head in the window boxes, and the net curtains hung in perfect pleats. She wondered if Effie and her mother had possibly been twins separated at birth.

"Are you going to knock or what?" Phil said.

"Sorry. I was just having a moment of déjà vu. Or something." Karen pressed the doorbell, feeling guilty for leaving her fingerprint on it.

The door opened almost at once. The sense of being in a time warp continued. Karen hadn't seen a woman with a scarf turbanning her head like that since her grandmother died. With her overall and rolled-up sleeves Effie Reekie resembled a pensioned-off version of Rosie the Riveter. She looked Karen up and down, as if gauging whether she was clean enough to be allowed across the doorstep. "Aye?" she said. It wasn't a welcome.

Karen introduced herself and Phil. Effie frowned, apparently affronted to have police officers at her door. "I never saw anything or heard anything," she said abruptly. "That's always been my policy."

"We need to talk to you," Karen said gently, sensing the fragility the elderly woman was desperately hiding.

"No, you don't," Effie said.

Phil stepped forward. "Mrs. Reekie," he said, "even if you don't have anything to say to us, I would be your pal for life if you could see your way to making us a cup of tea. I've a throat on me like the Sahara."

She hesitated, looking from one to the other with anxious eyes. Her face scrunched up with the wrestle of hospitality versus vulnerability. "You'd better come in, then," she said at last. "But I've got nothing to tell you."

The kitchen was immaculate. River could have conducted

an autopsy on the table without risk of contamination. Karen was pleased to see she'd guessed right. Like her mother, Effie Reekie viewed every available surface as a depository for ornaments and knick-knacks. It was, Karen thought, a desperate waste of the planet's resources. She tried not to think of all the crap she'd brought home from school trips. "You've got a lovely home," she said.

"I've always tried to keep it nice," Effie said as she busied herself with the kettle. "I would never let Ben smoke in the house. That was my man, Ben. He's been dead now five years, but he was somebody round these parts. Everybody knew Ben Reekie. There wouldn't be the bother there is in this street these days if my Ben was still alive. No, siree. There would not."

"It's Ben we need to talk to you about, Mrs. Reekie," Karen said.

She swung round, eyes wide, rabbit in the headlights. "There's nothing to talk about. He's been dead these five years. Cancer, it was. Lung cancer. Years of smoking. Years of branch committee meetings, all of them smoking like chimneys."

"He was the branch secretary, wasn't he?" Phil asked. He was studying a group of decorative plates mounted on the wall. They represented various milestones in trade union history. "A big job, especially during the strike."

"He loved the men," Effie said vehemently. "He'd have done anything for his men. It broke his heart to see the way that bitch Thatcher brought them down. And Scargill." She brought their tea to the table with a clatter of china. "I never had any time for King Arthur. Into the valley of death, that's where he led them. It would have been a different story if it had been Mick McGahey running the show. A very different story. He had respect for the men. Like my Ben. He had respect for his men." She gave Karen a look that bordered on the desperate.

"I understand that, Mrs. Reekie. But it's time now to set the record straight." Karen knew she was chancing her arm. Mick Prentice could have been mistaken. Ben Reekie might have kept his own counsel. And Effie Reekie might be determined not to think about the way her husband had breached the trust of the men he professed to love.

Effie's whole body seemed to clench. "I don't know what you're talking about." It was a shrill denial, its deceit obvious.

"I think you do, Effie," Phil said, joining the two women at the table. "I think it's been eating away at you for a long time."

Effie covered her face with her hands. "Go away," she said, her words muffled. She was shivering now, like a sheep that had just been sheared.

Karen sighed. "It can't have been easy for you. Seeing how hard everybody else had it, when you were doing all right."

Effie grew still and took her hands away from her face. "What are you talking about?" she said. "You surely don't think he took it for himself?" Affront had given her strength. That or made her careless.

Fuck, fuck, fuck. Karen realized she had completely misjudged the situation. But if she had, so could others. Others like Mick Prentice. Mick Prentice, whose best friend had been a union official. Who might even have been complicit in what Ben Reekie was doing. Thoughts racing, she pulled herself back into the conversation.

"Of course we don't think that," Phil said. "Karen just meant the fact that you still had a wage coming in."

Effie looked uncertainly at them both. "He only did it after they started sequestering the union funds," she said. The words spilled out as if it was a relief to let them loose. "He said, what was the point in passing money through to the branch when they'd just hand it on to Head Office. He said money raised locally should go to support local miners, not be shuffled off to Buffalo." She managed a piteous smile. "That's what he always used to say. 'Not be shuffled off to Buffalo.' He just took some here and there, not enough for the high-ups to notice. And he was very discreet about passing it out. He got Andy Kerr to go through the welfare request letters and he'd hand it out where it was most needed."

"Did anybody find out?" Phil asked. "Anybody catch him at it?"

"What do you think? They'd have strung him up first and asked questions afterwards. The union was sacred round here. He'd never have walked away in one piece if anybody had so much as suspected."

"But Andy knew." Karen wasn't ready to give up yet.

"No, no, he never knew. Ben never said he was giving them money. He just asked Andy to prioritize them, supposedly for branch relief. Except there wasn't any branch relief by then because all the funds were going to national level." Effie rubbed her hands as if they hurt. "He knew he couldn't trust anybody with that. You see, even if they'd believed he was doing it for the men and their families, they'd still have seen it as treason. Everybody was supposed to put the union first, especially officials. What he did, it would have been unforgivable. And he knew it."

San Gimignano

Bel finally found a bar that wasn't crammed with tourists, tucked away in a back street. The only patrons were half a dozen old men playing cards and drinking small glasses of dark purple wine. She ordered an espresso and a water and sat down by the back door, which was open on to a tiny cobbled yard.

She spent a few minutes looking at the catalogue she'd picked up at the gallery. Daniel Porteous had been an artist whose work she'd have happily lived with. But who the hell had he been? What was his background? And had his path truly crossed Cat's, or was Bel making bricks without straw? Just because Daniel Porteous was an artist and he had a loose connection to the place where the posters had been found didn't mean he was involved with the kidnapping. Maybe she was looking at the wrong man. Maybe the link was Matthias, the man who designed the puppets and their stage sets. The man who might either be a killer or a victim.

Still looking at the reproductions of Porteous's work, she called her work experience student Jonathan on her mobile.

"I tried to get hold of you last night," he said. "But your mobile was switched off. So I rang the ice maiden at Rotheswell and she said you were unavailable."

Bel laughed. "She does like to make herself important, doesn't she? Sorry I missed you last night. I was at a party."

"A party? I thought you were supposed to be being Nancy Drew?"

Part of her thought Jonathan's cheeky flirtatiousness was marginally inappropriate. But its absurdity amused her so she let him play. "I am. The party was in Italy."

"In *Italy*? You're in *Italy*?"

Bel quickly brought Jonathan up to speed. "So now you have the inside track," she wound up.

"Wow," Jonathan said. "Who knew this was going to be so exciting? None of my mates are having an internship like this. It's like Woodward and Bernstein, hot on the trail of Watergate."

"It's nothing like that," Bel protested.

"Of course it is. You told me there was blood on the villa floor. People generally don't run from household accidents or suicide, so that rather suggests that somebody was killed. And in a situation that ties in with murder and kidnap going back twenty-two years. Bel, there is at least one very unpleasant person out there and you are definitely hot on his trail."

"At the moment, Jonathan, what I'm on the trail of is a young man who's just lost his father. How scary can that be?" Bel said, her tone light and easy.

Suddenly serious, Jonathan said, "Bel, they're not all as charming and harmless as me. We can be savages. You've done enough stories about rape and murder to have no illusions about that. Stop treating me like a child. This isn't a game. Promise me you'll take it seriously."

Bel sighed. "When I get to something that looks serious, I will take it seriously, Jonathan. I promise. Now, meanwhile, I need you to do something for me."

"Of course, whatever you need. I don't suppose it involves a visit to Tuscany?"

"It involves a visit to the Family Records Centre in Islington to find out what you can about a man called Daniel Porteous. He'd be late forties, early fifties. He died in April in Italy, but I'm not sure where exactly. And besides, Italian death certificates have almost no information on them. So I'm looking for his birth certificate, maybe a marriage certificate. Can you do that for me?"

"I'm on it. I'll get back to you as soon as I've got anything. Thanks, Bel. It's great being involved in something as meaty as this."

"Thanks," Bel said to emptiness. She sipped her espresso and thought. She wasn't convinced the gallery owner would come up trumps as far as Gabriel Porteous was concerned. She was going to have to do some serious digging herself. The records would be in the provincial capital, Siena. There was no point in heading over there now. By the time she made it, everyone would have disappeared for the day. Afternoons and Italian bureaucracy were unhappy bedfellows.

There was nothing else for it. She was going to have to go back to Campora and lie by Grazia's pool. Maybe call Vivi-anne, catch up on family life. Sometimes life was just too, too hard.

EDINBURGH

Karen reclined the car seat back from bolt upright and settled herself in for the drive to Edinburgh. "I tell you," she said. "My head's nipping with this case. Every time I think I'm making sense of it, something trips me up."

"Which case did you have in mind? The one the Macaroon thinks you're prioritizing or the one you're actually working?" Phil said, turning on to the back road that would bring them to a farm tearoom by the motorway. One thing about cold cases was that you could generally manage to eat at regular times. There wasn't the pressure of the clock ticking before an-other offence was committed. It was a regime that suited both of them just fine.

"I can't do anything about Cat Grant until I get a proper report from the Italian police. And they're not exactly going hell for leather. No, I'm talking about Mick Prentice. First, ev-erybody thinks he's gone to Nottingham. But now it looks like he never left the Wemyss alive. He never went with the scabs, even though one of them confused the issue by sending money to Jenny. But the one thing we did learn from the scabs is that Mick was alive and well and walking round the Newton a good twelve hours after Jenny claims he walked out."

"Which is odd," Phil said. "If he was leaving her, you'd think he'd be long gone. Unless he was just trying to teach her a lesson. Maybe he'd stayed away for hours to wind her up. Maybe he was on the way back home and something happened to divert him."

"It certainly sounds like something knocked him out of character. The guys going scabbing obviously expected him to lose his head with them. When they saw him, they thought they were in for a tongue-lashing or a fight. But all they got was him pleading with them, looking like he was ready to burst into tears."

"Maybe that was the night he found out there was something going on between Jenny and Tom Campbell," Phil suggested. "That would have knocked his confidence for six."

"Maybe." She sounded unconvinced. "If you're right, he would have been in a state. He wouldn't have wanted to go home. So maybe he crashed with his pal Andy in the cottage in the woods."

"If he did, why did nobody see him again after that night? You know what it used to be like round here. When people split up, they didn't leave town. They just moved three houses down the street."

Karen sighed. "Fair enough. But he could still have gone to Andy's. It could have played out a different way. We know Andy was on the sick with depression. And we know from his sister that he liked to go up into the Highlands, walking. What if Mick decided to go with him? What if they both had an accident and their bodies are lying in some ravine? You know what it's like up there. Climbers go missing and they're never found. And that's just the ones we know about."

"It's possible." Phil signalled and turned into the parking lot. "But if that's what happened, whose body is it in the cave? I think it's a lot simpler than you're making out, Karen."

They walked into the café in silence. They ordered steak pie, peas, and new potatoes without looking at the menu, then Karen said, "Simpler how?"

"I think you're right, he did go to Andy's. I don't know if he was planning on leaving for good or just putting a bit of space between him and Jenny. But I think he told Andy about Ben Reekie. And I think there was some sort of confrontation. I don't know if Andy lost the place with Mick, or if Ben came round and it all got out of hand. But I think Mick died in that cottage that night."

"What? And they took him down the cave to get rid of him? That seems a bit elaborate. Why not just bury him in the woods?"

"Andy was a country man. He knew bodies don't stay buried in shallow graves in woodland. Putting him in the cave then engineering a rock fall was a much safer place to put him. And a lot more private than trying to dig a grave in the middle of the Wemyss woods. Remember what it was like back then. Every bit of woodland was alive with poachers trying to get a rabbit or even a deer to put on the table."

"You've got a point." Karen smiled an acknowledgement at the waitress who brought their coffees. She added a heaped spoonful of sugar to hers and stirred slowly. "So what happened to Andy? You think he went off and topped himself?"

"Probably. From what you've told me, he sounds like the sensitive kind."

She had to admit it made sense. Phil's distance allowed

him to see the case more clearly. Smart though she was, she knew when to step back and let someone else consider the facts. "If you're right, I suppose we'll never know how it panned out. Whether it was between Andy and Mick, or whether Ben Reekie was in the picture too."

Phil smiled, shaking his head. "That's one theory we can't run past Effie Reekie. Not unless we want another body on our hands."

"She'd stroke out on the spot," Karen agreed.

He chuckled. "Of course, this could all be a wild-goose chase if Jenny was telling the truth when she told you to lay off."

Karen snorted. "Fantasy island, that line. I reckon she's trying to shut down the aggravation. She wants us out of her hair so she can get back to her life of martyrdom."

Phil looked surprised. "You think she rates her own peace and quiet above her grandson's life?"

"No. She's incredibly self-absorbed, but I don't think she sees it in those terms. I think deep down she feels some responsibility for Mick disappearing. And that means she has to carry some of the guilt for his unavailability to be a donor for Luke. So she's trying to offload the guilt by getting us to stop looking for him so she can go back to hiding her head in the sand like before."

Phil scratched his chin. "People are so fucked up." He sighed.

"True enough. At least this jaunt will get us some answers."

"Maybe. But it makes you wonder," Phil said.

"Makes you wonder what, exactly?"

He pulled a face. "We're going all the way to Edinburgh to take a DNA sample so River can compare it to the corpse. But what if Misha's not Mick's kid? What if she's Tom Campbell's bairn?"

Karen gave him an admiring look. "You have a truly evil mind, Phil. I think you're wrong, but it's a beautiful thing all the same."

"You want to take a bet on the DNA showing it's Mick Prentice?"

They both leaned back to let the waitress put the piled plates of food in front of them. The aroma was killer. Karen wanted to pick up the plate and inhale it. But first she had to answer Phil. "No," she said. "And not because I think Misha might be Tom Campbell's kid. There's other possibilities. River says it's the back of the skull that's smashed in, Phil. If Andy Kerr killed Mick Prentice, it was in the heat of the moment. He would never have crept up behind him and caved his head in. Your theory's neat enough, but I'm not convinced." She smiled. "But then, that's why you love me."

He gave her an odd look. "You're always full of surprises."

Karen swallowed a divine mouthful of meat and pastry. "I want some answers, Phil. Real answers, not just the daft notions you and me dream up to fit what we know. I want the truth."

Phil cocked his head, considering her. "Actually," he said, "*that's* why I love you, ma'am."

An hour later, they were standing on the doorstep of the Marchmont tenement where Misha Gibson lived. Karen was still wondering whether there had been anything more than a tease in Phil's words. She'd thought for a long time that nothing was off limits between them. Apparently she'd been wrong. She certainly wasn't going to ask him what he'd meant. She pressed the buzzer again, but there was no reply.

A voice from behind them said, "Are you looking for Misha?"

"That's right," Phil said.

An elderly man stepped round them, forcing Karen to move away from the door or be trampled on. "You'll not find her in at this time of day. She'll be down at the Sick Kids' with the boy." He looked pointedly at them. "I'm not letting you in and I'm not putting my code in while you're standing there looking."

Karen laughed. "Very commendable, sir. But at the risk of sounding like a cliché, we are the police."

"That's no guarantee of honesty these days," the old man said.

Taken aback, Karen stepped away. What was the world coming to when people thought the police would burgle them? Or worse? She was about to protest when Phil put his hand on her arm. "No point," he said softly. "We've got what we need."

"I tell you," Karen said when they were out of earshot. "They sit watching their American cop shows where every other cop is bent and they think that's what we're like. It makes me mad."

"That's a bit rich, coming from the woman who put the assistant chief constable behind bars. It's not just the Americans," Phil said. "You get people who take the piss everywhere. That's where the scriptwriters get their ideas from."

"Oh, I know. It just offends me. All the years I've been in this job, Lawson's the only truly bad apple I've ever come up against. But that's all it takes for people to lose all respect."

"You know what they say: Trust is like virginity. You can only lose it once. So, you ready for 'good cop, bad cop'?" They paused on the kerb to wait for a break in the traffic and headed on down the hill to the hospital.

"Count me in," Karen said.

Finding Luke Gibson's ward was easy but harrowing. It was impossible to avoid the presence of ill children, the images of their sickness burning themselves into memory. It was, Karen thought, one of the few upsides of being childless. You didn't have to stand by impotent as your kid suffered.

The door to Luke's room was open and Karen couldn't stop herself watching mother and son together for a few minutes. Luke seemed very small, his face pale and pinched but still hanging on to a young boy's prettiness. Misha was sitting on the bed next to him, reading a Captain Underpants book. She was doing all the voices, making the story come alive for her boy, who laughed out loud at the bad puns and the daft storyline.

Finally, she cleared her throat and stepped inside. "Hi, Misha." She smiled at the boy. "You must be Luke. My name's Karen. I need to have a wee word with your mummy. Is that OK?"

Luke nodded. "Sure. Mum, can I watch my *Dr. Who* DVD if you're going away?"

"I'll be right back," Misha said, scrambling off the bed. "But yeah, you can have the DVD on." She reached for a personal DVD player and set it up for him.

Karen waited patiently, then led her into the corridor, where Phil was waiting. "We need to talk to you," Karen said.

"That's fine," Misha said. "There's a parents' room down the hall." She set off without waiting for a response, and they followed her into a small, brightly decorated room with a coffee vending machine and a trio of sagging couches. "It's where we escape to when it all gets too much." She gestured at the sofas. "It's amazing what you can catnap on after twelve hours sitting by a sick kid's bed."

"We're sorry to intrude—"

"You're not intruding," Misha interrupted. "It's good that you've met Luke. He's a wee doll, isn't he? Now you understand why I'm willing to pursue this even though my mother doesn't like you poking into the past. I told her she was out of order on Sunday. You need to ask these questions if you're going to find my dad."

Karen flashed a quick glance at Phil, who looked as surprised as she felt. "Did you know your mother came to see me this morning?" she said.

Misha frowned. "I had no idea. Did she tell you what you wanted to know?"

"She wanted us to give up looking for your father. She said she didn't think he was missing. That he'd walked out on the pair of you from choice and that he didn't want to come back."

"That makes no sense," Misha said. "Even though he did walk out on us, he wouldn't turn his back on his own grandson if he needed his help. All I've heard about my dad was that he was one of the good guys."

"She says she's trying to protect you," Karen said. "She's scared that if we do find him he'll reject you for a second time."

"Either that or she knows more about his disappearance than she's letting on," Phil said grimly. "What you probably don't know is that we've found a body."

Campora

Bel sat on her tiny terrace, watching the sky and the hills range through the spectrum as the sun set slowly and gloriously. She picked at the cold leftovers of pork and potato that Grazia had left in her fridge, considering her next move. She wasn't relishing the battle with Italian bureaucracy that lay ahead of her, but if she was to find Gabriel Porteous, it would have to be faced. She pulled out Renata's prints again, wondering whether she was imagining the resemblance.

But again, it leapt off the page at her. The deep-set eyes, the curved beak of the nose, the wide mouth. All mimicking Brodie Grant's distinctive features. The mouth was different, it was true. The lips were fuller, more shapely. Definitely more kissable, Bel thought, chiding herself instantly for the thought. The hair was a different colour too. Both Brodie Grant and his daughter had had hair so dark it was almost black. But this boy's hair was much lighter, even allowing for the bleaching of the Italian sun. His face was broader too. There were points of difference. You wouldn't mistake Gabriel Porteous for the young Brodie Grant, not judging by the photos Bel had seen around Rotheswell. But you might take them for brothers.

Her thoughts were interrupted by the phone. With a sigh, she picked it up. It was a pain that caller ID didn't always work abroad. You could never tell whether the person on the other end was someone you were trying to avoid. And letting calls go to voicemail so you could screen them soon became hideously expensive. Plus, being partly responsible for her nephew meant she could never ignore the mystery callers. "Hello?" she said cautiously.

"Bel? It's Susan Charleson. Is this a good moment?"

"Yes, perfect."

"I got your e-mail. Sir Broderick asked me to tell you he's very pleased with your progress so far. He wanted to know whether you needed anything at this end. We can organize record searches, that sort of thing."

Bel bit back a rueful laugh. She'd spent her working life doing her own dirty work, or else persuading others to do it for her. It hadn't occurred to her that working for Brodie Grant meant she could offload all the boring bits. "It's all in hand," she said. "Where you could give me a hand is on the personal stuff. I can't help thinking there must be a point in her past where Catriona's life intersected either with Daniel Porteous or this Matthias, who might be German or British. I suppose he might even be Swedish, given that's where Catriona studied. I need to find out when and where that happened. I don't know if she kept diaries or an address book? Also, when I get back, I could really do with tracking down her female friends. The sort of women she would confide in."

Susan Charleson gave a well-bred little laugh. "You're going to be disappointed, then. You might think her father plays things close to his chest, but Catriona made him look like a soul-barer. She was the ultimate cat who walks alone. Her mother was her best friend, really. They were very close. Apart from Mary, the only person who really got inside Cat's head was Fergus." She left the name dangling in the air between them.

"I don't suppose you know where I'll find Fergus?"

"You could talk to his father when you get back. He often visits his family around this time of year," Susan said. "It's not something Willie feels the need to communicate to Sir Broderick. But I'm aware of it."

"Thank you."

"And I'll see what I can do about diaries and address books. Don't hold your breath, though. The trouble with artists is that they let their work do the talking. When will you be back?"

"I'm not sure. It depends how I get on tomorrow. I'll let you know."

There was nothing more to say, no pleasantries. Bel couldn't remember the last time she'd failed so completely to make a connection with another woman. She'd spent her adult life learning how to get people to like her enough to confide things they didn't really want to tell anyone. With Susan Charleson, she had failed. This job that had started out as little more than an off-chance of persuading a famously reclusive man to talk had exposed her to herself in the most unexpected of ways.

What next, she wondered, taking a long sip of her wine. What next?

Wednesday, 4th July 2007; East Wemyss

Some American woman on the radio was belting out a cracking alt-country song about Independence Day. Only this wasn't about the Stars and Stripes, it was about a radical approach to domestic violence. As a police officer, Karen couldn't approve; but as a woman, she had to admit the song's solution had its appeal. If Phil had been there, she would have bet him a pound to a gold clock that the man she was about to meet wouldn't have had "Independence Day" blasting out of his car radio.

She drove slowly up the narrow street that led to what had been the pithead and offices of the Michael colliery. There was nothing there now apart from a scarred area of hard standing where the canteen and wages office had been. Everything else had been landscaped and transformed. Without the rust-red pylon of the winding gear it was hard to orientate herself. But at the far end of the asphalt, a single car sat pointing out to sea. Her rendezvous.

The car she pulled up beside was an elderly Rover, buffed to within an inch of its life. She felt faintly embarrassed about the collection of dead insects on her number plate. The Rover's door opened in synch with her own and both drivers got out simultaneously, like a choreographed shot from a film. Karen walked to the front of her car and waited for him to join her.

He was shorter than she expected. He must have struggled to make the five-feet-eight minimum for a cop. Maybe his hair had tipped him over the edge. It was steel grey now, but the quiff would have put Elvis to shame. He wouldn't have been allowed the DA and the sideburns when he was a serving officer, but when it came to hairstyle, Brian Beveridge had taken full advantage of retirement.

Like Elvis, he'd piled on the beef since his days of strutting his stuff on the streets of the Wemyss villages. The buttons of his immaculate white shirt strained over a substantial belly, but his legs were incongruously slim and his feet surprisingly dainty. His face had the florid tones and fleshiness of a man heading for a cardiovascular disaster. When he smiled, his cheeks became tight pink balls, as if someone had stuffed them with cotton wool. "DI Pirie?" he enquired cheerfully.

"Karen," she said. "And you must be Brian? Thanks for coming out to meet me." It was like shaking hands with the Pillsbury Dough Boy, all soft, engulfing warmth.

"It's better than dottering about in the garden," he said, his thick Fife accent untempered. "I'm always happy to help. I walked the beat in these villages for thirty years and, if I'm honest, I miss that sense of knowing every pavement and every house. Back then, you could make a career out of being a beat bobby. There was no pressure to go for promotion or the CID." He rolled his eyes. "There I go. I promised my wife I wasn't going to do my Dixon of Dock Green impersonation, but I can't help myself."

Karen laughed. She liked this cheery little man already, even though she was well aware that working alongside him back in the day would have been a different matter. "I bet you remember the Catriona Maclennan Grant case," she said.

Suddenly sombre, he nodded. "I'll never forget that one. I was there that night—of course, you know that, it's why I'm here. But I still dream about it sometimes. The gunshots, the smell of the cordite on the sea air, the screams and cries. All these years later, and what have we got to show for it? Lady Grant in her grave alongside her daughter. Jimmy Lawson in the jail for the rest of his life. And Brodie Grant, master of the bloody universe. New wife, new heir. Funny how things turn out, eh?"

"You can never tell," Karen said, happy to buy into the clichés for the time being. "So, can you talk me through it as we walk down to the Lady's Rock?"

They set off past a row of houses similar to Jenny Prentice's street in Newton of Wemyss, stranded and solitary now the reason for their existence was gone. Soon they entered the woods and the path began to descend, a waist-high stone wall on one side, thick undergrowth flanking it. In the distance, she could see the sparkle of the sea, the sun shining for once as they descended to shore level. "We had teams stationed up at the top here, and the same along at West Wemyss," Beveridge said. "Back then, you couldn't get along the shore towards East Wemyss for the pit bing. But when they made the coastal path, they got money from the EU and trucked all the pit red off the foreshore. You look at it now and you'd never know."

He was right. As they reached the level of the shore, Karen could see right along past East Wemyss to Buckhaven on its high promontory. In 1985, the view would not have existed. She turned towards West Wemyss, surprised that she couldn't actually see the Lady's Rock from where she stood.

Karen followed Beveridge along the path, trying to imagine what it must have been like that night. The file said it had been a new moon. She pictured the sickle sliver in the sky, the pinprick stars in the freezing night. The Plough like a big saucepan. Orion's belt and dagger, and all the other ones whose names she didn't know. The cops hidden in the woods, breathing with their mouths open so their breath would be chilled before it came out in puffs. She took in the high sycamores, wondering how much smaller they'd been then. Ropes hung from thick branches where kids would swing as they'd done when she was little. To Karen in her heightened state of imagination, they resembled hangman's nooses, motionless in the mild morning air, waiting for tenants. She shivered slightly and hurried to catch up with Beveridge.

He pointed up to the high cliffs where the treetops ended. "Up there, that's the Newton. You can see how sheer the cliffs are. Nobody was coming down there without us knowing. The guys in charge figured the kidnappers had to come along the path one way or the other, so they put most of the team here in the trees." He turned and pointed to what looked like a huge boulder by the side of the path. "And a guy with a rifle up there on top of the Lady's Rock." He gave a derisive snort of laughter. "Facing the wrong way, like."

"It's much smaller than I remember from when I was wee." Looking at it now, Karen found it hard to believe that anybody had bothered to name so insignificant a chunk of sandstone. The side next to the path was a straight cliff about twenty-five feet high, pitted with holes and striated with cracks. Small boy paradise. On the other side, it fell away in a forty-five-degree slope, dotted with tussocks of coarse grass and small shrubs. It had loomed much larger in her imagination.

"It's not just your memory playing tricks on you. I know it doesn't look much now, but twenty years ago, the shore was a lot lower, and the rock was a lot bigger. Come on, I'll show you what I mean."

Beveridge led the way down the side of the rock. The path was little more than grass bent by the passage of feet; a far cry from the EU's well-dressed track. They walked a dozen paces past the rock on to what seemed to be a narrow road made of coarse concrete. A few feet along, a rusted metal ring was set into the concrete. Karen frowned, trying to make sense of it. She let her eye follow the road, which bent at an angle before eventually meeting the sea. "I don't get it," she said.

"It was a quay," Beveridge said. "That's a mooring ring. Twenty years ago, you could bring a decent-sized boat along here. The shore was somewhere between eight and fifteen feet lower than it is now, depending on where you stand. This is how they did it."

"Jesus," Karen said, taking it all in; the sea, the rock, the quay, the splay of the woodland behind them. "Surely we must have heard them coming in?"

Beveridge smiled at her, like a teacher with a favourite pupil. "You'd think so, wouldn't you? But if they were using a small open boat, you could bring it in on the rising tide with just oars. With a good boatman, you wouldn't hear a thing. Besides, when you're up on the path, the rock itself acts as a baffle. You can hardly hear the sea itself. When it came to the getaway, you could give it full throttle, of course. You could be at Dysart or Buckhaven by the time they got the helicopter scrambled."

Karen studied the lie of the land again. "Hard to believe nobody thought about the sea."

"They did." Beveridge spoke abruptly.

"You mean, you did?"

"I did. So did my sergeant." He turned away and stared out to sea.

"Why did nobody listen to you?"

He shrugged. "They listened, I'll give them that. We had a briefing with DI Lawson and Brodie Grant. The two of them just didn't believe it could be done. A big boat would be too obvious, too easy to identify and chase down. A wee boat would be impossible because you couldn't subdue an adult hostage in an open boat. They said the kidnappers had shown forward planning and intelligence and they wouldn't take stupid risks like that." He turned back to her and sighed. "Maybe we should have pushed harder. Maybe if we had, there would have been a different outcome."

"Maybe," Karen said thoughtfully. So far, everyone had looked at the botched ransom operation from the point of view of the police and Brodie Grant. But there was another angle that deserved consideration. "They did have a point, though, didn't they? How did they manage it in a wee boat? They've got an adult hostage. They've got a baby hostage. They've got to handle the boat and keep the hostages under control, and there can't have been that many of them in a boat small enough to have avoided detection coming in. I wouldn't like to have been running that operation."

"Me neither," Beveridge said. "It would be hard enough getting that lot ashore if everybody was on the same side, never mind at odds with each other."

"Unless they were there a good long while before the actual handover. It would have been dark by four, and the quay itself would hide a wee boat from most lines of sight . . ." She pondered. "When did you guys set up?"

"We'd supposedly had the whole area under surveillance from two. The advance teams were in place by six."

"So theoretically, they could have sneaked in after it got dark and before your boys were on station," she said thoughtfully.

"It's possible," Beveridge said, sounding unconvinced. "But how could they be sure we didn't have the quay staked out? And how could you be sure of keeping a six-month-old kid quiet in the freezing cold for three or four hours?"

Karen walked out along the old quay, marvelling at the movement of the shoreline. The more she found out about the mechanics of this case, the less sense it made. She didn't think she was stupid. But she couldn't get things to add up. There had never been a single verified sighting of Cat or Adam after they'd been snatched. Nobody had witnessed anyone staking out her cottage, or the snatch itself. Nobody had seen them arrive at the ransom handover site. Nobody had seen them escape. If it hadn't been for the very real corpse of Cat Grant, she could almost believe it had never happened.

But it had.

ROTHESWELL CASTLE

Brodie Grant handed Bel's report to his wife and started fiddling with the espresso machine in his office. "She's doing surprisingly well," he said. "I wasn't sure about this arrangement of Susan's, but it seems to be paying off. I thought we should use a private investigator, but the journalist seems to be doing just as well."

"She has more at stake than a private eye would, Brodie. I think she's almost as desperate for a result as we are," Susan Charleson said, helping herself to a glass of water and sitting down on the window seat. "With her unparalleled access to you, I suspect she sees a bestseller in this."

"If she helps us get some answers after all this time, she deserves it," Judith said. "You're right, this is an impressive start. What does DI Pirie think?"

Grant and Susan exchanged a quick glance of complicity. "We've not passed it on to her yet," Grant said.

"Why ever not? I imagine she'd find it useful." Judith looked from one to the other, puzzled.

"I think we'll just keep it to ourselves for now," Grant said, pressing the button that forced pressurized hot water through the coffee to produce an espresso as perfectly as any Italian barista. "My experience with the police last time wasn't exactly a happy one. They cocked things up and my daughter ended up dead. This time, I'd rather leave as little up to them as possible."

"But this is a police matter," Judith protested. "You brought them in. You can't ignore them now."

"Can't I?" His head came up. "Maybe if I'd ignored them last time and done things my way, Cat would still be alive. And it would be Adam . . ." He stopped abruptly, realizing that nothing he said could get him out of the hole he'd just dug.

"Quite," Judith said, her voice sharp as a splinter. She tossed the papers on his desk and walked out.

Grant pulled a face. "Drum ice," he said as the door closed behind his wife. "I didn't handle that as well as I might have. Tricky things, words."

"She'll get over it," Susan said dismissively. "I agree. We should keep this to ourselves for now. The police are notoriously incapable of keeping a lid on information."

"It's not that I'm bothered about. I'm more worried about them cocking it up again. This could be the last chance we have of finding out what happened to my daughter and my grandson, and I don't want to take a chance on it going sour. It matters too much. I should have taken more control last time. I won't make that mistake again."

"We will have to tell the police eventually, if Bel Richmond comes up with a serious suspect," Susan pointed out.

Grant raised his eyebrows. "Not necessarily. Not if he's dead."

"They'll want to clear up the case."

"That's not my problem. Whoever destroyed my family deserves to be dead. Bringing the police into it won't make that happen. If they're already dead, well and good. If they're not—well, we'll cross that bridge when we come to it."

Little shocked Susan Charleson after three decades of working for Brodie Grant. But for once, she felt a tremor pass through her calm certainties. "I'm going to pretend I never heard that," she said.

"That's probably a good idea," he said, finishing his espresso. "A very good idea."

Glenrothes

Phil was on the phone when Karen got back to the office, handset tucked into his neck, scribbling in his notebook. "And you're sure about that?" she heard him say as she tossed her bag on the desk and headed for the fridge. By the time she returned with a Diet Coke, he was staring glumly at his notes. "That was Dr. Wilde," he said. "She got someone to do a quick and dirty on the DNA. There's no linkage between Misha Gibson and the body in the cave."

"Shit," Karen said. "So that means the body isn't Mick Prentice."

"Or else Mick Prentice wasn't Misha's father."

Karen leaned back in her chair. "It's a good thought, but, if I'm honest, I don't really think that Jenny Prentice was playing away when Mick was still on the scene. We'd have heard about it by now. A place like the Newton, it's a gossip factory. There's always somebody ready to shop their neighbour. I think the chances are that body's not Mick's."

"Plus you said the neighbour was adamant that Jenny was in love with him. That Tom Campbell was a poor second."

"So if we're right about him being Misha's dad, maybe Mick was the one that put the body there. He knew the caves, he probably could have got his hands on explosives. We need to find out if he had any experience of shot-firing. But burying a body in the Thane's Cave would be a pretty good reason for disappearing. And we know somebody else went on the missing list around the same time . . . " Karen reached for her notebook and flicked back the pages till she found what she was looking for. She glanced at her watch. "You think it's too late to ring somebody at half past eleven?"

Phil looked baffled. "Too late how? It's not even dinner time."

"I mean at night. In New Zealand." She reached for the phone and keyed in Angie Mackenzie's number. "Mind you, it's a murder inquiry now. That always comes ahead of beauty sleep."

A grumpy male voice answered. "Who is this?"

"I'm sorry to bother you, this is Fife Police. I need a word with Angie," Karen said, trying to sound ingratiating.

"Jesus. Do you know what time it is?"

"Yes, I'm sorry. But I do need to talk to her."

"Hang on, I'll get her." Off the phone, she could hear him calling his wife's name.

A full minute passed, then Angie came on the line. "I was in the shower," she said. "Is this DI Pirie?"

"That's right." Karen softened her voice. "I'm really sorry to bother you, but I wanted to let you know we've found human remains behind a rock fall in one of the Wemyss caves."

"And you think it might be Andy?"

"It's possible. The timescale looks like it might fit."

"But what would he have been doing in the caves? He was an outdoor kind of guy. One of the things he liked about being a union official was never having to go underground again."

"We don't know yet that it is your brother," Karen said. "Those are questions for later, Angie. We still have to identify the remains. Do you happen to know who your brother's dentist was?"

"How did he die?"

"We're not sure yet," Karen said. "As you'll appreciate, it's been a long time. It's a bit of a forensic challenge. I'll keep you informed, of course. But in the meantime, we have to treat it as an unexplained death. So, Andy's dentist?"

"He went to Mr. Torrance in Buckhaven. But he died a couple of years before I left Scotland. I don't even know if there's still a practice there." She sounded slightly panicked. Shock kicking in, Karen thought.

"Don't worry, we'll check it out," she said.

"DNA," Angie blurted out. "Can you get DNA from . . . what you found?"

"Yes, we can. Can we arrange for your local police to take a sample from you?"

"You don't need to. Before I left for New Zealand, I arranged with my lawyer to hold a certified copy of my DNA analysis." There was a crack in her voice. "I thought he'd gone off a mountain. Or maybe walked into a loch with his pockets full of stones. I didn't want him lying unclaimed. My lawyer has instructions to provide my DNA analysis to the police where there's an unidentified body the right age." Karen heard a sob from the other side of the world. "I always hoped . . . "

"I'm sorry," Karen said. "I'll get in touch with your lawyer."

"Alexander Gibb," Angie said. "In Kirkcaldy. I'm sorry, I need to go now." The line went dead abruptly.

"Not too late, then," Phil said.

Karen sighed. Shook her head. "Depends what you mean by 'too late.'"

HOXTON, LONDON

Jonathan speed-dialled Bel's mobile. When she answered, he spoke quickly. "I can't chat, I've got a meeting with my tutor. I've got some stuff to e-mail you, I'll get to it in an hour or so. But here's the headline news—Daniel Porteous is dead."

"I know that," Bel said impatiently.

"What you don't know is that he died in 1959, aged four."

"Oh, shit," said Bel.

"I couldn't have put it better myself. But here's the kicker. In November 1984, Daniel Porteous registered the birth of his son."

Bel felt light-headed, realized she was holding her breath, and released it in a sigh. "No way."

"Trust me, this is the business. Our Daniel Porteous somehow managed to have a son twenty-five years after he died."

"Wild. And who was the mother?"

Jonathan chuckled. "This just gets better, I'm afraid. I'm going to spell it out to you. F-R-E-D-A C-A-L-L-O-W is the name on the birth certificate. Say it out loud, Bel."

"Freda Callow." *Sounds like Frida Kahlo. The cheeky bastard.*

"He has a sense of humour, our Daniel Porteous."

DUNDEE

Karen found River at the university, sitting at her laptop in a small room lined with shelves of plastic boxes crammed with tiny bones. "What in the name of God is this place?" she said, plonking herself down on the only other chair.

"The professor here is the world's leading expert in the bones of babies and young children. You ever seen a foetus's skull?"

Karen shook her head. "And I don't want to, thank you very much."

River grinned. "OK, I won't make you. Let's just say when you've seen that, you understand where ET came from. So, I take it this isn't a social visit?"

Karen snorted. "Oh, sure. The anatomy department of Dundee University is my number one destination when I want a good day out. No, River, this is not a social visit. I'm here because I need a clear chain of custody on a piece of evidence in a homicide inquiry." She placed a sheet of paper on the desk. Angela Kerr's solicitor had been quick off the mark. "That is the DNA of Andy Kerr's sister Angie. I'm formally requesting that you compare it with the DNA extracted from the human remains discovered in the area known as the Thane's Cave lying between East Wemyss and Buckhaven. You'll get that in writing as soon as I get back to my desk."

River looked at it with curiosity. "Fast work, Karen. Where did this come from?"

"Angie Mackenzie is a woman of foresight," Karen said. "She lodged it with her lawyer. Just in case a body ever turned up." As she spoke, River was tapping keys on her laptop.

"I'll do you a detailed report in writing," she said slowly, distracted by what she was looking at. "And I'll need to scan this in to be certain . . . But quick and dirty says these two people are closely related." She looked up. "Looks like you might have an ID for your mystery man."

Siena

How, Bel wondered, could Italian investigative journalists cope? She'd thought British bureaucracy wearisome and cumbersome. But compared to Italian red tape, it was open access all areas. First there had been the office-to-office shuttle. Then the form-filling shuffle. Then the blank-stared shut-out from officials who clearly minded their leisure being interrupted by someone who wanted them to do their job. It was a miracle anyone ever managed to find out anything in this country.

Towards the end of the morning, she began to fear that time would run out before she had learned what she needed to know. Then, with minutes to go before the registry office closed for lunch, a bored-looking bottle blonde called her name. Bel rushed to the counter, fully expecting to be fobbed off till the next day. Instead, in exchange for a bundle of unreceipted euros, she was handed two sheets of paper that appeared to have been photocopied on a machine painfully short of toner. One was headed *Certificato di Morte,* the other *Certificato di Residenza.* In the end, she'd got more than she'd bargained for.

The death certificate of Daniel Simeon Porteous stated simply that he had died on 7th April 2007 at the age of fifty-two at the Policlinico Le Scotte, Siena. His parents were named as Nigel and Rosemary Porteous. And that was it. No cause of death, no address. About as much use as a chocolate teapot, Bel thought bitterly. She considered going to the hospital to see if she could find anything out, but dismissed the idea at once. Breaching the walls of officialdom would be impossible for someone who didn't know the system. And the chances of finding someone bribable who remembered Daniel Porteous after this much time were remote and probably beyond her command of the language.

With a sigh, she turned to the other certificate. It seemed to be a short list of addresses and dates. It didn't take her long to figure out that this was a record of where Daniel had lived since he had come to the Commune di Siena in 1986. And that the last address on the list was where he had been living when he died. Even more surprising was that she knew more or less where it was. Costalpino was the last village she'd driven through on her way from Campora. The main road twisted down through its main street in a series of curves, the road flanked with houses, the occasional shop or bar tucked alongside.

Bel practically ran back to the car in spite of the sweaty heat of the middle of the day. She gasped with gratitude as the air conditioning kicked in and wasted no time getting out of the parking lot and on to the road heading for Costalpino. The man behind the counter of the first bar she came to provided excellent directions, and a mere fifteen minutes after leaving Siena she was parking a few doors down from the house where she expected to find Gabriel Porteous. It was a pleasant street, wider than most in that part of Tuscany. Tall trees shaded the narrow pavements, and waist-high walls topped with iron railings separated small but well-kept villas from each other. Bel felt the pulse of excitement in her throat. If she was right, she could be about to come face to face with Catriona Maclennan Grant's lost son. The police had failed twice, but Bel Richmond was about to show them all how it was done.

So confident was she that she could hardly credit the sign on the front of the yellow stuccoed villa. She checked the numbers again to make sure she was standing before the right house, but there was no mistake. The dark green shutters were pulled tight. The plants in the tall terracotta pots that lined the driveway looked tired and dusty. Occasional weeds were poking through the gravel, and junk mail poked out of the mailbox. All of which reinforced the SE VENDE sign with the name and number of an estate agent in nearby Sovicille. Wherever Gabriel Porteous was, it looked like it wasn't here.

It was a setback. But it wasn't the end of the world. She'd overcome bigger obstacles than this on her way to the stories that had built her reputation as someone who could deliver. All she had to do was formulate a plan of campaign and follow it through. And for once, if she came up against stuff she couldn't do, she could call on Brodie Grant's resources to make it happen. It wasn't exactly a comforting feeling, but it was better than nothing.

Before she headed off for Sovicille, she decided to check out the neighbours. It wouldn't be the first time that somebody who knew they were being looked for went out of their way to make their home look uninhabited. Bel had already noticed a man on the loggia of a villa diagonally opposite the Porteous house. There had been nothing covert about the way he had been watching her walk up the street and study the sign. Time for a little stretching of the truth.

She crossed the road and greeted him with a wave. "Hello," she said.

The man, who could have been anywhere from mid-fifties to mid-seventies, gave her an appraising look, making her wish she'd worn a loose T-shirt rather than the close-fitting spaghetti-strapped top she'd chosen that morning. She loved

Italy, but God, she hated the way so many of the men eyed up women as if they were meat on the hoof. This one wasn't even good looking: one eye bigger than the other, a nose like an ill-favoured parsnip, and hair spurting out of the top of his vest. He smoothed down an eyebrow with his little finger and gave her a crooked smile. "Hello," he said, managing to make it sound freighted with meaning.

"I'm looking for Gabriel," she said. She gestured over her shoulder to the house. "Gabriel Porteous. I'm a friend of the family, from England. I haven't seen Gabriel since Daniel died, and this is the only address I have. But it's up for sale, and it doesn't look like Gabe's still living there."

The man stuck his hands in his pockets and shrugged. "Gabriel hasn't lived here for more than a year now. He's supposed to be studying some place, I don't know where. He was back for a while before his father died, but I haven't seen him for a couple of months now." His smile reappeared, a little wider than before. "If you want to give me your number, I could call you if he shows up?"

Bel smiled. "That's very kind, but I'm only going to be here for a few days. You said Gabe's 'supposed' to be studying." She gave him a look of complicity. "Like you think he's up to his old games?"

It did the trick. "Daniel, he worked hard. He didn't mess about. But Gabe? He's always messing about, hanging out with his friends. I never saw him with a book in his hands. What kind of studying is he going to be doing? If he'd been serious, he'd have signed up at the university in Siena, so he could live at home and only think about his studies. But no, he goes off some place he can have a good time." He tutted. "Daniel was sick for weeks before Gabe showed up."

"Maybe Daniel didn't tell him he was ill. He's always been

a very private person," Bel said, making it up as she went along.

"A good son would have visited regularly enough to know," the man said stubbornly.

"And you've no idea where he's studying?"

The man shook his head. "No. I saw him on the train one time. I was coming back from Firenze. So, somewhere up north. Firenze, Bologna, Padova, Perugia. Could be anywhere."

"Oh well. I guess I'll just have to try the estate agent. I really wanted to see him. I feel bad about missing the funeral. Were many of the old crowd here?"

He looked surprised. "It was a private funeral. None of us neighbours knew anything about it till it was all over. I spoke to Gabe afterwards. I wanted to pay my respects, you know? He said his father had wanted it that way. But now, you're talking like there was something to miss." He took out a pack of cigarettes and lit up. "You can't trust kids to tell you the truth."

There was no real reason why she should try to cover her tracks with someone she would never meet again, but she'd always believed in keeping her hand in. "What I was talking about was more of a gathering for some of Daniel's old friends. Not a funeral as such."

He nodded. "The arty crowd. Kept them separate from his friends in the village. I met a couple of them once. They turned up at the villa when a few of us were round there playing cards. Another English guy and a German woman." He hawked and spat over the stone balustrade. "I've got no time for the Germans. That Englishman, though. You'd have thought he was German, the way he acted."

"Matthias?" Bel guessed.

"That's the one. High-handed. Treated Daniel like he was dirt. Like he was the one with the brains and the talent. And very amused to find Daniel playing cards with the locals. The funny thing was, Daniel let him get away with it. We didn't stick around, just finished the hand and left them to it. If that's your arty intellectuals, you can keep them."

"I never had much time for Matthias myself," Bel said. "Anyway, thanks for your help. I'll head over to Sovicille and see if the agents can put me in touch with Gabe."

It was amazing how even the least promising encounter could add to your store of knowledge, Bel thought as she set off again. Now she had a second source who thought Matthias was English, in spite of his Teutonic name and German partner. A Brit who didn't acknowledge his roots, who had artistic leanings, a connection to the ransom notes, and a friendship with the man whose son looked eerily like Cat Grant and her father. It was starting to make a tantalizing shape in her mind.

Two young men, struggling artists, aware of Cat Grant because she moved in the same circles. Aware, too, of her father's wealth. They hatch a plan to feather their nests. Kidnap Cat and her kid, make it look like some political thing. Take off with the ransom and never have to paint for anyone but themselves ever again. Say it fast, it sounds like a great idea. Only it all goes horribly wrong and Cat dies. They're left with the kid and the ransom money, but now they're the focus of a murder manhunt.

Professional criminals would know what to do and be cold-hearted enough to do it. But these are nice, civilized boys who thought they were indulging in something only marginally more serious than an art college prank. They've got a boat, so they just keep going across the North Sea to Europe. Daniel ends up in Italy, Matthias in Germany. And somewhere along the line, they decide not to kill or abandon the child. For whatever reason, they keep him. Daniel brings him up as his son. Cushioned by the ransom money, he sets them up in comfort and then, ironically, becomes a reasonably successful artist. But he can't cash in on his success with media interviews and personality-based marketing because he knows he's a criminal on the run. And he knows his son is not Gabriel Porteous. He's Adam Maclennan Grant, a young man cursed with a distinctive face.

It was an attractive scenario, no doubt about it. It begged questions, true—How did they get their hands on the ransom, given that they were floundering round in the dark trying to find the dead woman who'd been carrying it? How did they outwit the tracking devices the cops had planted on the ransom? How did they get away by boat and not get spotted by the helicopter? How would a couple of art students have got hold of a gun back then? All good questions, but ones she was sure she could finesse one way or another. She'd have to; this was too good to pass by just for the sake of a few awkward details.

She'd known she was on to a good thing with her unique access to Brodie Grant, but this was infinitely better than she could have hoped for. This was the kind of story that would make her name. Establish her as one of that handful of journalists whose name alone stood for the story. Stanley with the discovery of Dr. Livingstone. Woodward and Bernstein with Watergate. Max Hastings with the liberation of Port Stanley. Now they'd be able to include Annabel Richmond with the unmasking of Adam Maclennan Grant.

There were lots of gaps in the story at this point, but they could be filled in later. What Bel needed now was the young man known as Gabriel Porteous. With or without his cooperation, she needed a sample of his DNA so Brodie Grant could establish whether this really was his missing grandson. And then her fame was assured. Newspaper features, a book, maybe even a movie. It was a thing of beauty.

The estate agent's office was tucked in a side street just off Via Nuova. The window was filled with A4 sheets displaying photographs and a few details of each property. The Porteous villa was there, its rooms and facilities enumerated without comment. Bel pushed open the door and found herself in a small grey office. Grey filing cabinets, grey carpet, pale walls, grey desks. The only inhabitant, a woman in her thirties, was like a bird of paradise by comparison. Her scarlet blouse and turquoise necklace blazed brightly, drawing the eye to her tumble of dark hair and perfectly made-up face. She was definitely making the most of what she had, Bel thought as they found their way through the pleasantries.

"I'm afraid I'm not actually in the market for a property," Bel said, with an apologetic gesture. "I'm trying to contact the owner of the villa you have for sale in Costalpino. I was an old friend of Gabriel Porteous's father, Daniel. Sadly, I was in Australia when Daniel died. I'm back in Italy for a while and I wanted to see Gabriel, to pay my respects. Is it possible for you to put me in touch with him?"

The woman rolled her eyes. "I'm really sorry. I can't do that."

Bel reached for her wallet. "I could pay for your time," she said, using one of the traditional formulae for corruption.

"No, no, it's not that," the woman said, not in the least offended. "When I say I can't, that's what I mean. Not that I won't. I can't." She sounded flustered. "It's very unusual. I don't have an address or a phone number or even an e-mail for Signor Porteous. Not even a mobile phone. I tried to explain this was very unconventional, and he said, so was he. He said now his father was dead, he planned to go travelling and he didn't want to be tied down to his past." She gave a wry little smile. "The sort of thing young men think is very romantic."

"And the rest of us think is impossibly self-indulgent," Bel said. "Gabriel always had a mind of his own. But how are you supposed to sell the house if you can't contact him? How can he agree to a sale?"

The woman spread her hands. "He phones us every Monday. I said to him, 'What if someone comes in on a Tuesday morning with an offer?' He said, 'In the old days people had to wait for letters to go back and forth. It wouldn't kill them to wait till the next Monday if they're serious about buying the house.'"

"And have there been many offers?"

The woman looked glum. "Not at that price. I think he needs to drop at least five thousand before anyone will get serious. But we'll see. It's a nice house, it should find a buyer. He's emptied it, too, which makes the rooms look so much bigger."

Since Bel's next suggestion had been that she take a look round to see if there were any clues to Gabriel's whereabouts, that last revelation came as a disappointment. Instead, she fished a business card from her Filofax. One of the ones that had her name, her mobile number, and her e-mail address. "Never mind," she said. "Perhaps when he rings on Monday you could ask him to get in touch? I knew his father for the best part of twenty years, I'd just like to get together." She handed the card over.

Scarlet fingernails plucked it from her hand. "Sure, I'll pass the message on. And if you ever want a property around here . . . ?" She waved at the array of details in the window. "We've got a great selection. I always say we are on the unfashionable side of the autostrada so the prices are lower but the properties are just as beautiful."

Bel walked back to the car, knowing there was nothing else she could do here. Five days until Gabriel Porteous would get her message, and then who knew whether he would get in touch? If he didn't, tracking him down would be a job for a private detective in Italy, someone who knew the ropes and the right hands to ply with brown envelopes of cash. It would still be her story, but someone else could do the grunt work. Meanwhile she needed to get back to Rotheswell to see if she could nail down a chat with Fergus Sinclair.

Time to exploit the resources Brodie Grant had put at her disposal. She dialled Susan Charleson's number. "Hello, Susan," she said. "I need a flight back to the UK asap."

GLENROTHES

The trouble with cold cases, Karen thought, was that there were so many brick walls to run into. When there really was nothing you could do next. No obvious witness to interview. No convenient forensic samples to organize. At times like this, she was at the mercy of her wits, twisting the Rubik's Cube of what she knew in the hope that a new pattern would emerge.

She'd interviewed everyone who might have been able to give her a lead on what had happened to Mick Prentice. In a way, that should have worked to her advantage when it came to investigating Andy Kerr's death because she'd been talking to them in the context of a missing-person inquiry. Unless they had something to hide, people were generally pretty open with the police when it was a matter of helping to track down those missing and missed. When it came to murder, they were more reluctant to talk. And what they did say was hedged with qualifications and anxieties. Theoretically, she knew she should go back to her witnesses and take fresh statements, statements that might lead her to other witnesses who remembered what Andy Kerr was saying and doing leading up to his death. But experience told her it would be a waste of time now suspicious death was on the agenda. Nevertheless, she'd sent the Mint and a bright new CID aide on a fresh round of interviews. Maybe they'd get lucky and pick up on something she'd missed. A girl could always hope.

She turned to the Cat Grant file. She was stalled there, too. Until she had a proper report from the Italian police, it was hard to see where she could make progress. There had been one stroke of luck in that area, however. She'd contacted Fergus Sinclair's parents, hoping to find out where their son was working so she could arrange to interview him. To her surprise, Willie Sinclair had told her his son would be arriving with his wife and children that very evening for their annual Scottish holiday. Tomorrow morning, she would have the chance to talk to Fergus Sinclair. It sounded as if he was the only person left who might be willing to unlock Cat Grant's personality. Her mother was dead, her father was unwilling, and the files offered no clue to any close friendships.

Karen wondered if the lack of friendships was a matter of choice or personality. She knew people so invested in their work that the lack of close human relationships was something they barely noticed. She also knew others who were desperate for intimacy but whose only talent was for driving people away. She counted her blessings; she had friends whose support and laughter filled an important place in the pattern of her days. It might lack a central relationship at its heart, but hers was a life that felt solid and comfortable.

What had Cat Grant's life felt like? Karen had seen women consumed by their children. Witnessing their adoring gaze, she'd felt uneasy. Children were human, not gods to be worshipped. Was Cat's child the centre of her world? Had

Adam occupied her entire heart? It looked that way from the outside. Everyone assumed Fergus was the baby's father, but even if he hadn't been, one thing seemed clear. Adam's father had been banished from his life; it appeared that his mother had wanted him for herself alone.

Or maybe not. Karen wondered if she was looking through the wrong end of the telescope. What if it hadn't been Cat who had cast out Adam's father? What if he'd had his own reasons for refusing to accept a role in his son's life? Maybe he didn't want the responsibility. Maybe he had other responsibilities, another family whose call on him was thrown into relief by the prospect of another child. Maybe he'd only been passing through and had gone before she even knew she was pregnant. There was no denying that there were other possibilities worth considering.

Karen sighed. She'd know more after she'd spoken to Fergus. With luck, he'd help her to narrow down some of her wilder ideas. "Cold cases," she said out loud. They'd break your heart. Like lovers, they tantalized with promises that this time it would be different. It would start out fresh and exciting, you'd try to ignore those little niggles that you felt sure would disappear as you got to understand things better. Then suddenly it would be going nowhere. Wheels spinning in a gravel pit. And before you knew it, it was over. Back to square one.

She glanced up at Phil, who was working computer databases, trying to track down a witness in another case. Probably just as well it had never come to anything between them. Better to have him as a friend than to end up with bitterness and frustration measuring the distance between them.

And then the phone rang. "CCRT, DI Pirie speaking," she said, trying not to sound as pissed off as she felt.

"This is Capitano di Stefano from the carabinieri in Siena," a heavily accented voice said. "You are the officer I have talk-ed to about the Villa Totti near Boscolata?"

"That's right." Karen sat bolt upright, reaching for pen and paper. She remembered di Stefano's style from their previous conversation. His English was surprisingly good as far as vocabulary and grammar were concerned, but his accent was atrocious. He pronounced English as if it were an opera libretto, the stresses in peculiar places and the pronunciation bordering on the bizarre. None of that mattered. What mattered was the content, and Karen was prepared to work as hard as necessary to nail that down precisely. "Thanks for calling."

"It is my pleasure," he said, every vowel distinct. "So. We have visited the villa and talk-ed to the neighbours."

Who knew you could get four syllables out of "neighbours"? "Thank you. What did you discover?"

"We have found more copies of the poster you e-mailed to us. Also, we have found the silk screen it was printed from. Now we are processing fingerprints from the frame and other areas inside the villa. You understand, many people have been here, and there are many traces everywhere. As soon as we have process-ed the prints and the other material, we will transmit our results as well as copies of prints and DNA sequences. I am sorry, but this aspect is not a priority for us, you understand?"

"Sure, I understand. Is there any chance that you can send us some samples so we can run our own tests? Just in the interests of time, not for any other reason." *Like, everybody in my department thinks you're useless.*

"*Sì.* This is already done. I have sent you samples from the bloodstain on the floor and other bloodstains in the kitchen and living area. Also, other evidence where we have multiple samples. So, I hope this will come to you tomorrow."

"What did the neighbours have to say?"

Di Stefano tutted down the phone. "I think you call these people lefties. They don't like the carabinieri. They're the kind of people who go to Genoa for the G8. They are more on the side of the people living illegally at the Villa Totti. So my men did not learn a great deal. What we know is that the people living here ran a travelling puppet show called BurEst. We have some photos from a local newspaper and my colleague is e-mailing them to you. We know some names, but these are the kind of people who can very easily disappear. They live in the world of the black economy. They don't pay taxes. Some of them are probably illegals."

Karen could almost see him spreading his hands in a frustrated shrug. "I appreciate how hard it is. Can you send me a list of the names you do have?"

"I can tell you now. We only have first names for these people. So far, no family names. Dieter, Luka, Maria, Max, Peter, Rado, Sylvia, Matthias, Ursula. Matthias was in charge. I am sending you this list. Some of them, we think we know their nationality, but it's mostly guessing I think."

"Any Brits?"

"It does not look like it, although one of the neighbours thinks that Matthias might have been English because of his accent."

"It's not a very English name."

"Maybe it wasn't always his name," Di Stefano pointed out. "The other thing about people like this, they are always trying to be born again. New name, new history. So, I am sorry. There does not seem to be very much here for you."

"I appreciate what you've been able to do. I know it's hard to justify manpower on something like this."

"Inspector, it looks to me as if there has been a murder in this villa. We are treating this as a possible murder investigation. We try to help you in the course of this, but we are more interested in what we think happened three months ago than what happened twenty-two years ago in your country. We are looking very hard for these people. And tomorrow, we bring in the body dogs and the ground-penetrating radar to see if we can find a burial site. It will be difficult because it is surrounded by woodland. But we must try. So you see, manpower is not the issue here."

"Of course. I didn't mean to suggest you weren't taking it seriously. I know what it's like, believe me."

"There is one more thing we have found out. I don't know if this matters to you, but there has been an English journalist here, asking questions."

Karen was momentarily at a loss. Nothing had been released to the media. What was a hack doing sniffing around in her case? Then suddenly it dawned on her. "Bel Richmond," she said.

"Annabel," di Stefano said. "She was staying at a farm up the hill. She left this afternoon. She is returning to England tonight. The neighbours, they said that she wanted to know about the BurEst people. A teenager told one of my men that she was also interested in a couple of friends of Matthias. An English painter and his son. But I have no names, no photos, no nothing. Maybe you can speak to her? Maybe the Boscolata neighbours think it's better to talk to a journalist rather than a cop, what do you think?"

"Tragically, I think you might be right," Karen said bitterly. They exchanged pleasantries and empty promises to visit, then the call was over. Karen screwed up a piece of paper and tossed it at Phil. "Can you believe it?"

"What?" He looked up, startled. "Believe what?"

"Fucking Bel Richmond," she said. "Who does she think she is? Brodie Grant's private police force?"

"What's she done?" He stretched his arms above his head, grunting as he unkinked his spine.

"She's only been to Italy." Karen kicked her bin. "Fucking cheeky bitch. Going out there and chatting up the neighbours. The neighbours that won't say much to the police because they're a bunch of unreconstructed lefties. Jesus Christ."

"Wait a minute," Phil said. "Shouldn't we be pleased about that? I mean, that we've got somebody getting the dirt, even if it's not our colleagues in Italy?"

"Can you come over here and look in my e-mail inbox and show me the message from Bel Richmond telling us what she's dug up in bloody Tuscany? Can you maybe let your fingers do the walking through my in-tray and show me the fax she sent with all the information she's gathered out there? Or maybe it's my voicemail that I've lost the ability to access? Phil, she might have found out all sorts. But we're not the ones she's telling."

Edinburgh Airport to Rotheswell Castle

Bel watched the empty luggage carousel circling, exhaustion rendering her incapable of thought. A drive to Florence airport, mysteriously hidden somewhere in the suburbs, a dismal journey via Charles de Gaulle, an airport surely designed by a latter-day Marquis de Sade, and still miles to go before she could sleep. And not even in her own bed. At last, suitcases and holdalls started to appear. Ominously, hers was absent from the first circuit. She was about to throw a tantrum at the ground services counter when her case finally came limping through, one latch hanging loose from its moorings. In her heart, she knew Susan Charleson had nothing to do with her miseries, but it was nice to have someone to lay irrational blame on. Please God she'd sent someone to pick her up.

Her spirits should have risen when she emerged in the arrivals area to see there was indeed a chauffeur waiting for her. But the fact that it was Brodie Grant himself only emphasized her weariness. She wanted to curl up and sleep or curl up and drink. She did not want to spend the next forty minutes under interrogation. He wasn't even paying her, now she came to think about it. Just fronting her exes and opening doors for her. Which wasn't exactly a bad gig. But in her book, it didn't entitle him to 24/7 service. *Like you're going to tell him that.*

Grant greeted her with a nod and they wrestled momentarily over the suitcase before Bel gave in gracelessly. As they hustled through the terminal, Bel was conscious of eyes on them. Brodie Grant clearly had street recognition. Not many businessmen achieved that. Richard Branson, Alan Sugar. But they were familiar TV faces, on screen for reasons that were nothing to do with business. She didn't think Grant would be noticed in London, but here in Scotland, the punters knew his face in spite of his media shyness. Charisma, or just a big fish in a small pond? Bel wouldn't have liked to hazard a guess.

It wasn't just the punters. Outside the terminal, where signs and PA announcements strictly banned the parking of cars, an armed police officer was standing next to Grant's Land Rover. He wasn't there to warn Grant or give him a ticket; he was there to make sure nobody messed with the Defender. Grant gave him a patriarchal nod as he loaded the case, then waved graciously as they drove off.

"I'm impressed," Bel said. "I thought it was just royalty that got that sort of treatment."

His face twitched as if he wasn't certain whether she was being critical. "In my country, we respect success."

"What? Three hundred years of English oppression hasn't knocked that out of you?"

Grant started upright, then realized she was teasing him. To her relief, he laughed. "No. You're much keener to knock success than we are. I think you like success too, Annabel. Isn't that why you're up here working with me instead of uncovering some ghastly tale of rape and sex trafficking in London?"

"Partly. And partly because I'm interested in finding out what happened." As soon as the words were out, she could have kicked herself for giving him the perfect opening.

"And what have you found out in Tuscany?" he asked.

As they raced through the night on empty roads, she told him what she had discovered and what she had surmised. "I came back because I don't have the resources to track Gabriel Porteous down," she concluded. "DI Pirie might be able to kick the Italian cops into action—"

"We're not going to be talking to DI Pirie about this," Grant said firmly. "We'll hire a private investigator. He can buy us the information we need."

"You're not going to tell the police what I've found out? You're not sharing the info with them? Or the photos?" She knew she shouldn't be shocked by the antics of the very rich, but she was taken aback by so adamant a response.

"The police are useless. We can wrap it up ourselves. If this boy is Adam, it's a family matter. It's not up to the police to find him."

"I don't understand," Bel said. "When we started this, you were the one who went to the police. Now you want to shut them out."

There was a long silence. The dashboard lit up his profile against the night, the muscles in his jaw tight and hard. At last, he spoke. "Forgive me, but I don't think you've entirely thought this through, Bel."

"What have I missed?" She felt the old clutch of fear that news editors had always induced with their questioning of her copy.

"You talked about a significant amount of blood on the kitchen floor. You thought someone who lost that much blood would probably be dead. That means there's a body somewhere, and now the police are looking, they'll probably find it. And when they find it, they'll be looking for a killer—"

"And Gabriel was there the night before they all disappeared. You think Gabriel will come under suspicion," Bel said, suddenly getting it. "And if he is your grandson, you want him out of the picture."

"You got there, Bel," he said. "More than that, I don't want the Italian police fitting him up because they can't find the real killer. If he's not around, the temptation is less, especially since there will be other, more attractive suspects on the ground. The Italian private eyes won't just be looking for Gabriel Porteous."

Oh my God, he's going to have someone else fitted up. Just as an insurance policy. Bel felt nauseous. "You mean, you're going to find a scapegoat?"

Grant gave her an odd look. "What an extraordinary suggestion. I'm just going to make sure the Italian police get all the help they deserve." His smile was grim. "We're all citizens of Europe now, Bel."

Thursday, 5th July 2007; Kirkcaldy

Karen had conducted interviews in strange places before, but Ravenscraig Castle would probably have made the top five. When she'd asked Fergus Sinclair to meet her, he'd suggested the venue. "That way, my wife can take the kids round the castle and down to the shore," he said. "This is our summer holiday. I don't see why we have to be cooped up just because you want to talk to me."

"The weather" would have been as good an answer as any. Karen was sitting on the remains of a wall with her anorak collar turned up against a sharp breeze coming off the sea; Phil sat next to her huddled into his leather jacket. "This better be worth it," he said. "I'm not sure whether it's rheumatism or piles I'm getting here, but I know it's not good for me."

"He's probably used to it. Working on a hunting estate like he does." Karen squinted up at the sky. The cloud was high and thin, but she'd still have put money on rain by lunchtime. "You know that, back in the Middle Ages, this was the St. Clair family seat?"

"That's why this part of Kirkcaldy's called Sinclairtown, Karen." Phil rolled his eyes. "You think he's trying to intimidate us?"

She laughed. "If I can survive Brodie Grant, I can survive a descendant of the St. Clairs of Ravenscraig. Do you think this is him?"

A tall, rangy man walked through the castle gatehouse followed by a woman almost as tall as him and a pair of small sturdy boys, each with a shock of bright blond hair like their mother. The lads looked around them and then they were off, running and jumping, clambering and exploring. The woman turned her face upwards and the man planted a kiss on her forehead, then patted her back as she turned to chase the boys. He looked around and caught sight of the two cops. He raised a hand in greeting and came towards them with quick, long strides.

As he approached, Karen studied a face she'd seen only in twenty-two-year-old photos. He'd aged well, though his face was weathered, the web of fine white lines round his sharp blue eyes a testament to time spent in the sun and the wind. His face was lean, the cheeks hollow, the outline of the bones clear beneath the skin. His light brown hair hung in a fine fringe, making him look almost medieval. He wore a soft plaid shirt tucked into moleskin trousers, lightweight walking boots on his feet. She stood up and nodded hello. "You must be Fergus Sinclair," she said, extending a hand. "I'm DI Karen Pirie and this is DS Phil Parhatka."

He took her hand in one of those tight grips that always made her want to slap the other's face with her free hand. "I appreciate you meeting me here," he said. "I didn't want my parents subjected to the bad old memories again." His Fife accent was almost completely gone. If she'd been pressed, Karen might even have placed him as a German with exceptionally good English.

"No problem," she lied. "You know why we've reopened the case?"

He sat down on a piece of masonry at right angles to Karen and Phil. "My dad said it was something to do with the ransom poster. Another copy's turned up?"

"That's right. In a ruined villa in Tuscany." Karen waited. He said nothing.

"Not that far from where you live," Phil said.

Sinclair raised his eyebrows. "It's hardly on my doorstep."

"About seven hours' driving, according to the Internet."

"If you say so. I'd have said more like eight or nine. But either way, I'm not sure what you're implying."

"I'm not implying anything, sir. Just setting the location in context for you," Phil said. "The people who were squatting the villa were a group of puppeteers. They called themselves BurEst. The leaders were a couple of Germans called Matthias and Ursula. Ever come across them?"

"Christ," Sinclair said, exasperated. "That's a bit like asking a Scotsman if he ever ran across your auntie from London. I don't think I've ever been to a puppet show. Not even with the kids. And I don't know anyone called Matthias. The only Ursula I know works in my local bank, and I doubt very much she's into puppets in her spare time." He turned to Karen. "I thought you wanted to talk about Cat."

"We do. I'm sorry, I thought you wanted to know why we were reopening the case," she said earnestly, slipping easily into the Good Cop role. "I suppose you've put it all behind you now. What with having a wife and kids."

He dropped his hands between his knees, interlocking his fingers. "I'll never put it behind me. I still loved her when she died. Even though she'd sent me packing, there wasn't a day went by that I didn't think of her. I wrote so many letters. Sent none of them." He closed his eyes. "But even if I could put Cat behind me, I'll never be able to do the same with Adam." He blinked hard and caught Karen's eye. "He's my son. Cat kept me from him when he was tiny, but the kidnappers have kept him from me for twenty-two and a half years."

"You think he's still alive?" Karen asked gently.

"I know the chances are that he was dead within hours of his mother. But I'm a parent. I can't help hoping that somewhere he's walking around in the world. Having a decent life. That's how I like to think of him."

"You were always sure he was your son," Karen said. "Even though Cat wouldn't acknowledge you as the father, you never wavered."

He twisted his hands together. "Why would I waver? Look, I know my relationship with Cat was on the skids by the time she got pregnant. We'd split up and got back together half a dozen times. We were hardly seeing each other at all. But we did spend the night together almost exactly nine months before Adam was born. When we were having our . . . difficulties, I asked her if there was someone else, but she swore there wasn't. And God knows she had no reason to lie. If anything, she'd have been better off saying she was seeing someone else. I'd have had to accept it was over then. So there wasn't anybody else in the frame." He unclenched his hands and splayed his fingers. "He even had my colouring. I knew he was mine the first time I clapped eyes on him."

"You must have been angry when Cat refused to admit Adam was yours," Karen said.

"I was furious," he said. "I wanted to go to court, to do all the tests."

"So why didn't you?" Phil said.

Sinclair stared down at the ground. "My mum talked me out of it. Brodie Grant hated the idea of me and Cat being together. Considering he came from dirt poverty in Kelty, he had some pretty high and mighty ideas about who was a fit partner for his daughter. And it certainly wasn't a ghillie's son. He was practically dancing a jig when we split up." He sighed. "My mum said if I fought Cat over Adam, Grant would take it out on her and my dad. They live in a tied cottage. Grant once promised my dad they could stay there for the rest of their lives. They've worked all their days for low wages. They've got no other provision for their old age. So I bit the bullet for their sakes. And I took myself off where I didn't have to face Cat or her father every day."

"I know you were asked this at the time, but did you ever consider taking revenge on these people who had wrecked your life?" Karen asked.

Sinclair's face screwed up as if he was in pain. "If I'd had any notion of how to take revenge, I would have. But I didn't have a clue and I didn't have any resources. I was twenty-five years old, I was working as a junior keeper on a hunting estate in Austria. I worked long hours, I spent my spare time learning the language and drinking. Trying to forget what I'd left behind. Believe me, Inspector, the idea of kidnapping Cat and Adam never crossed my mind. I just don't have that kind of mind. Would it have crossed yours?"

Karen shrugged. "I don't know. Happily I've never been put in that position. I do know that if I'd been treated like you were I'd have wanted to get my own back."

Sinclair's sideways nod conceded her point. "Here's what I know. My mum always used to say that living well is the best revenge. And that's what I've tried to do. I'm lucky to have a job I love in a beautiful part of the world. I can shoot and fish and climb and ski. I've got a good marriage and two bright, healthy boys. I don't envy any man, least of all Brodie Grant. That man took everything I valued away from me. Him and his daughter, they hurt me. No getting away from it. But I've rebuilt my life and it's a good one. I've got history that's left me with scars, but those three"—he pointed to where his wife and sons were scrambling up a grassy bank—"those three make up for a hell of a lot."

It was a pretty speech, but Karen wasn't entirely convinced by it. "I think I'd resent him more, in your shoes."

"Then it's just as well you're not. Resentment isn't a healthy emotion, Inspector. It'll eat you away like cancer." He looked her straight in the eye. "There are those who believe there's a direct connection between the two. Me, I don't want to die of cancer."

"My colleagues interviewed you after Cat died. I expect you remember that quite well?"

His face twisted, and suddenly Karen saw a glimmer of the fires that Fergus Sinclair kept well banked down. "Being treated as a suspect in the death of the woman you love? That's not something you forget very easily," he said, his voice tight with contained anger.

"Asking someone for an alibi isn't necessarily treating them as a suspect," Phil said. She could tell he'd taken a dislike to Sinclair and hoped it wouldn't derail the interview. "We have to exclude people from our inquiries so we don't waste time investigating the innocent. Sometimes alibi evidence is the quickest way to take someone out of the picture."

"Maybe so," Sinclair said, his chin jutting forward defensively. "It didn't feel like that at the time. It felt like your people were putting a hell of a lot of effort into proving I wasn't where I said I was."

Time for the oil on the water, Karen thought. "Is there anything that has occurred to you since then that might be helpful?"

He shook his head. "What could I know that would be helpful? I've never been remotely interested in politics, never mind anarchist splinter groups. The people I mix with don't want a revolution." He gave a self-congratulatory little smile. "Unless maybe it's a revolution in ski design."

"To tell you the truth, we don't think it was an anarchist group," Karen said. "We have pretty good intelligence on the kind of people who believe in direct action in the furtherance of their political ambitions. And the Anarchist Covenant of Scotland was never heard from before or since."

"Well, they weren't going to draw attention to themselves afterwards, were they? Not with charges of murder and kidnap hanging over their heads."

"Not under that name, no. But they walked away with a million pounds in cash and diamonds. That would be over three million in today's money. If they were dedicated political animals, you'd expect to see chunks of that money turning up in the coffers of radical groups with similar aims. My predecessors on this case asked MI5 for a watching brief. In the five years after Cat's murder, it never happened. None of the groups of fringe nutters suddenly came into money. So we don't think the kidnappers were really a bunch of political activists. We think they were likely closer to home."

Sinclair's expression said it all. "And that's why I'm here." He couldn't keep the sneer off his face.

"Not for the reason you think," Karen said. "You're not here because I suspect you." She held up her hands in a gesture of surrender. "We never managed to put you anywhere near the kidnap or the ransom scene. Your bank accounts never showed any unaccountable funds. Yes, I know, you're pissed off to hear we checked your bank accounts. Don't be. Not if you really care about Cat or Adam. You should be pleased that we've been doing our job the best we can all these years. And that it's pretty much put you in the clear."

"In spite of the poison Brodie Grant has tried to plant about me."

Karen shook her head. "You might be pleasantly surprised on that score. But anyway, here's the point. You're here because you are the only person who really knew Cat. She was too like her father; I suspect they might have ended up best pals, but they were still in the fighting phase. Her mother's dead. She didn't seem to have close female friends. So that leaves you as my only way in to Cat's life. And I think that's where the secret of her death lies." She pinned Sinclair with the directness of her gaze. "So what's it going to be, Fergus? Are you going to help me?"

Sunday, 14th August 1983; Newton of Wemyss

Catriona Maclennan Grant spun round on one toe, arms outstretched. "Mine, all mine," she said in mock wicked witch tones. Suddenly she stopped, staggering slightly with dizziness. "What do you think, Fergus? Isn't it just perfect?"

Fergus Sinclair surveyed the dingy room. The gatehouse on the Wemyss estate was nothing like the plain but spotless cottage he'd grown up in. It was even further removed from Rotheswell Castle. It wasn't even as appealing as the student houses he'd lived in. Having stood empty for a couple of years, it held no sense of its previous occupants. But even so, he found it hard to feel enthusiastic about it. It wasn't how he'd imagined them setting up home together. "It'll be fine once we've gone through it with a bucket of paint," he said.

"Of course it will," Cat said. "I want to keep it simple. Bright but simple. Apricot in here, I think." She headed for the door. "Lemon for the hall, stairs, and landing. Sunshine yellow in the kitchen. I'm going to use the other downstairs room as an office, so something neutral." She ran up the stairs, and leaned over the banister, smiling down at him. "Blue for my bedroom. A nice Swedish sort of blue."

Sinclair laughed at her enthusiasm. "Don't I get a say?"

Cat's smile faded. "Why would you get a say, Fergus? It's not your house."

The words slammed into him like a physical blow. "What do you mean? I thought we were going to live together?"

Cat dropped on to the top step and sat there, knees tight together, arms folded round herself. "Why did you think that? I never said anything about that."

The ground beneath his feet seemed not to be stable. Sinclair clutched at the newel post for support. "It's what we always talked about. We'd finish our training and move in together. Me keepering, you doing the glasswork. It's what we planned, Cat." He stared up at her, willing her to admit he was right.

And so she did, but not in a way that made him feel any better. "Fergus, we were hardly more than children then. It's like when you're little and your big cousin says he's going to marry you when you're older. You mean it all when you say it, but then you outgrow the promise."

"No," he protested, starting up the stairs. "No, we weren't children. We knew what we were saying. I still love you as much as I ever did. Every promise I've made to you—I still want to keep them." He pushed himself down next to her, forcing her to shift right up against the wall. He put his arm round her shoulders. But still she kept her arms wrapped round her body.

"Fergus, I want to live by myself," Cat said, staring down to where he'd been a moment before as if she was still speaking directly to him. "This is the first time I've had my own work space and my own living space. My head is bursting with ideas for things I want to make. And for how I want to live."

"I won't interfere with your ideas," Sinclair insisted. "You can have everything just the way you want it."

"But you'll be *here*, Fergus. When I go to bed at night, when I wake up in the morning. I'll have to think about things like what we're going to eat and when we're going to eat it."

"I'll do the cooking," he said. He could feed himself; how hard could it be to feed both of them? "We can do this on your terms."

"I'll still have to think about mealtimes and things happening at set times, not when it feels natural or right for my creative rhythms. I'll have to think about your washing, when you need to be in the bathroom. What you're going to watch on the TV." Cat was rocking to and fro now, the natural anxiety she'd always worked to hide coming to the surface. "I don't want to have to deal with all that."

"But, Cat . . . "

"I'm an artist, Fergus. I'm not saying that like it's some precious state that sets me above everybody else. What I mean is that I'm kind of fucked up. I'm not good at being with people for extended periods of time."

"We seem to do OK together." He could hear the pleading in his voice and he wasn't ashamed. She was worth shaming himself for.

"But we don't actually spend huge chunks of time together, Fergus. Look at the last few years. I've been in Sweden, you've been in London. We've spent the occasional weekend together, but mostly we've seen each other at Rotheswell. We've hardly ever spent more than a couple of nights together. And that suits me fine."

"It doesn't suit me," he said gruffly. "I want to be with you all the time. Like I said, we can do it on your terms."

She slipped out from under his arm and dropped down a couple of steps, turning so she could look at him. "Can't you see how scary that is for me? Just hearing you say it makes me feel claustrophobic. You talk about doing it on my terms, but none of my terms include having someone under the same roof as me. Fergus, you mean so much to me. There isn't anyone else who makes me feel the way you do. Please, please don't spoil that by pushing me or guilt-tripping me into something I can't bear the thought of."

His face felt frozen, as if he was standing on top of Falkland Hill in a gale, the skin whipped hard against his bones, his eyes flayed to tears. "It's what people do when they love each other," he said.

Now she reached out her hand and put it on his knee. "It's one model for loving," she said. "It's the most common one. But part of the reason for that is economic, Fergus. People live together because it's cheaper than living apart. Two can live as cheaply as one. It doesn't mean it's the best way for everybody. Lots of people have relationships that don't conform to that pattern. And those other ways of doing it work just as well. You think me not wanting to live with you means I don't love you. But Fergus, it's the other way round. Living with you would destroy our relationship. I'd go crazy. I'd want to kill you. It's because I love you that I don't want to live with you."

He pushed her hand away and stood up. "You've spent too fucking long in Sweden," he shouted, feeling his throat tighten. "Listen to yourself. Models for loving. Conforming to patterns. That's not what love is. Love is . . . Love is . . . Cat, where does affection and kindness and helping each other find a place in your world?"

She stood up and leaned against the wall. "Same place they always have. Fergus, we've always been kind to each other. We've always cared for each other. Why do we need to change the shape of our relationship? Why risk all those beautiful things that work so well between us? Even sex. Everybody I know, once they start living together, the sex stops being so exciting. Two, three years down the line, they hardly ever fuck any more. But look at us." She sidestepped up so she was level with him. "We don't take each other for granted. So when we see each other, it's still electric." She stepped forward, one hand flat on his chest, the other cupped under his balls. In spite of himself, he felt the hardening rush of blood. "Come on, Fergus—fuck me," she whispered. "Here. Now."

And so she got her own way. As usual.

Thursday, 5th July 2007

"Like her father, she was very good at getting her own way. She was more subtle than him, but the end result was the same," Sinclair concluded.

For the first time since the Macaroon had briefed her, Karen felt she had a sense of who Catriona Maclennan Grant had been. A woman who knew her own mind. An artist with a vision she was determined to realize. A loner who took pleasure in company when she was in the mood for it. A lover who learned how to accept being pinned down only after she became a mother. A difficult woman but a brave one, Karen suspected. "Can you think of anybody whose life touched hers that might have wanted to punish her?" she asked.

"Punish her for what?"

"You name it. Her talent. Her privilege. Her father."

He thought about it. "It's hard to imagine. The thing is, she'd just spent four years in Sweden. She just called herself Cat Grant. I don't think anybody over there had the faintest idea who Brodie Maclennan Grant is." He stretched his legs out and crossed them at the ankles. "She did summer school over here the first couple of years she was in Sweden. She hooked up with some of the people she knew from when she was at the Edinburgh College of Art."

Karen sat up straight. "I didn't know she was at the Edinburgh College of Art," she said. "There was nothing in the file about that. All it says is that she studied in Sweden."

Sinclair nodded. "Technically, that's right. But instead of doing the sixth year at her fancy private school in Edinburgh, she did a foundation course at the College of Art. It's probably not on the file because her old man didn't know about it. He absolutely didn't want her to be an artist. So it was a big secret between Cat and her mum. She'd go off every morning on the train and come home at more or less the usual time. But instead of going to school she went to the college. You really didn't know?"

"We really didn't know." Karen looked at Phil. "We need to start looking at the people who were on that foundation course."

"The good news is that there weren't many of them," Sinclair said. "Only ten or a dozen. Of course, she knew other students, but it was the ones on her course that she mainly hung out with."

"Can you remember who her pals were?"

Sinclair nodded. "There were five of them. They liked the same bands, they liked the same artists. They were always going on about modernism and its legacy." He rolled his eyes. "I used to feel like a complete hick from the sticks."

"Names? Details?" Phil putting the pressure on again. He reached for his notebook and flipped it open.

"There was a lassie from Montrose: Diana Macrae. Another from Peebles, what was her name . . . ? Something Italian . . . Demelza Gardner."

"Demelza's not Italian, it's Cornish," Phil said. Karen silenced him with a look.

"Whatever. It sounded Italian to me," Sinclair said. "There were two lads as well. A guy from Crieff or some arsey place in Perthshire like that: Toby Inglis. And finally, Jack Docherty. He was a working-class toe-rag from Glasgow. They were all nice middle-class kids and Jack was their performing monkey. He didn't seem to mind. He was one of those people who don't care what kind of attention they get as long as they get some."

"Did she stay in touch with any of them when she went to Sweden?"

Sinclair stood up, ignoring her, as his boys raced across the grass towards him. They threw themselves on him in an excited torrent of what Karen took to be German. Sinclair clung on to them, struggling forward a couple of steps with them hanging on like baby chimps. Then he dropped them, said something to them, ruffled their hair, and sent them off in pursuit of their mother, who had disappeared towards the steps down to the shore. "Sorry," he said, coming back and sitting down again. "They always like to be sure you know what you're missing. To answer your question—I don't really know. I vaguely remember Cat mentioning one or other of them a few times, but I didn't pay much attention. I had nothing in common with them. I never met any of them again after Cat left the college." He ran a hand over his jaw. "Looking back at it now, I think that, the older we got, the less Cat and I had in common. If she'd lived, we would never have got back together again."

"You might have found some common ground over Adam eventually," Karen said.

"I'd like to think so." He looked longingly at the gateway his boys had disappeared through. "Is there anything else? Only, I'd kind of like to get back to my life."

"Do you think there was anyone from her art college days who might have harboured ill feeling towards her?" Karen asked.

Sinclair shook his head. "Nothing she ever said would make me think that," he said. "She had a strong personality, but she was a hard person to dislike. I don't remember her ever complaining that she'd been given a hard time by anybody." He stood up again, smoothing down his trousers. "I have to say, I can't believe anyone who knew her would think they could get away with kidnapping her. She was far too good at getting her own way."

GLENROTHES

The Mint stabbed the keyboard with his index fingers. He didn't know why they called that fast business "touch typing." Because you couldn't type without touching the keyboard. It was all touch typing, when you got down to it. He also wasn't sure why the boss kept lumbering him with the computer searches unless it was just pure sadism. Everybody thought young guys like him were totally at home in front of a computer, but for the Mint it was like a foreign country where he didn't even know the word for beer.

He'd have been much happier if she'd sent him off with the Hat to the College of Art to talk to real people and pore through yearbooks and physical records. He was better at that. And besides, DS Parhatka was a good laugh. There was nothing funny about trawling through the message boards and membership lists of www.bestdaysofourlives.com searching for the names the boss had dropped on his desk on a tatty page torn from a notebook.

This was so not what he'd joined up for. Where was the action? Where were the dramatic car chases and arrests? Instead of excitement, he got the boss and the Hat acting like they were some ancient comedy partnership, like French and Saunders. Or was it Flanders and Swann? He could never get them straight in his head.

He hadn't even had to monster anybody to get full access to the website. The woman he'd spoken to had fallen over herself to be helpful. "We've helped the police before, we're always happy to do what we can," she'd gabbled as soon as he'd made his request. Whoever she'd dealt with before had clearly left her in a state of shivering submission. He liked that in a source.

He checked the list of names again. Diana Macrae. Demelza Gardner. Toby Inglis. Jack Docherty. 1977–78 the year he was looking for. After a couple of false clicks, he finally made it to the membership list. Only one of them was there. Diana Macrae was now Diana Waddell, but it wasn't hard to figure that out. He clicked on Diana's profile.

> *I followed my foundation course at the College of Art with a degree from Glasgow School of Art, specializing in sculpture. After graduating, I started working in the field of art therapy for people with mental illness. I met Desmond, my husband, when we were both working in Dundee. We married in 1990 and we have two children. We live in Glenisla, which we all adore. I have started sculpting in wood again and have a contract with a local garden centre as well as a gallery in Dundee.*

A gallery in Dundee, the Mint thought scornfully. Art? In Dundee. About as likely as peace in the Middle East. He skimmed through more rubbish about her husband and kids, then clicked through to her messages and e-mails from fellow ex-students. Why did these people bother? Their lives were as dull as an East Fife home game. After scrolling through a couple of dozen innocuous exchanges, he found a message from someone called Shannon. *Do you ever hear from Jack Docherty?* she asked.

Darling Jack! We swap Christmas cards. Her smugness penetrated the notoriously nuance-free e-mail. *He's out in Western Australia now. He has his own gallery in Perth. He does a lot of work with Aboriginal artists. We have a couple of pieces from him, they're remarkable. He's very happy. He has an*

Aboriginal boyfriend. Quite a few years younger than him and very handsome, but he sounds like a sweetheart. Once our two are off to uni, we're planning a trip out to visit.

Two birds with one stone, the Mint thought, scribbling the details down. He continued to the end of Diana's wittering correspondence, then decided he needed a break while he came up with his next move.

A cup of coffee later, he got back to his search. Neither Toby Inglis nor Demelza Gardner showed up anywhere on the College of Art area of the website. But thanks to the way his contact had rolled over, he was able to search the entire website. He typed in the woman's name and to his complete astonishment, he got a hit. He clicked on the result and discovered Gardner described as "totally my favourite teacher." The message was on the site of a high school in Norwich.

At least he had the sense to Google the school. And there was Demelza Gardner. Head of Art. God, this computer stuff was a piece of piss once you got the hang of it. He tried Toby Inglis's name in the search engine and again came up with a hit. The Mint followed the link to a forum where former pupils of a private school in Crieff could rabbit on to their hearts' content about their fabulous bloody lives. It took him a while to unravel the threads of correspondence, but at last he found what he was looking for.

Feeling rather pleased with himself, the Mint tore off the top sheet from his notepad and went off in search of DI Pirie.

It had, Karen thought, gone something like this. She had called Bel Richmond and invited her to come to CCRT for an interview as soon as possible. Preferably within the hour. Bel had refused. Karen had mentioned the small matter of police obstruction.

Then Bel had gone to Brodie Grant and complained that she didn't want to trot off to Glenrothes at Karen Pirie's beck and call. Then Grant had called the Macaroon and explained that Bel didn't want to be interviewed and DI Pirie had better stop threatening her. Then the Macaroon had summoned her and given her a hard time for upsetting Brodie Grant, and told her to lay off Bel Richmond.

Then Karen had called Bel Richmond again. In her sweetest voice, she had told Bel to present herself at CCRT at two o'clock. "If you're not here," she said, "there will be a squad car at Rotheswell ten minutes after that to arrest you for police obstruction." Then she'd put the phone down.

Now it was a minute to two and Dave Cruickshank had just called her to say Bel Richmond was in the building. "Get a uniform to take her up to Interview One and wait with her till I get there." Karen got herself a Diet Coke out of the fridge and sat down at her desk for five minutes. She took a last swig from her can, then headed down the hall to the interview room.

Bel was sitting at the table in the grey windowless room, looking furious. A red pack of Marlboros sat in front of her, a single cigarette lying next to it. Clearly she'd forgotten the Scots had banned smoking ahead of the English until the uniformed officer had reminded her.

Karen pulled a chair out and dropped into it. The foam cushion had been worn into its shape by other buttocks than hers, and she wriggled to get comfortable. Elbows on the table, she leaned forward. "Don't ever try to fuck with me again," she said, her voice conversational, her eyes like glittering granite.

"Oh, please," Bel said. "Let's not make this a pissing contest. I'm here now, so let it go."

Karen didn't take her eyes off Bel. "We need to talk about Italy."

"Why not? Lovely country. Fabulous food, wine's getting better all the time. And then there's the art—"

"Stop it. I mean it. I will charge you with police obstruction and put you in a cell and leave you there till I can bring you before a sheriff. I am not going to be jerked around by Sir Broderick Maclennan Grant or his minions."

"I'm not a minion of Brodie Grant," Bel said. "I'm an independent investigative journalist."

"Independent? You're living under his roof. Eating his food, drinking his wine. Which I bet is not Italian, by the way. And who paid for that little jaunt to Italy? You're not independent, you're bought and paid for."

"You're wrong."

"No, I'm not. I've got more freedom of action than you have right now, Bel. I can tell my boss to shove it. Come to think of it, I just have. Can you say the same? If it wasn't for the Italian police, I wouldn't even know you'd been talking to people in Tuscany about the Villa Totti. The very fact that you've been reporting to Grant and not talking to us tells me that he owns you."

"That's bullshit. Reporters don't talk to cops about their investigations till their work is finished. That's what's going on here."

Karen shook her head slowly. "I don't think so. And, to tell you the truth, I'm surprised. I didn't think you were that kind of woman."

"You don't know anything about me, Inspector." Bel settled herself more comfortably in the chair, as if she was getting ready for something pleasurable.

"I know you didn't earn your reputation spouting clichés like that." Karen pulled her chair closer to the table, cutting the distance between them to less than a couple of feet. "And

I know that you've been a campaigning journalist for almost the whole of your career. You know what people say about you, Bel? They say you're a fighter. They say you're someone who does the right thing even if it's not the easiest. Like the way you took your sister and her boy under your roof when they needed looking after. They say you don't care about the popularity of your position, you drag the truth out kicking and screaming and make people confront it. They say you're a maverick. Somebody who operates to her own set of rules. Somebody who doesn't take orders from the Man." She waited, staring Bel down. The journalist blinked first, but she didn't look away. "You think they'd recognize you now? Taking your orders from a man like Sir Broderick Maclennan Grant? A man who epitomizes the capitalist system? A man who resisted his daughter's every attempt at self-determination to the point where she ended up putting herself in harm's way? Is that what you've come down to?"

Bel picked up her cigarette and tapped it end to end on the table. "Sometimes you have to find a place inside the enemy's tent so you can find out what he's really like. You of all people should understand that. Cops use undercover all the time when there's no other way of getting a story. Do you have any idea how many press interviews Brodie Grant has given in the last twenty years?"

"Taking a wild guess, I'd say . . . none?"

"Right. When I found a piece of evidence that might just crack this cold case open, I figured there would be a lot of interest in Grant. Publisher-type interest. But only if someone could get alongside Grant and see what he was like for real." She raised one corner of her mouth in a cynical half-smile. "I thought it might as well be me."

"Fair enough. I'm not going to sit here and pick holes in your self-justification. But how does your quest to give the world the definitive book about that miserable family grant you the right to stand above the law?"

"That's not how I see it."

"Of course it's not how you see it. You need to see yourself as the person who's acting on behalf of Cat Grant. The person who's going to bring her son home, dead or alive. The hero. You can't afford to see yourself in a true light. Because that true light shows you up as the person who is standing in the way of all of those things. Well, here's the scoop, Bel. You haven't got the resources to bring this to an end. I don't know what Brodie Grant's promised you, but it's not going to be clean. Not in any sense." Karen could feel her anger coiling inside her, getting ready to spring. She pushed her chair back, putting some space between them.

"The Italian police don't care about what happened to Cat Grant," Bel said.

"You're right. And why should they?" Karen felt her face flush. "But they do care about the person whose blood is all over the kitchen floor of the Villa Totti. So much blood that that person is almost certainly dead. They care about that, and they're doing everything they can to find out what happened there. And in the course of that, there will be information that will help us. That's how we do things. We don't hire private eyes who tailor their reports to what the client wants to hear. We don't construct our own private legal system to serve our own interests. Let me ask you a question, Bel. Just between the two of us." Karen turned to the uniformed constable who was still standing by the door. "Could you give us a minute?"

She waited till he had closed the door behind him. "Under Scots law, I can't use anything you say to me now. There's no corroboration, you see. So here's my question. And I want you to think about it very carefully. You don't need to tell me the answer. I just want to be sure that you've thought about it honestly and sincerely. If you were to find the kidnappers, what do you think Brodie Grant would do with that information?"

The muscles round Bel's mouth tightened. "I think that's a scurrilous implication."

"I didn't imply. You inferred." Karen got up. "I'm not a numpty, Bel. Don't treat me like one." She opened the door. "You can come back in now."

The constable took up his station by the door, and Karen returned to her chair. "You should be ashamed of yourself," she said. "Who the hell do you people think you are, with your private law? Is this what you've spent your career working for? A law for the rich and powerful that can thumb its nose at the rest of us?" *That hit home. About bloody time.*

Bel shook her head. "You misjudge me."

"Prove it. Tell me what you found out in Tuscany."

"Why should I? If you people were any good at your job, you'd have found it out yourself."

"You think I need to defend my ability? The only thing I have to defend is that our investigations struggle under the weight of rules and regulations and resources. That sometimes means it takes me and my team a while to cover the ground. But you can be sure that, when we do, there's not a blade of grass goes unexamined. If you give a toss about justice, you should tell me." She gave Bel a cold smile. "Otherwise, you might find yourself on the other end of the reporters' notebooks."

"Is that a threat?"

To Karen's ear, it sounded like bluster. Bel was close to spilling, she could sense it. "I don't need to threaten," she said. "Even Brodie Grant knows what a leaky sieve the police are. Stuff just seems to slip out into the public domain. And you know how the press love it when someone camped out on the moral high ground gets caught up in a mudslide." Oh yes, she was right. Bel was definitely growing uneasy.

"Look, Karen—I can call you Karen?" Bel's voice dropped into hot chocolate warmth.

"Call me what you like, it makes no odds to me. I'm not your pal, Bel. I've got six hours to question you without a lawyer and I plan to make the most of every minute. Tell me what you found out in Italy."

"I'm not telling you anything," Bel said. "I want to go outside for a cigarette. I'll just leave my bag here on the table. Careful you don't knock it over, things might spill out." She stood up. "Is that OK with you, Inspector?"

Karen struggled not to smile. "The constable will need to keep you company. But take your time. Make it two. I've got plenty to keep me occupied." Watching Bel leave the room, she couldn't help a momentary flash of admiration for the other woman's style. Give it up without giving in. *Nice one, Bel.*

Her arm brushed against the straw shopping bag, which fell over on its side, fanning a wedge of paper out on the table. Without reading it, Karen scooped it up and hustled down the hall to her office. Into the photocopier, the whole bundle copied inside ten minutes, a set of copies locked in her drawer, the originals in her hand. And back to the interview room, where she settled down to read.

As she digested Bel's report for Brodie Grant, her mind arranged the bullet points. Mongrel bunch of puppeteers squatting the Villa Totti. Daniel Porteous, British painter, not so much friend of the house as friend of Matthias the boss and his girlfriend. Matthias the set designer and poster maker. Gabriel Porteous, son of Daniel. Seen with Matthias the day before Bur-Est scattered to the four winds. Blood on the kitchen floor, fresh that morning. Daniel Porteous a fake. Already a fake in November 1984, when he registered his son's fake birth.

She stumbled for a moment on the mother's name, knowing she'd come across it but struggling for context. Then she said it out loud and it clicked. Frida Kahlo. That Mexican artist that Michael Marra wrote the song about. "Frida Kahlo's Visit to the Taybridge Bar." She had a bad time with her man. So, nothing new there, then. But somebody was being a smartarse with the registrar, laughing up his sleeve at some minor civil servant who wouldn't know Frida Kahlo from Michelangelo. Showing off. Thinking he was being clever but not realizing he was saying something about himself in the process. He must have been a skilful forger though, this Daniel Porteous, to turn up with all the necessary documentation to convince the registrar. And bold, to carry it through.

It was all very interesting, but what had convinced Bel that Gabriel Porteous was Adam Maclennan Grant? And, by logical extension, Daniel Porteous his biological father? And by extending the logic further, that Daniel Porteous and Matthias were the kidnappers? Still in touch after all these years, still in possession of the original silk screen. Based on the poster, you could draw the thread through, but it was only circumstantial.

Aware that Bel would be back any moment, Karen flicked forward through the pages, skimming for sense, hunting for something that might anchor the theory to solid fact. The last few pages were photographs—originals taken at some party, and enlarged sections with captions.

Her stomach flipped and her mind at first refused to accept what she was looking at. Yes, it was true that the boy Gabriel bore a striking resemblance to both Brodie and Cat Grant. But that wasn't what had provoked the turmoil inside. Karen stared at the image of Daniel Porteous, nausea churning her guts. Dear God, what was she to make of this? And then with the suddenness of a light coming on, she realized something that turned everything on its head.

Daniel Porteous had registered the birth of his son three months before the kidnap. He'd assumed a fake identity at least three months ahead of the time that he was going to use it to make his getaway. Fair enough. It demonstrated forethought. But he'd also established the right to take his son with him. "You don't do that if you're planning to ransom him," she said under her breath.

Karen stuffed Bel's papers back in the straw bag and headed for the door. This was insane. She needed to talk to someone who could help her make sense of this. Where the hell was Phil when she needed him?

As she burst out of the interview room, she practically collided with the Mint. He sidestepped, looking startled. "I was looking for you," he said.

Definitely not mutual. "I can't stop now," she said, pushing past him.

"I've got this for you," he said plaintively.

Karen whirled round, grabbed the sheet of paper, and broke into a run. She felt as if an army of messengers were running round inside her head, each with a jigsaw piece. Right now, none of the matching pieces were joining up. But she had a shrewd suspicion that, when they did, the picture would rock everybody back on their heels.

Rotheswell Castle

There had been a shift change in the security team since Bel left for her interview with Karen Pirie, so the guard on duty at the gate had to clear her return via taxi with the castle. That knocked on the head any hopes of slipping back quietly. As she paid off the cab, the front door swung open to reveal a grim-faced Grant. Bel assumed a look of pleasure and walked towards him.

No pleasantries today. "What did you tell her?" he demanded.

"Nothing," Bel said. "A good journalist protects her sources and her information. I told her nothing." It was, technically, the truth. She had told Karen Pirie nothing. She hadn't had to. The inspector had come haring out of the building, pausing only to tell Bel she was free to go.

"Something's just broken on another case I'm working, I've got to go to Edinburgh. I'll be in touch. You can go back to Rotheswell as soon as you like," Karen had said. Then she'd given Bel a wink. "And you can put your hand on your heart and tell Brodie you didn't talk."

Secure in the knowledge that she wasn't actually lying, Bel moved into the house, leaving him no choice but to grab her or follow her.

"You're telling me you told her nothing and she just let you go?" He had to extend his stride to its full length to keep up with her as she bustled down the hall to the stairs.

"I made it clear to DI Pirie that I was not going to talk. She recognized there was no point in prolonging the stalemate." Bel glanced over her shoulder. "This isn't the first time in my career I've had to hold information back from the police. I told you there was no need to try and put the frighteners on her."

Grant conceded with a nod. "I'm sorry I didn't take you at your word."

"So you should be," Bel said. "I—" She broke off to reach for her ringing phone. "Bel Richmond," she said, holding a finger up to still Grant.

A torrent of Italian poured into her ear. She made out "Boscolata," then recognized the voice of the youth who had seen Gabriel with Matthias the night BurEst had done a runner. "Slowly, just take your time," she protested gently, switching to his language.

"I saw him," the boy said. "Yesterday. I saw Gabe in Siena again. And I knew you wanted to find him, so I followed him."

"You followed him?"

"Yeah, like in the movies. He got on a bus, and I managed to sneak on without him seeing me. We ended up in Greve. You know Greve in Chianti?"

She knew Greve. A perfect little market town stuffed with trendy shops for the rich English, redeemed by a few bars and trattorie where the locals still ate and drank. A meeting place for young people on Fridays and Saturdays. "I know Greve," she said.

"So, we end up in the main piazza and he goes into this bar, sits down with a bunch of other guys about the same age. I stayed outside, but I could see him through the window. He had a couple of beers and a bowl of pasta, then he came out."

"Were you able to follow him?"

"Not really. I thought I could, but he had a Vespa parked a couple of streets back. He went off down the road that heads east out of town."

Near, but not near enough. "You did well," she said.

"I did better. I left it about twenty minutes, then I went into the bar he'd been in. I said I was looking for Gabe, I was supposed to meet him there. His mates said I'd not long missed him. So I went all innocent and said, could they direct me to his place, only I didn't know how to get there."

"Amazing," Bel said, genuinely taken aback by his initiative. Grant started to walk away, but she beckoned him back.

"So they drew me a map," he said. "Pretty cool, huh? Apparently it's, like, one step up from a shepherd's hut."

"What did you do?"

"I got the last bus home," he said, as if it was blindingly obvious. Which she supposed it was if you were a teenage boy.

"And you've got this map?"

"I brought it back with me," he said. "I thought it might be worth something to you. I thought maybe a hundred euros?"

"We'll talk about it. Listen, I'll be back as soon as I can. Don't talk to anybody except Grazia about this, OK?"

"OK."

Bel ended the call and gave Grant the thumbs-up. "Result," she said. "Forget the private eyes. My contact has discovered where Gabriel is living. And now I need to get back to Italy to talk to him."

Grant's face lit up. "That's tremendous news. I'm coming with you. If this boy is my grandson, I want to see him face to face. The sooner the better."

"I don't think so. This needs to be handled carefully," Bel said.

From behind her, a voice chimed in. "She's right, Brodie. We need to know a lot more about this boy before you put your head over the parapet." Judith stepped forward and laid a hand on her husband's arm. "This could all be an elaborate set-up. If these are the people who kidnapped Adam and robbed you twenty-two years ago, we know they're capable of the most cruel behaviour. We don't know anything else for sure. Let Bel handle it." Grant made a protest, but she shushed him. "Bel, do you think you can get a DNA sample without this young man realizing?"

"It's not so hard," Bel said. "One way or another, I'm sure I can manage it."

"I still think I should go," Grant said.

"Of course you do, darling. But the women are right this time. And you will just have to possess your soul in patience. Now, where's the plane?"

Grant sighed. "It's at Edinburgh."

"Perfect. By the time Bel's packed a bag, Susan will have everything arranged." She glanced at her watch. "You said you would take Alec fishing after school, so I can drive Bel over." She smiled at Bel. "Better get cracking. I'll see you downstairs in fifteen?"

Bel nodded, too gobsmacked to argue. If she'd ever wondered how Judith Grant held her own in her marriage, she'd just witnessed a spectacular demonstration. Grant had been totally sandbagged and, short of throwing a temper tantrum, there was no way back for him. She turned and ran up the stairs. *Add another zero to the advance.* This was turning into the story of her career. Everyone who had ever dissed her was going to have to eat their words. It was going to be blissful. OK, there was some tedious legwork to be got through, but there was always tedious legwork. There just wasn't always glory at the end of it.

KIRKCALDY

Karen paced the floor, an unwavering ten steps across the living room, then a swivel and ten steps back. Usually movement helped her get her thoughts lined up in order. But this evening, it wasn't working. The jumble in her head was intractable, like herding cats or wrestling water. She suspected it was because, at some deep level, she was resisting the inevitable conclusion.

She needed Phil here to hold her hand while she thought the unthinkable.

Where the hell was he? She'd left a message on his voicemail almost two hours ago, but he hadn't got back to her. It wasn't like him to go off the radar. As that thought circled for the hundredth time, her doorbell pealed out.

She'd never covered the distance to the front door faster. Phil stood on the doorstep, looking sheepish. "I'm sorry," he said. "I went to the National Library in Edinburgh and I had to turn my phone off. I forgot to turn it back on again till a few minutes ago. I thought it would be quicker to just come straight over."

Karen was ushering him into the living room as he spoke. He looked around curiously. "This is nice," he said.

"No, it's not. It's just a machine for living in," she said.

"But it's a good one. It's relaxing. The colours all work with each other. You've got a good eye."

She didn't have the heart to tell him it was someone else's eye. "I didn't ask you round to appreciate the décor," she said. "Do you want a beer? Or a glass of wine?"

"I've got the car," he said.

"Never mind that. You can always get a cab home. Believe me, you are going to need a drink." She thrust the photocopy of Bel's notes at him. "Beer or wine?"

"Have you got some red wine?"

"Read that. I'll be right back." Karen went through to the kitchen, chose the best of the half-dozen reds she had in the rack, unscrewed the cap, and poured two big glasses. The jammy spice of the Australian shiraz tickled her nose as she picked up the drinks. It was the first external thing she'd noticed since she'd left the office.

Phil had made his way through to the dining area and was

sitting at the table, intent on the report. She put the glass down by his hand. Absently, he took a swig. Karen couldn't keep still. She sat down, then she stood up. She went through to the kitchen and returned with a plate of cheese crackers. Then she remembered the sheet of paper the Mint had given her. She'd stuffed it in her bag without looking at it.

She tracked her bag down in the kitchen. The Mint's notes weren't exactly the most clear or succinct that she'd ever read, but she got the gist of what he had found out. Three of Cat's friends were clearly of no interest. But the forum message he'd copied about Toby Inglis leapt out at her with all the force of a coiled spring . . . *just like Kate Mosse's book. But you'll never guess who we bumped into in a bistro in Perpignan. Only Toby Inglis. You remember how he was going to set the world on fire, be the next Olivier? Well, it obviously hasn't worked out quite the way he planned. He was pretty evasive when it came to the details, but he said he's a theatre director and designer. IMHO he was being a bit economical with the truth. Brian said he looked more like a superannuated hippy. He certainly smelled like one, all patchouli and dope. We asked where we could see one of his productions, but he said he was taking a summer break. I was dying to do some more digging but then this German woman arrived. I think she thought they were eating there, but he hustled her out of the door as fast as he could. I think he didn't want us talking to her and finding out the truth. Whatever that is. So, after Perpignan . . .*

Karen re-read the Mint's scrawl. Could this be Matthias? It certainly sounded like the mysterious Matthias who hadn't been seen since he was spotted in Siena with Gabriel Porteous. Another piece that appeared to belong with the jigsaw but didn't seem to fit.

Karen forced herself to breathe deeply, then joined Phil at

the dining table. He'd spread the prints in front of him. He poked one with his finger to align it with the others. "It's him, isn't it?" he said.

"Adam?"

He flapped an impatient hand at her. "Well yes, of course it's Adam. It's got to be Adam. Not just because he looks like his mother and his grandfather. But because the man who's brought him up is Mick Prentice."

Karen experienced a moment of weightlessness. The agitation stilled and she could think straight again. She wasn't losing her mind or letting her imagination run away with her. "Are you sure?"

"He's not actually changed that much," Phil said. "And look, there's the scar—" He traced it with his fingertip. "The coal tattoo through his right eyebrow. The thin blue line. It's Mick Prentice. I'd put money on it."

"Mick Prentice was one of the kidnappers?" Even to her own ears, Karen sounded a bit wobbly.

"I think we both know he was more than that," Phil said.

"The registration," Karen said.

"Exactly. This was all planned even before Mick left Jenny. He'd set up his fake identity so he could start a new life. But there can be only one reason why he needed to set up a fake identity for Adam."

"He wasn't planning to ransom him at all," Karen said. "Because he was Adam's father. Not Fergus Sinclair. Mick Prentice." She took a gulp of red wine. "It was a set-up, wasn't it? There were no anarchists, were there?"

"No." Phil sighed. "It looks like there were two miners. Mick and his pal Andy."

"You think Andy was part of the plot?"

"It looks that way. How else do you account for him ending up buried in the cave at just the right time?"

"But why? Why kill him? He was Mick's best mate," Karen protested. "If he could trust anyone, he could trust Andy. The way you guys operate, he could probably have trusted Andy more than Cat."

"Maybe it was an accident. Maybe he hit his head getting in or out of the boat."

"River said the back of his head was smashed in. That doesn't sound like an accident getting into a boat."

Phil threw his hands in the air in a "whatever" gesture. "He could have tripped, smacked his head on the quay. It was chaos that night. Anything could have happened. I'd put my money on Andy being the co-conspirator."

"And Cat? Was she part of the plan or was she the victim? Were she and Mick still an item or was he trying to get his kid and enough of Brodie Grant's money to set the pair of them up for life?"

Phil scratched his head. "I think she was in on it," he said. "If they'd split up and he'd taken them both, she'd never have let Adam out of her arms. She'd have been too scared of him taking the bairn away from her."

"I can't believe they got away with it," she said.

Phil gathered the prints together and straightened the edges. "Lawson was looking in the wrong direction. And with good reason."

"No, no. I don't mean the kidnap. I mean the affair. Everybody knows everybody else's business in a place like the Newton. Easier to get away with murder than an extra-marital affair, I'd have said."

"So it looks like we've done what Lawson couldn't do. Solved the kidnapping, tracked down Adam Maclennan Grant."

"Not quite," Karen said. "We don't actually know where he is. And there's the small matter of a lot of blood spilled in Tuscany. Which could be his."

"Or it could have been spilled by him. In which case he's not going to be very keen on being found."

"There's one thing we haven't factored in," Karen said, passing Phil the result of the Mint's searches. "It looks like Matthias the puppeteer might actually be a friend of Cat's from art college. Toby Inglis has a description that you could stretch to cover Matthias, the leader of the motley crew. Where does he fit in the picture?"

Phil looked at the paper. "Interesting. If he was involved in the kidnap, it might be more than embarrassment at his less-than-glittering career that's making him keep a low profile." He finished his glass of wine and tipped it towards Karen. "Any more where that came from?"

She fetched the bottle and refilled his glass. "Any bright ideas?"

Phil took a slow mouthful. "Well, if this Toby is Matthias, he was an old pal of Cat's. Could be that's how he met Mick. It didn't have to be planned, he could just have turned up out of the blue when Mick was there. You know what artists are like."

"I don't, actually. I don't think I've ever met anyone who was at art college."

"My brother's girlfriend was. The one who's doing the makeover at my place."

"And is she prone to being unreliable?" Karen asked.

"No," Phil admitted. "Unpredictable, though. I never know what she's going to inflict on me next. Maybe I should have got you to do the job instead. This is definitely more easy on the eye."

"What I live for," Karen said. "Easy on the eye." There was a charged moment of silence between them, then she hastily cleared her throat and said, "But here's the thing, Phil. If they'd met when Mick was with Cat, then ran into each other by chance in Italy, how the holy fuck did Mick explain what had happened to Cat and how he'd ended up with the kid?"

"So you're saying he must have been involved in the kidnap too?"

She shrugged. "I don't know. I really don't know. What I do know is that we need to get the Italian police to find the person whose blood isn't on the floor of that villa so we can ask them some pertinent questions."

"Another tall order for the woman who put Jimmy Lawson behind bars." He raised his glass to her.

"I'm never going to live that down, am I?"

"Why would you want to?"

Karen looked away. "Sometimes it feels like a millstone round my neck. Like the man who shot Liberty Valance."

"It's not like that," Phil said. "You nailed Lawson fair and square."

"After somebody else did all the work. Just like this time, with Bel doing the legwork."

"You did the work that mattered, both times. We'd still be back at square one if you hadn't had the cave excavated and the Nottingham guys properly questioned. If you're going to quote the movies, remember how it goes. 'When the legend becomes fact, print the legend.' You are a legend, Karen. And you deserve to be."

"Shut up, you're embarrassing me."

Phil leaned back in his chair and grinned at her. "Do they deliver pizza round here?"

"Why? Are you buying?"

"I'm buying. We deserve a wee celebration, don't you think? We've come a long way towards solving two cold cases. Even if we're landed with Andy Kerr's murder as a sick kind of bonus. You order the pizza, I'll check out your DVDs."

"I should speak to the Italians," Karen said half-heartedly.

"With the time difference, it's nearly eight o'clock there. Do you really think there's going to be anyone with any seniority around? You might as well wait till morning and talk to the guy you've been dealing with. Relax for once. Switch off. We'll finish the wine, knock off a pizza, and watch a movie. What do you say?"

Yes, yes, yes! "Sounds like a plan," Karen said. "I'll get the menus."

Celadoria, near Greve in Chianti

The sun was heading for the hills, a scarlet ball in her rearview mirror as Bel drove east out of Greve. Grazia had met her in a bar in the main piazza and handed over the paper directing her to the simple cottage where Gabriel Porteous was living. Just over three kilometres out of town, she found the right turn indicated on the scrawled map. She drove up slowly, keeping an eye out for a pair of stone gateposts on the left. Immediately after them, there was supposed to be a dirt road on the left.

And there it was. A narrow track weaving between rows of vines that followed the contour of the hill; you'd pass it without a second glance if you weren't looking for it. But Bel was looking, and she didn't hesitate. The map had a cross on the left side of the track, but it clearly wasn't drawn to scale. Anxiety began to creep upon her as the distance from the main road grew. Then suddenly, tinted pink by the setting sun, a low stone building appeared in her sights. It looked one step above complete dilapidation. But that wasn't unusual, even somewhere as fashionable as the Chiantishire area of Tuscany.

Bel pulled over and got out, stretching her back after hours of sitting. Before she'd taken a couple of steps, the plank door creaked open and the young man in the photographs appeared in the doorway dressed in a pair of cut-off jeans and a black muscle vest that emphasized evenly bronzed skin. His stance was casual; a hand on the door, the other on the jamb, a look of polite enquiry on his face. In the flesh, the resemblance to Brodie Grant was striking enough to seem eerie. Only the colouring was different. Where the young Brodie's hair had been as black as Cat's, Gabriel's was caramel coloured, highlighted with sun-streaks of gold. Other than that, they could have been brothers.

"You must be Gabriel," Bel said in English.

He cocked his head to one side, his brows lowering, shading his deep-set eyes even further. "I don't think we've met," he said. He spoke English with the music of Italian underpinning it.

She drew closer and extended a hand. "I'm Bel Richmond. Didn't Andrea from the gallery in San Gimi mention I'd be stopping by?"

"No," he said, folding his hands over his chest. "I don't have any of my father's work for sale. You've wasted your time coming out here."

Bel laughed. It was a light, pretty laugh, one she'd worked on over the years for doorstep moments like this. "You've got me wrong. I'm not trying to rip off you or Andrea. I'm a journalist. I'd heard about your father's work and I wanted to write a feature about him. And then I discovered I was too late." Her face softened and she gave him a small, sympathetic smile. "I am so sorry. To have painted those paintings, he must have been a remarkable man."

"He was," Gabriel said. It sounded as if he begrudged her both syllables. His face remained inscrutable.

"I thought it might still be possible to write something?"

"There's no point, is there? He's gone."

Bel gave him a shrewd look. Reputation or money, that was the question now. She didn't know this lad well enough to know what would get her across the door. And she wanted to be across the door before she dropped the bombshell of what she really knew about him and his father. "It would enhance his reputation," she said. "Make sure his name was established. And that would obviously increase the value of his work too."

"I'm not interested in publicity." He moved backwards, the door starting to inch closed.

Time to throw the dice. "I can see why that might be, Adam." She'd hit home, judging by the swift spasm of shock that passed across his features. "You see, I know a lot more than I told Andrea. Enough to write a story, that's for sure. Do you want to talk about it? Or shall I just go away and write what I know without you having any say in how the world sees you and your dad?"

"I don't know what you're talking about," he said.

Bel had seen enough bluster in her time to recognize it for what it was. "Oh, please," she said. "Don't waste my time." She turned and started to walk back to the car.

"Wait," he shouted after her. "Look, I think you've got hold of the wrong end of the stick. But come in and have a glass of wine anyway." Bel swung round without a second's hesitation and headed back towards him. He shrugged and gave her a puppy-dog grin. "It's the least I can do, seeing as you've come all the way out here."

She followed him into the classic dim Tuscan room that served as living room, dining room, and kitchen. There was even a bed recess beyond the fireplace, but instead of a narrow mattress, it housed a plasma-screen TV and a sound system that Bel would have been happy to have installed in her own home.

A scarred and scrubbed pine table sat off to one side near the cooking range. A pack of Marlboro Lights and a disposable lighter sat next to an overflowing ashtray. Gabriel pulled out a chair for Bel on the far side, then brought over a couple of glasses and an unlabelled bottle of red wine. While his back was turned, she lifted a cigarette butt from the ashtray and slipped it into her pocket. She could leave any time now and she would have what she needed to prove whether this young man really was Adam Maclennan Grant. Gabriel settled down at the head of the table, poured the wine, and raised his glass to her. "Cheers."

Bel clinked her glass against his. "Nice to meet you at last, Adam," she said.

"Why do you keep calling me Adam?" he said, apparently bewildered. He was good, she had to admit. A better dissembler than Harry, who'd never been able to stop his cheeks pinking whenever he lied. "My name's Gabriel." He took a cigarette from the pack and lit it.

"It is now," Bel conceded. "But it's not your real name, any more than Daniel Porteous was your father's real name."

He gave a half-laugh, flipping one hand in the air in a gesture of incomprehension. "See, this is very bizarre to me. You turn up at my house, I've never seen you before, and you start coming out with all this . . . I don't mean to sound rude, but really, there's no other word for it but bullshit. Like I don't know my own name."

"I think you do know your own name. I think you know exactly what I'm talking about. Whoever your father was,

Daniel Porteous wasn't his name. And you're not Gabriel Porteous. You're Adam Maclennan Grant." Bel picked up her bag and pulled out a folder. "This is your mother." She extracted a photo of Cat Grant on her father's yacht, head back and laughing. "And this is your grandfather." She added a publicity head shot of Brodie Grant in his early forties. She looked up and saw Gabriel's chest rising and falling in time with his rapid and shallow breathing. "The resemblance is striking, wouldn't you say?"

"So you found a couple of people who look a bit like me. What does that prove?" He drew hard on his cigarette, squinting through the smoke.

"Nothing, in itself. But you turned up in Italy with a man using the identity of a boy who'd died years before. The pair of you showed up not long after Adam Maclennan Grant and his mother were kidnapped. Adam's mother died when the ransom handover went sour, but Adam vanished without trace."

"That's pretty thin," Gabriel said. He wasn't meeting her eyes now. He drained his glass and refilled it. "I don't see any real connection to me and my father."

"The ransom demand was made in a very distinctive format. A poster of a puppeteer. The same poster turned up in a villa near Siena that was being squatted by a puppet troupe led by a guy called Matthias."

"You've lost me." His eyes might be focused over her shoulder, but his smile was charm itself. Just like his grandfather's.

Bel placed a photo of Gabriel at the Boscolata party on the table. "Wrong answer, Adam. This is you at a party where you and your father were guests of Matthias. It ties the pair of you to a ransom demand that was made for you and your mother twenty-two years ago. Which is more than suggestive, don't you think?"

"I don't know what you're talking about," he said. She recognized the stubborn line of the jaw from her encounters with Brodie Grant. Really, she could leave now and rely on the DNA to do all that was necessary. But she couldn't help herself. The journalist's instinct for running the game and gaining the scoop was too strong.

"Of course you do. This is a great story, Adam. And I am going to write it with or without your help. But there's more, isn't there?"

There was nothing friendly in the look Gabriel gave her. "This is bullshit. You've taken a couple of coincidences and built this fantasy out of them. What are you hoping to get out of it? Money from this Grant guy? Some crappy magazine story? If you've got any reputation at all, you're going to destroy it if you write this."

Bel smiled. His feeble threats told her she had him on the run. Time to go for the throat. "Like I said, there's more. You might think you're safe, Adam, but you're not. There's a witness, you see . . . " She left the sentence dangling.

He crushed out his cigarette and immediately began fiddling with another. "A witness to what?" There was an edge to his voice that made Bel feel she was on the right track.

"You and Matthias were seen together the day before the BurEst troupe disappeared from the Villa Totti. You were at the villa with him that night. The next day, they'd all gone. And so had you."

"So what?" He sounded angry now. "Even if that's true, so what? I meet up with a friend of my father. My father, who's just died. Next day, he leaves town with his crew. So fucking what?"

Bel let his words hang in the air. She reached for his cigarettes and helped herself to one. "So there's a bloodstain the size of a couple of litres on the kitchen floor. OK, you already know that bit." She sparked the lighter, the flame's brightness revealing how much darker it had become in the short time since she'd arrived. The cigarette lit, she drew smoke into her mouth and let it trickle out of one corner. "What you probably don't know is that the Italian police have launched a murder hunt." She tapped the cigarette pointlessly against the edge of the ashtray. "I think it's time you came clean about what happened back in April."

Thursday, 26th April 2007; Villa Totti, Tuscany

Until the last few days of his father's life, Gabriel Porteous hadn't understood his closeness to the man who had brought him up single-handed. The bond between father and son had never been something he'd thought much about. If he'd been pressed, polite rather than passionate was how he'd have characterized their relationship, especially when he contrasted it with the dynamic rapport that most of his mates shared with their fathers. He put it down to Daniel's Britishness. After all, the Brits were supposed to be uptight and reserved, weren't they? Plus, all his mates had vast extended families, ranging vertically and horizontally through time and space. In an environment like that, you had to stake your claim or sink without trace. But Gabriel and Daniel had only each other. They didn't have to compete for attention. So being undemonstrative was OK. Or so he told himself. Pointless to acknowledge a longing for the sort of family he could never have. Grandparents dead, the only child of only children, he was never going to be part of a clan like his mates. He'd be stoic, like his dad, accepting what couldn't be changed. Over the years, he'd shut the door on his desire for something different, learning to bow to the inevitable and reminding himself to count the blessings that came with his solitary status.

So when Daniel had told him about the prognosis of his cancer, Gabriel had gone into denial. He couldn't get his head round the thought of life without Daniel. This horrible information didn't make sense in his vision of the world, so he simply went on with his life as if the news hadn't been delivered. No need to come home more often. No need to snatch at every possible opportunity to spend time with Daniel. No need to talk about a future that didn't contain his father. Because it wasn't going to happen. Gabriel wasn't going to be abandoned by the only family he had.

But finally it had been impossible to ignore a reality that was bigger than his capacity for defiance. When Daniel had phoned him from the Policlinico Le Scotte and said in a voice weaker than a whisper that he needed Gabriel to be there, the truth had hit him with the force of a sandbag to the back of the neck. Those final days at his father's bedside had been excruciating for Gabriel, not least because he hadn't allowed himself to prepare for them.

It was too late for the conversation Gabriel finally craved, but in one of his lucid moments, Daniel had told him that Matthias was keeping a letter for him. He could give Gabriel no sense of what the letter contained, only that it was important. It was, Gabriel thought, typical of his father the artist to communicate on paper rather than face to face. He'd given his instructions for his funeral previously in an e-mail. A private service prearranged and paid for in advance in a small but perfect Renaissance church in Florence, Gabriel alone to see him to his grave in an undistinguished cemetery on the western fringes of the city. Daniel had attached an MP3 file of Gesualdo's *Tenebrae Responsories* for his son to upload to his iPod and listen to on the day of his burial. The choice of music puzzled Gabriel; his father always listened to music while he painted, but never anything like this. But there was no explanation for the choice of music. Just another mystery, like the letter left with Matthias.

Gabriel had planned to visit Matthias at the dilapidated villa near Siena once the first acerbity of his grief had passed. But when he emerged from the graveyard, the puppeteer was waiting for him. Matthias and his partner Ursula had been the nearest to an uncle and aunt that Gabriel had known. They'd always been part of his life, even if they'd never stayed in one place long enough for him to grow familiar with it. They hadn't exactly been emotionally accessible either; Matthias was too wrapped up in himself and Ursula too wrapped up in Matthias. But he'd spent childhood holidays with them while his father went off for a couple of weeks on his own. Gabriel would end the holidays with suntanned skin, wild hair, and skinned knees; Daniel would return with a satchel bursting with new work from further afield: Greece, Yugoslavia, Spain, North Africa. Gabriel was always pleased to see his father, but his delight was tempered by having to say goodbye to the light touch of Ursula and Matthias's childcare.

Now the two men fell into a wordless embrace at the cemetery gates, clinging to each other like the shipwrecked to driftwood, not caring how unstable. At last, they parted, Matthias patting him gently on the shoulder. "Come back with me," he said.

"You've got a letter for me," Gabriel said, falling into step beside him.

"It's at the villa."

A bus to the station, a train to Siena, then Matthias's van back to the Villa Totti, and hardly a word exchanged. Sorrow blanketed them, bowing their heads and slumping their shoulders. By the time they reached the villa, drink was the only solution either of them could face. Thankfully, the rest of the BurEst troupe had set off earlier for a gig in Grossetto, leaving Gabriel and Matthias to bury their dead alone.

Matthias poured the wine and placed a fat envelope in front of Gabriel. "That's the letter," he said, sitting down and rolling a spliff.

Gabriel picked it up and set it down again. He drank most of his glass of wine, then ran a finger round the edge of the envelope. He drank some more, shared the spliff, and continued drinking. He couldn't imagine anything Daniel had to tell him that would need so much paper. It hinted at revelation, and Gabriel wasn't sure he wanted revelation right now. It was painful enough holding on to the memory of what he had lost.

At some point, Matthias got up and put a CD in a portable player. Gabriel was surprised by the same music he'd listened to earlier, recognizing the strange dissonances. "Dad sent that to me," he said. "He told me to play it today."

Matthias nodded. "Gesualdo. He murdered his wife and her lover, you know. Some say he killed his second son because he wasn't sure if he was really the father. And his father-in-law too, supposedly, because the old man was out for revenge and Gesualdo got his retaliation in first. Then he repented and spent the rest of his life writing church music. It just goes to show. You can do terrible things and still find redemption."

"I don't get it," Gabriel said, uneasy. "Why would he want me to listen to that?" They were already on the second bottle of wine and the third joint. He felt a little fuzzy round the edges, but nothing too serious.

"You really should read the letter," Matthias said.

"You know what's in it," Gabriel said.

"Kind of." Matthias stood up and made for the door. "I'm going out on the loggia for some fresh air. Read the letter, Gabe."

It was hard not to feel there was something portentous about a letter delivered in such circumstances. Hard to avoid the fear that the world would be changed for ever. Gabriel wished he could pass; leave it unopened and let his life move on, unaltered. But he couldn't ignore his father's final message. Hastily, he grabbed it and ripped it open. His eyes watered at the sight of the familiar hand, but he forced himself to read on.

Dear Gabriel,

I always meant to tell you the truth about yourself but it never felt like the right time. Now I'm dying, and you deserve the truth but I'm too scared to tell you in case you walk away and leave me to face the end by myself. So I'm writing this letter that you'll get from Matthias after I'm away. Try not to be too hard on me. I've done some stupid things but I did them out of love.

The first thing I am going to say is that although I've told you a lot of lies, the one thing that is the truth, the whole truth, and nothing but the truth is that I am your father and I love you more than any other living soul. Hang on to that when you wish I was alive so that you could kill me.

It's hard to know where to start this story. But here goes. My name is not Daniel Porteous and I'm not from Glasgow. My first name is Michael, but everybody called me Mick. Mick Prentice, that's who I used to be. I was a coal miner, born and raised in Newton of Wemyss in Fife.

I had a wife and a daughter, Misha. She was four years old when you were born. But I'm getting ahead of myself here because the two of you have different mothers and I need to explain that.

The one thing I was any good at, apart from digging coal, was painting. I was good at art at school but there was no way somebody like me could do anything about that. I was headed for the pit and that was that. Then the Miners' Welfare ran a class in painting and I got the chance to learn something from a proper artist. It turned out I had a knack for watercolours. People liked what I painted and I could sell them for a couple of quid now and again. At least, I could before the miners' strike in 1984, when folk still had money for luxuries.

One afternoon in September 1983, I came off the day shift and the light was amazing, so I took my paints up on the cliffs on the far side of the village. I was painting a view of the sea through the tree trunks. The water looked luminous, I can still remember how it looked too beautiful to be real. Anyway, I was totally into what I was doing, not paying attention to anything else. And suddenly this voice said, "You're really good."

And the thing that got me right away was that she didn't sound surprised. I was used to folk being amazed that a miner could paint a beautiful landscape. Like it was a monkey doing it or something. But not her. Not Catriona. Right from that first moment, she spoke to me like I was on an equal footing to her.

I just about shat myself, mind. I thought I was all alone, and suddenly somebody right next to me was speaking to me. She saw how freaked out I was and she laughed and said she was sorry to disturb me. By then,

I'd noticed she was bloody gorgeous. Hair black as a jackdaw's wing, bone structure like it had been carved with a flawless chisel. Eyes set deep so you'd have to get right up close to be sure of the colour (blue like denim, by the way) and a big smile that could wipe out the sun. You look so like her sometimes it catches my heart and makes me want to cry like a bairn.

So there I am in the woods, face to face with this amazing creature and I can't find a word to say. She stuck her hand out and said, "I'm Catriona Grant." I practically choked myself clearing my throat so I could tell her my name. She said she was an artist too, a sculptor in glass. I was even more amazed then. The only other artist I'd ever met was the woman who took the painting classes, and she was no great shakes. But I just knew Catriona would live up to the job description. She walked about with this ring of confidence, the sort of thing you only have when you're the real thing. But I'm running ahead of myself again.

Anyway, we talked a bit about the kind of work we were interested in making, and we got along pretty well. Me, I was just grateful to have anybody to talk to about art. I'd not seen much art in the flesh, so to speak, just what they had at Kirkcaldy Art Gallery. But it turns out they had some pretty good stuff there, which maybe helped me a bit in the early days.

Catriona told me she had a studio and a cottage on the main road and told me to come round and see her set-up. Then she went on her way and I felt like the light had gone out of the day.

It took me a couple of weeks to build up to going to see her studio. It wasn't hard to get to—only a couple of miles through the woods—but I wasn't sure if she really meant me to come or if she was just being polite. Shows how little I knew her back then! Catriona never said anything she didn't mean. And by the same token, she never held back when she had something to say.

I went across to see her one day when it was raining and I couldn't get painting. Her cottage was an old gatehouse on the Wemyss estate. It was no bigger than the house I was living in with my wife and kid, but she'd painted it in vibrant colours that made the rooms feel big and sunny even on a miserable grey day. But best of all was the studio and gallery she had out the back. A big glass kiln and plenty of working space, and at the other end, display shelves where people could come and buy. Her work was beautiful. Smooth, rounded lines. Very sensual shapes. And amazing colours. I'd never seen glass like it and even here in Italy you'd be hard pressed to find colours so rich and intense. The glass seemed to be on fire with different colours. You wanted to pick it up and hold it close to you. I wish I had a piece of hers but I never thought I'd need part of her until it was too late. Maybe one day you'll be able to track down something she made and then you'll understand the power of her work.

It was a good afternoon. She made me coffee, proper coffee like you didn't find much in Scotland back then. I had to put extra sugar in, it tasted funny to me at first. And we talked. I couldn't believe the way we talked. Everything under the sun, or so it seemed. It was obvious from the first time she opened her mouth that day in the woods that she was a different class from me, but that afternoon it didn't seem to make a lot of difference.

We arranged to meet again at the studio a few days later. I don't think either of us had any notion that there might be risks in what we were doing. But we were playing with fire. Neither of us had anybody else in our lives that we could talk to the way we could talk to each other. We were young—I was 28 and she was 24, but back then we were a lot more innocent than you and your friends at the same age. And from the very first moment we met, there was electricity between us.

I know you don't want to think about your mum and dad being in love and all that goes with it, so I won't trouble you with the details. All I will say is we became lovers soon enough and I think for both of us it was like coming out into bright sunlight after you've been used to electric lights. We were daft about each other.

And of course it was impossible. I learned soon enough the truth about your mother. She wasn't just any nice middle-class lassie. She wasn't just plain Catriona Grant. She was the daughter of a man called Sir Broderick Maclennan Grant. It's a name that everybody in Scotland knows, like everybody in Italy knows Silvio Berlusconi. Grant is a builder and developer. Everywhere you go in Scotland, you see his company's name on cranes and hoardings. Plus he owns chunks of things like radio stations and a football club and a whisky distillery and a haulage company and a chain of leisure centres. He's a bully as well. He tried to stop Catriona becoming a sculptor. Everything she did, she did in spite of him. He would never have stood for her having a relationship with someone as common as a miner. Never mind a miner who was married to somebody else.

And yes, I was married to somebody else. I'm not try-

ing to excuse myself. I never meant to be a cheating bastard, but Catriona swept me off my feet. I never felt that way about anybody before or since. You might have noticed I've never been one for girlfriends. The thing is that nobody could ever match up to Catriona. The way she made me feel, I don't think anybody else could do that.

And then she fell pregnant with you. You see, son, you're not Gabriel Porteous. You're really Adam Maclennan Grant. Or Adam Prentice, if you prefer that.

When that happened, I would have left my wife for Catriona, no question. I wanted to and I told her so. But she wasn't long out of a relationship that had been going for years, on and off. She wasn't ready to live with me and she wasn't ready for another fight with her father. I don't think anybody even suspected we knew each other. We were careful. I always came and went through the woods, and everybody knew I was a painter, so nobody paid any attention to me wandering about.

So we agreed to keep things as they were. Most days we saw each other, even if it was only for twenty minutes or so. And once you were born, I spent as much time with the two of you as I could. By then, I was on strike so I didn't have work to keep me from you.

I'm not going to do your head in by telling you all about the year-long miners' strike that broke the union and the spirits of the men. There's plenty of books about it. Go and read David Peace's GB84 *if you want an idea of what it was like. Or get the DVD of* Billy Elliot. *All you need to know is that every week that passed made me long for something different, some life where the three of us could be together.*

By the time you were a few months old, Catriona had

changed her mind too. She wanted us to be together. A fresh start somewhere nobody knew us. The big problem was that we had no money. Catriona was making a pretty bare living from her glasswork and I wasn't working at all because of the strike. She could only afford her cottage and studio because her mother paid the rent. That was a kind of bribe, to get Catriona to stay near at hand. So we knew her mum wouldn't be paying for us to set up home anyplace else. We couldn't stay put either. Me walking out on my wife and daughter at the height of the strike to go and live with somebody from the bosses' class would have been seen as worse than being a scab. They'd have put bricks through our windows. So without a bit of money to get us started, we were screwed.

Then Catriona had this idea. The first time she mentioned it, I thought she'd lost her mind. But the more she talked about it, the more she convinced me it would work. The idea was that we'd fake a kidnap. I'd walk out on my family, make it look like I'd gone scabbing, and hide at Catriona's. A few weeks later, you and Catriona would disappear and her father would get a ransom note. Everybody would think you'd been kidnapped. We knew her father would pay the ransom, if not for her then for you. I would take the money, you and Catriona would go back, then a few weeks later, Catriona would take you away, saying she was too upset by the kidnapping to carry on living there. And we'd all meet up and start our life together.

It sounds simple when you say it fast. But it got complicated, and things went to shit. As it turns out, your mother couldn't have had a worse idea if she'd spent her whole life working on it.

The first thing we realized when we started making the detailed plans was that we couldn't do it with just two of us. We needed an extra pair of hands. Can you imagine trying to find somebody we could trust to join in with a plan like that? I didn't know anybody who would be mad enough to join us, but Catriona did. One of her old pals from the College of Art in Edinburgh, a guy called Toby Inglis. One of those upper-class mad bastards who are up for anything. You've always known him as Matthias, the puppeteer. The man who will have given you this letter. And he's still a mad bastard, by the way.

He had the bright idea of making the kidnapping look like a political act. He came up with these posters of a sinister puppeteer with his marionettes and used them to deliver the ransom notes as if they were from some anarchist group. It was a good idea. It would have been a better idea if he'd destroyed the screen he used to print them, but Toby's always thought he was one degree smarter than everybody else. So he kept the screen and he still uses that same poster sometimes for special performances. Every time I see it, my bowels turn to water. All it would take is one person to recognize where it comes from and we'd have found ourselves up to our necks in it.

But I'm getting ahead of myself again. I really wasn't sure whether I should tell you all of this, and Toby thought maybe it would be better to let sleeping dogs lie, especially since you'll be having to cope with me not being around any more. But the more I thought about it, the more it seemed to me that you have a right to know the whole truth, even if it's hard for you to deal with. Just remember the years we've had together. Remember the good stuff, it's what redeems all the crap I did. At least, I hope that's how it works.

A very bad thing happened the night I left my wife and daughter. I walked out in the morning without saying anything about leaving. I'd heard there was a bunch of scabs going down to Nottingham that night and I figured everybody would think I'd gone with them. I went straight round to Catriona's and I spent the day looking after you while she was working. It was bloody cold that day, and we were going through a lot of wood. After dark, I went out to chop some more logs.

This is hard for me. I haven't talked about this for twenty-two years and still it haunts me. When I was growing up, I had two pals. Like you and Enzo and Sandro. One of them, Andy Kerr, had become a union official. The strike was hard on him and he was off work with depression. He lived in a cottage in the woods about three miles west of Catriona's place. He loved natural history, and he used to walk the woods at night so he could watch badgers and owls and that kind of thing. I loved him like a brother.

I was chopping the wood when he came round the end of the workshop. I don't know who got the bigger shock. He asked what the hell I was doing, chopping wood for Catriona Maclennan Grant. Then he twigged. And he lost it. He came at me like a madman. I dropped the axe and we fought like stupid wee boys.

The fight's all a bit of a blur to me. The next thing I remember is Andy just stopping. Collapsing into me so I had to put my arms round him to stop him falling. I just stared at him. I couldn't make sense of it. Then I saw Catriona standing behind him holding the axe. She'd hit him with the blunt end, but she was strong for a woman and she'd hit him so hard she'd smashed his skull.

I couldn't believe it. A few hours before, we'd been on top of the world. And now I was in hell, holding the dead body of my best pal.

I don't know how I got through the next few hours. My brain seemed to work independent of the rest of me. I knew I had to sort things, to protect Catriona. Andy had a motorbike and sidecar combination. I walked back through the woods to his place and drove the bike back to Catriona's. We put him in the sidecar and I drove down to the Thane's Cave at East Wemyss. There's a set of caves down there that have been used by humans for 5,000 years, and I was involved in the preservation society so I knew what I was doing. I could get the bike right up to the entrance to the Thane's Cave. I carried Andy in the rest of the way and buried him in a shallow grave in the back part of the cave.

I went back a couple of days later and brought the roof down so nobody would find Andy. I knew where to get my hands on some pit explosives—my wife's pal had been married to a pit deputy and I remembered him boasting about having a couple of shots of dynamite in his garden shed.

But back to that night. I wasn't finished. I drove the bike back through East Wemyss and along to the pit bing. I jammed the throttle open and let it pile into the side of the bing. The slag covered it while I stood there.

I walked home in a total daze. Ironically, I ran into the scabs as they were setting off. I've no idea what I said to them, I was deranged.

When I got to Catriona's, she was in a hell of a state.

I don't think either of us slept that night. But by the time morning came, we knew we had to go through with her idea. As well as wanting to start a new life, we needed to put some distance between Andy and us. So we started to make our plans.

Ironically, Andy being dead solved one problem we'd had about faking the kidnap—where we could hide you and Catriona without anybody knowing. I hit on the idea of forging a note in Andy's handwriting in case any of his family came by to see why they hadn't heard from him. It wasn't a straight-out suicide note. I didn't want to upset them, so I left it kind of ambiguous. I know that sounds weird, but I'm telling it like it was, not trying to make myself look like the good guy. Like I said, I've done things I'm ashamed of, but I did all of them out of love.

We let some time pass before we set up the kidnap because we didn't want anybody making a connection between me leaving and the kidnap. Also, we wanted to be sure Andy's family had accepted he'd gone away and wouldn't be coming round on the off-chance. I'm ashamed to say I forged a couple of postcards in his writing and went up north to post them after the New Year so they'd stay away from his cottage and not come looking to see if he was back. We needed to make sure we'd be safe there.

On the day we'd agreed, the three of us went off to Andy's with your toys and your clothes and there we stayed until the night of the ransom handover. Toby wasn't around much—he was sorting out the boats. We'd decided to do the handover in a place where we could escape by boat. We'd told Grant not to tell the police, but we weren't sure if he'd stick to that, so we thought we'd leave the police flat-footed if we got away on the water.

At the time, Toby was living on his father's boat, a four-berth cabin cruiser. He knew about boats, and he'd decided we needed to make our getaway in an inflatable with an outboard engine. He knew somebody who had one up in a boathouse in Johnstown. He reckoned nobody would even notice it was missing until May, so that seemed like a good idea.

Anyway, the night of the handover came and we set off. We'd agreed Catriona was going to get the money, then we'd hand you over to her mother. We'd go off with Catriona, then the next day, she'd turn up by some roadside, supposedly having been dumped once the kidnappers knew the ransom was the real thing. Meanwhile I'd give Toby his third share, he'd go his way, and I'd go mine, finding us somewhere to live and work up in the Highlands.

Nothing went like it was supposed to. The place was crawling with armed police, though we didn't realize it. Toby had a gun too, though I didn't realize that either until we got out the boat at the rendezvous. And Grant had a gun. It was a recipe for disaster. And a disaster was what we got.

Even after all this time, thinking about it makes me choke up. Everything was going to plan, but for some reason, Catriona's mum made a big performance about handing the ransom over. Grant lost the place and started waving his gun around. Then Toby turned off the spotlight and the shooting started. Catriona got caught in the crossfire. I had night-vision goggles from the army surplus and I saw her fall just a few yards away from me. I ran to her. She died in my arms. It was all over in seconds. She'd dropped the bag with the ransom when she was shot, and Toby grabbed it. I didn't know what to do. You were back by the boat, in your carry cot. We'd planned to leave you there. But I knew I couldn't leave you, not with your mother dead. I couldn't leave you behind for Grant to bring up in his image. So we ran for the boat. I got a hold of your carry cot and threw it back aboard and we got out of there as fast as we could.

The only thing that went according to plan was what we'd decided to do to avoid anyone using tracking devices to follow us. We put the money in another bag that we'd brought with us and tossed the original over the gunwale. Then I dredged the bag with the diamonds through the sea. We figured the water would knock out any transmitter they might have put in amongst them. It seemed to do the trick, because there was nobody on our tail as we shot down the coast to Dysart where Toby's boat had already been moored for a few days. It was just a few miles, so we got there before the helicopter was in the air. We could hear it and see it from the boat. After it had gone, Toby took the inflatable out of the harbour and sank it off the beach. Then we holed up there till dawn and set off on the morning tide. I was in a state of shock, to tell you the truth. A couple of times, I was on the point of walking to the nearest police station and giving myself up. But Toby held himself together and saved all of us.

It took us a few weeks to get to Italy. We laundered most of the money in automatic cash machines and casinos along the French coast. The lion's share of the ransom was in uncut diamonds, and we hung on to those.

Once we got here, we split up. I left Toby with the boat and I rented a house in the hills outside Lucca for a few months till I decided where I wanted to live. I don't re-

member much about that time. I was dazed with grief and guilt and the terrible pain of losing Catriona. If it hadn't been for you, I might not have made it through. I still can't believe how it all went so wrong.

I know you probably look at my life and think I had it pretty good. The ransom money bought us the house in Costalpino, and a bit left over that I've got invested. The income from that put the jam on the bread and butter I earned from the painting. I got to spend the rest of my life in a beautiful place, bringing up my son and painting the things I wanted to paint without ever having to worry too much about money.

The only reason you can think I had it pretty good is that you never knew your mother. When she died, she took the light away. You have been the only real light in my life since then, and don't underestimate what a joy it has been for me to spend these years with you. It breaks my heart that I will not live to see what you achieve with the rest of your life. You're a very special person, Adam. I call you that because it is the name we chose together for you.

There's one last thing I want you to do. I want you to make contact with your grandfather. I Googled him last week for the first time: Sir Broderick Maclennan Grant. His friends call him Brodie. He lives in Rotheswell Castle in Fife. His first wife, your grandmother, committed suicide two years after Catriona died. He's got a new wife now, and a son called Alec. So you see, you have a family. You have a grandfather and an uncle who is quite a few years younger than you! Make the most of them, son. You've got a lot of time to make up for, and you're enough of a man now to stand up to a bully like Brodie Grant.

So now you know it all. Blame me or forgive me, it's up to you. But never doubt that you were conceived and born in love, and that you have been loved every single day of your life. Take care of yourself, Adam.

All my love,
Your father, Mick the miner

Gabriel dropped the last sheet on top of the others. He went back to the first page and read it all again, aware that Matthias had come back in at some point. It was like reading the synopsis of a movie. Impossible to connect to his life. Too absurd to be true. He felt as if the foundations of his life had been removed, leaving him hanging in the air like a cartoon character holding his breath for the inevitable catastrophic fall. "Does Ursula know all this?" he said, knowing it wasn't that important a question, but wanting to know the answer anyway.

"Some of it." Matthias sat down heavily opposite Gabriel, another bottle of wine in his hand. "She doesn't know who your mother was, or all of Daniel's story. She knows he set up a fake kidnap because he wanted to be with you and your mother. But she doesn't know about the shoot-out at the OK Corral."

The flippancy of Matthias's description of his mother's death gave Gabriel a jolt. *Toby had a gun too.* He gave a half-hearted snort of derision. "All these years, I thought I was living among a bunch of old hippies with a load of outdated leftie ideals. And it turns out you lot are actually a bunch of criminals on the run after the worst kind of capitalist crime." He knew there were more important things to talk about, but he had to work his way round to them, like a dog faced with a hot dinner who starts off nibbling at the edges because that's all he can cope with. *Toby had a gun too.*

"You're looking at it all wrong, Gabe, my man," Matthias said, fingers busy with another joint. "Think of us as latter-day Robin Hoods. Robbing the seriously rich to spread the money round more fairly."

"You and my dad living the life of Riley, doing exactly what you want—how exactly does that further the fight against international capitalism?" Gabriel didn't even try to keep the sneer from his face or his voice. "If my grandfather had been supportive of my mother's art, none of this would have happened. Don't tell me you all did this for some higher purpose. You did it because you wanted your own way and you saw how you could make somebody else pay for it." He waved the joint away impatiently. He didn't want to lose any of the shreds of clarity left to him.

"Hey now, Gabe, don't be rushing to judgement on us."

"Why not? Isn't that what the Gesualdo is all about? It's like the last thing he did was invite me to judge him. Should I see him as a killer or as a man redeemed by his painting? Or redeemed by loving me and bringing me up the best he could?" Gabriel scrabbled through the letter, looking for the last page. "Here it is, in his own hand: 'Blame me or forgive me, it's up to you.' He wanted me to make up my own mind about what you did." The heat of anger was spreading through him, filling him up and making it harder to be reasonable. *Toby had a gun too.*

"And you should forgive him," Matthias said. "You doubt our motives, but I tell you, all he wanted was to make a life with you and Cat. Circumstances were against them. We just tried to redress the balance, that's all, Gabe."

His easy complacency was like a goad to Gabriel. "And when did that give you the right to make my choices for me?"

"What are you talking about?"

"You and Daniel, you chose what I got to know about who I am and when I got to know it. You kept me away from my family. You lied about my history, made me think all I had was Daniel and you and Ursula. You took away my chance of growing up knowing my grandfather. My grandmother might still be alive if she'd had me with her."

Matthias blew out a plume of smoke. "Gabe, there was no going back for us. You think growing up under Brodie Grant's thumb would have been better than the life you've had?" He snorted derisively. "You wouldn't say that if you had any idea how tough he made Cat's life." He got up and fetched a block of dope and a sharp knife to cut off a fresh slice.

"But I don't, do I? Because I never got the chance to find out, thanks to you two and the choices you made for me." Gabriel slammed the flat of his hand down on the table. "Well, I'm going to make up for lost time. I'm going back to Scotland. I'm going to find my grandfather and get to know him for myself. Maybe he's the ogre you and Daniel make him out to be. Or maybe he's just someone who wanted the best for his daughter. And judging by this"—he batted the letter, making the papers flutter in the dim light—"he wasn't so far off the mark, was he? I mean, my dad wasn't exactly a model citizen, was he?"

Matthias dropped the knife and stared at Gabriel. "I don't think going back is that great an idea."

"Why not? It's time I got to know my family, don't you think?"

"That's not the issue."

"Well, what is?"

Matthias made a small helpless gesture with his hands. "They're going to want to know where you've been for the last twenty-odd years. And that's kind of a problem for me."

"What's it got to do with you?"

"Think about it, Gabe. There's no statute of limitations for murder or kidnap. They're going to come after me and put me away for the rest of my life."

Toby had a gun too. "I won't tell them anything that implicates you," Gabriel said, contempt in the curl of his mouth. "You don't have to worry about your own skin. I'll take care of that."

Matthias laughed. "You really have no fucking idea who your grandfather is. You think you can just refuse Brodie Grant? He'll chase down your history, he'll backtrack and find out every move you've made all these years. He won't stop till he's nailed me to a fucking cross. This isn't just about you."

"This is my life." They were both shouting now, outrage and fear stoking the paranoia of dope and the abandon of alcohol. "If he gets me back, why the hell would my grandfather care about you?"

"Because he'll never give up the chance for revenge so he doesn't have to take responsibility."

"Responsibility? Responsibility for what?"

"For killing Cat." Even as he spoke, Matthias's face stretched in horror. He knew the enormity of what he'd said as soon as the words were out of his mouth.

Gabriel stared at him in disbelief. "You're crazy. You're saying my grandfather shot his own daughter?"

"That's exactly what I'm saying. I don't think he meant—"

Gabriel jumped to his feet, sending the chair crashing to the floor. "I can't believe—You lying piece of—You'd say anything," he shouted incoherently. "You brought a gun. You're the one who shot her, aren't you? That's what really happened. Not my grandfather. You. That's why you don't want me to go back, because you'll finally have to face what you did."

Matthias stood up, walking round the table towards

Gabriel, hands outstretched. "You've got it so wrong," he said. "Please, Gabe."

Gabriel's face was a mask of rage and shock. He reached down for the knife on the table and rushed Matthias. Nothing in his mind but anger and pain, nothing as coherent as intent. But the result was as incontrovertible as if it had been the result of a meticulous plan. Matthias crumpled and fell backwards, a dark red blemish quickly spreading to a stain across the front of his T-shirt. Gabriel stood above him, panting and sobbing, not caring to make any effort to staunch the blood. *Toby had a gun too.*

Matthias clutched at his failing heart as it slowly ran out of blood to pump round his body. His heaving chest gradually subsided till it grew motionless. Gabriel had no idea how long it took Matthias to die, only that, by the end, his legs were so tired they could scarcely hold him up. He slumped to the floor where he stood, just beyond the margin of the slowly congealing pool of blood that had spread beyond Matthias's body.

Time drifted past. Finally, what roused him was footsteps and lively chatter approaching along the loggia. Max and Luka swaggered in, full of the success of the evening's performance. When they saw the gory tableau in front of them, they stopped short. Max cursed, Luka crossed himself. Then Rado walked in with Ursula. She caught sight of Matthias and opened her mouth in a soundless scream, falling to her knees and crawling towards him.

"He killed my mother," Gabriel said, his voice flat and cold.

Ursula swung her head round to him, her lips curled back in a snarl. "You killed him?"

"I'm sorry," he whispered. "He killed my mother."

Ursula whimpered. "No. No, it's not true. He couldn't hurt a fly." She stretched out her hand tentatively, her fingertips brushing Matthias's dead hand.

"He had a gun. It's in the letter. Daniel left me a letter."

"What the fuck are we going to do?" Max yelped, breaking the macabre intimacy between them. "We can't call the cops."

"He's right," Rado said. "They'll pin it on one of us. One of the illegals, not the painter's son."

Ursula pressed her hands to her face, fingers splayed, as if she was going to claw her features apart. Her body heaved in a spasm of dry retching. Then somehow she visibly drew her strength together. Her face smeared with Matthias's blood like a terrible parody of night camouflage, she launched herself at Gabriel with a harrowing scream.

Max and Luka instinctively threw themselves between her and Gabriel, dragging her back, keeping her clawing fingers from his eyes. Panting, she spat on the floor. "We loved you like a son," she wailed. Then something in German that sounded like a curse.

"He killed my mother," Gabriel insisted. "Did you know that?"

"I wish he'd killed you," she screamed.

"Get her out of here," Rado shouted.

Max and Luka hauled her to her feet and half-carried her towards the door. "Pray I never see you again," Ursula screamed as she disappeared.

Rado crouched beside Gabriel. "What happened, man?"

"My dad left me a letter." He shook his head, dazed with shock and drink. "It's all over now, isn't it? He killed my mother, but I'm the one who's going to jail."

"Fuck, no," Rado said. "No way is Ursula going to the cops. It goes against everything she believes in." He put his arm round Gabriel. "Besides, we can't let her drag us all into this shit. No way I'm going back where I came from. Matthias is dead, there's nothing we can do to help him. No need to make things worse."

"She's not going to let me get away with this," Gabriel said, leaning into Rado. "You heard her. She's going to want to hurt me."

"We'll help her," Rado said. "We love you, man. And eventually she'll remember she does too."

Gabriel dropped his head into his hands and let the tears come. "What am I going to do?" he wailed.

Once his sobbing had subsided, Rado pulled him to his feet. "I hate to sound like a cold-hearted bastard, but the first thing you need to do is help me get rid of Matthias's body."

"What?"

Rado spread his hands. "No body, no murder. Even if we can't keep Ursula away from the cops, they're not going to sweat it if there's no body."

"You want me to help you bury him?" Gabriel sounded faint, as if this was one step more than he could manage.

"Bury him? No. Buried bodies have a way of turning up. We're going to carry him down to the field. Maurizio's pigs will eat anything."

By morning, Gabriel knew Rado had been right.

Thursday, 5th July 2007; Celadoria, near Greve in Chianti

Remembering that night now, Gabriel felt as though Bel Richmond was hollowing his stomach out with a spoon. Losing his father had been bad enough. But Daniel's letter and what it had led to had been devastating. It was as if his life was a piece of fabric that had been ripped from top to bottom and tossed in a heap. If the letter had plummeted him into a state of turmoil, killing Matthias had made matters infinitely worse. His father had not been the man he thought he was. His lies had poisoned so much. But Gabriel himself was worse than a liar. He was a killer. He'd committed an act that he would never have believed himself capable of. With such fundamental elements of his life exposed as a fantasy, how could he cling to any of it with confidence?

He'd grown up thinking his mother was an art teacher called Catherine. That she'd died giving birth to him. Gabriel had struggled with that guilt for as long as he could remember. He'd seen his father's isolation and sadness and had shouldered the blame for that too. He'd grown up carrying a weight that was completely bogus.

He didn't know who he was any more. His history had been just a story, made up to protect Daniel and Matthias from the consequences of the terrible thing they'd been part of. For their sake, he'd been wrenched out of the country where he belonged and brought up on alien soil. Who knew what his life would have been if he'd grown up in Scotland instead of Italy? He felt cast adrift, rootless and deliberately cheated out of his birthright.

His torment was made worse by constant fear, shivering behind him like the backdrop in a puppet booth. Every time he heard the sound of a car, he was on his feet, back to the wall, convinced that this time it was the carabinieri come for him at Ursula's insistence. He'd tried to cover his tracks, but he didn't have his father's experience, and he was afraid he hadn't succeeded.

But time had crawled past and after a few weeks of being holed up like a sick animal, he had started to put himself back together. Gradually, he'd managed to find a way to distance the guilt, telling himself Matthias had lived free and clear for over twenty years, never paying a penny of the debt that was owed for Catriona's death. All Gabriel had done was force him to make amends for the life he'd stolen from all of them—Catriona, Daniel, and Gabriel himself. It wasn't entirely satisfactory from the perspective of the morality Daniel had instilled in him, but holding fast to this conviction made it possible for Gabriel to attempt to move forward, accommodating his remorse and assimilating his pain.

One overwhelming imperative drove him forward. He wanted to find the family that was his by rights, the clan he'd always craved, the tribe he belonged to. He wanted the home he'd been denied, a land where people looked like him rather than escapees from medieval paintings. But he'd known he wasn't ready yet. He had to get his head straight before he attempted to take on Sir Broderick Maclennan Grant. The little he had been able to glean from his father's letter, from Matthias, and from the Internet had left him certain that Grant would not give any claimant an easy time. Gabriel knew he needed to be able to hold his own and to keep his story straight in case that terrible April night ever came back to haunt him.

And now it looked as if it had. Fucking Bel Richmond with her digging and her determination was going to destroy the one hope he'd been clinging to for the past weeks. She knew she was on to something. Gabriel hadn't had much to do with the media, but he knew enough to realize that now she had the threads of her story, she wouldn't give up till she had nailed him. And when she published her scoop, any hope he had of making a new life with his mother's family would be dead in the water. Brodie Grant wouldn't be happy to embrace a murderer. Gabriel couldn't let it happen. He couldn't lose everything for a second time. It wasn't fair. It so wasn't fair.

Somehow, he remained composed, meeting her long, level stare. He had to find out exactly what she knew. "What do you think happened?" he said, a sneer on his face. "Or should I say, what are you planning to tell the world happened?"

"I think you killed Matthias. I don't know whether you planned it or it was a spur-of-the-moment thing. But, like I said, there's a witness who can put you two together earlier that day. The only reason he hasn't told the police is that he doesn't understand the significance of what he saw. Of course, if I was to explain that to him . . . Well, it's not rocket science, is it, Adam? It took me three days to find you. I know the carabinieri have a reputation for being a bit slow on the uptake, so it might take them a bit longer. Time enough to get yourself under the protective wing of your grandfather, I'd have thought. Oh, but he's not your grandfather, is he? That's just my little fantasy."

"You can't prove any of this," he said. He poured the last of the wine into her glass, then went over to the wine rack to fetch another. He felt cornered. He'd come through a terrible ordeal. And now this fucking woman was going to steal the one hope that had held him together. His challenge was his way of giving her a chance to prevent his having to do whatever it took to stop her.

He glanced over his shoulder. Bel wasn't really paying attention to him now; she was absorbed in the chase, focused on turning the interview in the direction she sought. Absently, she said, "There are ways. And I know all of them."

He'd given her the chance and she'd deflected it. His past was corrupt beyond redemption. All he had left was the future. He couldn't let her take that from him. "I don't think so," he said, coming up behind her.

At the last minute, some primitive warning signal hit her brain and she swung round just in time to catch a flash of the blade as it headed unwaveringly for her.

KIRKCALDY

After Phil had made the first move, things had progressed at breakneck speed. Clothes stripped. Skin to feverish skin. Him on top. Her on top. Then to the bedroom. Face down, his hands cupping her breasts, her hands clinging to the struts of the bed-head. When they finally needed to pause for a second wind, they lay on their sides, grinning stupidly at each other.

"Whatever happened to foreplay?" Karen said, a giggle in her voice.

"That's what working together all these years has been," Phil said. "Foreplay. You getting me all het up. Your mind's as sexy as your body, you know that?"

She slid a hand down between them and let her fingertips caress the soft skin below his belly button. "I have wanted to do this for so long."

"Me too. But I really didn't want to fuck things up between us at work. We're a good team. I didn't want to chance spoiling that. We both love our work too much to risk it. Plus it's against the rules."

"So what's changed?" Karen said, a hollow feeling in her stomach.

"There's an inspector's job coming up in Dunfermline and I've been told unofficially that it's mine for the asking."

Karen pulled away, leaning on one elbow. "You're leaving CCRT?"

He sighed. "I've got to. I need to move up and there's not room for another inspector in the CCRT. Besides, this way I get to have you too." His face screwed up in anxiety. "If that's what you want. Obviously."

She knew how much he loved working cold cases. She also knew he was ambitious. After she'd blocked his career path with her promotion, she'd expected him to go sooner or later. What she hadn't bargained for was that she might figure in his calculations. "It's the right move for you," she said. "Better get out quick before the Macaroon realizes he should hate you as much as he hates me. I'll miss working with you, though."

He wriggled close to her, gently rubbing the palms of his hands against her nipples. "There will be compensations," he said.

She let her hand drift downwards. "Apparently," she said. "But it's going to take a lot to make it up to me."

Boscolata, Tuscany

Carabiniere Nico Gallo crushed the cigarette under the heel of his highly polished boot and pushed himself off the olive tree he was leaning against. He brushed off the back of his shirt and his tightly fitting breeches and set off again along the path that bordered Boscolata's olive grove.

He was fed up. Hundreds of miles from his home in Calabria, living in a barracks only marginally better than a fisherman's shack, and still getting the shitty end of every assignment, he could hardly get through a day without regretting choosing a career in the carabinieri. His grandfather, who had encouraged him in his choice, had told him how women fell for men in uniform. That might have been the case in the old man's day, but it was the polar opposite now. All the women his age he seemed to meet were feminists, environmentalists, or anarchists. To them, his uniform was a provocation of a very different kind.

And to him, Boscolata was just another hippy commune

inhabited by people with no respect for society. He bet they didn't pay their taxes. And he bet that the killer who had claimed the unknown victim at the Villa Totti wasn't far from where he was walking now. It was a waste of time, having a night patrol out here. If the killer had wanted to cover his tracks, he'd had months to do it. And even now, Nico reckoned everybody in Boscolata knew how to get inside the ruined villa without his having a clue they were in there. If this were his village back in the south, that's exactly how it would be.

Another round of the olive grove and he was going back to his car for a cup from the flask of espresso he'd thoughtfully brought with him. These were the milestones that made it possible to stay awake and alert: coffee, cigarettes, and chewing gum. When he got to the corner closest to the Villa Totti, he could have another cigarette.

As the sound of his match died away, Gallo realized there was another noise on the night air. This far up the hill, the night was silent but for the crickets, the odd night bird, and the occasional dog barking. But now the silence had been invaded by the straining sound of an engine climbing the steep dirt road to Boscolata and beyond. But curiously, it wasn't matched with the brilliance of headlights on full beam. He could make out pale glimmers through the trees and hedgerows, as if the vehicle was travelling on sidelights. Only one reason for that, in his books. The driver was up to something he didn't want to draw attention to.

Gallo glanced ruefully at his cigarette. He'd made sure he had enough for the night's duty, but that didn't mean he wanted to waste one. So he cupped it in his hand and moved closer to the villa to cut off anyone attempting to enter the crime scene.

It soon became clear he'd made the wrong choice. Instead of heading towards Boscolata and the villa, the lights swerved off to the right at the far end of the olive trees. Cursing, Gallo took a last drag on his cigarette, then started down the side of the grove as quickly and as quietly as he could.

He could just about make out the shape of a small hatchback. It stopped at the end of the trees, where the Totti property butted up against the substantial acreage farmed by the guy with the pigs. Maurizio, wasn't that the old man's name? Something like that. Gallo, about twenty metres away, edged closer, trying not to make a sound.

The car's interior light came on as the driver's door swung open. Gallo saw a tallish guy wearing dark sweats and a baseball cap get out and open the tailgate. He seemed to be dragging out a rolled-up carpet or something similar, bending down to get his back underneath to take the weight. As he straightened up, staggering a little under the weight of his burden and approaching the sturdy wire fence that kept the pigs penned in, Gallo realized with a horrible lurch of his stomach that this wasn't an instance of midnight trash-dumping but something much more serious. The evil fucker was about to feed a body to the pigs. Everyone knew pigs would eat bloody anything and everything. And this was indisputably a body.

He grabbed his flashlight and turned it on. "Police! Freeze!" he shouted in the most melodramatic style he could muster. The man stumbled, tripped, and fell forward, his burden landing athwart the fence. He regained his feet and raced back to the car, reaching it seconds before Gallo. He jumped in and started the engine, throwing it into reverse just as Gallo hurled himself at the hood. The carabiniere tried to hang on, but the car was speeding backwards towards the track, jouncing and jittering every metre of the way, and he finally slid off in an ignominious heap as the car disappeared into the night.

"Oh God," he groaned, rolling over so he could reach his radio. "Control? This is Gallo, on guard at the Villa Totti."

"Roger that, Gallo. What's your ten?"

"Control, I don't know the ten-code for this. But some guy just tried to dump a body in a pig field."

Friday, 6th July 2007; Kirkcaldy

The phone penetrated Karen's light sleep on the first ring. Dazed and disorientated, she groped for it, thrilled into full consciousness by the mumble of "Phone," next to her ear. He was still here. No hit and run. He was still here. She grabbed the phone, forcing sticky eyelids apart. The clock read 05:47. She was CCRT. She didn't get calls at this time of the morning any more. "DI Pirie," she grunted.

"Morning, DI Pirie," a disgustingly bright voice said. "This is Linda from Force Control. I've just had a Capitano di Stefano on from the carabinieri in Siena. I wouldn't usually have woken you, but he said it was urgent."

"It's OK, Linda," Karen said, rolling away from Phil and trying to get her head into work mode. What the hell could be quarter-to-six-in-the-morning urgent on a three-month-old maybe murder? "Fire away."

"There's not much to fire, Inspector. He said to tell you he's e-mailed you a photo to see if you can ID it. And it's urgent. He said it three times, so I think he meant it."

"I'll get right on to it. Thanks, Linda." She replaced the phone and Phil immediately pulled her to him with a different kind of urgency.

She squirmed round, trying to free herself from his grip. "I need to get up," she protested.

"So do I." He covered her mouth with his and started kissing her.

Karen pulled away, gasping. "Can you do quickies?"

He laughed. "I thought women didn't like quickies."

"Better learn how if you're going back on front-line policing," she said, drawing him into her.

Feeling only mildly guilty, Karen logged on to her e-mail. The promised message from di Stefano was the latest addition to her inbox. She clicked it open and set the attachment to download while she read the brief note. *Someone tryed to feed a body to Maurizio Rossi's Cinta di Siena pigs. Maybe this is where the other victim went. Here is a picture of the face. Maybe you know who it is?* God, that was a nasty thought. She'd heard that pigs had been known to eat everything but the belt buckle when unfortunate farmers had had accidents inside their pens, but it would never have occurred to her to consider it as a means of body disposal.

And then an even nastier thought occurred to her. *Pig eats victim. Pig incorporates human into its own meat. Pig gets turned into salami. And people end up eating people.* Somehow, she didn't think the farmer was going to have much of a business left once this got out.

Karen hesitated, wondering why di Stefano thought she might recognize the victim. Could this be Adam Maclennan Grant, his future with his grandfather snatched from him at the last moment? Or the mysteriously disappeared Matthias, aka Toby Inglis? Anxiety dried her mouth, but she clicked on the attachment.

The face that filled her screen was definitely dead. The spark that animated even coma patients was entirely absent.

But it was still shockingly unmistakable. The day before, Karen had interviewed Bel Richmond. And now she was dead.

A1, Firenze–Milano

There had been no reason to ditch Bel's hire car, Gabriel had decided. Not at this point. That mad bastard cop had shaken the living daylights out of him, but he couldn't have seen the licence plate. Nobody would be connecting a car hired by an English journalist with what had happened on the Boscolata hillside. Putting distance between himself and Tuscany was the most important thing now. Leave the past and its terrible necessities behind. Make a clean break and drive straight into the future.

It had been horrible, but he'd stripped the body, partly to make it easier for the pigs to do his dirty work for him, and partly to make it harder to identify her in the unlikely event that she was found soon enough to make identification a possibility. As it turned out, that had been a great decision. It had been bad enough when that crazy cop appeared out of nowhere. It would have been a million times worse if he'd left anything on the body that could make it easier to work out who she was.

And so the car would be safe for now. He'd park it in the long-stay at Zurich airport and pick up a flight. Thanks to Daniel's insistence that there was nothing for him there but pain and ghosts, he'd never been to the UK before, had no idea what the security would be like. But there was no reason for them to look twice at him and his British passport.

He wished he hadn't had to kill Bel. It wasn't like he was some stone-cold killing machine. But he'd already lost everything once. He knew what that felt like, and he couldn't bear it to happen again. Even mice fight when they're cornered, and he definitely had more bottle than a mouse. She'd left him no choice. Like Matthias, she'd pushed him too far. OK, it had been different with Matthias. That time, he'd lost control. Realizing that someone he'd loved since childhood had been his mother's killer had cracked open some well of pain in his head, and he'd stabbed him before he even knew he had a knife in his hand.

With Bel, he'd known what he was doing. But he'd acted in self-preservation. He'd been on the very point of contacting his grandfather when Bel barged into his life, threatening everything. The last thing he needed was her spilling the beans, linking him to Matthias's murder. He wanted to arrive at his grandfather's house with a clean sheet, not have the life he'd been denied fucked up by some muck-raking journalist.

He kept telling himself that he'd done what he had to do. And that it was good that he felt bad about it. It showed he was basically a decent person. He'd been ambushed by events. It didn't mean he was a bad person. He desperately needed to believe that. He was on his way to start a new life. Within days, Gabriel Porteous would be dead and Adam Maclennan Grant would be safely under the wing of his rich and powerful grandfather.

There would be time to feel remorse later.

ROTHESWELL CASTLE

Susan Charleson clearly didn't like the police turning up without prior invitation. The few minutes' notice between Karen's arrival at the gate and her presence on the front doorstep hadn't been quite long enough for Grant's right-hand woman to disguise her affront. "We weren't expecting you" replaced the welcome that had been uttered previously.

"Where is he?" Karen swept in, forcing Susan to take a couple of quick steps to the side.

"If you mean Sir Broderick, he is not yet available."

Karen made an ostentatious study of her watch. "Twenty-seven minutes past seven. I'm betting he's still at his breakfast. Are you going to take me to him, or am I going to have to find him myself?"

"This is outrageous," Susan said. "Does Assistant Chief Constable Lees know you're here, behaving in this high-handed manner?"

"I'm sure he soon will," Karen said over her shoulder as she set off down the hall. She threw open the first door she came to: a cloakroom. The next door: an office.

"Stop that," Susan said sharply. "You are exceeding your authority, Inspector." The next door: a small drawing room. Karen could hear Susan's running feet behind her. "Fine," Susan snapped as she overtook Karen. She stopped in front of her, spreading her arms wide, apparently under the illusion that would stop Karen if she was seriously minded to continue. "I'll take you to him."

Karen followed her through to the rear of the building. Susan opened the door on to a bright breakfast room that looked over to the lake and woods beyond. Karen had no eyes for the view or for the buffet laid out on the long sideboard. All she was interested in was the couple sitting at the table, their son perched between them. Grant immediately stood up and glowered at her. "What's going on?" he said.

"It's time for Lady Grant to get Alec ready for school," Karen said, realizing she was sounding like a bad script but not caring how foolish that felt.

"How dare you barge into my home shouting the odds." His was the first raised voice, but he appeared not to notice.

"I'm not shouting, sir. What I have to say, it's not appropriate for me to say in front of a child." Karen met his glare, not backing down. Somehow, this morning she had lost what little fear of consequences she possessed.

Grant gave a quick, nonplussed look at his son and wife. "Then we'll go elsewhere, Inspector." He led the charge to the door. "Susan, coffee. In my office."

Karen struggled to keep up with his long stride, barely catching up as he stormed into a spartan room with a glass desk which held a large spiral-bound notebook and a slim laptop. Behind the desk was a functional, ergonomically designed office chair. Filing drawers lined one wall. Against the other were two chairs Karen recognized from a trip to Barcelona, where she'd mistakenly got off the city tour bus at the Mies van der Rohe pavilion and been surprisingly captivated by its calm and simplicity. Seeing them here grounded her somehow. She could hold her own against any big shot, she told herself.

Grant threw himself into his chair like a petulant child. "What the hell is all this in aid of?"

Karen dropped her heavy satchel on the floor and leaned against a filing cabinet, arms folded across her chest. She was dressed to impress in her smartest suit, one she'd bought from Hobbs in Edinburgh at the sales. She felt absolutely in control and to hell with Brodie Grant. "She's dead," she said succinctly.

Grant's head jerked back. "Who's dead?" He sounded indignant.

"Bel Richmond. Are you going to tell me what she was chasing?"

He attempted a nonchalant half-shrug. "I've no idea. She was a freelance journalist, not a member of my staff."

"She was working for you."

He waved a hand at her. The brush-off. "I was employing her to act as press liaison should anything come of this cold case inquiry." He actually curled his lip. "Which doesn't seem very likely at this point."

"She was working for you," Karen repeated. "She was doing a lot more than press liaison. She wasn't a publicist. She was an investigative journalist, and that's precisely what she was doing for you. Investigating."

"I don't know where you get your ideas from, but I can assure you, you won't be having any more of them about this case after I've spoken to Simon Lees."

"Be my guest. I'll enjoy telling him how Bel Richmond flew out to Italy on your private jet yesterday. How she picked up a hire car on your company account at Florence airport. And how her killer was disturbed by the police while trying to feed her naked body to the pigs a couple of hundred yards from the house where Bel herself found the poster that kick-started this whole inquiry." Karen straightened up and crossed to the desk, leaning on it with her fists. "I am not the fucking numpty you take me for." She gave him glare for glare.

Before he could work out how to respond, a young woman in a black dress arrived with a tray of coffee. She looked around uncertainly. "On the desk, lassie," Grant said. Somehow Karen didn't think she was going to be offered a cup.

She waited till she heard the door close behind her, then she said, "I think you'd better tell me why Bel went to Italy. It's likely what got her killed."

Grant tilted his head back, thrusting his strong chin towards her. "As far as I am aware, Inspector, Fife police's jurisdiction doesn't stretch to Italy. This is nothing to do with you. So why don't you fuck off?"

Karen laughed out loud. "I've been told to fuck off by better men than you, Brodie," she said. "But you should know, I am here at the request of the Italian police."

"If the Italian police want to talk to me, they can come here and talk to me. Organ grinders, not monkeys. That's my way. Besides, if this was in any way official, you'd have your wee boy with you, taking notes. I do know my Scots law, Inspector. And now, as I previously requested, fuck off."

"Don't worry, I'm going. But for the record, I don't need corroboration for a witness statement for the Italian police. I'll tell you something else for nothing. If I was your wife, I'd be seriously unhappy about all these women's bodies in your slipstream. Your daughter. Your wife. And now your hired gun."

His lips stretched back in a reptilian rictus. "How dare you!"

In spite of her determination, Grant had got under her skin. Karen reached for her bag and drew out the scale map of the ransom handover scene. "This is how I dare," she said, spreading it out on Grant's desk. "You think your money and your influence can buy anything. You think you can bury the truth like you've buried your wife and your daughter. Well, sir, I'm here to prove you wrong."

"I don't know what the hell you think you're talking about." Grant had to force out his words between stretched lips.

"The received account," she said, stabbing the map with her finger. "Cat takes the bag from your wife, the kidnappers fire a shot that hits her in the back and kills her. The police fire a shot that goes high and wide." She glanced up at him. His face was motionless, frozen in a mask of rage. She hoped her expression was giving as good as it got. "And then there's the truth: Cat takes the bag from your wife, she turns to take it back to the kidnappers. You start waving your gun around, the kidnappers plunge the beach into darkness, you fire." She looked him straight in the eye. "And you kill your daughter."

"This is a sick fantasy," Grant hissed.

"I know you've been in denial all these years, but that's the truth. And Jimmy Lawson is ready to tell it."

Grant slammed his hand down on the desk. "A convicted murderer? Who's going to believe him?" His lip quivered in a sneer.

"There's others who know you had a gun that night. They're retired now. There's nothing you can hold over their heads any more. You can maybe get Simon Lees to shut me up, but the genie's out of the bottle now. It wouldn't hurt you to start cooperating with me over Bel Richmond's murder."

"Get out of my house," Grant said. "Next time you come back, you'd better have a warrant."

Karen gave him a tight little smile. "You can count on it." She still had plenty of shots in reserve, but this wasn't the time to fire them. Mick Prentice and Gabriel Porteous could wait for another day. "It's not over, Brodie. It's not over till I say so."

The about-to-be-former Gabriel Porteous had no problem entering the UK. The immigration official at Edinburgh Airport swiped his passport, compared his image to the photograph, and nodded him through. He had to stick with his old ID for the car hire too. This collision of past and future was hard to balance. He wanted to let go of Gabriel and all he had done. He wanted to enter his new life clean and unencumbered. Emotionally, psychologically, and practically, he wanted no connection to his past life. No possibilities of awkward questions from the Italian authorities. Please God, his grandfather would accept that he wanted a clean break with his past. One thing was certain—he wouldn't have to exaggerate the shock and pain his father's letter had inflicted on him.

He had to stop at a petrol station and ask directions to Rotheswell Castle, but it was still only mid-morning when he approached the impressive front gate. He pulled up and got out, grinning at the CCTV. When the intercom asked who he was and what his business might be, he said, "I'm Adam Maclennan Grant. That's my business."

They kept him waiting almost five minutes before they opened the outer gate. At first, it pissed him off. His anxiety had reached an intolerable level. Then it dawned on him that you took precautions like this only when there was something serious to protect. So he waited, then he drove into the pen between the two sets of gates. He tolerated the security patdown. He didn't complain when they searched his vehicle and asked him to open his holdall and his backpack so they could rummage around. When they finally let him through the inner gate and he caught his first glimpse of what he'd lost, his breath caught in his throat.

He drove slowly, making sure he had his emotions under control. He wanted this fresh start so badly. No more fuck-ups. He parked on the gravel near the front door and climbed out of the car, stretching luxuriously. He'd been folded into seats for too long. He squared his shoulders, straightened his spine, and walked up to the door. As he approached, it swung open. A woman in a tweed skirt and a woollen sweater stood in the doorway. Her hand flew up to her mouth involuntarily and she gasped, "Oh my God."

He gave her his best smile. "Hello. I'm Adam." He extended a hand. One look at this woman and he knew the kind of uptight manners expected in this house.

"Yes," the woman said. Training overcame emotion, and

she took his hand in a firm grip and held on tight. "I'm Susan Charleson. I'm your gran—, I mean, I'm Sir Broderick's personal assistant. This is the most extraordinary shock. Surprise. Bolt from the blue." She burst out laughing. "Listen to me. I'm not usually like this. It's just that—well, I never imagined I'd see this day."

"I appreciate that. It's all been a bit of a shock for me too." He gently freed his hand. "Is my grandfather at home?"

"Come this way." She closed the door and ushered him down a hallway.

He'd been in some fine houses in Italy thanks to his father's business, but this place was utterly foreign. With its stone walls and its spare décor, it felt cold and naked. But it didn't hurt to make nice. "This is a beautiful house," he said. "I've never seen anything like it."

"Where do you live?" Susan asked as they turned into a long corridor.

"I grew up in Italy. But I'm planning on returning to my roots."

Susan stopped in front of a heavy studded oak door. She knocked and entered, beckoning Adam to follow. The room, a book-lined refuge, was a blur to him. His total focus was on the white-haired man standing by the window, deep-set eyes unreadable, face immobile.

"Hello, sir," Adam said. To his surprise, he found it hard to speak. Emotion that he hadn't expected welled up, and he had to swallow hard to avoid tears.

The old man's face seemed to disintegrate before his eyes. An expression somewhere between smiling and sorrow engulfed him. He took a step towards Adam, then stopped. "Hello," he said, his voice choked too. He looked beyond Adam and waved Susan from the room.

The two men stared hungrily at each other. Adam managed to get himself under control, clearing his throat. "Sir, I'm sure you've had people claiming to be Catriona's son before. I just want to say that I don't want anything from you and I'm happy to undergo any tests—DNA, whatever—that you want. Until my father died three months ago, I had no idea who I really was. I've spent those three months wondering whether I should contact you or not . . . And, well, here I am." He took Daniel's letter from the inside pocket of his one good suit. "This is the letter he left me." He stretched out his arm to Grant, who took the creased sheets of paper. "I'll happily wait outside while you read it."

"There's no need for that," Grant said gruffly. "Sit down there, where I can see you." He took a chair opposite the one he had indicated and began to read. Several times he paused and scrutinized Adam, who forced himself to stay still and calm. At one point, Grant covered his mouth with his hand, the fingers visibly trembling. He came to the end and gazed hungrily at Adam. "If you're a fake, you're a bloody good one."

"There's also this—" Adam took a photograph from his pocket. Catriona sat on a kitchen chair, hands folded over the high curve of a heavily pregnant belly. Behind her, Mick leaned over her shoulder, one hand on the bump. They were both grinning. It had the slightly awkward look of something posed for the timer. "My mum and dad."

This time, Grant couldn't hold back his tears. Wordlessly, he held out his arms to his grandson. Adam, his eyes wet, got up and accepted the embrace.

It felt as if it went on forever and lasted no time at all. Finally they drew apart, each wiping their eyes with their hands. "You look like I did fifty years ago," Grant said heavily.

"You should still have the DNA test done," Adam said. "There are some bad people out there."

Grant gave him a long, measured look. "I don't think they're all on the outside," he said with an air of melancholy. "Bel Richmond was working for me."

Adam struggled not to show he recognized the name, but he could tell from his grandfather's face that he'd failed. "She came to see me," he said. "She never mentioned that you were her boss."

Grant gave a thin smile. "I wouldn't say I was her boss. But I did hire her to do a job for me. She did it so well it killed her."

Adam shook his head. "That can't be right. It was only last night that I spoke to her."

"It's right enough. I've had the police here earlier. Apparently her killer tried to feed her to the pigs right next door to the villa where your pal Matthias was squatting until round about the time when your father died," Grant continued grimly. "And the police are also investigating a presumed murder there. That one happened round about the time Matthias and his little troupe of puppeteers disappeared."

Adam raised his eyebrows. "That's bizarre," he said. "Who else is supposed to be dead?"

"They're not sure. The puppeteers scattered to the four winds. Bel was planning to track them down next. But she never got the chance. She was a good journalist. Good at sniffing things out."

"It sounds like it."

"So where is Matthias?" Grant asked.

"I don't know. The last time I saw him was the day I buried my father. I went back to the villa so he could give me the letter. I was upset when I realized he had known my real identity all along. I was angry and upset that he and my dad had conspired to keep me from you all those years. When I left, I said I didn't want to hear from him again. I didn't even know they'd left Boscolata." He gave a delicate little shrug. "They must have fallen out with each other. I know the others sometimes got restive because Matthias took a bigger cut of the take. It must have got out of hand. Somebody got killed." He shook his head. "That's harsh."

"And Bel? What's your theory there?"

Adam had had a night drive and a flight to figure out the answer to that one. He hesitated for a moment, as if thinking about the possibilities. "If Bel was asking questions around Boscolata, word might have got back to the killer. I know at least one of the group was having sex with someone who lived there. Maybe his girlfriend told him about Bel and they were keeping tabs on her. If they found out she was coming to see me, they might have thought she was digging too deep and needed to be got rid of. I don't know. I've no idea how people like that think."

Grant's expression was as unreadable as it had been when Adam had first seen him. "You're very plausible," he said. "Some might say you're a chip off the old block." His face twisted momentarily in pain. "You're right about the DNA. We should have that done as soon as possible. Meanwhile, I think you should stay with us. Let us start getting to know you." His smile was disturbingly ambivalent. "The world's going to be very interested in you, Adam. We need to prepare for that. We don't necessarily need to be entirely frank. I've always been a great believer in privacy."

That had been a shaky moment when the old man revealed Bel was in his pocket. His questions were tougher than Adam had expected. But now he understood that a decision had been taken, a decision to opt for complicity. For the first time since Bel had walked through his door, the unbearable tension began to dissipate.

FRIDAY, 13TH JULY 2007; GLENROTHES

The latest summons to the Macaroon's office wasn't entirely unexpected. Karen had been refusing to take no for an answer from him since she'd had a terse e-mail from Susan Charleson revealing the return of the prodigal. She badly wanted to talk to Brodie Grant and his murderous grandson, but of course she'd been warned off before she could even make her case to Lees. She'd known confronting Grant about his actions on the beach all those years ago would bring repercussions. Unsurprisingly, Grant had got his retaliation in first, accusing her of desperately looking for somebody to charge with something in a case where all the criminals were dead. Karen had had to listen to the Macaroon lecturing her on the importance of good relationships with the public. He reminded her that she had resolved three cold cases even though nobody would be tried for any of them. She had made the CCRT look good, and it would be extremely unhelpful if she pushed Sir Broderick Maclennan Grant into making them look bad.

When she'd raised the issue of Adam Maclennan Grant's possible involvement in two murders in Italy, the Macaroon had turned green and told her to back off a case that was none of her business.

Di Stefano had been in regular contact with Karen via phone and e-mail over the previous weeks. There was, he said, plenty of DNA on Bel's body. One of the teenagers who lived at Boscolata had identified Gabriel aka Adam as the man he'd seen with Matthias on the presumed day of the assumed murder at the Villa Totti. They'd found the house near Greve where a man answering to that description had been living. They'd found DNA there that matched what was on Bel's body. All they needed to bring a case before an investigating magistrate was a sample of DNA from the former Gabriel Porteous. Could Karen oblige?

Only when hell froze over.

Now, finally, the Macaroon had summoned her. Marshalling her thoughts, she walked into his office without knocking. This time, she was the one who got the shock. Sitting to one side of the desk, at an angle to the Macaroon but facing the visitor's chair, was Brodie Grant. He smiled at her discomfiture. Friday the thirteenth, right enough.

Without waiting to be asked, Karen sat down. "You wanted to see me, sir," she said, ignoring Grant.

"Karen, Sir Broderick has very kindly brought us his grandson's notarized statement about the recent events in Italy. He thought, and I agree with him, that this would be the most satisfactory way to proceed." He brandished a couple of sheets of paper at her.

Karen stared at him in disbelief. "Sir, a simple DNA test is the way to proceed."

Grant leaned forward. "I think you'll find that once you've read the statement, it's clear that a DNA test would be a waste of time and resources. No point in testing someone who's manifestly a witness, not a suspect. Whoever the Italian police are looking for, it's not my grandson."

"But—"

"And another thing, Inspector; my grandson and I will not be discussing with the media where he's been for the past twenty-two years. Obviously, we will be making public the fact that we have had this extraordinary reunion after all this time. But no details. I expect you and your team to respect that. If information leaks into the public domain, you can rest assured that I will pursue the person responsible and make sure they are held accountable."

"There will be no leaks from this office, I can assure you," the Macaroon said. "Will there, Karen?"

"No, sir," she said. No leaks. Nothing to contaminate Phil's imminent promotion or her own team.

Lees waved the papers at Karen. "There you go, Inspector. You can forward this on to your opposite number in Italy and then we can draw a line under our own solved cases." He smiled winningly at Grant. "I'm glad we've been able to clear this up so satisfactorily."

"Me too," Grant said. "Such a pity we won't be seeing each other again, Inspector."

"Indeed. You take care, sir," she said, getting to her feet. "You want to take very good care of yourself. And your grandson. It would be tragic if Adam had to endure any more losses." Seething, Karen stalked out of the room. She steamed back to her own office, ready to rant. But Phil was away from his desk and nobody else would do. "Fuck, fuck, fuck," she muttered, slamming into her office just as the phone rang. For once, she ignored it. But the Mint stuck his head round the door. "It's some woman called Gibson looking for you."

"Put her on." She sighed. "Hello, Misha. What can I do for you?"

"I just wondered if there was any news. When your sergeant came round a couple of weeks ago to tell me you were pretty sure my father died earlier this year, he said there was a possibility he might have had children that we could test for a match. But then I didn't hear from you . . . "

Fuck, fuck, fuck, and fuck again. "It's not looking hopeful," Karen said. "The person in question is refusing to give any samples for testing."

"What do you mean, refusing? Doesn't he understand a child's life is at stake here?"

Karen could feel the emotional intensity down the phone line. "I think he's more concerned about keeping his own nose clean."

"You mean he's a criminal? I don't care about that. Does he not get it? I'm not going to give his DNA to anybody else. We can do it confidentially."

"I'll pass the request on," Karen said wearily.

"Can you not put me in direct touch with him? I'm begging you. This is my wee boy's life at stake. Every week that goes past, he's got less and less chance."

"I do understand that. But my hands are tied. I'm sorry. I will pass the request on, I promise."

As if she sensed Karen's frustration, Misha changed her approach. "I'm sorry. I appreciate how hard you've tried to help. I'm just desperate."

After the call, Karen sat staring into space. She couldn't bear the thought that Grant was protecting a murderer for his own selfish emotional ends. It wasn't exactly a surprise, given the way he'd covered up his own culpability in his daughter's death. But there had to be a way to get round this barrier. She and Phil had gone over their options so often during the past couple of weeks that it felt as if they'd worn a groove in her brain. They'd talked about stalking Adam, going for the publicly discarded Coke can or water bottle. They'd discussed stealing the rubbish from Rotheswell and having River go through it till she found a match for the Italian DNA. But they'd had to concede they were not so much clutching at straws as at shadows.

Karen leaned back in her chair and thought about the place where all this had started. Misha Gibson desperate for hope, prepared to do anything for her child. Just as Brodie Grant was for his grandson. The bonds between parents and children . . .

And then, suddenly, it was there in front of her. Beautiful and cunning and deliciously ironic.

Almost tipping herself on to the floor, Karen shot up straight and grabbed the phone. She keyed in River Wilde's number and drummed her fingers on the desk. When River answered, Karen could hardly speak in sentences. "Listen, I just thought of something. If you've got half-siblings, you'd be able to see the connection in the DNA, right?"

"Yes. It wouldn't be as strong as with full siblings, but you'd see a correlation."

"If you had some DNA, and you got a sample that showed that degree of correlation, and you knew that person had a half-sibling, do you think that would be enough to get a warrant to take samples from the half-sibling?"

River hummed for a moment. "I could make the case," she said. "I think it would be enough."

Karen took a deep breath. "You know when we got Misha Gibson's DNA to check against the cave skeleton?"

"Yes," River said cautiously.

"Have you still got that?"

"Is your case still open?"

"If I was to say yes, what would your answer be?"

"If your case is still open, I'm legally entitled still to have possession of the DNA. If it's closed, the DNA should be destroyed."

"It's still open," Karen said. Which, technically, it was, since the only evidence against Mick Prentice in the death of Andy Kerr was circumstantial. Enough to close the file, certainly. But Karen hadn't actually returned it to the registry, so it wasn't closed as such.

"Then I still have the DNA."

"I need you to e-mail me a copy ASAP," Karen said, punching the air. She got to her feet and did a little dance round the office.

Fifteen minutes later, she was e-mailing a copy of Misha Gibson's DNA to di Stefano in Siena with a covering note. *Please ask your DNA expert to compare these. I believe this to be the half-sibling of the man known as Gabriel Porteous. Let me know how you get on.*

The next hours were a form of torture. By the end of the working day, there was still no word from Italy. When she got home, Karen couldn't leave the computer alone. Every ten minutes she was jumping up and checking her e-mail. "How quickly it fades," Phil teased her from the sofa.

"Yeah, right. If I wasn't doing it, you would be. You're as keen as I am to nail Brodie's grandson."

"You got me bang to rights, guv."

It was just after nine when the anticipated reply from di Stefano hit her inbox. Holding her breath, Karen opened the message. At first, she couldn't believe it. "No correlation?" she said. "No fucking correlation? How can that be? I was so sure . . ."

She threw herself down on the sofa, allowing Phil to cuddle her close. "I can't believe it either," he said. "We were all so sure that Adam was the killer." He flicked a finger at the anodyne statement Karen had brought home to show him. "Maybe he's telling the truth, bizarre though it sounds."

"No way," she said. "Murderous puppeteers following Bel through Italy? I've seen more credible episodes of *Scooby Doo*." She curled up, disconsolate, head tucked under Phil's chin. When the new idea hit, her head jerked so suddenly he nearly bit through his tongue. While he was moaning, Karen kept repeating, "It's a wise child that knows its father."

"What?" Phil finally said.

"What if Fergus is right?"

"Karen, what are you talking about?"

"Everybody thought Adam was Fergus's kid. Fergus thinks so. He shagged Cat around the right time, just a one-off. Maybe she'd had a row with Mick. Or maybe she was just pissed off because it was a Saturday night and he was with his wife and kid and not her. Whatever the reason, it happened." Karen was bouncing on her knees on the sofa, excitement making her a child again. "What if Mick was wrong all these years? What if Fergus really is Adam's dad?"

Phil grabbed her and gave her a resounding kiss on the forehead. "I told you right at the start I love your mind."

"No, you said it was sexy. Not quite the same thing." Karen nuzzled his cheek.

"Whatever. You are so smart, it turns me on."

"Do you think it's too late to ring him?"

Phil groaned. "Yes, Karen. It's an hour later where he lives. Leave it till the morning."

"Only if you promise to take my mind off it."

He flipped her over on to her back. "I'll do my best, boss."

Wednesday, 18th July 2007

Karen stretched out in the bath, enjoying the dual sensations of foam and water against her skin. Phil was playing cricket, which she now understood meant a quick game followed by a long drink with his mates. He'd stay at his own house tonight, rolling home at closing time after a skinful of lager. She didn't mind. Usually she met up with the girls for a curry and a gossip. But tonight she wanted her own company. She was expecting a phone call, and she didn't want to take it in a crowded pub or a noisy restaurant. She wanted to be sure of what she was hearing.

Fergus Sinclair had been suspicious when she'd called him out of the blue to ask for a DNA sample. Her pitch had been simple—a man had turned up claiming to be Adam, and Karen was determined to make every possible check on his bona fides. Sinclair had been cynical and excited by turns. In both states, he'd been convinced that he was the best litmus test available. "I'll know," he kept insisting. "It's an instinct. You know your own kids."

It wasn't the right time to share River's statistic that somewhere between 10 and 20 per cent of children were not actually the offspring of their attributed fathers and, in most of those cases, the fathers had no idea they weren't the dad. Karen kept falling back on appropriateness. Finally, he'd agreed to go to his local police station and give a DNA sample.

Karen had managed to persuade the German police duty officer to have the sample taken and couriered directly to River. The Macaroon would lose his mind when he saw the bill, but she was past caring. To speed things up, she'd persuaded di Stefano to e-mail a copy of the Italian killer's DNA to River.

And tonight, she would know. If the DNA said Fergus was the Italian killer's father, she'd be able to get a warrant to take a sample from Adam. Under Scots law, she could have detained him and taken a DNA sample without arresting or charging him. But she knew her career would be over if she attempted to treat Adam Maclennan Grant like any other suspect. She wouldn't go near him without a sheriff's warrant. But once his DNA was in the system, even Brodie Grant's power couldn't keep him out of the clutches of the law. He'd have to pay for the lives he'd cut short.

Her thoughts stuttered to a halt when the phone rang. River had said nine o'clock, but it was barely half past seven. Probably her mother or one of the girls trying to persuade her to change her mind and join them. With a sigh, Karen stretched to pick up the phone from the stool by the bath.

"I've got Fergus Sinclair's DNA analysis in front of me," River said. "And I've also got one from Capitano di Stefano."

"And?" Karen could hardly breathe.

"A close correlation. Probably father and son."

Thursday, 19th July 2007; Newton of Wemyss

The voice is soft, like the sunlight that streams in at the window. "Say that again?"

"John's cousin's ex-wife. She moved to Australia. Outside Perth. Her second husband, he's a mining engineer or something." Words tumbling now, tripping over each other, a single stumble of sounds.

"And she's back?"

"That's what I'm telling you." Exasperated words, exasperated tone. "A twenty-fifth school reunion. Her daughter, Laurel, she's sixteen, she's come with her for a holiday. John met them at his mother's a couple of weeks ago. He didn't say anything because he didn't want to raise my hopes." A spurt of laughter. "This from Mr. Optimism."

"And it's right? It's going to work?"

"They're a match, Mum. Luke and Laurel. It's the best possible chance."

And this is how it ends.

Acknowledgments

It started when Kari "Mrs. Shapiro" Furre made a bizarre discovery in the *casa rovina* down the hill. The Giorgi family of the Chiocciola contrada offered their suggestions; the wonderful Mamma Rosa fed us like kings and taught us like little children; Marino Garaffi continues to breed the finest pigs, even the ones that get stuck. Their friendship, their kindness, and their generosity brightens my summers.

In Fife, I owe thanks to my mother for her memories; to the many miners and musicians whose songs and stories weave in and out of my childhood memories; to the fellow Raith Rovers supporter who suggested it was about time I wrote another book set in the Kingdom; and to the communities I grew up among who were shattered by the 1984 strike and its aftermath. Professor Sue Black was generous as ever with her expertise and reminds me that the mistakes are mine.

Some of the people who made this book possible are beyond thanks. My father Jim McDermid, my miner grandfathers Tom McCall and Donald McDermid, and my brevet uncle Doddy Arnold all opened doors into the world of working men, a world whose demands cut short their lives.

And finally, a nod of appreciation to the team who always push me to make the book the best I can manage—my editor, Julia Wisdom; my copy editor, Anne O'Brien; and my agent, Jane Gregory. Not forgetting Kelly and Cameron, whose patience is entirely remarkable.

About the Author

Scottish crime writer **Val McDermid** is the author of twenty-three novels. Her books have won the Gold Dagger Award for Best Crime Novel of the Year and a *Los Angeles Times* Book Prize, have been selected for the *New York Times*' 100 Notable Books of the Year list, and have been nominated for the Edgar Award. She lives in the north of England.

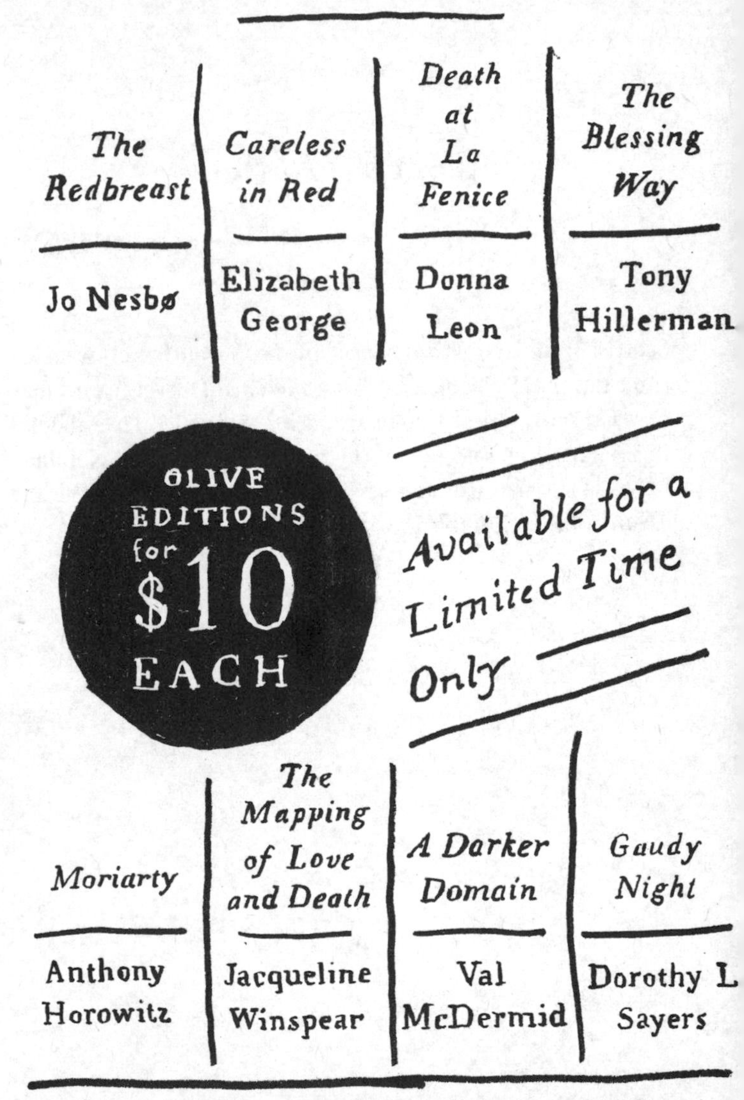

"Must-read mysteries, thrilling new look!"
The Redbreast
Jo Nesbø
Careless in Red
Elizabeth George
Death at La Fenice
Donna Leon
The Blessing Way
Tony Hillerman
OLIVE EDITIONS for $10 EACH
Available for a Limited Time Only
Moriarty
Anthony Horowitz
The Mapping of Love and Death
Jacqueline Winspear
A Darker Domain
Val McDermid
Gaudy Night
Dorothy L. Sayers
Available for a limited time wherever books are sold, or call 1-800-331-3761 to order.